I've travelled the world twice over,
Met the famous: saints and sinners,
Poets and artists, kings and queens,
Old stars and hopeful beginners,
I've been where no-one's been before,
Learned secrets from writers and cooks
All with one library ticket
To the wonderful world of books.

GREEN MONEY

George Ferrier unexpectedly becomes trustee to the lovely Elma Green. As a background the life in George's country home is delightfully described. His very Irish mother; the green paddocks with the mares and their foals; early morning rides, the very human family of neighbours who live at Rival's Green, tying up the peach trees with Cathie Seeley; giving a party in the garden for her schoolgirl sister. There is a freshness and charm about the whole story.

D. E. STEVENSON

Green Money.

Complete and Unabridged

ULVERSCROFT
Leicester

First published 1939

First Large Print Edition
published July 1981
by arrangement with
Collins, London & Glasgow
and
Holt, Rinehart & Winston, CBS Inc.
New York

British Library CIP Data

Stevenson, Dorothy Emily
    Green money.—Large print ed.
    (Ulverscroft large print series: romance)
    I. Title
    823'.9'1F

    ISBN 0-7089-0649-4

Published by
F. A. Thorpe (Publishing) Ltd.
Anstey, Leicestershire

Printed and Bound in Great Britain by
T. J. Press (Padstow) Ltd., Padstow, Cornwall

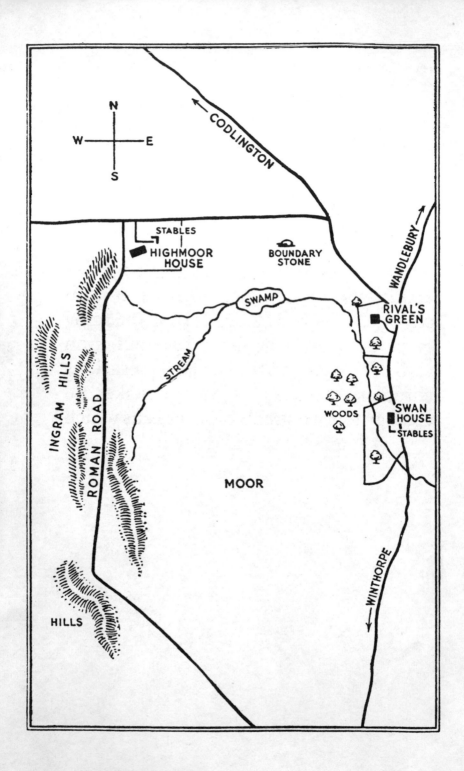

Part 1

1

ENTER THE HERO

IT was a May morning. The sun shone brightly. It shone down upon the Home Counties, upon fields and woods and gardens; it shone upon meadows, so that a faint, shimmering haze quivered over the new green carpet, starred with buttercups. Cows, knee-deep in grass, munched contentedly, aware in their own slow bovine way that winter was really past. Even in London it was obvious that summer was on her way: there was a liveliness in the air, women's hats were more jaunty, men's gaits more brisk, and here and there in the gardens, and in the back-greens, an apple tree with a load of snowy blossom astonished and delighted the eye, or a whiff of heady hawthorn astonished and delighted the nose. The sun shone down upon the streets, so that all at once they were white and glaring, it glittered on a million plate-glass windows and was reflected from the silver-plated fittings of a hundred thousand cars.

George Ferrier was twenty-five today, and it seemed to him that the sun was shining with peculiar brilliance on that account. The sun was shining for him, and the shops were displaying their most treasured wares for him, and the cars, crawling slowly down Bond Street, were winking at him with their glittering headlamps and wishing him many happy returns of the day.

It was a pleasant conceit, and George toyed with it as he strolled along. The absurd fancy made his eyes sparkle, and turned up the corners of his mouth in a whimsical smile at his own foolishness and at the colossal egotism which had inspired it. Several young women who were taking the air (if you could call it air, laden as it was with carbon monoxide and scented with petrol fumes) in Bond Street that fine spring morning glanced at him sideways as he passed, and registered a mental picture of his personal appearance (not exactly good looking, perhaps, but distinctly worth looking at, with his long limbs and broad shoulders and easy carriage), and George, becoming aware of these glances, returned them with a slightly impudent grin, for he was not backward in his dealings with the opposite sex, nor had he any illusions about them.

4

The shop windows were fascinating. George spent several minutes gazing into Asprey's, where a marvellous assortment of crocodile leather handbags, silver cigarette-cases and fitted picnic baskets was displayed. He chose with great care the handbag which he would have bought for his mother (if he had happened to have any money left): that brown, shiny, crocodile leather one with the silver clasp. Yes, that was the one. He would tell Paddy when he got home that he had chosen a bag for her at Asprey's, and Paddy would be pleased. She would be just as pleased to hear that he had chosen the bag and had wanted to buy it for her as if he had really bought the bag—mothers were like that—perhaps she would be *more* pleased than if the bag had really been bought. For, as a matter of fact, now that George thought about it seriously, he could not "see" Paddy with that bag under her arm. She would never use it. She would put it away carefully in a drawer and go on using her old shabby bulging bag which was always full of unanswered letters, and catalogues of plants, and all sorts of odds and ends which Paddy always declared might come in useful, but seldom did. It was much better as it was. He would tell her about the bag, and she would know that he had thought of her.

George had spent ten days in London, and having also spent all his money, he was going home tomorrow. Ten days in London was an expensive pleasure—so George had found. He had not stinted himself, of course, and he had had a really tremendous time, staying with Tom Clitheroe at his comfortable bachelor flat and going with Tom to dances and sherry parties and plays. He had met several delightful girls, and enjoyed it all immensely. It was over now, and he was sorry. It seemed rather sad to think that he would drop out of their lives and they would forget him. If he had had any money he would have liked to buy that shagreen cigarette-case for Clarice Morton (it would suit her, he thought); and the little white doe-skin purse with the bead pattern on it would be just right for Betty Holmes. Clarice and Betty were both darlings, and George was not at all sure which he liked best. That day on the river he had decided he was in love with Betty—she was so sweet and full of fun; but then he met Clarice at the dance. Clarice danced divinely. They would both forget him quite soon, of course. . . . It was a pity he could not afford to give them something nice to remember him by.

George sighed. He lifted his eyes and saw his reflection in the window-pane (not a bit good looking, he thought, but not exactly ugly, either. . . . I'm glad my ears don't stick out like Tom's. . . .)

He strolled on now, savouring Bond Street, as an epicure savours an especially succulent dish. He would not be here again for months, and he wanted to be able to shut his eyes and see it, and to feel the subtle stimulation, the sort of challenge to be and look one's brightest and best.

There was, of course, a "special feeling" about Bond Street, a *difference*, a quality of glamour which obtained nowhere else. Bond Street was a sort of legend, George thought. It was a shrine in the hearts of exiles; it was the hub of London—or at least of a certain romantic legend of London—just as London was the hub of the world. It was narrow and congested, and its shops were necessarily small, but they were full of expensive luxuries, of treasure from every country under the sun. The very paving-stones, thought George (though, as a matter of fact, they looked exactly like the paving-stones of any other street in any other town) were somehow sacred, or almost sacred,

7

so full of history were they. How long had they lain here? Who had walked upon them? Giants of history who were long since dust.

And all this was for him—thought George, as he strolled along—this golden effulgence, this pleasant warmth, this marvellous display of treasure, this cavalcade of brave cars. All Bond Street was his, and the Spirit of Bond Street gave him joy of his birthday.

One might have thought, to see George, that he had nothing whatever to do this fine spring morning, but such was not the case. George was making, slowly but surely, for a definite point, where he had a definite and extremely important appointment. He was due at Foxton's at twelve-thirty, to try on an exceedingly fine pair of riding boots, and it was exactly twelve-thirty-one when he pushed open the glass door and went in.

Foxton's is not a large establishment, but it is full of tradition; it has the atmosphere—almost—of a church, only, instead of the somewhat musty smell of a church, it has an oily, leathery smell, a smell to which several centuries of concentrated leather have contributed.

George, received with smiling courtesy, was led into a small fitting-room at the back of the shop, and invited to divest himself of his dark grey lounge suit with the pin stripe, and to don the riding breeches which he had sent by a messenger boy for the trying on process. Mr. Foxton himself (high priest of the god of leather) attended the fitting and chatted with George in a friendly manner while the boot-maker put on the boots.

"Your father is well, I hope," Mr. Foxton said. "We have not seen him here for some time."

"He never comes to town now," George explained, holding out his foot. "He likes the country best . . . can't stand the noise."

"London has changed."

"Yes," said George; "but it's still exciting—at least it is to me. I suppose if you lived here always it wouldn't be. Your place doesn't change much," he added.

"Ah, but it has," said Mr. Foxton sadly. "In my grandfather's day Foxton's was very different. He would turn in his grave if he knew that we had been obliged to branch out—to stock fancy leather goods. *Fancy leather goods!*" said Mr. Foxton with scornful emphasis. "If he could see the front shop full of pekinese dog-collars and ladies' purses, and

9

fitted suitcases, my grandfather would turn in his grave."

"There," said the bootmaker. "If you would just stand up, sir——"

George stood up, and old Mr. Foxton was forgotten.

"A bit bulgy in the calf, isn't it?" George suggested anxiously.

"Ah . . . just a bit, perhaps," agreed Mr. Foxton, kneeling down and pinching the boot with experienced fingers. "Here, Ditton, d'you see that? Perhaps just a shaving off the calf—eh?"

"Just the merest shaving, perhaps, sir," agreed Ditton, frowning.

"Don't go and make it too fine!" said George hastily.

"And there," continued Mr. Foxton, prodding George's right instep, "it's going to break across there. . . . See that, Ditton?"

Ditton saw.

"I like a good boot," George declared, admiring his long legs in the carefully adjusted mirror.

"Sets off your leg, sir," agreed Ditton gravely. "It's a pleasure to make a boot for a leg like yours, sir—if you'll excuse me saying so."

George excused him magnanimously.

"Good boots are an investment, really," declared George, who had told himself this several times already in order to assure himself that he was not being extravagant. "A really good pair of boots like this . . ."

". . . will last you for years," completed Mr. Foxton.

"Yes, they will jolly well have to," agreed George ruefully.

There was a short stout gentleman waiting in the shop when George, still attended by Mr. Foxton, emerged from the fitting-room, a short, stout gentleman with a purple face and quantities of snow-white hair.

"I'm going home tomorrow," George was saying. "You know the address, of course."

"Swan House, Winthorpe," recited Mr. Foxton proudly.

The stout gentleman wheeled round. "What?" he cried. "Excuse me, but I couldn't help hearing—you must be Ferrier's son!"

"Yes," said George, smiling.

"I'm Green!" cried the gentleman eagerly.

"You're green?" exclaimed George, looking at the purple face in amazement.

"I see you're surprised!" cried the old

11

gentleman seizing his hand and shaking it heartily. "You've heard your father speak of me, of course, and you're astonished to meet me here like this. It *is* astonishing, of course, and yet you must admit that coincidences are bound to happen sometimes. London!" cried the old gentleman excitedly, still shaking George's hand, "London—it's a city of co-incidences! Everybody meets everybody in London! Why shouldn't they? Tell me that. If nobody ever met anybody in London it would be an even more astonishing thing."

"Perhaps it would," agreed George feebly.

"It would, it would! But never mind that now. The point is, where are you going? What are you doing, eh? I want to hear all your news. Come and have lunch."

"But I've got some things to do."

"You can do them afterwards," declared the old gentleman, following George out of the shop.

"I really must . . ." George began.

"No, no. I won't take a refusal."

"It's awfully kind of you, but really . . ."

"No, no—my club—we'll lunch there." He seized George's arm and signalled wildly with his stick to a taxi which was passing down the street. "Damn the fellow!" he

12

cried. "Damn the fellow. Why doesn't he stop? He saw me and he didn't stop. . . ."

"He's engaged."

"Engaged, was he?"

"Yes," said George. He was conscious of amused glances from passers-by and his skin prickled uncomfortably. He gazed longingly down Bond Street and wondered whether it would be possible to make a bolt for freedom; but his companion had him so tightly by the arm that it would have required actual violence to escape from his clutches, and George was not prepared to exert violence here in Bond Street upon a gentleman who claimed to be his father's friend. It was therefore a great relief to his mind when a taxi drew up at the curb and deposited a young woman at the hairdresser's establishment next door.

"Here's a taxi!" he said.

"Splendid! Come on, come on!" cried his new friend, darting across the pavement and dragging George after him. "Come on . . . mustn't stop here . . . block the traffic. . . . Come on, Ferrier."

There was nothing for it but to allow himself to be carried off, and George, seeing

that escape was impossible, gave in as grace-
fully as he could.

They moved off slowly down the street.

"Well," said the old gentleman. "This is
splendid! It was smart of you to seize on to
it like that. Well, here we are. I've always
wanted to see you—George, isn't it?"

"George it is."

"You've heard your father speak of me, of
course?"

"Yes, of course," agreed George. "Er—
what was the name, sir?"

"Green," declared the purple-faced old
gentleman, hitting himself violently on the
chest. "John Green—G R double E N. We
were in Mespot together—great days, those."

"Of course," George said. He had not the
faintest recollection of hearing his father
speak of John Green; but, being an exceedingly kind-hearted young man, he felt bound
to lie, and lie convincingly. He was in the
middle of his fabrications when the taxi
turned into Piccadilly and came to rest
behind a furniture van.

"Is it a block?" inquired Mr. Green fret-
fully.

George thought it was, and said so, but his
companion was not satisfied. He rapped on

14

the window and yelled at the top of his voice: "Is it a block, driver?"

The driver turned, and George saw with surprise that his face was quite as purple as that of his fare. "Oh, no," he said with elaborate sarcasm. "We're jus' 'avin' a bit of a rest, that's what. There ain't never no blocks 'ere."

"Try and get round," shouted Mr. Green. "Back up Bond Street. Go round the other way."

"Wouldn't you rather I 'opped over the 'ouses?"

"We're in a hurry," declared Mr. Green.

"Spread yer wings an' fly, gov'nor," suggested the driver patiently.

"We'll get out, then!" cried Mr. Green. "Dammit, we can't sit here all day——"

At that moment the furniture van moved on and the taxi started with a jerk which pitched Mr. Green backwards into his seat.

"Good!" he said, gathering himself together and retrieving his hat from the floor, "Good, we're moving. Shan't be long now."

15

2

THE YOUTHFUL TRUSTEE

THE taxi drew up in front of the Die Hards Club and deposited Mr. Green and George upon the pavement. George had never before set foot inside these somewhat gloomy portals. He was aware, of course, that the Die Hards was the most exclusive club in town, and that all its members were said to have one foot in the grave, and this rumour was confirmed when George strolled into the dining-room in the wake of his new friend and beheld the members at meat—red faced, yellow faced or grey faced, the members of the Die Hards were all old and gouty and disagreeable. They looked up from their plates of food and eyed young George with disapproving stares.

"Here we are!" cried Mr. Green, quite oblivious of the unfavourable impression produced by his guest. "Here we are! Here's a table! Now, what are you going to have?"

The food was excellent and George was

hungry. He began to feel more charitably inclined towards his host. Mr. Green was rather a nice old boy and quite amusing; and his fussiness, which had annoyed George considerably, was really an emanation from his good nature and kindliness. He gave George all sorts of absurd messages for his father: "Ask him if he remembers the night we let down the adjutant's tent," said Mr. Green, chuckling; "and ask him if he remembers the night we went round Cairo and painted the town red. . . , Oh, and be sure to ask him if he remembers Dusty—a fellow called Dusty. Got that?"

"Yes," said George. "I'll ask him."

"Good lad," said Mr. Green approvingly.

A bottle of excellent hock accompanied their repast, and a glass of port followed. They were very friendly indeed by now. George had told his new-found friend all the Ferrier news in answer to searching questions.

"Your mother—is she still alive?"

"Very much so," declared George, smiling. "She's tried to kill herself several times, but hasn't succeeded yet."

"What!" cried Mr. Green in amazement.

"Hunting," explained George. "She's

Irish, you know, and rides like the devil.''

"Oh, hunting," nodded Mr. Green. "You hunt, too?"

"Rather."

"What else d'you do?"

"Nothing much, I'm afraid," admitted George, somewhat shamefacedly. "I mean, I've got no brains. I look after the place for Dad, of course, and Paddy and I breed horses—and all that. There's quite a lot to do, as a matter of fact."

"I dare say there's a lot in it."

"Quite a lot," said George. "Dad's busy, of course. He writes books on astronomy——"

"I've read them all," declared Mr. Green with pride—and his pride was not without justification, for Mr. Ferrier's output was large and erudite.

George looked at Mr. Green with increased respect. "I say!" he exclaimed. "I wish I had. The truth is, I can't read Dad's books. I can't understand them."

"I didn't say I understood them, did I? But never mind that now. Tell me about yourself. You aren't married, are you?"

"Good life, no!"

"Engaged—eh?"

"No," said George.

"In love, then?" Mr. Green inquired, and his eyes were so kind and so sincerely interested that it was impossible to be annoyed.

"Well . . ." George began, smiling in a deprecating way. "Well, I thought I was, you know, and then I met another girl and——"

"Ha—you young rascal!" cried Mr. Green delightedly.

"They're all nice," George declared. "All in different ways——"

"Why, of course they are!"

"—And sometimes I wonder whether I shall ever find one who's nice in all the different ways together."

"Oh!" said Mr. Green, quite serious now. "And what if you did find her, eh? What if you found someone to fit the bill?"

"Why, then, I'd marry her, of course," said George simply.

When they were settled in the smoking-room Mr. Green began to speak of his own affairs:

"I'm a rich man," he told George in a suitably lowered voice. "You won't find many men saying that; but I'm proud of it. I made every penny of it myself—every penny. I went to America after the war and made my pile, and I got out of business at the right moment and came home to spend it. I was lucky in a way, but it wasn't all luck, by any means."

George was suitably impressed.

"I built a house near Codlington," continued Mr. Green. "It's right up on the moors—a fine, healthy situation. I had to carry the electric cable three miles. That cost something."

"Codlington!" George said. "Why, it's quite near us—not more than six miles or so."

"You must come over," declared Mr. Green enthusiastically. "Bless my soul, I had no idea of that—six miles! You must come over and stay, and bring your father. We could sit up all night talking about Mespot. You will, won't you?"

"Rather," said George. "At least I will. Dad's very hard to move nowadays."

"We'll move him," declared Mr. Green. "It's a comfortable house—central heating and everything up to date—five bathrooms. I go down there myself for weekends. It's too far to come to town every day, besides, it's a bit dull in the country; very quiet, it is—you can hear yourself breathe."

"Plenty of noise here," said George, smiling.

"I like it—makes me feel alive," said Mr. Green.

"Do you live there alone?" inquired George, who had somehow become aware that there was no Mrs. Green in the offing.

"I have a daughter," he replied. "My wife died when she was born. Her governess keeps house for me—an admirable woman. I'd like you to meet my little girl some time."

George replied suitably.

"We must fix it," Mr. Green declared. "You're just the sort of fellow. As a matter of fact——" He broke off suddenly and looked at George with a strangely intent stare.

George met the stare with a contented expression. He had fed extremely well and his body felt drowsy and happy. He saw the sun streaming in through the windows and billions of motes moving gently in its beam. He saw the old dusty furniture, and the huge dark pictures of dead and gone Die Hards through a sort of golden haze.

"It's my birthday!" said George suddenly.

"By Jove, is it?" exclaimed Mr. Green. "What a coincidence! What an extraordinary coincidence!"

"A coincidence?"

"With meeting you, of course. Fancy me

meeting you on your birthday! Why didn't you tell me before? We'd have had fizz."

"I never meant——"

"Of course not," Mr. Green said. "But I tell you what: we'll have brandy now. They've an excellent——"

"No," said George.

"Yes, to drink your health."

"No, I say, really . . ."

"We must," declared Mr. Green, calling the waiter impatiently and giving his order.

"And now," said Mr. Green, when the brandy had arrived in enormous bubble-like glasses, and George's health had been drunk with due ceremony. "And now, George, I want to ask you something."

For a moment George was startled—most of his friends prefaced a request for a loan with these ominous words—but almost immediately he remembered that Mr. Green had claimed to be a rich man, and the beginnings of a frown changed into a smile.

"Yes, I want to ask you something," repeated Mr. Green. "It's like this, you see: I'm a rich man with an only daughter, and when I die she'll be a rich woman. I've got the money tied up in trust, with trustees to look after it for her. Well, here's the position,

George: One of the trustees has died—he's the second to fall out, and, to tell you the truth, I'm sick of it. Costs money, too. Well, what about it, eh?"

"What about what?"

"What about you taking on?"

George was struck dumb with amazement. He was used to censure from the older generation, to pointed reference to his extravagance and unreliability; he was used to lectures about the gravity of life and the need to take things seriously, and now here was a man—quite an old man, and obviously belonging to the censorious age—who was actually prepared to entrust George with the responsibility of administering his fortune.

"Well, what about it?" inquired Mr. Green.

"Me?" asked George incredulously.

"Yes, you."

"But I'm—you w-want somebody older."

"I do *not*," cried Mr. Green in such loud tones that an ancient member who had been slumbering off the effects of a heavy lunch leapt out of his chair and glared round the room in a fury. "I do *not* want an old doddering dotard," Mr. Green amplified in a lower voice. "Haven't I just said I was sick of the way the trustees were dying off—haven't I?"

"Yes, but——"

"There isn't any 'but' about it. I *am* sick of it. I want somebody young, somebody who's going to outlive me. I'm good for another twenty years," declared Mr. Green confidently. "I'm fit and hearty, and as active as a cricket. Now, in another twenty years, you'll be forty-five—exactly the right age for a trustee."

George saw the point. "But you don't know me," he objected. "I might be the most awful——"

"Know you! Of course I know you. Your father used to talk about you by the hour—used to show me pictures of you. I remember one of you lying on a tiger skin without any clothes on."

George shuddered.

"How I envied Ferrier!" continued Mr. Green reminiscently. "I said to myself, 'One day I'll marry and have a son.' But it wasn't to be."

"You've got a daughter," said George comfortingly.

"Yes," agreed his companion, "I've got a daughter; but it isn't the same. You've got to be careful with daughters—always on your best behaviour, and no swear words—you

24

can't chat with a daughter like we're doing now."

"Why not?" inquired George, who found the fair sex quite companionable.

"You've got to shield them, George," declared his new friend gravely. "Shield them from harm. Women are like flowers, delicate, virginal, easily shocked and frightened."

George had not thought of women in this light before, but he was always willing to consider a fresh point of view. He thought of the various girls he knew: were they like flowers? Not noticeably. Were they delicate, virginal, easily shocked and frightened? No, no, no. He thought of his mother and smiled involuntarily. "Oh, well!" he said. "I dare say some girls may be like that. I've always found them fairly hard-boiled——"

Mr. Green shuddered. "Hard-boiled!" he exclaimed. "That's just it! That's the ruin of the country. We don't want hard-boiled women. We want tender, gracious ladies. How are we to get what we want? Tell me that, George."

George could not tell him.

"Now, listen to me," said Mr. Green earnestly. "I've brought up my little girl as a girl *should* be brought up. I've sheltered her

25

from the world. She's uncontaminated by the modern ideas—uncontaminated. What d'you think of that?"

George did not know what to think.

Mr. Green sighed. "There's only one thing that worries me," he said with a confidential air. "Only one thing. I shall have to be damned careful in choosing a husband for her. She's so innocent, you see."

"Yes," nodded George. "But perhaps she'll have something to say about——"

"She does what she's told," interrupted Mr. Green. "Obedience is the chief attribute of a woman. Oh, I can tell you, the man who marries my little girl will be a lucky fellow." He was silent for a moment, and then he added: "You must come over to Highmoor House, George."

"Yes," said George. "Thank you, I should like to."

"Good. And now to business. You *will* do it, won't you, George? You'll take on this trusteeship?"

George thought about it seriously. "How long would it take to—er—fix?" he asked.

"We'll ginger them up," declared his new friend excitedly. "We'll get the thing fixed in half no time."

26

"I don't know anything about business," George pointed out.

"You don't have to know anything. Old Wicherly, the lawyer, does all the work. All you have to do is to sign a few papers and pocket five hundred pounds."

"Five hundred pounds?" inquired George, pricking up his ears.

"When I'm dead, of course," Mr. Green reminded him. "Nothing happens until I'm dead—and I don't intend to pass out for a bit yet."

"No, of course not," agreed George hastily.

"I'm full of beans," Mr. Green assured him, laughing. "Brimful of beans. 'A good life,' that's what I am."

"A good life?" inquired George, who was singularly ignorant of business matters.

"That's what they call it," explained Mr. Green. "When a man's got reasonable expectations of living to a ripe old age the insurance companies say he's 'a good life'— nothing to do with his morals, you know."

"Oh, I see," said George.

Mr. Green dropped his voice and added confidentially: "As a matter of fact, my life's insured for twenty thousand. I took out the policy ten years ago as an insurance against

27

death duties. But never mind that now. The question is, *are you on?*"

George hesitated, but not for long. Five hundred pounds was well worth having—not to be sneezed at by any means. Five hundred pounds twenty years hence was not so attractive a proposition as five hundred pounds here and now, of course; but, all the same, George could not envisage a time when such a sum of money would not be acceptable.

"If you really want me, I'll do it," said George.

"Good lad!" cried Mr. Green. "Good lad, we'll go to old Wicherly and fix the whole thing."

They drove to the lawyer's office in a taxi and were shown into a dusty, fusty waiting-room, and here they sat and waited for at least twenty minutes before anything further befell. George had already formed the opinion that his new friend was impulsive and impatient, and this opinion was amply confirmed now; for Mr. Green ramped up and down the room like a madman, cursing the delays of the law.

"Kicking our heels here!" cried Mr. Green. "Kicking our heels!"

It was not merely a figure of speech. Mr. Green was actually kicking his heels; and

George, who had never seen the thing happen before, was at first somewhat amused. Soon, however, the countenance of his new friend became so lurid in hue that George was quite alarmed, and he began to think that Mr. Green might die of apoplexy before the business was completed.

At last Mr. Wicherly appeared. He was a small, wizened creature with a domed head, bald as a coot, and his eyes were screened by spectacles with enormously magnified lenses.

"If you had warned me of your visit," he said mildly, in answer to his client's upbraidings, "if you had let me have notice of your intention——"

"Well, never mind," said Mr. Green, sinking into a chair and mopping his brow. "You're here now, and we don't want any more time wasted. This young man has things to do. You can't expect him to kick his heels in a lawyer's office all day."

"This young gentleman——" began Mr. Wicherly doubtfully.

"He's going to be the new trustee," said Mr. Green.

Mr. Wicherly looked at George, and an expression of horror appeared upon his face.

George sighed. He was not surprised at all,

"I told you I was too young," he said.

"Much too young," agreed Mr. Wicherly promptly.

"Not too young at all," declared Mr. Green, and thereupon he produced all his former arguments in favour of appointing young trustees to administer his estate.

George looked on and listened (and hid a smile) while the two old gentlemen wrangled over his body. At first he was of the opinion that the lawyer would gain the day; but, after a few minutes, he perceived that the lawyer's hands were tied. He hadn't the ghost of a chance. It was impossible for Mr. Wicherly to produce his best argument in favour of old and experienced trustees, for he could not say to his client, "You may die at any moment," or "I don't believe you've got twenty years of life in you." George also saw that Mr. Wicherly was receiving quite an erroneous impression of his intimacy with Mr. Green.

"I've known George since he was knee-high to a grasshopper," declared that gentleman, confident in his own mind that this was nothing but the truth. "The Ferriers live at Winthorpe—six miles from my little place in the country. Mr. Ferrier and I were in Mespot together—this young fellow's father, I mean."

Mr. Wicherly, not unnaturally, assumed that the Greens and the Ferriers had been living in each other's pockets for at least a quarter of a century.

He sighed and gave in. "Come back tomorrow," he said. "I will communicate with Mr. Millar immediately. You are aware, of course, that Mr. Millar had suggested Mr. Chiverman as the new trustee?"

"I know, I know," replied Mr. Green testily. "But I can appoint George if I want to."

"Mr. Chiverman is an exceedingly experienced——"

"I said I could appoint George if I wanted to."

"Oh, undoubtedly."

"Well, then, go ahead."

"Come back tomorrow," repeated Mr. Wicherly. "I will prepare the papers and——"

"Nonsense!" cried Mr. Green. "We'll fix it now. You've got all the papers ready because we intended to have old Chiverman—but George is far better. Get the papers and fix it up."

"I can't come back tomorrow," added George.

"Why not?"

31

"I'm going home."

"But we must consult the other trustees," objected Mr. Wicherly. "We cannot appoint Mr. Ferrier without consulting the other trustees——"

"Why not?"

"Mr. Millar might—er—resent it."

"Let him."

"I beg your pardon!"

"I said *let him*," repeated Mr. Green.

"But, my dear sir——"

Mr. Green thumped on the desk. "Can I, or can I not appoint George here and now?"

"Oh, if you put it like that . . ."

"I do put it like that," said Mr. Green firmly.

3

THE WANDERER'S RETURN

GEORGE was on his way home. Having caught the train by the skin of his teeth, he found himself in a compartment with two elderly ladies, and there was no corridor to offer him an escape. Fortunately they were quite pleasant old ladies, and had no objection when George asked if he might smoke.

"It is a smoking compartment," the elder lady pointed out. "My sister and I were unable to obtain seats in a 'Ladies Only.'"

"Well, if you're sure you don't mind," said George, and he smiled at them charmingly.

The ladies were a little fluttered by the smile, and flattered, too, for they were unused to charming smiles from large young men with brown faces and flashing white teeth. The younger and more dashing of the two requested George to open the window a little, and, having thus broken the ice, confided to him that they were going to Codlington for a holiday.

"I'm going to Winthorpe," George said. "It's the station before Codlington. My home is four miles from Winthorpe, right out in the country."

"It is lovely country," said the younger lady. "Our sister is married and lives at Codlington, and we are going to stay with her. We have had influenza," she added confidingly.

George commiserated with them. He would have been quite glad to go on talking, for he had no paper to read; but the elder lady handed her sister a copy of *The Queen* with a significant glance, and no more was said.

Thrown back upon himself, George surveyed the country, which seemed more than usually green and verdant after his stay in town, and began to wonder what had happened at Swan House during his absence. He felt as if he had been away for months, and it was really quite exciting to be going home. How had the young colt come on, he wondered, and would Nadia's puppies have arrived? Paddy would probably meet him at the station and give him all the news. He hoped Paddy would meet him. It would depend upon what was happening at home, whether or not there was a domestic crisis on, and whether she could get the car to start at the right moment——

As they approached Winthorpe, George let down the window and stuck out his head. He saw his mother at once. She had come. She was standing talking to a porter. Yes, there she was, a small, slight figure in comfortably shabby tweeds. George had not seen her for ten whole days, and he seemed to see her with the eyes of a stranger—her small dark face, her flashing eyes, the almost foreign gestures of her thin hands. How eager she was, how full of life. . . .

Suddenly, as the engine steamed in, she spun round and saw him, and was off like a rocket down the platform, running lightly after the still-moving train. "George!" she cried. "George, darling, your bitch has whelped! It was this very morning as ever was. I've had a hell of a time——"

George cast a hasty glance at the scandalised faces of his travelling companions and hurled himself out of the train.

The car was waiting for them at the station entrance. It was a large Rolls of ancient vintage, very high in the body and covered with brass fittings. It boasted a cape hood, but this was scarcely ever employed, owing to the fact that almost superhuman strength was necessary to raise or lower it. Even in the pouring rain Mrs. Ferrier drove the car open, though she had been known to drive it through the streets of Winthorpe with an umbrella wedged between the seats to protect her best hat. In spite of the obvious disadvantage of the car, Mrs. Ferrier was devoted to it, and had been heard to declare that she would not part with it for a king's ransom. She called it Meredith, because it reminded her, so she said, of an old Irish gentleman who had wanted to marry her when she was seventeen. George called it Grandpa.

"How lovely to see you again!" sighed Mrs. Ferrier as she turned out of the station yard. "I declare I'd almost forgotten what you looked like, darling."

"And I'd forgotten how awful you were," retorted George, smiling. "Those poor old ladies, Paddy!"

"I was elated," she declared apologetically. "It was seeing you again, and your dear face and all."

The way to Swan House led through narrow winding roads with high hedges on either side. They were full of wild flowers, and the scent of them was heady and sweet. It was beautiful country all round: undulating country with great trees standing solitary in meadows, or clustered together in woods. Here and there small villages nestled in hollows, their tiny gardens bright with flowers. The trees were at their best, with fresh foliage of a dozen different shades of green. The may was in bloom. There were orchards with trees laden with blossoms like snow.

As they went George learnt a good deal more about the interesting event which had taken place that morning. His mother described it with a wealth of detail and a raciness of language which was all her own.

"She escaped me, the creature," declared Mrs. Ferrier, "and the house was *wrecked* before I could lay hands on her again. . . . But they're little beauties, George. There's not a hair of them you'd want altered, not a hair. . . ."

George, lounging by her side, listened to the tale with an amused smile. He was interested in the tale, but perhaps even more interested in the teller. He enjoyed the deep, husky voice with its contralto notes, and the extravagant exaggerations which were never intended to deceive. And he enjoyed the soft brogue which she could put on at will, and which still (after twenty-six years in England) came naturally to her Irish tongue in moments of pleasure or stress. Her dark eyes were fixed on the road as she talked, and her thin nervous hands gentled the big unwieldy car— almost as if it were one of her beloved horses. It was worth while going away, thought George, if only for the pleasure of returning home and finding Paddy more Paddyish than ever.

He was used to his mother's driving; but today even he was frightened. Paddy was elated, and was therefore inclined to take risks.

"Paddy—great heavens!" he cried as they turned a blind corner on two wheels.

"Is it scared you are?" she inquired, cramming on her brakes and swerving violently to avoid a dog. "It's a new thing for you to be scared. What have you been doing to upset your nerves?"

"Dancing," said George.

"And the girls?" she asked. "Were they all in love with you—the poor pets?"

"Head over heels," declared George, laughing.

"Look at that, now," she said seriously, but with twinkling eyes. "And you can laugh at them—the playboy you are!"

For a little while no more was said, and then George asked suddenly, "How old are you, Paddy?"

"What a question!" she cried, gurgling suddenly with deep laughter. "Forty-five, if you must be knowing—but it's inelegant of you to be asking a lady's age."

"Twenty years older than me! You don't look it, Paddy."

"I don't mind much," said Mrs. Ferrier, suddenly serious. "My pleasures were never in my looks, and as long as I can sit a horse and enjoy the company of my friends I'll be happy. Wrinkles don't trouble me, George; it's a queer thing, but it's the truth."

"Were you ever like a flower?" inquired George. "Were you ever delicate and virginal and easily shocked?"

"George. Who is she?"

"Who?"

"The girl—the woman. . . ."

"It was a man——" began George.

"A man!" screamed Paddy. "For the love of Mike!"

George laughed. "If you'd only listen," he

said. "If you'd only listen for half a minute instead of jumping to conclusions——"

"But a man," she interrupted, "a man to be delicate and easily shocked—and like a flower——"

"It was a man *told* me about a girl who was——"

"Ah!" said Paddy, understandingly. "If you'd said that at first——"

"Look out!" yelled George. "Look out, Paddy!"

"All right," she said, as she twisted the wheel and scraped past a farm-cart with half an inch to spare. "All right, George. Keep cool. You should *not* shout at me suddenly—we might have had an accident."

They had now arrived at the gates of Swan House and George looked at it with affection. It stood close by the road, for it had once been an inn, or posting-house, called the White Swan, on the route from London to Wandlebury. George's great-grandfather had bought the place more than a hundred years ago when trains had begun to take the traffic off the roads and the mail coaches had stopped running. He had altered it and renovated it and turned it into a gentleman's residence.

He could not move it back from the road, but he had planted trees to give it a measure of privacy. It was an old rambling house, a rabbit warren of twisting passages and stairs, and there were several large pleasant rooms on the ground floor which had once been used to entertain passengers from the coaches. The spirit of hospitality which inhabits all good inns had not departed from the precincts of Swan House. There was a comfortable feeling about the place, an atmosphere of comfort, of kindliness, and of good cheer. So that, although the house was old, it had quite a different personality from that of most ancient buildings, such as old fortresses and castles which were used for defence. Swan House had always opened its arms to strangers, and it still did. There was a large cobbled yard at one side of the house with stables and outhouses, and behind were large fields and paddocks with high hedges and great trees. Beyond the fields stretched the moor, sweeping up to a line of hills against the skyline.

Paddy stopped the car with a jerk in the middle of the gravel sweep, and without a word they both got out and made a bee-line for the stables.

"I put her in the loose-box," Paddy said as

they crossed the cobbled yard. "I was at my wits' end, George."

"You've done splendidly," George declared. "I meant to be back in time. Paddy, darling, I'm so sorry you had all the bother. . . ."

"I didn't mind," she answered. "They're all right, and that's the main thing. Look at them, George."

He peeped over the high door of the loose-box and saw Nadia, the spaniel, surrounded by her babies. They were not really pretty yet—in fact, they were rather ugly—mere balls of fur, with huge tummies and huge mouths.

Mrs. Ferrier stood on a conveniently placed box and rested her arms on the loose-box door. "Aren't they lambs?" she whispered.

"No, they're puppies," he replied, but he was pleased with them, too.

"Horrid creature!" she said affectionately, and then she added in a significant tone: "Forbes asked for one."

"He did, did he?"

"It shows he thought they were good," Mrs. Ferrier pointed out. "He said he'd take one instead of his fee."

"Good of him," said George dryly.

"Oh, George! He was very decent. I was thankful to see him——"

"In that case he must have one, I suppose. But I'm not giving away any more. I want to *sell* them, see?"

"I know," she agreed hastily. "But there might be one not so good as the others—there's sure to be—and Harry Coles——"

"I'm not giving any of them away," said George again. He knew only too well the extent of Paddy's generosity. The puppies were his, and Paddy knew that, but she was generous with other people's belongings no less than with her own. It must be clearly understood from the beginning that the puppies were to be sold and not given away to any impecunious young man who happened to be in need of a shooting dog. As it was, George had promised one to his great friend, Peter Seeley, and another had been promised to the vet in the heat of the moment. He did not blame Paddy for this, of course.

"Don't change," said Paddy as they walked back to the house arm-in-arm. "I won't change, either. We'll walk down to the West Paddock after dinner and have a look at Snowball's colt."

4

THE FERRIERS AT HOME

DINNER at Swan House was the only ceremonial meal of the day. It was the only meal at which Mrs. Ferrier ate more than a few mouthfuls of food. At breakfast she consumed a grapefruit, standing at the mantelpiece in front of the fire; and her lunch was usually a cup of coffee and a bowl of salad and a buttered roll. But dinner was a different affair altogether; and unless Swan House was visited by a major domestic crisis, the three Ferriers sat down to a well-appointed table and consumed four courses in a civilised manner.

The dining-room was large, with a low ceiling and a stone floor; the furniture was dark oak, shabby, and scratched by generations of stirring Ferriers; the rugs, though good, were old and worn. Mr. Ferrier was too vague and other-worldly to notice the deterioration of his household goods, and Mrs. Ferrier too Irish to mind.

On this particular evening, the evening of George's return from the delights of the Metropolis, the three Ferriers sat down to dinner in great contentment. George was pleased to be home, and his parents were delighted to have him; Swan House was a dull place without George. The french windows opened westwards on to a pleasant lawn shaded by trees, and the declining sun shone in through the windows and lighted up the room. Belt, the spaniel, lay on the floor near the fireplace. He was the father of the puppies in the stable. It seemed strange to be home, George thought, and not to have Nadia at his heels, following him up and down the stairs like a small brown shadow, or lying on the floor by his feet, perfectly content to be near him. There was a "special feeling" between Nadia and George, for he had had her since she was six weeks old, and had trained her himself. She understood every tone of his voice and gave him undivided devotion. George felt almost jealous of the puppies which were now usurping her attention; it was an absurd feeling, of course—he realised that himself.

"How quiet it is!" George said as he dipped the spoon into his soup.

"Yes," agreed Paddy, "I dare say it is—after London. What were you doing all the time? Tell me about it."

George complied at once with this somewhat comprehensive request. He knew that Paddy loved to hear all the news. He told her where he had gone and what he had done, and described the bag which he had chosen for her at Asprey's. Her reactions to this particular episode were exactly what he had expected:

"Darling!" she cried. "And you thought of me in Bond Street. It's almost as if I'd been there myself—so it is!"

Mr. Ferrier, sitting in the big carved chair at the head of the table, glanced from his wife to his son, and listened to their prattle as a benignant grandfather might listen to the prattle of four-year-old babes. He was so much older than either of them—not only in years, but in mind—that sometimes it seemed to him that they were the same age and of the same generation, separated from him by a thousand ages of time.

"How goes the book, Dad?" inquired George, realising suddenly that his father was being neglected.

"It is going well, thank you," replied Mr.

Ferrier, smiling; "but I have not been writing today. I walked over to Ingram Hill and sat there in the sun. It occurred to me that a holiday would be pleasant."

"Quentin—if you'd told me!" cried his wife, "I would have come with you—indeed I would!"

"I was aware of that, my dear; but you were fully occupied—and, to tell you the truth, I wanted to think."

"What did you think about?" George inquired.

"I thought about the future," replied Mr. Ferrier musingly. "It is a fascinating employment to envisage what may come. One sees how the practice of genethliacs, and other forms of astrology, obtained so strong a hold upon the immature intelligence of mediaeval peoples."

The serious and scholarly reply was typical of Mr. Ferrier. He would never force his ideas upon any one, but neither would he withhold a straightforward answer to a straightforward question. He was aware that he thought more deeply than most of his neighbours, and indeed that most of his neighbours preferred not to think at all; but he could not believe that they had not the power to think, or the capacity to understand. The depth of his own thought engendered in Mr. Ferrier a certain vagueness of manner, but his inattention seldom gave offence, for he possessed great charm, and his kindliness was too obvious to be disregarded. George remembered the classical occasion when the Ferriers had been entertaining a certain Mrs. Fry, who had come down to speak at the local Unionist meeting. She had sat next to Mr. Ferrier at luncheon, and, resentful of his abstraction, had turned to him suddenly and demanded, "Mr. Ferrier, what do *you* think of Hitler?" There was a sudden lull in the conversation, and the host's quiet tones had dropped into the silence like pebbles into a pool. "Hitler?" queried Mr. Ferrier. "I am afraid I have not the pleasure of his acquaintance, Mrs. Fry."

"Dad," said George after a short silence. "Dad, I met a friend of yours in town—a man called Green with a purple face—rather a nice old boy."

"A man called Green with a purple face!" echoed Mr. Ferrier, aroused from the contemplation of genethliacs as practised by mediaeval sages.

"John Green," said George patiently. "Do you know him?"

"Green? Dear me, yes."

"You were in Mespot together."

"We were indeed. We shared a tent for some months, I remember. Green! Dear me, I have not thought of young Green for years."

"He's thought of you," said George. "He's read all your books, Dad."

"How very gratifying!" exclaimed Mr. Ferrier, whose public was so limited as to be almost invisible to the naked eye.

George, having thus prepared the ground and gained his father's attention, proceeded to deliver the messages with which he had been entrusted, and he had the satisfaction of seeing all trace of Mr. Ferrier's vagueness disappear. In fact, Mr. Ferrier became quite human and jocular, and was able to add a good many amusing details to the tale of the adjutant's tent.

"And Dusty," said George. "He said I was to ask if you remembered a fellow called Dusty. Do you, Dad?"

The happy smile faded from Mr. Ferrier's face. "Dusty!" he said slowly. "Why did Green want to remind me of *him*?"

It was said in such a way that it was

49

obviously not a question, or at any rate not a question to George. Perhaps it might have been a question to some higher power, or perhaps only the musing of a man looking back at the past.

Mrs. Ferrier had been silent for some time, listening to all that was said; but now she leant forward suddenly.

"Wasn't there something about Dusty?" she asked, wrinkling her forehead in her effort to remember. "Didn't he do something—something odd? What was it, Quent?"

"He was—er—not quite straight, my dear," declared Mr. Ferrier in such a final sort of tone that George, who was itching to know what Dusty had done, realised that the subject was closed.

"*Not quite straight*," thought George. It was a sufficiently damning indictment; for Mr. Ferrier was a mild, gentle creature and—unlike his wife—was given to understatement. If he liked a man immensely he had been known to say that so-and-so was a pleasant sort of man; and, of an out-and-out ruffian, he would probably remark that he did not care for the fellow very much. George made a mental note that Dusty must resemble a corkscrew, and passed on to other things.

He had decided not to tell his parents about the trusteeship—they would only laugh and say it was absurd. In twenty years he would be forty-five, thought George, and nobody could say that a man of forty-five was too young to be a trustee.

After dinner Mrs. Ferrier and her son walked down to the West Paddock and stood at the rails looking at Snowball and her colt. It was getting dark now, the hour when darkness closes gently upon the woods, yet leaves the fields untouched, and when light-coloured objects shine in the surrounding gloom with almost phosphorescent effect. Snowball was a grey, and her colt was dove-coloured, so the two quiet forms were easily discernible as they stood against the darkness of the hedge. Paddy and George watched them for a few moments without speaking. It was an extraordinarily peaceful scene.

"She's getting old," said Paddy at last with a sigh.

George agreed. "You'll want another hunter next winter," he told her, speaking in a low tone which the intense stillness seemed to demand.

"Forbes has a young horse," said Paddy,

"a darling thing. He needs a little schooling, but we could manage that."

"We'll have a look at him," George declared.

"Yes," said Paddy, "but I hate it, you know. I don't like to admit that Snowball's old."

In spite of the low tone in which their conversation had been held, Snowball pricked up her ears and came across the paddock, walking delicately, with her colt at her heels. She accepted the greetings of her human friends, and also a lump of sugar which George had filched from the cupboard in the dining-room. When Paddy offered her a second lump, however, she hesitated a moment and turned her head towards the colt, which was standing a few yards off watching the proceedings with interest.

"The darling lamb!" cried Mrs. Ferrier. "She wants her child to have it!"

It certainly looked like that; but, if it were the case, her altruism was of short duration, for, when the colt, tempted by cooing noises, sidled up to Paddy's hand, Snowball leaned over and took the titbit from under his nose. "You must learn to be a bit quicker, young man," she seemed to say as she crunched it up.

George and Paddy laughed wholeheartedly at the incident.

"It's a lesson to mothers," declared George. "There's no foolish sentiment about Snowball. She's all out for number one."

"But she wanted him to have it at first," Paddy pointed out. "She did, indeed—you saw her. I declare the creature's human."

But this was mere trifling. Paddy and George had come down to the paddock with a definite object, and they were both aware that the moment for an important decision was at hand.

"Have you thought about it, George?" inquired his mother anxiously.

"Well, no," replied George; "but we'll think about it now. Let's see," he continued, eyeing the colt, whose light hide gleamed softly in the ever-increasing gloom, "Snowflake, Soapflake. What about Lux?"

"I thought of Noah," said Mrs. Ferrier diffidently. "He's the colour of a dove; it was *that* made me think of it."

"Noah!" said George, holding out his hand. The colt approached sideways. Perhaps he approved of the name, or perhaps he was under the impression that the outstretched hand contained a cube of that white shiny stuff which his mother was munching with such obvious enjoyment.

Mrs. Ferrier was of the former opinion. "He likes it," she whispered excitedly. "He came when you called him Noah. . . ."

"Noah it is," said George. "Give me some sugar for him, Paddy."

He was aware that Paddy's pockets could usually yield stray lumps of sugar when required, and his faith was justified; she produced a dark-coloured object and put it into his hand. "I've had it for years," she declared, and for once her exaggerated statement rang true.

"Noah won't mind," said George comfortingly.

Mrs. Ferrier watched the coaxing of the shy colt, and suddenly she loved George unbearably—he was so good and gentle, so kind. Her heart twisted in her breasts, and the physical pain of the emotion was such that she was forced to cling to the rails. Oh, God, said Mrs. Ferrier silently. Oh, God, let him be happy for ever and ever and all the time.

"There," said George, wiping his hand on a tuft of grass. "You'll know another time, old chap. You won't be so backward the next time you see sugar, will you?"

5

THE POOR OLD WOMAN

THE following morning, George was very late for breakfast. He had been down to the stables to have a look at Nadia, and, finding her in the mood for a little conversation, he had stayed by her sick bed for a chat. "You've done splendidly, old girl," George had told her. "The babies are lovely. We'll keep one—or perhaps two, if Paddy doesn't mind, and I don't think she will mind, somehow. She's so proud of them, you'd think she'd had them herself. . . ."

"It's awfully dull here," Nadia had complained, licking the hand that was fondling her smooth brown head. "You've been away so long, and now that you're home again I've got to look after these tiresome children."

These tender passages had run away with a good deal of time, and when George reached the dining-room, Paddy had eaten her grapefruit and gone, and Mr. Ferrier was at the marmalade stage with *The Times* propped up against the coffee-pot.

"Anything in the paper?" inquired George cheerfully.

"Nothing at all," replied Mr. Ferrier from force of habit.

There was a little silence, and then he inquired, "What did you say, George?"

"I only said was there anything in the paper?" declared George as he helped himself to a plate of bacon and eggs and took his seat at the table.

"There's the Budget, of course," Mr. Ferrier said, looking at his son over the tops of his spectacles. "The Budget is—er—there is a new tax on tobacco; and this is somewhat unfortunate in view of the fact that your mother's small income is invested in tobacco. She is—er—a trifle upset——"

"Good Lord, is she?" exclaimed George, looking round the room for evidence of the storm, and noting with relief that, except for an overturned chair and a couple of cushions on the floor near the window, everything seemed much as usual.

"Yes," said Mr. Ferrier. "I gathered there was some project on foot to purchase a young

56

horse from Forbes, and that the project may have to be abandoned."

"Oh, hell!" said George dejectedly. "She'd set her heart on the beast."

"A little walk," continued Mr. Ferrier gently. "Yes, George, I think if you could persuade her to take a little walk with you through the woods—er—the fact is, I should prefer to think of her walking than riding this morning."

"Absolutely," agreed George, nodding emphatically, with his mouth full of bacon.

"She mentioned selling Snowball," Mr. Ferrier went on; "but there will be no necessity for any such drastic measure. . . ."

"I'll tell her," said George understandingly.

Mr. Ferrier sighed with relief. It was a great comfort to have George. He could leave the whole situation in George's hands and retire to his study for a morning's work with an easy mind. There had been a time when he had been disappointed to find that his son had no love of learning, and no ambition to make his mark in the world; but for some years now he had been completely satisfied with George. He realised that it took all sorts to make a world, and George had his own particular kind of brains—quite different from Mr. Ferrier's kind, but perhaps no less valuable.

"Perhaps more valuable," said Mr. Ferrier aloud. And then, thinking of his Herculean labours and the minute public to which his books appealed, he added firmly, "Definitely more valuable than mine."

George looked up from his breakfast; but, seeing that his father was immersed in thought, he looked down again and smiled. What was more valuable than what, George wondered—the discovery of some new star, perhaps, or some astronomical calculation about the speed of a comet, or some new-fangled idea about the atmosphere of Mars! "He's forgotten Paddy's storm by now," thought George; "and it's even chances she's forgotten it herself; but all the same I shan't let her ride this morning—he's right about that."

But Paddy had not forgotten her storm; he was aware of this directly he emerged from the back door and saw her in the stable-yard. She was standing with her hands clasped behind her back, waiting for a bucket to fill with water from the trickling tap, and she was singing the song of "The Poor Old Woman, the Shan Van Voght." It was an ominous sign.

> "Oh, the French are on the say,
> Says the Shan Van Voght,
> Oh, the French are on the say,
> Says the Shan Van Voght.
> The French are on the say,
> They'll be here by break of day,
> And the Rose it will decay,
> Says the Shan Van Voght."

Paddy sang it defiantly in her slightly husky contralto, and when she came to the penultimate line she gave the bucket a good hard kick:

> "And the *Rose*, it will decay,
> Says the Shan Van Voght."

The bucket was full now, and the rebel seized it up and disappeared into the stable. George followed her.

It took a great deal of finesse to inveigle Paddy into a walk that morning, for Paddy wanted to ride—and ride like hell! She wanted to trample on the Chancellor of the

59

Exchequer, to ride him down and trample upon him with iron-shod hooves. She wanted to trample upon the Rose, and see it broken in the mud.

"It's Irish I am," she declared. "And how was I to be knowing that I'd lose my country when I married an Englishman? Taking my money, they are, and be damned to them for it! And me, an Irishwoman, to be paying for their English guns!"

George listened gravely, walking up and down the cobbled yard with his hand through her arm and putting in the right interjections at suitable moments. Presently they were through the gate which led to the woods and climbing the steep stony path . . . and Paddy was still talking. . . .

They were half-way through the woods when at last she stopped for want of breath, and aroused by the sudden silence—as a passenger on an Atlantic liner is aroused from his slumbers by the sudden cessation of the ship's engines—she looked at George, and looked around her, and laughed. . . .

George laughed, too. "Has the poor old woman gone?" he asked her.

"It seems like it," Paddy said, giving herself a little shake. "But it's a bad, wicked, ugly-tempered old woman you've got for a mother, George."

George let go of her arm and lighted a cigarette. He was aware that the fight was over and the battle won. Paddy would not turn back now, but would concede his victory with a good grace. There was never any aftermath of bitterness to Paddy's storms—they passed like thunderclouds and were forgotten.

"You've been making a mountain out of a molehill, haven't you?" he said as they walked on.

"A mountain out of a hill," amended Paddy. "It's like this, George, darling: if you make a mountain and look at it, the hill seems smaller when you come to your senses again; that's the way of it, you see."

George saw. He thought it was rather interesting. There was something deep and psychologically sound in this method of dealing with troubles.

"Dad says he'll stand you Snowball's oats," said George.

"The treasure!" said Paddy tenderly. "Ah, the treasure!"

They walked on together through the woods, and the sun, shining through the new leaves, dappled the ground with light. There were wood violets here, half-hidden beneath their round, shiny leaves, and the bluebells were in bud. A cuckoo called softly and was answered by another in the valley, and, as they came out upon the green hillside, a lark rose from beneath their feet and soared upwards, bursting into song. . . .

"Now that we're here we might call at Rival's Green," said Paddy suddenly. "I want to ask Mrs. Seeley about eggs—eggs for pickling. Peter's there," she added, offering him as an enticement.

George was quite ready to fall in with his mother's wishes. He had always liked Rival's Green, and, being an only child, he had revelled in the companionship of the young Seeleys. They had played together as children, quarrelled and fought and made it up again, and the friendship was cemented for all time.

Mr. Seeley was a shadowy sort of figure to George. He was a small, thin man with shaggy eyebrows. He travelled daily to town, and George was vaguely aware that he was a lawyer. Mrs. Seeley was large and very fat. Her feet seemed too small to support her body, and perhaps this was why she used them so little. Mrs. Seeley was immobile. She sat in the drawing-room all day and radiated good nature. There were five young Seeleys. The eldest, Peter (George's great friend) had just passed his finals in medicine with flying colours. The second was Catherine, who looked after the house; then came the twins— Jim and Joan—aged sixteen; and lastly Diana, the "baby." George had always entertained rather a special feeling for Diana—or Dan, as she was usually called; he had seen her grow up, and she had grown with startling rapidity. The mere fact that he had held her in his arms when she was less than a fortnight old seemed to give him a feeling of responsibility towards her. He was aware, too, that Dan was fond of him and admired him, and that she really liked him better than Peter, her own brother. (This was not so strange as it might appear, for Peter had not much use for Dan except as a fag, and was wont to declare that Dan, as the "baby," enjoyed privileges which had been denied to older members of the family).

One of the pleasant things about Rival's Green was the fact that you could be sure of finding Mrs. Seeley at home. You did not trouble to ring the bell—unless you were a stranger, of course—but simply walked across the lawn to the drawing-room door. Mrs.

Seeley was always there, sitting in a large chintz-covered chair with a high back and low arms; sometimes she was sitting there reading, and sometimes doing fancy work, and sometimes she was just sitting there.

Today she was reading, but she dropped the book when she saw Paddy and George, and her fat face creased into a large good-natured smile. "Nice people!" she said. "Come and talk to me. What has George been doing in London?"

"All sorts of things," said George. "It was marvellous; but it's nice to be home."

"The children are somewhere about," said Mrs. Seeley vaguely. "I think Cathie is rolling the lawn. Peter went to Winthorpe——"

"I'll see," said George.

He looked back from the door and saw that the two friends had already started to talk. How funny they were—Mrs. Seeley so large and fat and placid, and Paddy so small and fiery! Their heads were close together in earnest conclave, and George was pretty certain that the subject under discussion was yesterday's interesting event.

6

CATHERINE SEELEY

THE Seeley's garden was looking very pretty. It was not so burnt up as the garden at Swan House, for it lay in a hollow and was shaded by large trees. At Swan House the garden was Paddy's responsibility, and sometimes Paddy took a violent interest in it and dug and hoed like a maniac, and sometimes she sat back and let it rip; but at Rival's Green the garden was under the management of an old and experienced gardener called Cobham, and was cared for with solicitude and skill. George, looking at the bright array of flowers, wished that they could afford an experienced gardener at Swan House. He was fond of flowers, and liked to see them blooming luxuriantly in properly tended beds.

He went down through the rose garden to the tennis lawn and found it rolled and marked. It was obvious that Cathy had finished that job and gone on to something else. The question was *what*. She might be in the kitchen garden—a large rectangular garden encircled by high red-brick walls—or she might be feeding the ducks near the stream which flowed past the bottom of the garden, or, again, she might have gone back to the house. George tried the kitchen garden first, and found her standing on a ladder, tying up the little branches of the peach trees.

Catherine Seeley was very fair. Her skin was a little tanned by the sun, but her hair was like floss silk, and fluffy as the downy feathers of a chicken. Her eyes were very blue and her mouth well shaped, but on the large side for beauty. George had known Cathy since she was a small girl in crumpled overalls; he knew her and liked her in the same casual way as one knows and likes a sister. He was four years older than Cathy, which made her twenty-one; but, perhaps because she was so fair, she looked younger. Sometimes he and Peter had allowed Cathy to take part in their games, and sometimes they had not, and Cathy had always accepted whatever treatment was meted out to her, and made the best of it. He remembered her in small unrelated pictures—as a leggy child and as a fat and somewhat pudding-faced girl—and always she had been somewhere about, either playing with him and Peter and meekly accepting the least interesting rôle, or playing by herself with a row of battered dolls.

George had never thought of it before, but today as he went towards her down the path, beneath the blossom-laden branches of the apple trees, he wondered whether Cathy ever felt lonely. The twins were everything to each other, and Peter was sufficient unto himself. Cathy was the odd man out of the Seeley family.

"Hallo, George!" she said, looking down from the ladder and smiling at him in a friendly way.

"Hallo, Cathy!"

"I've promised Cobham to tie these up. He's getting old, you know, and I don't think he's very fit for ladders now."

"I want to talk to you."

"You can talk while I work."

George did not think that would be easy. He was not used to talking up at people, for he was usually a good bit taller than the person he happened to be talking to. He explained this to Cathy, but she was adamant.

"It will do you good," she declared. "You know now how uncomfortable it is for other people to talk to you—pass me up that ball of bass, please."

George passed it up.

"Has Nadia had her puppies yet?" inquired Cathy.

"Yes," said George. "Six beauties. Look here, I'll come and help you——"

He found another ladder and reared it against the wall, and in another moment he was on a level with Cathy. Her fair face was flushed, and some tendrils of her silky hair were flattened on her forehead.

"You *do* look hot," he said.

"No," she replied. "I mean I don't feel hot—or at least I didn't until you said the word. Look, George, each of these little twigs, with the peaches forming, has got to be tied on to the iron grid."

"What a frightful job!" he exclaimed.

"If we didn't tie them up, the peaches wouldn't form properly, and the branches would sag with their weight."

"D'you mean it has to be done every year?"

"Every single year," nodded Cathy.

He watched her at work for a moment or two.

"What neat fingers!" he said, taking her hand and spreading it out so that he could see it properly. "Mine are huge and clumsy, aren't they?"

"Huge, but not clumsy," she replied, removing her hand firmly.

"Why did you do that?" he inquired.

"Because I want to get on with the work, silly," said Cathy, laughing.

They worked away together for a little, talking in the desultory fashion of old friends. George soon got into the way of it, for, as Cathy had said, his fingers were not clumsy— they were slim and tensile.

"I like this work," he said. "It's very more—ish."

Cathy agreed. "You feel you must do just one more, and then another one more. It's just as well."

"Are you going to do the whole wall?"

"I expect so," said Cathy.

"Why doesn't Peter help?"

"Why should he? He's here for a holiday. Oh, George, you can't imagine how glad I am that he's through. He's worked so hard."

"Is he tired?"

"Yes, I think so, but he doesn't realise it himself. I wish you would do something about Peter: you're good for him."

"No brains, that's why," replied George.

"He can't talk to me about his work. He's got to descend to my level, and that's a rest for his brain. I wish I was clever."

"You're quite clever in your own way," she told him. "Clever about horses—and people, too. Really brainy people are sometimes awful fools about their kind."

George conceded that. "D'you know Clarice Morton?" he asked.

"We were at school together," said Cathy.

George had felt pretty certain that Cathy did not like Clarice, and now he was sure of it. He smiled to himself.

"What's the joke?" Cathy inquired.

"Nothing much—only people *are* interesting," George replied. "Clarice dances like an angel," he added with an innocent air.

"She always did," agreed Cathy, rather too heartily. "Look, George, can you reach that high one?"

George reached it quite easily and tied it into place.

"Tell me about London," Cathy said. "Tell me what you did."

"London was absolutely wizard," declared George. "Tom knows such crowds of people. We danced and we went to Henley, and we

70

did some plays—we pub-crawled a bit, too. It was fun."

"It must have been."

"But you'd soon get sick of it if you lived there always."

"I suppose you would," said Cathy wistfully.

George noticed the wistfulness, and it struck him that Cathy had rather a poor time.

"Look here," he said, "what about a ride some time? You haven't ridden for ages, have you?"

"I'm so busy——" she began.

"Before breakfast," George explained. "You aren't busy before breakfast, are you? Do come, Cathy. You used to ride quite well."

Now that he had formulated the idea, he was enchanted with it and wondered why he had not thought of it before. It would be fun for Cathy, and she could help him to exercise the horses—two birds with one stone, as it were.

"I'd like to, thank you," Cathy was saying in a cool little voice.

"Tomorrow?"

"Yes."

"That's settled, then."

There was silence for a while, and the work went on.

"How's my friend Dan?" asked George at last. "Haven't seen her for ages."

"She's back at school now—at Winthorpe, of course—she goes in every morning in the bus. I don't like it."

"I thought that school in Winthorpe was supposed to be quite good," said George gravely.

"It's the girls," Cathy said. "Dan doesn't make friends easily. She ought to go to boarding school."

George considered the matter. "Won't they do it?" he asked.

"No, they won't. The parents won't part with her because she amuses them, and Peter backs them up."

"I should have thought Peter——"

She interrupted quickly: "Peter is against it because he says it would be a waste of money. He's always so down on Dan. It isn't fair. He says she's spoilt. But she isn't, really; she's just sort of—neglected."

"Neglected?" echoed George in surprise.

"Oh, the parents *adore* her, of course, but they don't *worry* about her," Cathy explained. "They think it's funny if she's cheeky, and they let her do what she likes, more or less, as long as she doesn't bother them. It's so frightfully bad for her—it would be bad for any one."

"They weren't like that with you," said George thoughtfully.

Cathy agreed. "They were absolutely different. They *worried* over us. They worried over our reports. They sent us to bed if we were rude . . . but I believe we were happier, really. At any rate, we knew that they really minded."

"It's very odd, isn't it?" said George.

Cathy did not reply, and, glancing sideways, he saw that her brows were drawn together in a little frown. Cathy was worrying about Dan. Mrs. Seeley sat complacently in the drawing-room, and Mr. Seeley lived in a world apart, so it was left to Cathy to bear the burdens of the family on her slim shoulders.

"Dan's all right," said George comfortingly. "I *mean* that, Cathy. She's made of the right stuff!"

They had just moved their ladders and started another tree when Peter came strolling down the path with his hands in his pockets.

"Hallo!" he said. "What on earth are you doing?"

"Hallo, Dr. Seeley!" cried George. "We're setting the peaches. Come and help."

"No, thank you. But I'll set your leg if you fall off the ladder—it'll be good practice for me."

"Thanks awfully," retorted George.

Peter stood and looked at them for a moment or two. "I say, come on," he said at last. "Cathy can finish that. Come and see my new car. At least it isn't really new—only new to me. I bought it for ten pounds."

George climbed down the ladder and followed Peter without a word (he had always followed Peter), but he paused at the door in the garden wall and looked back, for it had suddenly occurred to him that he had not been polite. This was an odd thought, because, of course, there really wasn't any need to be polite to Cathy. He was Peter's friend and always had been, and Cathy knew that. . . . Still, he might have said something. . . .

He saw her blue dress against the pink wall—it was the colour of the sky—and he remembered suddenly that her eyes were that colour, too. The garden was full of blossom, white and pink, great masses of it like white and pink snow.

"Come on," said Peter. "What are you looking at?"

"Nothing," said George.

"Come on, then," said Peter.

7

"THE DROUGHT CONTINUES"

THE moor stretched westwards and northwards from Swan House, rising gradually to the low rolling hills, and it was here that George and Cathy took their early morning ride. The moor was very dry; even the boggy places were hard and cracked across and across with gaping fissures, for England was enjoying—or enduring—a prolonged drought, and day after day of brilliant sunshine had sucked up the moisture from the land.

Cathy and George cantered gaily over the level stretches of the moor and skirted sand-pits at a sober walk. It was necessary to use caution near these sand-pits, for they were riddled with rabbit-holes, and sometimes the turf gave way beneath the horses' hooves and they sank up to their fetlocks. The rabbits were all out this morning; there were hundreds of them flopping about and playing games and nibbling the close-growing turf, and for some reason these rabbits were so tame that they did not vanish at the sight of human beings, but only hopped away a little and sat with cocked ears as the horses went past.

"This is lovely," Cathy said. "The world seems much fresher in the early morning, doesn't it? Why don't we always get up early like this? Why doesn't everybody?"

"I've often wondered that," said George.

He was more than ever glad that he had asked Cathy to ride with him. She was an ideal companion, for she neither talked too little nor too much. She rode well and she looked comfortable, and, what was even more important from George's point of view, her mount looked comfortable as well. He glanced at her now, sitting astride the brown mare, and approved of her well-fitting corduroy breeches and brown leggings. They were shabby, of course, but that was all to the good. Her cap had blown off and she had tucked it into the pocket of her saddle, and her fluffy hair stood out like a nimbus round her flushed happy face.

"You look just right," he said.

Cathy smiled at him.

"It was a good idea," he added.

She nodded, and he saw that she knew what he meant. That was one of the nice companionable things about Cathy—you never had to cross your t's or dot your i's.

"What a hideous house!" she exclaimed, pointing to a huge red-brick building on the lower slopes of the hill. "Who on earth lives there, I wonder?"

"I know, it's frightful," agreed George. "I've often wondered who could have built it. Look at those ghastly turrets! Paddy and I call it the Architect's Nightmare."

"I suppose you ride here often," Cathy said.

"It's the best ride," he replied, "nice places to canter. Paddy doesn't ride in the early morning now—except for cubbing. It takes all my time to keep the horses exercised. We've got three boarders at present."

The "boarders" to which George referred were hunters belonging to a London business man who found it convenient to board out his horses with the Ferriers. Swan House was a good centre for hunting, and the pasture was excellent during the summer months. In addition to the boarders, Paddy and George had a couple of brood-mares, and a couple of hunters for their own use. George did a good

78

deal himself in the way of feeding and grooming and exercising, and it kept him busy.

"This is a darling mare," Cathy remarked, patting the brown, shiny neck of her steed as she spoke.

"Yes, she is," agreed George. "I'm awfully fond of her. There's something very special about her—she's so human—I wouldn't let everybody ride her."

"Why did you call her Port?" Cathy wanted to know. "Or was she called that when you got her?"

"I called her that," he replied.

"But why?" she persisted. "Did you think she was the colour of old brown port, or what?"

"It isn't that kind of Port at all," said George. "It's 'Port After Stormy Seas.' She had the devil of a time before I bought her. . . . It's a long story," he added after a little pause.

"Tell me about it," Cathy said.

By now they had reached the limit of their ride—an old mossy stone which at one time must have marked a boundary on the moor. They stopped here and dismounted and, lighting companionable cigarettes, they sat down side by side on the mossy turf.

"Tell me about 'Port After Stormy Seas,' " said Cathy again. "It sounds awfully interesting."

"Well, it all began by Paddy having to go to the dentist," said George obediently. "We went up to town together and I left her there to be tortured. I had to go down to the Strand to a book-shop for Dad. I found the shop all right and got the book, and when I came out a horse had fallen down. It had just fallen down that minute, as a matter of fact. It was a horse in a sort of coal-cart with bags of coal—frightfully heavy—and as I came out I saw the man leap off the cart and start beating the wretched brute with a whip. I think he was a bit mad or drunk, or something."

"How frightful!" Cathy exclaimed in horror-stricken tones.

"Yes, it was. I rushed across the street and seized hold of his arm, and all at once a policeman sprang up out of the ground—you know how they do in London—and there was a man sitting on the horse's head, and there was a crowd.

"Well, the policeman took hold of the coalman and I started to cut the harness—it was all tied up with string—and we got the poor brute up. It stood there, shaking with

80

fright and its knees bleeding and its side all scraped and muddy, and there was something about the look in the poor brute's eyes that made me absolutely see red: it looked as if it had been through hell, it looked *hopeless*.

"It was in a frightful condition, of course, with its ribs almost sticking through its hide; but, all the same, I could see that the brute had breeding—it was no cart-horse.

"By this time the policeman had got the man pretty cowed, and was taking his name and address—a horrible, bloated-looking bully of a man, he was—and the crowd was melting away. I said to the policeman, 'That horse ought to be shot. It isn't fit to drag a heavy cart. It isn't fit for anything.' The policeman was quite decent. 'I can see that,' he said. 'It's nothing but a skeleton; but I can't make him shoot it.' I asked him what he could do, and he said something about the Cruelty to Animals Society. It all seemed pretty vague. *There* was the beast of a man, and *there* was the wretched, miserable animal. I couldn't stand it.

"I said, 'I'll buy it and shoot it myself.'

"The coalman pricked up his ears when I said that, and he began to say it was a valuable animal; but the policeman cut him short. 'If the gentleman gives you two pounds for it you'll be lucky,' he said.

"The man argued a bit, but in the end I gave him two quid and he went off—and there was I, standing in the middle of the Strand, holding on to the poor wretched bag of bones and wondering what on earth to do next. I was all in my London clothes, of course, which made it a lot worse. People were laughing, and I don't blame them— must have been damn' funny, if you think of it.

"Luckily for me, the man who had sat on its head—Dunn, his name was—came to the rescue. He was a grocer, and he had a little place in one of those narrow back streets— there's a sort of network of narrow, sordid little streets down there. Dunn had a stable for his own nag and the other stall was empty. We took the wretched brute there. I meant to shoot her, of course, but I wanted to give her a square meal first—she looked as if she hadn't had one for months—so we gave her a bran mash; and you should have seen the way the stuff disappeared. Then we washed her knees and bound them up. I don't know why we did that when we meant to shoot her; but it seemed as if we had to, somehow. Dunn had been a groom before he bought his grocery business, so the two of us soon had her cleaned up.

"She looked more human, after that—not so absolutely down and out, somehow. Dunn said, 'You're not going to shoot her now, are you?' I said I didn't know. 'I'll buy her,' he said. He was quite keen, really. He wanted to buy her and feed her up a bit and rest her. He said he'd use her as a second string. I knew he'd be decent to her, of course, but I felt—well, I felt as if the poor brute had done enough. I felt—sort of ashamed—ashamed of being a man—of being one of the two-legged creatures who had used her so badly and brought her to this pass. I was so sorry for her, and so ashamed, that I felt I wanted to keep her in clover for the rest of her life—to make up a bit if I could.

"Well, the upshot was, I arranged with Dunn to keep her that night and then box her down to Winthorpe—and he did. Paddy and I met her at the station. When she came out of the box and stood there, with her bones almost through her skin and her legs bandaged, and her head drooping and that awful hopeless look about her—Paddy had a fit. Paddy wanted to shoot her straight off. But I wouldn't. I took off her shoes and turned her into a paddock with some cows and left her there—and, by jove, didn't she improve! My hat, in a month you wouldn't have known her!

"Well, there she is, you see. She'll never be very strong—no stamina at all—but she enjoys life now. I had her re-shod and I ride her a bit and—well, there you are! She's been a hunter in her day—that's obvious—but don't ask me how she got into that man's hands. I can't tell you. She could tell you a good deal if she could speak. Well, that's why I called her 'Port After Stormy Seas.' "

"It was wonderful!" Cathy said, looking at him with wide eyes.

"Yes," said George. "Yes, it was, really. It just shows—well, I don't know what it shows, except that things happen in a funny way sometimes."

Cathy thought it showed a good deal more than that, but she did not put her thoughts into words.

It became a habit, and a very pleasant one, for them to ride together every morning.

The Ferriers had had their dinner, and now George and Paddy were busy watering the garden. (It was very dry; the ground had opened in great cracks, and the seedlings were withering.) They filled their buckets from the stream and carried them across the lawn to the garden. It was hard work.

"And it's useless, really," Paddy declared.

"Useless?" inquired George, straightening his back and looking at her in surprise.

"They're dead already," she explained. "Dead and done for. The garden is like the Desert of Sahara, without so much as an oasis."

George laughed half-heartedly.

"It's cacti we ought to have planted," continued Paddy bitterly. "Cacti and gourds—or whatever they have in deserts—and not sweet peas at all. Whoever heard of sweet peas in deserts?"

At this moment Mr. Ferrier appeared from the house. He stood and looked at them for a little.

"You look a trifle warm," he said mildly.

"Is it *warm*?" inquired Paddy. "And wouldn't you be warm working your arms off to carry buckets of water in the Desert of Sahara? Come and help, Quentin, darling. George and I are exhausted. There will not be a single flower in the garden this summer—nor a leaf, either."

Mr. Ferrier was too used to his wife's exaggerations to take this appalling statement at its face value.

"I have been listening to the news," he said. "The drought continues."

"Could they not think of something different?" cried Paddy. "Could they not call it some other name, even?"

"I could call it several other names," put in George significantly. "In fact, I did, this morning, when I saw that the pond in the lower paddock was bone dry—and so did Bolton when I told him he must fill the trough."

"Was that all the news?" demanded Paddy. "Just, 'The drought continues,' and nothing more at all?"

Mr. Ferrier smiled: "There was the usual bulletin, and several S O S messages—it is strange how individuals seem to vanish from their families for years."

"And are called back because their fathers or mother or sisters or brothers are 'dangerously ill,'" nodded George.

"Exactly," agreed Mr. Ferrier. "But that was not the piece of information which I came out to give you."

"It was to tell us the drought continues, you

came," said Paddy bitterly—so bitterly that you might have thought the lack of rain was Mr. Ferrier's fault.

"No," he said patiently. "I should not have come for that. The fact that there is to be no break in the drought is self-evident, I am afraid."

"What is it, then?" inquired George bluntly.

"Green is dead," said Mr. Ferrier in a lower tone.

"Green!" echoed George in bewilderment.

"Yes, John Green. The B.B.C. has just announced his demise with the usual conventional regrets."

"Green!" repeated George incredulously. Mr. Green—dead?"

Mr. Ferrier nodded. "It appears that he was an exceedingly wealthy man, and well known in business circles—"

"But he said—" began George, rubbing his dirty wet hand across his forehead and leaving a streak of mud—"but he said he was good for another twenty years."

Mr. Ferrier shook his head sadly. "Poor fellow!"

"Was it an accident?"

"No, it appears to have been apoplexy. . . . I think you mentioned that he was excitable,

George? An excitable man with a tendency to apoplexy? . . . Very sad. . . ."

"Frightfully sad!" agreed George.

"Strange that I had heard nothing of Green for so many years, and then to hear of him from you so shortly before his death!"

George was astounded at the news. His feelings were so mixed that he did not know what he felt. He was sorry about Mr. Green, for he had liked the little man, and it seemed hard that he had been done out of his twenty years of life; but, on the other hand, there was the five hundred pounds, which was now (so George supposed) as good as in his pocket. Five hundred pounds—a princely sum—he could buy Paddy that young horse that she had set her heart on, and he could put a new door to the stable yard. He could . . . but there was no limit to the things he could do with the money.

George leant on a spade and gazed at the ground. His parents looked at each other.

"You are—er—naturally upset," said his father kindly.

"Yes," he replied. "Yes, I am. I mean he was so awfully full of life. . . . but the fact is—I didn't tell you before—he asked me to be a trustee."

"A trustee!"

"Yes, and I said I would."

"Well, it is too late now," Mr. Ferrier said.

"But it isn't—I am," said George incoherently.

Mr. Ferrier was bewildered by these apparently contradictory statements. "It isn't—you are," he murmured hopelessly; but Paddy understood.

"For the love of Mike!" she cried. "What will you have to do?"

George explained the whole thing from beginning to end, standing on the path surrounded by buckets and watering cans and withered plants; he told them how he had met Mr. Green and what he had said, and all about the lunch at the Die Hards Club, and he told them about Mr. Green's proposition and his reaction to it, and how at last he had consented and they had driven straight to the lawyer's office and fixed it up. His parents listened, enthralled. They were not nearly as surprised as he had expected, nor did they laugh at the idea of George as a trustee of Mr. Green's fortune. Perhaps this was because they had a better opinion of their son than he was aware of, or perhaps it was because they were both, in their different ways, unpractical and inexperienced in worldly affairs.

"I know little of these matters," said Mr. Ferrier when the saga came to an end; "but I had always imagined that it was an essential part of the position of a trustee that no benefits should accrue to him from the estate. This being so, I do not see how you are to obtain the money you speak of."

"It's a legacy, or something," said George vaguely, and then he added: "Oh, it's absolutely O.K. I shall get the money. We'd better ring up Forbes at once about that horse."

"What horse?" inquired Mr. Ferrier in surprise.

"No," cried Paddy. "No, I couldn't dream of letting you—treasure that you are——"

"But, Paddy, you really need——"

"No, I couldn't let you——"

"But, Paddy——"

Mr. Ferrier went away and left them arguing. It crossed his mind that human beings were very strange—and his own family no exception to the rule. George had liked Green—he had said so quite definitely—and yet, before the man was cold, George was cheerfully engaged in spending the legacy which had been left to him. On the other hand, it must be admitted that George was extremely unselfish, for his first thought upon hearing of the unexpected legacy had been to buy his mother a horse. Not many young fellows would have thought of that first, reflected Mr. Ferrier. Human nature was extremely queer—a mixture of good and evil, of kindness and callousness, of Jekyll and Hyde—and even George, an apparently uncomplex creature, was no exception to the rule.

Mr. Ferrier sighed and returned to the contemplation of the heavenly bodies, which moved according to a definite and orderly plan.

Mr. Ferrier was not altogether right about his son's heartlessness, for George, although he dropped no tears over Mr. Green's demise, was certainly a good deal more upset over it than he seemed. Indeed, he lay awake for quite ten minutes that night, thinking about his benefactor, and musing over the precariousness of life. Mr. Green had seemed so full of vitality, so eager and confident, and (what seemed even more pathetic) he had so enjoyed his food.

George fell asleep and dreamed that Mr. Green was enjoying a banquet in heaven.

8

THE FOUR YOUNG SEELEYS

ONE afternoon, about a fortnight after Mr. Green's death, the Seeleys arrived at Swan House to play tennis. They arrived quite unexpectedly soon after lunch, saying that their own court had been watered that morning and was therefore unfit for play. Mrs. Ferrier was delighted to see them, but George was not quite so pleased. He liked the Seeleys, of course, but he did not like rushing about a tennis court directly after lunch in the hottest part of the day. He therefore suggested that the four Seeleys—Peter, Cathy and the twins—should set to and play a mixed four.

"You don't want me," he declared firmly.

"Yes, we do," said Jim. "We *do* want you. Cathy's no good, and it'll make a much better game if you play. Joan and I can play a single while you change."

Jim Seeley was already, at seventeen, one of those people who enjoy arranging other people's affairs. He found that people usually did what they were told if you told them firmly enough. People were like sheep; they strayed about vaguely and wasted valuable time, so it was much better to arrange things for them. Jim was fair and plump—very like his mother—and it was his one fear in life that he would become really fat. He played tennis violently, and swam, but, as he was apt to be a little greedy, and these exercises whetted his appetite for rich foods, his weight continued almost imperceptibly to increase. Joan was very like him, only thin, and Mrs. Seeley sometimes said, rather unkindly, that it was a pity she couldn't roll them out and divide them into two ordinary children.

Jim's arrangement was accepted by everybody concerned. He and Joan started their game. Peter went off with George to talk to him while he changed, and Cathy sat down on the seat under the May tree.

Cathy did not mind being left out. If she had minded that sort of thing she would have been a very unhappy person, so it was fortunate that her temperament was unselfish and sweet. She sat there for a little, watching the game, and then Mrs. Ferrier came out to talk to her.

"Dear lamb!" said Paddy affectionately.
"It's like spring, you are, with your pretty
short frock and your golden hair!" And, she
thought to herself, friendly eyes, kind eyes.
The eyes of young girls are not always kind.
It's gold all through, she is, and not only her
hair. I'd have been different if I'd had a little
daughter like Cathy.

Peter and George went up the narrow winding stairs to the top of the old house. George
had two rooms here, a bedroom and a sitting-
room. The latter was always referred to by his
parents as "George's study," though they
were well aware that no serious brainwork
ever took place in it. The room had been
renamed when it had ceased to be "George's
nursery," and the name continued to be used
quite seriously and in all good faith. It was a
long-shaped room with a low ceiling and an
oak floor, which sloped a bit to one corner in
the fashion of ancient floors. Its walls were
covered with beaver boarding (George had
done this himself and had made a very good
job of it) and were hung with various trophies
of an interesting nature: bridles and whips
and spurs, faded rosettes which had been won
at horse shows, a fox's brush or two, and the

mounted mask of a large dog otter which George had been awarded when he was twelve years old. There were a good many photographs of horses mounted in passe-partout, and school groups in which George, large and brawny and intensely serious, could be recognised amongst a team of equally serious but not so brawny contemporaries. The furniture consisted of a few somewhat battered basket chairs, with cushions on them, a desk with some silver cups on the top of it, a table, two straight-backed chairs and a bookcase containing a heterogeneous collection of Percy Westerman, Herman Melville, Dorothy Sayers and Agatha Christie. On the floor was a couple of shabby rugs—one of which still retained the scars of a bygone Fifth of November when George, confined to the house with mumps, had been unwilling to postpone his display of fireworks. There was in addition a large old-fashioned cupboard which was always kept locked, and only George knew its disgraceful secret. It contained a teddy bear and a gollywog, six boxes of soldiers and some building blocks. George was always saying to himself that he must clear them out and give them to Paddy for the hospital; but somehow or other he never did.

The windows of George's study were small and almost square with wide window seats let into the thick walls; they faced west and looked out over the garden and the fields, and farther still, over rolling undulating country to the hills. George often watched the horses grazing in the fields, or cantering aimlessly about, or lying in the shade. He possessed an old-fashioned naval telescope which had once belonged to a great-uncle of Paddy's—a seafaring man.

"I love this den of yours," said Peter, as he followed George into the room. "I wish I had a place like this. It's so quiet and peaceful."

"We've had lots of good times here, haven't we?" replied his friend. "And that makes you fond of a place doesn't it?"

"It's peaceful," said Peter, sitting down.

"Because it's high up and far away from everybody, and because the walls are thick."

"It's because it's your own," said Peter, "because nobody comes here unless you want them. You aren't surrounded by a horde of noisy brats."

"No," agreed George, a little uncomfortably. "It must be—but, as a matter of fact, I don't believe I'd mind. I mean, I'm different from you—no brains."

96

"You would mind," Peter told him.

"Well, perhaps," said George doubtfully. "Only I rather like lots of people about the place; it's more cheerful. Look here," he went on, "there are the papers I've got to sign. Take a look at them while I change."

The papers were lying on the table, and Peter glanced at them casually. He knew all there was to know about this trusteeship which George had undertaken so light-heartedly, and he thought it was "rather queer." Peter was very fond of old George, of course, but fond of him in a slightly patronising way, and he thought that George was the last person he would have chosen to look after his money—if he had had any money to look after. He glanced over the papers casually, reading a bit here and a bit there, but after a few minutes he became more interested and, pulling a chair up to the table, he began to study them in sober earnest.

"Are you going to sign these papers?" Peter asked when George returned, ready for tennis, in spotless whites.

"Yes, that's what I'm getting paid for, old cock," replied George, swinging his racquet in a shadow service. "Gosh, I feel fine now.

I'll take you on at a single for half a crown. What say?"

"Have you read them?"

"I've skimmed through them," admitted George. "I don't understand all those aforesaids and so forth, but the five hundred doesn't include that. I'm getting the money for signing my name, not for understanding the beastly thing. 'George Ferrier' half a dozen times, and the dibs are mine."

"It's an easy way of earning money," Peter said, and there was an undercurrent of significance in the words—or tone—which George did not miss.

"Too easy, you think?" he inquired, suddenly grave.

"Too easy, George."

"You know I'm a fool," said George after a little silence. "I don't understand the damn' things."

"You could if you wanted to."

"You mean I'm just lazy?"

"Damn' lazy," replied Peter, with the frankness of long friendship.

George digested that. "Can you understand them?" he asked.

"Well—yes," said his friend somewhat

98

diffidently. "I'm not a lawyer, of course, but I'm used to . . . I'm used to . . ."

"Using your brain," suggested George helpfully.

Peter laughed. "I'm used to paper work," he said. "I'll tell you what I make of these, if you like."

"Go ahead," said George, sitting down and preparing to listen with all his ears.

He expected Peter to translate the papers word for word into plain English. But Peter did not; he sat for a few moments looking thoughtfully into space.

"I don't like it, George," he said at last. "I don't like the vagueness of it all. There's one paper especially that seems rather . . . odd. Yes, here it is. If you sign this paper, you give the other trustees the power to act without you."

"It's in case I can't go to the meeting," George explained. "Mr. Arbuthnot Millar told me that in his letter. It saves me the sweat of going up to town."

"But what's the *good* of you if they can act without you?" Peter inquired in perplexity, and he ran his fingers through his dark curly hair so that it stood up on end.

"I don't suppose I'm *any* good."

99

"Then you're getting the money for nothing," Peter pointed out.

"I suppose I am," agreed George with a little frown, and then he added, "But Mr. Green said it didn't matter whether I understood or not. He said the lawyer fellow understood, and all I had to do was to sign on the dotted line."

"I wouldn't like that."

George was beginning to dislike it, too. "Hell!" he said unhappily. "You've upset me, Peter."

They were silent for a few moments and the cries of the tennis players disporting themselves far below drifted in at the open window:

"Love thirty . . . out . . . fifteen thirty."

"What shall I do?" said George.

Peter considered the matter. "Why don't you go to the meeting? You'd feel, then, that you'd earned the money—or at least tried to earn it."

"I suppose I'd better," said George with a sigh.

"And what about the girl?" inquired Peter.

"The girl?"

"The girl who gets all the money," Peter explained. "Mr. Green's daughter—what's she like?"

"I don't know," replied George, somewhat shamefacedly. "To tell you the truth, I never thought about her at all. I suppose I ought to have."

Peter did not reply. He thought George was taking his responsibilities much too lightly—it was a thing he could not understand. If he had been in George's position he would have . . .

"What would you do?" asked George.

For a moment Peter was startled, for he was not used to having his thoughts read. He looked up and met his friend's straight glance, "I'd go and see the girl," he said. "You're her trustee, aren't you? I'll take you over in the car, if you like."

"What a bore!" George said. "But—well—perhaps I'd better. Old Green would have liked me to go—in fact, he said as much." He was silent for a few moments, thinking of old Green and all he had said about his little girl, of how he had brought her up so carefully and kept her sheltered from the world. . . .

"Well?" inquired Peter. "Are you on?"

"Yes," said George. "Yes, I'm on."

They arranged to go over to Codlington the following afternoon.

9

THE FIFTH YOUNG SEELEY

BY the time that George and Peter had strolled down to the tennis court the singles was over and Jim was getting restive.

"Come on!" he cried. "What an age you take to change!"

"You four play," said George. "I'll sit out and watch."

"No, you play," insisted Peter.

This was the sort of foolish argument that wasted time, and Jim immediately took the situation in hand.

"You can both play," he said. "Cathy won't mind sitting out again. Joan and I will take you on. Hurry up."

But George had lost all desire to play tennis. His conversation with Peter had upset him. "I tell you what," he said, "I'll go down to Winthorpe and fetch the child from school. It's just about time, isn't it?"

"Don't be an ass," said Jim. "We don't

want Dan *here*. Besides, she always comes in the bus. . . ."

But for once Jim found his orders unheeded. George did not argue, he simply put down his racquet and went off to get the car. It had suddenly come over him that he wanted to see Dan; he hadn't seen her for weeks. Besides, Cathy was worried about Dan for some reason. . . .

"Bring her back here to tea," Paddy called out.

The run to Winthorpe through the quiet country lanes soothed George. He was not fond of driving, and in fact he never drove a car if he could find somebody else to drive him, but today he rather enjoyed himself. The old car ran sweetly, and there was no hurry—none at all. He was glad he had thought of fetching Dan from school.

George drew up a little short of the big school gates and waited patiently. It was not so hot here, and there was a little breeze. He looked at the big grim building and wondered what it would be like to be a girl and go there every day and mix with crowds of other girls. And then he wondered what Mr. Green's daughter was like, and whether she was older or younger than Dan. It would be rather nice if he could make friends with her and have her over to Swan House, and have Dan to meet her. George decided that he would do that. The money part of the business was beyond him, but here was something he *could* do, and poor old Mr. Green would be pleased if he knew that George was going to take an interest in his little girl.

Presently the iron gates opened and three girls came out. They looked at George with curiosity and then looked away. One of them whispered to the others and they all three giggled. They were all exactly the same height, and were dressed in navy blue gym tunics with long black stockings and thick black shoes. George noticed that their legs were bulgy—he was a connoisseur in legs. Two other girls now appeared and joined the group, one tall and thin with legs like broomsticks, and the other short and incredibly fat. The fat one looked at George and smiled—she seemed more human than the others—and George smiled back at her. He was just preparing to get out of the car and make inquiries as to when Dan might be expected to emerge from the prison gates when Dan emerged. She came out alone, swinging her books by a strap, and although she was dressed exactly like the others, she looked completely different—or so George thought. The hideous tunic and the coarse black stockings seemed like a part of the other girls; but, where Dan was concerned, they were merely a sort of disguise. Inside that disguise was Dan herself, wrapped in her own personality.

Dan was too fat, of course, and her legs were far from perfect examples of what legs should be, and the good Seeley features which she had inherited from her father were somewhat obscured in the plump curves of her rosy cheeks; she was by no means beautiful—even to the fond eye of her friend—but there was something very clean and wholesome about her and her eyes were the same clear blue as Cathy's eyes. George decided that he liked the way her hair grew—it was brown hair, and as straight as a pound of candles—and Dan swept it back from her wide forehead to the nape of her neck.

He was able to watch her for a few moments before she saw him, and he watched her carefully, for he wanted to discover if all was well with her. She stood at the gate, speaking to the other girls and swinging her books against her leg, and it seemed to George that she was a little apart from her companions, as if she did not belong, and he thought she looked a little sad—or was it bored?

"Hullo, Dan!" he called.

She looked round and saw him, and immediately her face was transfigured. "George!" she cried, rushing towards him like an impetuous puppy. "Oh, George, how gorgeous of you!"

He was so moved by her pleasure that he put his arm round her waist and kissed her fair rounded cheek—it was cool and as soft and smooth as velvet—and Dan returned the kiss with interest.

"Hop in," George said. "I've come to fetch you home to tea."

Dan hopped in and slammed the door. She waved gaily to the other girls as they drove off.

"This is gorgeous," she said, snuggling down beside him. "This is simply gorgeous. It just shows . . ."

"What does it show?"

"Prayers *are* answered sometimes," said Dan seriously.

"Prayers!" exclaimed George, and he gave an involuntary hoot of laughter at the idea of

106

himself as an answer to a maiden's prayer.

"Yes," said Dan. "Oh, I don't mean I prayed for you to come and fetch me—not *actually*, you know—I never thought of it, for one thing. I just prayed for something nice to happen—and it did."

George did not know what to say.

Presently Dan continued: "You know how some days everything goes wrong—everything is perfectly beastly and you wish you were dead?"

"I know," said George sympathetically.

"Today was like that."

"What happened, exactly?" he inquired.

"All sorts of things. It started when I got up. I lost my hair slide, and I was late for breakfast, and it was kippers. I hate kippers."

"So do I," agreed George.

"I'm so glad you hate them, too," said Dan with a sigh. "Nasty, salty, bony things! Then, when I got on to the bus, my suspender burst—you can't think how horrible that is—and when I was in class I found I'd forgotten my pen—and then I found it was algebra, which I hate, instead of geography, which I love—and I hadn't done my algebra because I thought it was tomorrow."

"How awful!" exclaimed George, when he

had listened to the chapter of accidents.

"But all that isn't anything, really."

"It sounds a good deal to me."

"It isn't anything *much*," she declared. "I mean, it's just details." She was silent for a moment and then she went on: "I suppose boys' schools are different—you wouldn't understand."

"Couldn't you try me?" asked George.

They were getting near Swan House now, so George stopped the car beneath the shade of a chestnut tree and lighted a cigarette. He lay back in the driving seat and blew the cool grey smoke through his nose. It was very quiet there, in the narrow lane; even the birds were silent in the heat.

Dan was looking straight in front of her at the curving white road. Her hands were clenched in her lap and her round, soft face wore an earnest, strained expression.

"You must have Something at a girls' school, or you're Nothing," she said cryptically.

"What sort of Something?" asked George.

"You must be very pretty, or frightfully marvellous at Lacrosse, or you must give nice parties, or it even helps if your mother has a car of her very own and fetches you home every day, and you can say to somebody, 'Shall I give you a lift?' And it's Something if your mother takes you to London to get your clothes, or you have lunch at the Berkeley and go to the theatre. . . ."

"I see," said George rather carefully. "Yes, I think there's quite a lot of that in boys' schools, too—only not quite the same things, perhaps."

"Well, you see, I've got Nothing," Dan said.

George was dumb. It was quite beyond him.

After a few moments Dan continued: "It's funny, isn't it, how some people have Everything and other people have Nothing. There's a girl called Mary Byrd, and she's got Everything. It's a nice name, too, isn't it?"

"Er—yes," said George. "Mary Byrd—yes, it is, rather. Is she nice?"

"She's a gorgeous person," Dan told him. "But, of course, she never looks at me. . . . Well, why should she? I can't even ask her to tea. . . . Mother doesn't like the girls—it's a bother having them—and so, of course, nobody ever asks *me* when they have parties."

"But, Dan——"

"And mother isn't even coming to the school concert!" wailed Dan.

It was out now, and George realised,

somehow, that this was the worst—the supreme and unbearable limit—and that all that had gone before was as nothing compared to the fact that Mrs. Seeley refused to leave her chintz-covered chair and sit on a hard bench in the school hall. George, glancing sideways, saw a large crystal tear sliding down his companion's cheek. He was moved beyond measure at the sight.

"Oh, Dan, *don't*!" he exclaimed.

"I'm not," she said quickly. "I'm not crying. It's nothing at all. It doesn't m-matter."

"Oh, Dan!" he said miserably. "Oh, hell, this is awful! What can we do? Would it be any good at all if I came?"

She looked up incredulously. "You?" she asked.

"Yes, *me*. Would it?"

"You don't mean it, George?"

"Of course I mean it," said George stoutly. "I should like to come. Would it be any good?"

She slipped her hand through his arm and leaned against him. "It would be marvellous," she said, with a little catch in her breath. "It would be the most marvellous thing that could possibly happen. They saw you today—and *that* was marvellous, really, because they'll all be wondering who you are. You *do* look so—so marvellous in your nice white tennis things and your *lovely* O.E. blazer—and I shouldn't wonder if your calling for me like that would help a good deal—in fact, I'm sure it will—especially when you kissed me. . . . Perhaps I could even tell them that we're secretly engaged."

"No," said George firmly.

"Oh, well," she said. "Oh, well, they'll see you at the concert, anyhow—they'll *all* see you."

"Are you going to sing?" inquired George, with the idea of changing the subject.

"Yes," said Dan, "but only in the chorus. I'm not much good, you see. You won't mind, will you?"

George did not mind. He was going to the concert to give Dan "face," and not to enjoy himself; he had no illusions at all about school concerts.

"It's marvellous!" said Dan again.

"You'll get me a ticket, then," said George, squeezing her hand in a comforting way. "And I'll tell you another thing we might do. What about asking some of your pals to come to tea at Swan House? I'll speak to Paddy about it."

111

"Oh, George!" whispered Dan.

Suddenly her tears began to fall thick and fast. They gushed from her eyes like a fountain in full play, and splashed down her cheeks. George was at first astounded and then alarmed. He had never seen anything like it before.

"I say!" he began. "I say, look here"—and he took out a large silk handkerchief and endeavoured to staunch the flow—"I say, don't cry like that," he added.

"I c-can't help it."

"Do try to stop," he besought her earnestly. "Do *please* try. It's all fixed now—everything's all right, isn't it?"

"That's *why*," she sobbed. "It's b-because I'm so h-happy. I was so m-miserable, and now I'm so h-happy."

"People don't cry when they're happy," said George firmly.

"I seem to," she sobbed, "and it's making me feel b-better, too."

"That's splendid," he said. "But do stop now, or we shall both be drowned. I never knew anybody could have so much water in them."

Dan gave a little snort of laughter and her tears stopped falling.

"That's better," said George. "Buck up, old girl. We'll have to go on now, or they'll wonder where we've got to. . . . You can keep my hankie," he added quickly, eyeing with disfavour the wet, dirty rag which Dan was offering him.

She crammed it into her pocket and smiled at him bravely. "Are my eyes red?" she inquired.

"No," said George, "but your face is frightfully dirty. We'll have to go in the back way so that you can wash before they see you. They might think I'd been beating you, or something."

"Beating me!" she said tenderly, and she rubbed her dirty face against his arm. "I wouldn't mind if you *did* beat me, George. You can beat me to a jelly if you like."

"Don't be an ass," said George.

10

ELMA GREEN

THERE was a thunderstorm raging on the moors. The heavy black clouds had come up suddenly from the west and were emptying themselves upon the solid slate roof of Highmoor House. It was strange to see rain after such a long period of drought, and almost stranger to hear the patter of it on the high windows, and the sizzle of it as it splashed down the chimneys and fell into the fire. Elma Green was sitting in the drawing-room doing embroidery, and Miss Wilson was sitting near her in a high-backed chair. Miss Wilson had been reading aloud to her charge; but now *Pendennis* had been put aside and they were conversing; or perhaps it would be truer to say that Miss Wilson was conversing and Elma was listening—Elma was a good listener.

"There is no need for any change in our mode of life," declared Miss Wilson earnestly. "Your dear father has passed on to a better life, but he has left you capital in trust to ensure a steady income, more than sufficient for our modest needs. It is not always so," added Miss Wilson with a sigh.

"No," agreed Elma. She was aware that Miss Wilson's father had failed in this respect, for his daughter made no secret of the fact. Her presence at Highmoor House as companion to Elma was entirely due to the fact that no capital, and therefore no steady income, had accrued to Miss Wilson on her father's death.

"Your father was a most estimable man," continued Miss Wilson fervently, "and you are a fortunate young woman. You are now eighteen years old—quite old enough to understand and be suitably grateful to Providence for your benefits."

"Yes," said Elma meekly. She was embroidering a leaf now, and her dark head was bent over the tangle of silks; it was important to choose exactly the right shade of green for her work.

"I am glad that you are sensible of your benefits," Miss Wilson declared. "Your father is here no longer, but you can still show your gratitude to him by continuing to carry out his wishes. Your gratitude to

Providence can be shown by charity—by distributing money to Those in Need."

"Yes," said Elma. It was difficult to feel as sad as she ought, because she had never really known her father. He had come and gone, but he had remained quite outside her life. There had been no intimacy between them. Elma was not aware that there had been any lack in their relationship, for she had never expected anything different. She accepted the conditions of her life without question like a six-year-old child. Her father had been alive, and now he was dead. It was rather difficult to believe that he was dead, and that she would never see him again; but she did her best to believe it. She smoothed down her black silk dress and looked thoughtfully at the fire and wondered how long she would have to wear black clothes—they were so ugly.

"What were you thinking about?" inquired Miss Wilson.

Elma hesitated. She was aware that her thought was unsuitable for Miss Wilson's ears. "Nothing," she said at last.

"Nonsense," replied Miss Wilson firmly. "You were thinking of something. I have told you before that it is impossible to think about nothing. What were you thinking about?"

"About my pony," said Elma, turning her head sideways.

"You must be patient," Miss Wilson said. "There is no hurry about your new pony. Carruthers must try it thoroughly first. In any case, you have no desire to ride."

"No," said Elma without conviction.

"You are feeling too sad."

"Yes," said Elma. She wondered about this for a few moments and then she smiled in a secret way. "Would Father like me to be sad?" she asked innocently.

Miss Wilson looked at her in surprise. She was about to reply in the affirmative when a sudden doubt stopped the word on her lips.

"Father always told me to be happy," Elma pointed out.

Again Miss Wilson opened her mouth to speak, and again no words came. She was extremely like a cod at the best of times, and her perplexity increased her resemblance to this useful but far from ornamental fish.

Shortly before this, a small car had turned in at the gates at Highmoor House. It was an ancient Morris with a dilapidated hood, through which the rain was dripping steadily, and it was driven by a young man with curly hair. Beside him sat another young man whose unusually long legs were curled up in an excruciatingly uncomfortable position necessitated by the lack of room.

"We're nearly there, Peter," said the long-legged young man with a sigh. "That moron with the barrow must have told us right by mistake. This is the avenue."

"Not really?" inquired his companion with elaborate sarcasm. "You don't mean the *avenue*, George?"

"It is the avenue of a rich man," continued George seriously. "You can always tell a man's income by his avenue—that's one advantage of having no avenue at all, like us—note the smooth surface and the excellent banking at the bends."

"I have," said Peter promptly.

"I've seen this house before," George declared, looking at the tall red-brick building which had suddenly burst upon their view.

"Perhaps you saw it in a nightmare," suggested his friend.

"My hat, you've said it. This is the Architect's Nightmare seen from the other side. It's that awful house that you see when you're riding on the moor. There couldn't be two red-brick houses with turrets like that."

Peter looked at it and shuddered. "Well, all I can say is we must have gone miles out of our way," he declared.

"Miles and miles. It's because this house is this side of Codlington and we're this side of Winthorpe," George pointed out. "Now, if this house had been the other side of Codlington—like the first man we asked said it was—"

"The man with the wart on his nose," Peter put in.

"No, the man with the Dalmatian puppy."

"But I thought *he* said——"

"No, that was the other man," declared George firmly. "And if he'd been right about it—well, then, it *would* be at *least* six miles away. As it is, we've done a sort of circle and come back again."

Peter agreed that it was so. He pulled up at the door and they both surveyed the gloomy portal with aversion. George uncurled his legs and groaned.

"Well, if you will insist on having such long legs!" said Peter with complete lack of sympathy.

"It's a question of thyroid glands——"

"Pituitary," corrected Peter.

"Not my fault anyhow," said George, adding as he straightened himself: "Thank you, Peter."

"What for?"

"For bringing me here so nicely. Your driving is somewhat dull and uninspired compared with Paddy's, and our trip has been lacking in incident, but I know you've done your best, and I'm obliged to you."

"Thank *you*," said Peter gravely. "And now, shall I ring the bell, or will you? Or would you rather stand out here in the rain?"

"I'd rather stand out here in the rain; but I suppose we'd better get it over. . . . You ring."

Peter rang, and after a few minutes the door was opened to them by an elderly parlourmaid. She stared at them in amazement.

"Is Miss Green at home?" inquired George politely.

"Miss Green? Yes."

"I should like to see her."

There was reluctance—almost suspicion—in the woman's manner; but Peter was tired of the rain. He pushed past her into the hall and began to take off his waterproof.

"Please tell Miss Green that Mr. George

Ferrier—her trustee—would like to see her," said Peter firmly. It was the voice which he assumed with recalcitrant patients—patients in the hospital who refused to take castor oil, or objected to having their wounds dressed— and he had never known it to fail.

"Yes, sir," said the elderly parlourmaid meekly. "This way, please." And she opened the drawing-room door and showed them in.

They walked in at the very instant when Miss Wilson, taken aback by Elma's un- expected question, was opening and shutting her mouth soundlessly in an attempt to find a suitable and veracious answer. For a moment Miss Wilson was glad of the interruption— but for only a moment. When she managed to focus her short-sighted eyes and realised the nature of the interruption, she leapt to her feet and faced the two young men like an angry bear protecting her cub. George was frankly terrified, but Peter was used to handling difficult situations.

"This is Mr. Ferrier," he said. "Mr. Ferrier has come to see Miss Green."

"That is impossible," declared Miss Wilson firmly. "Quite impossible. Miss Green cannot see any one. I must ask you to leave at once."

"It's—er—on business," said Peter.

"Business!" she cried. "What business, may I ask? You have pushed your way in. You have intruded upon Miss Green. The business—if business there is—must be discussed elsewhere. Miss Green does not understand business."

"Oh, it isn't that kind of business," he replied, holding his ground with commendable courage. "It was just that my friend thought it was his duty to call upon Miss Green and make her acquaintance. He's her trustee, you see."

"Mr. Arbuthnot Millar is the trustee."

"There are three trustees, and my friend Mr. Ferrier is one of them," said Peter firmly. He looked round to see what his friend Mr. Ferrier was doing and why he was not pulling his weight in the conversation, and found that he had made good use of his time. Somehow or other, he had managed to dodge the dragon and make his way through the maze of occasional tables and uncomfortable looking chairs which filled this positively astounding Victorian room, and was now actually in conversation with Miss Green herself, bending over her chair and talking to her in a low voice which, owing to the size of

122

the room and the muffling furniture, was completely inaudible. Peter could see the back of Miss Green's head above the low shell-shaped chair upon which she was seated, and he could see that she wore her smooth black hair in a knot upon the nape of a curving milky-white neck, and he was quite sure—judging by the earnest and admiring expression of George's face, and by the unctuous manner in which he was bending down—that Miss Green's front view must be something quite out of the ordinary. Good old George, he thought; and, like a true friend, he proceeded further to engage the attention of the chaperon.

"I am Doctor Seeley," said Peter, trying to look elderly and reliable. It was a feat which he practised daily in front of his mirror, and he had begun to hope that the effort was bearing fruit.

Miss Wilson destroyed this illusion. "*Doctor* Seeley?" she inquired incredulously.

"Yes, Doctor Seeley," replied Peter in disgust. He would have liked to point out that quite a number of eminent medical men were afflicted with curly hair and pink-and-white complexions, but managed to refrain. It was more dignified. "I brought Mr. Ferrier over in my car," he told her. "Mr. Ferrier was anxious to make the acquaintance of his—er—his ward."

Miss Wilson was impressed by these words; she was also reassured by the calm demeanour of the speaker. "It is unfortunate that you did not warn me of your intention," she said doubtfully. "The fact is, Miss Green is hardly fit to receive visitors so soon after the demise of her devoted father."

"Very sad," put in Doctor Seeley gravely.

"Sad indeed," agreed Miss Wilson; and then she added in a different tone: "If I had known of your intention to visit Highmoor House, I could have arranged to see Mr. Ferrier myself at a more suitable hour. I am Miss Wilson."

Peter bowed gravely—or as gravely as he could, for if Miss Green were unfit to receive visitors, it seemed that she hid her feelings well. He could see by the back of her neck that she was quite enjoying George's conversation. (The back of a neck can be full of expression.) Good old George!

"How fortunate that Miss Green has you!" Peter exclaimed, for he was certain that this was the sort of person who liked it laid on thick.

"Oh!" said Miss Wilson, shaking her head. "Poor little Elma would be lost without me. I fear you may think it somewhat presumptuous of me to say this openly. . . ."

"No, no!"

"But it is only too true. Fortunately, there is no need for her to do without me. I shall give up my life to her. In fact, I have done so already—dedicated myself," said Miss Wilson, smiling sadly as a vestal virgin might.

"Wonderful!" Peter declared. He was getting awfully tired of Miss Wilson now and beginning to feel that he had suffered enough for friendship's sake. He was also increasingly anxious to obtain a front view of Miss Green.

The conversation, which had seemed so long to Peter, had in reality lasted but a few minutes. It was terminated now by the sudden appearance of the elderly parlourmaid accompanied by a slightly younger assistant carrying a silver tea-tray. Miss Wilson saw them and wavered.

"Now that you are here, perhaps you would care to join us. We are about to have tea," she said doubtfully.

Peter accepted with alacrity, and his acceptance broke the spell. The pattern of human beings rearranged itself round the tea-table, and introductions were made with the ceremony of a bygone age.

Although he was prepared for something unusual, Peter was absolutely stunned by the sheer loveliness of Elma Green. He sat down where he was told and accepted the pale yellow tea in a Spode teacup, and a thin piece of bread and butter from a silver plate. He was vaguely aware that George was now chatting agreeably to Miss Wilson, and that it was therefore his duty—as well as his opportunity—to chat agreeably to Miss Green; but, alas! Peter could not chat, he could think of nothing to say, and even if he could have thought of something to say, he would not have been able to say it. Fortunately, Miss Green did not seem to expect conversation from her guest; she ate thin bread and butter and drank tea with delicate composure. Her eyes were downcast, so that her long dark lashes lay on her cheeks. Peter looked at her and looked away—and then he looked at her again. He could not help looking at her; in fact, he felt as if he could sit and look at her for the rest of his life. Her skin was pearly white, except for a faint pink flush on her cheeks; her mouth was very small, it was a rose-bud mouth and innocent of lip-stick as the mouth of a new-born babe; her hair was black, absolutely jet black, with the greeny iridescent sheen of a raven's plumage, and it was parted in the middle and drawn back smoothly without a ripple to the simple knot which he had already seen on the nape of her neck. Whether in profile or full face, her features were perfect, exquisitely formed, delicately chiselled, and the line of her throat was something of which to dream.

For some little time it was enough—nay, it was more than enough—for Peter to steal glances at this beauty; but after a while it became absolutely imperative that he should see her eyes. Would they be brown eyes or blue? That was the question, and Peter found it difficult to decide which would be more delightful. Suddenly—it was almost as if she had guessed his thoughts—Elma raised her eyes and looked at him, and he saw that they were neither brown nor blue, but a deep rich violet.

"Oh!" said Peter, starting back in his chair as if somebody had hit him in the chest.

"What's the matter?" inquired George anxiously.

"Nothing," replied Peter. The shock of his amazing discovery and the solicitude of his friend did him good. He realised all of a sudden that his behaviour must seem odd, and he pulled himself together and tried to join in the conversation.

". . . Such a doting parent," Miss Wilson was saying in the lowered voice which she had used before in speaking of the late lamented Mr. Green. "His last thoughts were of his little girl, and almost his last act was to buy her a pony—such a sweet-looking creature it is!"

"How nice," said George uncomfortably.

"Elma is anxious to ride it," continued Miss Wilson, smiling at her charge; "but, although I feel certain that Mr. Green must have taken steps to assure himself of the reliability of the animal before purchasing it, I confess I am a trifle nervous about the matter."

"I'll try it for her," declared George, who was always in his element when horses became the subject of conversation.

"I could not dream of troubling you."

"But I'm her trustee," George pointed out; "and I know a good bit about horses. Don't I, Peter?"

128

"Yes," said Peter huskily.

"You see!" said George. "I'm the very fellow for the job."

Miss Green looked at him and smiled. Her smile was dazzling.

"You like riding, don't you?" said George heartily, "Why, of course, *everybody* does. It's absolutely the limit to have a new pony in the stable and not be able to ride it. I can't think how you can bear it."

"Elma is aware that I know best," said Miss Wilson sweetly.

The rain had stopped, and George was eager to have a look at the pony and try it there and then; but Miss Wilson would not hear of it. She pointed out with her usual apposite choice of words that Mr. Ferrier was not suitably attired for equestrian exercise, and, as this was perfectly true, Mr. Ferrier gave in with a good grace. It was arranged, however, that he should come over early the following morning and take his ward for a ride.

"I'll ride over," he said as they rose to go. "It's no distance at all if you come across the moor. In fact, I've often ridden this way and seen the house and wondered who it belonged to."

"Such a beautiful house," sighed Miss Wilson, looking round at the Victorian furniture with affectionate pride.

"Oh, rather," agreed George without conviction.

Miss Wilson accompanied the young men to the door.

"You think this riding will be quite *right*?" she asked as they stood on the step together.

"Perfectly all right," declared George. "I know all about horses. Don't I, Peter?"

"Yes," said Peter dully.

"I mean, in view of her father's recent demise," whispered Miss Wilson. "You do not consider it would be disrespectful to his memory?"

George opened his eyes. "Oh, I say!" he exclaimed. "What a funny idea; I mean, I'm sure the old—er—I'm sure Mr. Green wouldn't have wanted her to mope about the place and make herself ill. He wasn't like that, was he?"

"You knew him intimately?"

"Oh—er—oh, yes, *rather*."

"In that case——" said Miss Wilson with smiling consent.

"I'm her trustee, you know," added George.

"Yes," said Miss Wilson; "and Carruthers

130

will accompany you. He has been for many years in Mr. Green's service, and is eminently trustworthy."

George was half-way down the steps by now, and Peter had already started the car and was waiting for him. He half-turned back and opened his mouth to point out that it was quite unnecessary for the groom to ride with them; but Miss Wilson was walking away. "I can fix it tomorrow," thought George. He crawled into the car sideways and doubled up his legs, and they chugged off down the drive.

"She wants dressing," said George suddenly as they turned out of the big gates on the way home. "If somebody took her in hand she'd be beautiful."

"She is beautiful," Peter growled.

"I know," agreed George; "but what I meant was that if she had her hair done—waved or something—and a touch, just the merest touch, of make-up——"

"You're mad," Peter said. "Mad and blind. She's perfect as she is, and you want to go and mess her up with cosmetics. You want to go and make her like every other girl. She's unique. She's—she's virginal, delicate as a flower——"

131

"That's what Green said!" exclaimed George.

"Green! Who's Green?" inquired Peter suspiciously.

"Her father, of course."

"Oh, her *father*. Well, her father was right, and you've no business to interfere with her."

"I thought you wanted me to take an interest in the girl," said George patiently, "I thought that was the idea."

"Is that why you're going to take her for a ride?" inquired Peter with unusual and somewhat uncalled-for bitterness.

There was silence for a moment or two and then George replied, "It was your idea—for me to get to know her, I mean—and I thought riding with her was the only way. Perhaps I'll get her to say more than yes and no. It was chiefly yes, wasn't it?"

"She doesn't need to talk," declared Peter, treading on the accelerator with unnecessary violence. "Flowers can't talk, can they? Nobody wants them to. All you want of flowers is just to sit and look at them."

An apt retort rose to George's lips—he might point out that this was the first time he had heard of the pleasure derived by Peter from the contemplation of a flower, and inquire what time of day was best for this simple and aesthetic pastime—but George denied himself the pleasure of this witty utterance. For some unknown reason, old Peter was cross; and when Peter was cross, he was unable to see a joke.

"Her eyes," Peter continued, slowing down to pass some cows which were straying vaguely across the road, "Her eyes! . . . I never knew anybody *could* have violet eyes—or, if they had, that it would be so marvellous!"

"I thought her eyes were brown," George declared.

"They're violet," said Peter dreamily. "I don't mean that pinky colour that some people *call* violet. I mean the colour of real wood violets—English wood violets."

George made a mental note to have a good look at her eyes. He did not speak for a moment, and then he said, "So, you see, the only way I could get her away from Miss Wilson was to suggest the riding idea. It's up to me to get to know her because of being her trustee. You said so yourself, Peter."

Peter grunted.

"I should never have thought of it," continued George earnestly. "It was your idea

133

entirely; but, of course, I see now how absolutely right you were. It's my duty to get to know her." He paused a moment and added: "But I should *never* get to know her with that woman sitting there listening to every word I said, should I?"

Peter made no reply—perhaps it was because he was negotiating a blind corner at the time—and there was another little silence, broken only by the rattle of the ancient car. They passed the gates of Rival's Green and sped on.

"Oh, you're taking me straight home!" George exclaimed.

"Yes," said Peter between his teeth.

"Oh . . . all right; but you might tell Cathy I can't ride with her tomorrow morning. Tell her—tell her it's business connected with my trusteeship," said George grandly.

"I'll tell her the truth," Peter said. "Cathy won't mind."

11

THE FIRST RIDE

THE next day was bright and sunny. The thunderclouds had passed, and in many districts the drought was still unbroken. George rode over to Highmoor House in accordance with the arrangement which had been made. He rode across the moor, for it was much quicker than the road and much more pleasant, too. The moor had been so dry that the heavy rain of the previous day had not sunk in at all, but had run off the ground and collected in the hollows and the boggy places, or coursed into the stream, raising its level and muddying its limpid waters. The ground was as hard as ever, iron hard, and already the sun had sucked up what little moisture was left in the close-cropped grass. Still, there was a sort of freshness, a sort of washed feeling in the air as if the world had indulged in a much-needed bath.

Elma Green was ready and waiting in the

stable yard. She was dressed in a dark grey habit and a bowler hat, and her patent leather riding boots were beautifully new and shiny. Indeed, she looked exactly as if she were going to ride in the Row.

The groom was waiting, too, and when George arrived he led out the new pony. It was a showy chestnut polo pony of about twelve hands.

"Nice-looking beast, ain't 'e, sir?" said the groom proudly.

"Yes," said George, casting a professional eye over his points.

"There's no vice about 'im," the man continued, "Miss Elma can manage 'im easy."

But George was not taking any chances until he saw if Miss Green could ride, so they changed the saddles and mounted her on George's hunter.

"Now we'll see," said George, "and we'll change over later when I've tried your pony out." He mounted as he spoke and found that—as he had expected—his legs were almost trailing on the ground.

"It'll do 'im good to carry some weight," said the groom thoughtfully. " 'Asn't 'ad much exercise since 'e come 'ere."

"H'm, I look a bit of a fool, don't I?"

"There'll be nobody on the moor," replied the man, and then he added, "You ride on, sir, with Miss Elma. I've got my own 'orse ready. I'll be after you direckly."

"Oh, there's no need for you to come," declared George.

They rode off slowly. George was pleased to see that his ward had a good seat. She looked well, perched up on his hunter, neat and straight.

"Did your groom teach you to ride?" he inquired.

"Yes," replied Miss Green.

"He has taught you well," said George.

Miss Green remained silent. There was no need to reply, of course, because it was not a question; still . . .

"You like riding?" George asked.

"Yes," said Miss Green.

"So do I," said George.

They rode in silence for several minutes. George remembered that he had hoped to get to know Miss Green if he had her alone—he had found that you could get to know most girls pretty easily under these circumstances—but now he was beginning to feel a little doubtful about the success of his plan. He cudgelled his brains for some remark which would require a definite reply, and which could not be answered by a mono-syllable, but he could think of nothing. The silence grew. It became absolutely unbear-able.

"I love the moor," said George. He waited a moment and then, as Miss Green made no comment, he added a question: "Don't you?"

"Yes," said Miss Green.

George suggested that they should canter, so they cantered across a smooth stretch of turf and pulled up near the moss-grown stone where he had told Cathy about Port. The rush of wind through his hair had raised George's spirits, and he was encouraged to find that the chestnut pony had good paces and an excellent mouth.

"We'll change over," George said. "Your pony's all right. What's his name?"

"I don't know," she said.

They dismounted, and George changed the saddles. He noticed that she made no attempt to help.

"You should learn to saddle your own horse," he said to her. "Everybody should be able to."

"Yes," she said meekly.

He looked up and met her eyes, and saw

138

with interest that they really *were* violet and she *was* absolutely beautiful—just as Peter had said. Surely it was impossible that anybody who looked like that could be stupid. He had a mad impulse to take her slim shoulders and shake her—perhaps that would wake her up.

"Look here," he said. "Can't you talk? D'you think this 'yes' business is clever? D'you think it's any fun for me to ride with a yes machine? For heaven's sake, pull up your socks and take a little interest in things."

Miss Green smiled. "I like you," she said.

George was a little taken aback. It was the last thing he expected. He hardly knew what he *had* expected from Miss Green in answer to his outburst; but he certainly had not expected her to like him; nor was it usual for any young woman to express her feelings with such simple frankness; and this particular young woman had been so extremely reserved. . . . However, George managed to pull himself together and rise to the occasion.

"You see, I'm your trustee," he explained, "so I think we should get to know each other a bit; but we'll never manage it unless you talk. You see that, don't you?"

"Yes," said Miss Green.

139

"There you go again," said George, a trifle unreasonably.

Miss Green threw back her head and laughed, and her laugh was so pretty and spontaneous that George was forced to join in.

When they had finished laughing, they remounted and rode on. The ice was broken now, and Miss Green was more companionable. By dint of searching questions, George discovered that Miss Green had been brought up in the old-fashioned manner—she had been taught to be reserved and maidenly in the presence of the opposite sex. George thought that she was carrying the maidenly reserve too far, and he told her so.

"It's all different now," he explained gravely. "There's none of that old-fashioned nonsense now. Girls and men can be good friends. They can talk to each other. It's much better."

"Yes," agreed Miss Green, and then she added hastily, "much better."

"So we're friends now, aren't we?" said George. "And you can call me George—because I'm your trustee—and I shall call you Elma. We can ride together quite often like this."

140

"Yes—George," said Miss Green obediently.

"D'you think Miss Wilson will mind?" he inquired, stricken by a sudden thought.

"No, she will not mind," said Miss Green with confidence (for it is manifestly impossible to "mind" something of which you are unaware).

The groom was waiting for them when they returned from their ride, and George lingered for a few minutes, talking to him. Anybody who knew about horses and could talk about them sensibly was *persona grata* to George.

"Miss Green has a good seat," he said. "I hear you taught her."

The groom's brown monkey-face creased into a pleased smile. "Yes, sir, she does sit nice an' straight; but 'er 'ands is a bit 'eavy. It's a funny thing 'ow a light, delicate lady can 'ave 'eavy 'ands."

George agreed that it was. "What's your name?" he inquired.

"Carruthers, sir. I been 'ere twelve years. I looked after the two 'orses an' drives the car."

"My name's Ferrier," George told him. "I'm one of Miss Green's trustees."

"Is that so?" said Carruthers with interest. He paused a moment and then inquired a

141

trifle diffidently, "Then perhaps you could see your way to 'elping me, sir?"

"In what way?"

"Well, sir, it's like this—shall I 'ave to be looking for another job?"

George liked the frank way he had spoken.

"You see, sir," continued Carruthers, "you see, I'm not as young as I was. I'm fit an' strong as the best of 'em; but people ain't too keen on takin' a chap what's getting on in years. That's 'ow it is, sir, an' if you could give me an idea—well, then——"

"I shall certainly do what I can for you," declared George. "I can't say anything definite, because I'm only one of the trustees, but if I can manage it, you'll be kept on."

"Thank you, sir, you can't say fairer," said the man with a friendly smile. "It's a weight off my mind, that is."

"I'll do what I can," said George again. "You've been here twelve years." He put his foot in the stirrup and mounted lightly. "We'll be riding at the same time tomorrow," he added.

"Yes, sir," agreed Carruthers gravely. "You can depend on me, sir."

George thought about his morning's work as he rode home. It was, he thought, a

142

satisfactory morning's work. He had laid the foundations of his friendship with his ward; it remained to build the edifice. The chauffeur-groom was a decent fellow and must be kept on; he was pleasant and friendly without being familiar. "You can depend on me," he had said, and George was willing to believe that this was true—though what exactly Carruthers had meant by the words it was difficult to see. George thought about it for a few moments and then dismissed it from his mind; the man was only trying to impress Miss Green's trustee with the fact that he was reliable and honest, and that he would take no liberties in the absence of a master, that was all.

12

THE THIRD RIDE

SEVERAL days of brilliant weather ensued, and George rode over to Highmoor House every morning and took his ward for a canter on the moors. He had plumed himself upon laying the foundations of the friendship, and it seemed that he had laid them well and truly. Elma was no longer monosyllabic; in fact, she very soon began to take a major part in the conversation. He was much intrigued by the way she spoke, for her conversation was a mixture of Elma Green and Miss Wilson, and one could never be sure, when her rosebud mouth opened, whether she would let fall some simple Elma-ish remark, or whether she would utter a complex sentence full of the long words and pedantic expressions which she had culled from her instructress and from her reading of the classics.

It was on the third day that George and Elma decided to ride in a different direction, and, instead of turning south-eastwards, towards Swan House, they turned almost due south and rode along the edge of the hills. It was a stony path, an old Roman road, overgrown with heather and encroached upon by trailing brambles, but still wide enough for two horses to walk abreast.

Elma began to prattle almost at once. "I like riding with you," she said, smiling at George with a flash of pearly teeth. "I like the new-fashioned way best. It is very pleasant indeed. I think you resemble Pendennis. We are reading *Pendennis* just now, and I thought at once that you resembled him. Miss Wilson misses out bits when she reads to me—the bits about when he goes to Vauxhall Gardens and gets drunk. But I look them up and read them afterwards, so it does not matter."

George made an unintelligible sound. He had already become aware that Elma was not as meek and biddable as her instructress believed her to be, and he did not know how to deal with the matter. It was no part of his plan to encourage her to deceive, and yet, if he made any strong protest, he might forfeit Elma's friendship, which he had been at such pains to secure.

"Do you ever get drunk?" inquired Elma sweetly.

"No," said George. "The fact is, it's such a beastly feeling."

"Have you ever been to Vauxhall Gardens?"

"No. Where is it?"

"Oh, quite near London," replied Elma, who was unaware that London had changed since the days of Mr. Thackeray. "You go out to it by way of Shepherd's Inn."

"Is it a good place—amusing?"

"Indeed it is."

"I must ask Tom about it," said George thoughtfully. "Tom Clitheroe—he's a friend of mine. If it's worth going to, Tom will know all about it."

"Will you take me?" she asked eagerly.

George hesitated.

"Oh, please say yes!" cried Elma. "I know it is not supposed to be correct for ladies to go to Vauxhall Gardens; but we need not tell Miss Wilson."

"No, I couldn't do that," said George firmly.

"Why not?"

"Because I'm your trustee."

Elma sighed and looked sideways at her trustee. "Do you like being my trustee?" she inquired.

146

"Oh, yes, rather," he replied; "but it's a big responsibility, you know. That's why I couldn't let you do anything Miss Wilson wouldn't like."

"There are fireworks," urged Elma in a wheedling voice. "I should enjoy them, I'm sure. They went to a restaurant and had lobster and raspberry tart—Pendennis and Fanny did—and then they danced."

"I say, it sounds rather a good spot," said George with increased interest. "I must speak to Tom. Tom will know. He took me all over the place. We went to a road house near Maidenhead, where there was a clinking good swimming pool."

"How fortunate you are!" she exclaimed. "I have been nowhere and seen nothing. I have never ever been to London."

"Good Lord! You've *never* been to *London*?"

"No," said Elma, sighing. "But I have seen pictures of London. . . . I can imagine what it is like."

"I don't believe you can," George declared. "I don't believe anybody could imagine London unless they'd seen it."

"What is it like?"

George tried to describe it to her, but it was

147

quite beyond his powers of description, and he had to give it up.

"Like Winthorpe, only much bigger," suggested Elma.

"No, not a bit like Winthorpe," said George firmly.

When they reached the crest of the hill they tied the horses to a tree and sat down for a while on the soft turf. The moor was spread out before them like a coloured map, or like country seen from an aeroplane. They could see Winthorpe hiding amongst the trees, and George pointed out Swan House to his companion, and Rival's Green.

"Peter Seeley lives there," he said. "You remember he brought me over to tea?"

"Yes, I remember him," said Elma, and she added thoughtfully, "His hair is curly—dark and curly—and his eyes are blue."

George did not reply to this, and there was silence for a few minutes; but it was a companionable silence and not in the least uncomfortable.

"This is an extremely pleasant spot," said Elma at last. "There is a delightful breeze, and the view is entrancing."

George smiled to himself at the expression.

"Yes," he said. "Yes, by Jove, it is—er—entrancing, isn't it?"

"Why are you laughing at me?" she inquired.

"I'm not," he replied. "It was only—you use such odd words. People don't say 'entrancing' nowadays."

"What do they say?"

"Oh, I don't know; but, as a matter of fact, it's a very good word, and there's no reason why you shouldn't use it."

"I shall not use it again," said Elma gravely. "I intend to become modern in every way. That is what you would like, isn't it, George?"

"Well, I don't know . . ." began George.

"You will teach me," Elma said. It was a statement rather than a question—in fact, it was almost a command—and George was suddenly a trifle uneasy.

"I shall soon learn," she continued with sublime confidence. "Indeed, I have learned a great deal already. It was an excellent plan of yours that we should ride together every morning."

"You see, I wanted to get to know you," George explained.

Elma turned towards him and smiled. (Her eyes were so large and soft and dewy that a

149

little thrill coursed up George's spine.) "And now you know me," she said softly.

"Er—yes," said George. If she had not been such a child, and if he had not been her trustee, George would have responded differently. Any other girl saying a thing like that, and *looking* like that, would have been asking for it, and would most certainly have got it. George was no Benedictine Monk. He felt an almost over-mastering impulse to put his arm round her shoulders to tilt her head slightly backwards and kiss her firmly and lingeringly on her small rosy mouth. The whole movement was so clear to him that he could almost feel himself doing it. He was obliged to clench his hands firmly and to remind himself of the sacred duties he had undertaken on her behalf.

"Shall we go back now?" he inquired hoarsely.

"Oh, please let us stay a little longer," Elma said persuasively. "I do so love talking to you like this."

"Yes . . . it *is* nice, isn't it?"

"It is so much better than the *old* way."

"Yes," agreed George without conviction.

"The old way was very, very stupid—I see that now."

150

"Yes," said George; "but, you know——"
He stopped suddenly.

"What were you going to say, George?"

"Oh—nothing," he replied. What could he say? Could he eat his words? Could he point out that a little—just the least soupçon—of maidenly reserve was still desirable in contacts with the opposite sex? No, the thing was impossible.

"You are not unhappy, George?" she inquired with sudden anxiety.

"Good Lord, of course not."

"I thought you looked a little sad."

"Sad!" exclaimed George. "Good Lord, no."

Elma was reassured. "It *is* so wonderful," she said dreamily. "It is like something out of a book. I could sit here for ever and ever talking to you."

George rose. "We must really go back now," he said with all the firmness at his command.

Elma smiled up at him. "Why?" she asked. "Why must we, George?"

"Because it's nearly breakfast-time," he replied.

She sighed, and got up with obvious reluctance.

The ride back was accomplished without incident. George monopolised the conversation, keeping it to strictly inpersonal topics. In fact, he gave Elma a sort of impromptu lecture on the breeding and care of horses. She looked a trifle bored, as perhaps was natural, for the breeding and care of horses was not a subject that interested her (she liked riding them, of course), but fortunately Miss Wilson had trained her to listen to boring monologues, and she had trained herself to listen to them with one ear, while her thoughts strayed down other, more romantic, paths.

George took leave of her at the stable gate. "I can't ride tomorrow," he told her, "because I've got to go to town—*early*. I have to attend a meeting of your trustees," he added grandly.

"Oh, dear, how unfortunate!" Elma exclaimed. "How extremely vexatious!"

"Yes, isn't it?" said George.

"But we'll ride on Wednesday," she added.

"Thursday," said George firmly.

Elma sighed. "What a long time to wait!" she said.

As George rode home he found his heart unexpectedly light, and traced this feeling to the fact that he would not be riding with his ward for two days. Elma, who had been so slow off the mark, was now going a little too fast for George. He liked her quite a lot, of course—she interested him and intrigued him—but he welcomed an interval for reflection.

George was wont to bewail his lack of brains, but he had more than his share of intuition where human nature was concerned. He loved his neighbour, and therefore understood him (and her) far better than a scholar or a misanthrope. He was aware that Elma liked him; but he was also aware that this was probably due to the fact that he was the first friend of either sex she had ever had. Most girls had girl friends by the dozen with whom to exchange confidences. Elma had none. Most girls possessed or acquired some sort of technique which they employed in dealings with the opposite sex. Elma had none. He realised that the latter lack was in some part his fault, a fact which did not make things any easier.

George thought it over as he cantered home across the moor, and the more he thought about it the more glad he became of the two days' respite. Elma was absolutely defence-less, and unless he intended to go all the way, and take her for better or worse, he must stop now and not go one inch further.

It was easy to say, and easy to do if he could only make up his mind about it. The trouble was that he couldn't make up his mind. How could he possibly know whether or not he wanted to marry Elma Green when he scarcely knew her? How could he know whether she was the sort of girl that you could go on loving and living with all your life? Love at first sight? Well, yes, George *did* believe in it in a way (he was forced to believe in it, for it had actually happened to him once or twice), but you wanted more than that sort of glamorous business when you were choosing your wife. Not a very romantic young man, perhaps, but surely an eminently sensible one! A product of the modern system of freedom! When young men and young women dash about together in small cars, and dance together, and talk together, and play games together without let or hindrance, they get to know each other in a way that they could never get to know each other before, and look at each other—and at life—with eyes unblinded by glamour. To be honest, there is little glamour left in the relation of the sexes, for glamour requires a certain degree of mystery. A man thrills no longer at the sight of a shapely ankle peeping from beneath the sweeping folds of an evening gown. He has probably seen that ankle—not to speak of the legs and body to which it is attached—seen it bare (or as bare as makes no odds) sunbathing on the shore or stretched out upon a raft in the middle of a swimming pool. Or if he has not seen that particular ankle, he has seen others like it—dozens of them—and seen them with admiration, but without the smallest sensation of thrill.

George did not reason it out, of course, nor weigh the pros and cons of glamour and common sense; he did not bother himself as to whether his attitude was romantic or otherwise. He only knew that, although Elma intrigued him, and was indubitably the most beautiful creature he had ever seen, he wanted a little time.

13

BUYING A HORSE

THE five hundred pounds to which George was entitled for his arduous work in connection with the Green estate had now come appreciably nearer. It was not actually in his pocket yet, but it was definitely on its way. George had spent many pleasant and profitable moments trying to decide how he could use it to the best advantage, and the first item on every list was Paddy's horse. He and Paddy had argued about this horse for days, and at last, in a weak moment, Paddy had consented to go over to Winthorpe with him and look at it. "There's no harm in looking at it," Paddy had admitted reluctantly; "but you're not going to buy it for me—it's quite absurd."

"There's no harm in looking at it," agreed George, dissembling his pleasure. He felt pretty certain that once he got her over to Winthorpe and she started to bargain with Mr. Forbes, her scruples would vanish into thin air and she would allow him to buy the horse.

Paddy had consented to go, and it was important to follow up this partial victory and consolidate it into a complete one before she changed her mind again; so after breakfast was over George sought for her diligently and at last ran her to earth in the lamp-room.

The cleaning of the lamps was a job which Paddy had taken into her own hands. She had never found any servant who could be trusted to look after lamps and to keep them in that state of absolute cleanliness which was desirable. Modern servants were unused to lamps, and hated them like poison, and Paddy was of the opinion that nothing—not even a lamp—would give of its best to an unfriendly hand. Paddy loved lamps. She had been familiar with them all her life—first in her old Irish home, and later in her English one. It was not because their soft light was becoming that Paddy loved them; her affection for them was unselfish and objective. Lamps were friendly; lamps were peaceful and homely; lamps required care and repaid it a thousand-fold. There was something human and mutable about lamps—and they were so pretty. The drawbacks which many people find in this archaic form of illumination were no drawbacks to Paddy. She even had a secret and somewhat disgraceful predilection for their smell—that queer smoky tasty smell when they were first lighted and burnt up strongly and flaringly, with their flames all jagged and edged with grey—but what she liked most of all was to fuss over them a little, turning them up to the exact and absolute apex of their light-giving powers, or turning them down till they burned clear and gold like small domestic suns for ever setting.

When George discovered her, Paddy had just finished her self-appointed labour of love, and was wiping her hands on a piece of cotton waste. She had therefore no excuse to offer when George suggested a visit to Winthorpe to see the horse. They went over in the car, and as they went they argued.

"I don't want the horse," Paddy declared, "and if I wanted it I could buy it myself, for I could sell out some of that Building Society Loan. . . . But I don't want the horse. . . ."

"Paddy, dear . . ." began George.

". . . So why we're going to see it, I don't know at all," she added firmly, and stopped the car suddenly in the middle of the road.

A large Rolls which had been following

them for a mile and had been unable to pass them—partly owing to the winding road and partly to Paddy's erratic driving—very nearly ran into them, and was able to avert catastrophe only by the excellence of its brakes.

"Great Scott!" cried George. "Go on, Paddy; get into the side, for mercy's sake."

"How you fuss!" said Paddy.

"Get into the side; he wants to pass."

"All right," she said, pulling in. "All right, George."

The chauffeur of the Rolls frowned upon her portentiously as he passed.

"Horrid man!" she said. "It was all his fault for following so close behind—and then to give me a look like that!"

"If he hadn't been one of nature's gentlemen he'd have given you more than a look," said George with feeling. "What possessed you to stop like that?"

"Because I don't know why we're going," Paddy replied.

"Oh, Paddy——"

"I do *not*," she declared, taking a cigarette out of her case and lighting it with practised skill. "It's a waste of Mr. Forbes's time—and him a busy man."

"I'm giving you that horse," George said. "Do you hear me, Paddy? *I'm giving you that horse.*"

"You are not, then."

"I am. I want to do it. Oh, Paddy, we've argued this out already—dozens of times," declared George in exasperation.

"It's a nest egg," declared Paddy, referring, as George was aware, to his five hundred pounds. "It's a nest egg, and let's not break it."

"I'm not a hen," said George.

Paddy chuckled appreciatively.

"Come on, now, Paddy," he continued, changing the tone of his voice to the wheedling purr which Paddy could never resist. "Come on, now, you *know* I want to give you the horse. I want to with all my heart. You'll let me do it, won't you?"

"I'm not happy about it," she said with a sigh. "It seems wrong for you to spend the money on me."

"Who else should I spend it on?"

"You should keep it for a rainy day."

"I've got a waterproof for that."

"Smart, you are!" she retorted. "And Forbes won't part with the horse for less than fifty. It's a robber, the man is."

"We'll beat him down," said George.

"We'll get the beast for forty—I bet you we will. Come on, Paddy."

They did not go on at once, because it was nice sitting there in the shade, and Paddy wanted to finish her cigarette. George was reminded of the day he had sat by the road-side with Dan and, consequently, of his promise to her. He had already spoken to Paddy about the tea-party, and Paddy—though somewhat surprised—had agreed to entertain Dan's friends. The whole thing was now arranged for Saturday week, and George was looking forward to it with no little trepi-dation. He was very anxious that it should be a success, for an unsuccessful party would defeat its own object, and Dan would be more miserable than before.

"Have you thought any more about Satur-day week?" he inquired anxiously.

"Have I not?" retorted Paddy. "If it was boys, now, I'd know where I was. But girls!— I know nothing about the creatures."

"You were one yourself, I suppose."

"Not that sort of girl. I'm a female, of course, and I was young once—a long time ago, it seems—but I never had anything to do with another young female. There were none to be had in the neighbourhood at all, and

161

from one year's end to another I never beheld one of me own kind. Dragged up, I was, in a houseful of men and boys and dogs, with a cat or two thrown in for luck, and a stable full of horses. It was in the stable I spent the most of me time, if the truth were told, or running wild over the hills—and not a crumb of solid education to me name."

George smiled. He enjoyed Paddy in a reminiscent mood.

"Those were great days, George, darling," she continued. "I declare the sun always seems to be shining when I look back—unless it was the moon. A great, round, silver moon it was, and hung over the mountains like a great, round silver lamp. There must have been grey days and rainy nights galore, but I disremember them. It's the sun I remember best, out on the hills, and I can smell the warm smell of bog myrtle when I shut my eyes. Great days, George. . . . Still and all, I'd have been better for a little more discipline and a little less freedom—I can see it now."

She sighed, and her thoughts came back to the present. "Is it forward or back we go?" she asked.

"It's forward," George said. "I want to give you that horse. I want it—tremendously."

Mr. Forbes was out in the field. He was watching a stable-boy exercising one of his hunters and schooling it over some jumps, but he was pleased to see George and Paddy—especially the latter. Mrs. Ferrier amused him a good deal.

"How's Nadia?" he inquired, coming towards them and smiling all over his large ruddy face.

They reassured Mr. Forbes as to the welfare of his patient, and after some preliminary skirmishing they got down to business. The young horse was sent for and its paces displayed. Paddy began to enjoy herself thoroughly, for, like most of her fellow-countrywomen, she was in her element when she was buying a horse. She pointed out its blemishes, both real and imaginary, and Mr. Forbes denied that any blemishes existed. To listen to him, one would have thought the animal was perfect in every respect. To listen to Paddy, one would have thought it was worthless. Yet, curiously enough, Mr. Forbes wanted to sell the horse, and Paddy wanted to buy it. Of course, Paddy did not say she wanted to buy it—that was not the way the thing was done; she said that she did not care whether she bought it or not; she assured him that they had plenty of horses—too many, in fact—and she was doubtful whether they had room for it in the stables, and whether it could be given sufficient exercise.

"It would be eating its head off—and that's the truth," she declared flatly.

Mr. Forbes pretended to believe this, though he knew it to be untrue, and, what's more, he knew that Mrs. Ferrier knew that he knew it to be untrue. It was unfortunate, he said, because the horse was a bargain.

"A bargain!" exclaimed Paddy with scorn.

Mr. Forbes said that fifty pounds was not much for a horse with such marvellous possibilities as this.

What did he call *much*, Paddy wanted to know?

Mr. Forbes said he had just sold a hunter for an English gentleman to an Irish gentleman for a hundred and thirty pounds. Paddy did not pretend to believe him—he had never thought she would—she declared that if he had said it "the other way round" she might have believed him, but that neither Irish gentlemen nor Irish ladies were in the habit of throwing away their money on English horses. What was the use of them when there was hardly one that had ever seen a decent bank in its life, far less been schooled to change its feet on the top of it?

Mr. Forbes was quite unmoved. He said that it was a pity she did not like the horse, for he thought it would suit her, but that it didn't matter to him, because he had received a good offer for it that morning from a gentleman at Bicester. He would rather Mrs. Ferrier had the horse, but it couldn't be helped.

Mrs. Ferrier was quite unmoved, because she was aware that if Mr. Forbes had had a good offer for the horse that morning he would have accepted it, and they would not be standing here now. She hesitated whether to point this out or to ignore it completely.

At this moment George galloped past on the horse, and she received inspiration.

"Was that a noise it was making?" she inquired sweetly.

"A noise!" cried Mr. Forbes. "It was no such thing. The horse is perfectly sound, or I shouldn't offer it to you."

"A little squeak, it was," she declared innocently.

"It must have been the saddle."

Paddy had known it to be the saddle all along. "Ah, was that it?" she said.

165

"It's a new saddle," Mr. Forbes pointed out.

Mrs. Ferrier was aware of that already. She thought for a moment, and then in a casual voice she offered him thirty-five pounds for the horse—and Mr. Forbes nearly fainted. When he recovered a little, he said she could have the horse for forty-five—because she was a friend, and he would like her to have it—and Mrs. Ferrier cried out in horror at the bare idea.

While this interesting and wholly amicable discussion was in progress George had not wasted his time. He had examined the horse thoroughly—its mouth, its eyes, its legs, etc.—he had ridden it round the field and tried its paces. He had spoken to the stable-boy and had culled quite a lot of useful information from him, and he had come to the conclusion that Paddy was right. The horse would do quite nicely; it was green, of course, and required a good deal of schooling, but if they could get it for forty pounds it was not a bad bargain. It would never win a race—that much was certain—but it was sound in wind and limb and was a pleasant ride.

George dismounted and, relinquishing the horse to the stable-boy, he walked across the

166

field to where his mother and Mr. Forbes were still talking.

"I'll give you forty pounds for the beast," he said frankly. "It's not worth more."

Mr. Forbes knew George, and was therefore aware that George said what he meant. He thought in his own mind that George's method was crude and indelicate and lacked finesse, and he much preferred the time-honoured chaffering of which Mrs. Ferrier was such a brilliant exponent, but it came to the same thing in the end, for forty pounds was exactly the figure that Mr. Forbes had decided on when he first saw the Ferriers walking towards him across the field.

14

BUSINESS MATTERS

THE meeting of Miss Green's trustees was due to take place the following day at Mr. Millar's office, and George had been invited—or, rather, commanded—to attend. He had received a letter from Mr. Millar pointing out that, as he was unwilling to sign the paper giving his co-trustees the power to act without him, his presence at the meeting was essential. George saw that he would have to go—the thing was a confounded nuisance, but it was too late to back out now—so he donned his London garments and went up to town by a suitable train.

Mr. Millar's office was in the heart of the city and, long before George had found it, he had begun to wish more earnestly than ever that he had not listened to Peter's advice. The city was full of hurrying people with earnest and business-like faces, and George, as he looked at them, became aware that his own face was out of place here—it was the face of a country bumpkin. He was hot and dusty, and the noise of the street made him feel quite dazed.

He stood still for a moment and took Mr. Millar's letter from his pocket to make sure of the address, and, while he was standing there, somebody barged into his back and knocked him off the edge of the pavement and a passing taxi stopped within a foot of him with a screech of brakes. George leapt back in confusion, he felt a fool, and the taxi-driver's remarks did not help him to regain his composure. This isn't my country, he thought wretchedly. . . . His morale was extremely low when at last he found the right office and pushed open the swing-door.

It was a large office, full of busy clerks, but George was evidently expected, for he was seized upon immediately and whirled up in a lift and ushered into the private room of Mr. Arbuthnot Millar without waste of time. Three gentlemen were seated in comfortable leather chairs, waiting for him.

George knew Mr. Wicherly, of course, for he had seen him on the fateful day when he had gone with Mr. Green to the lawyer's office. George had not been favourably impressed with him on that occasion, and today the bald-headed lawyer was even less pleasant.

"Here he is at last!" said Mr. Wicherly, with the air of a man who has been waiting for hours.

"It was the traffic . . ." began George. "And I didn't know where——"

"You should have taken a taxi," Mr. Wicherly said.

"I never thought . . . I mean, I thought a tube would be quicker. . . ."

"Quite so," said Mr. Wicherly dryly, and with that somewhat inscrutable remark he proceeded to make the introductions. "Mr. Millar—Mr. Bennett—Mr.—er—er—Ferrier."

They all bowed.

Mr. Millar was a tall, well-padded gentleman with a red face. He had very little hair, but what there was of it was jet black, and he had a small black moustache and black eyebrows. An elderly man with black hair always looks a little odd, and Mr. Millar was no exception to the rule. Mr. Bennett was old—in fact, he was obviously very old indeed—his face was the colour of old ivory and his eyes were a watery blue.

George was horrified to find that he had kept three elderly, and presumably busy gentlemen waiting for him. He continued to apologise profusely and to explain about the traffic as they took their seats round the large table.

Mr. Millar was quite nice about it. "Sit down, sit down," he said. "We all know what the traffic is like. Say no more about it. Very good of you to come so far. I wanted to save you the trouble."

"I know," babbled George nervously; "but, you see, I felt I ought——"

"Wicherly and I could have settled everything quite easily—and Mr. Bennett, of course—it's plain sailing, isn't it, Wicherly?"

"Oh, quite, quite," quacked the old lawyer. "Just a few routine matters——"

"Perhaps I should explain," said Mr. Millar in a conversational tone of voice, "that all the late Mr. Green's affairs are in Mr. Wicherly's hands. Mr. Wicherly and I are the executors. We therefore opened his desk and examined his papers. There was no need to trouble Miss Green's trustees in the matter."

George found that Mr. Millar was looking at him, so he nodded hastily. "No, of course not," he said.

"Mr. Wicherly has collected the share certificates—I believe he has them in that large case of his."

Mr. Wicherly smiled bleakly. "That is so," he declared. He opened the case and in a moment the table was strewn with documents.

Mr. Millar drew in his chair and assumed a businesslike manner. He began to read through the various papers, tossing them about and sorting them into piles. On the table at his side was a typewritten sheet of foolscap, and he ticked off the papers as he sorted them, saying to Mr. Wicherly:

"Nine thousand Brazils; two thousand five hundred Union Pacifics; five thousand U.S. Steels. . . ." And Mr. Wicherly scrabbled about amongst the papers and jotted down figures, and made similar and equally unintelligible rejoinders.

George was completely at sea. He sat there with his hands gripping the edge of the table and looked on. They knew all about it and he knew nothing at all; it was hopeless to try to understand what they were doing. He glanced at Mr. Bennett and saw that he was sitting back in his chair staring before him with a vague expression in his pale-blue eyes. Mr. Bennett was obviously miles away. There was no help in him.

"These Bonds," said Mr. Millar, throwing down a packet of documents bound together by a couple of elastic bands. "They're quoted at nineteen and a half today. Shall I sell them?"

"Just as you say," rejoined Mr. Wicherly. "That's three thousand five hundred," he added, figuring rapidly.

"Three thousand five hundred and thirteen," retorted Mr. Millar.

George picked up a paper at random and tried to look as if he knew all about it.

"What's that, Ferrier?" inquired Mr. Millar. "Oh, the Railway Debentures. We'll sell those."

"Why?" inquired George. "Why have we got to sell anything?"

He saw a surprised expression flit over Mr. Millar's large red face. "Death Duties," he replied. "We've got to sell out sufficient stock to meet them. Twenty thousand pounds' worth of stock. Isn't it, Wicherly?"

"Quite," agreed Mr. Wicherly. "Oh, quite. Mr. Ferrier will realise that the sooner we get it settled, the better."

"Oughtn't we to consult a stockbroker?" inquired George.

There was a moment's horrified silence

and then Mr. Wicherly replied, "Mr. Miller is a stockbroker."

George was dumbfounded. He wished that the floor would open and swallow him. He had known that Mr. Millar was a stockbroker, of course, because it was printed at the head of the letter which was reposing peacefully in his pocket. Why on earth had he made such a fool of himself?

"I forgot," he mumbled.

"We are fortunate in having Mr. Millar to advise us," continued the lawyer reprovingly. "His—er—knowledge is at our disposal, most—er—fortunately for us."

"Oh, yes—of course," George said.

"Twenty thousand pounds," said Mr. Bennett suddenly. "It's a lot of money."

They all looked at him in surprise; but, even as they looked, the film descended over his eyes and he was lost again.

"Quite," said Mr. Wicherly.

Mr. Millar laughed pleasantly. "It certainly is a great deal of money," he agreed; "but, fortunately, there's a great deal more behind it. Miss Green will be extremely well off even after the duties are paid."

They had stopped sorting out the papers

while they were speaking, but now the work went forward again.

"Sign there, please," said Mr. Wicherly, passing the papers round the table.

George signed where he was told. He realised now that some of the securities were being sold to pay the Death Duties, and that the others were being transferred to the trustees to hold in trust for Elma. The sums were so enormous that they frightened him. It was a big responsibility to deal with such sums, especially when he only knew vaguely what he was doing.

"I suppose you've got a—a list of them," he said.

Mr. Millar laughed. "Well—naturally," he replied, holding up the typewritten sheet with which he had been working. "Have you got another list, Wicherly?"

Mr. Wicherly took out another list and handed it across the table to George.

Now that he had got the list, George did not know what to do with it, but it seemed only reasonable to do something with it, so he began to tick off the securities as he signed them, and this took up a good deal of time, for the list was long. Mr. Green had his money well spread.

"My dear boy," said Mr. Millar, smiling very pleasantly, "don't you think you could leave that to us? We shall be here for hours if you go all through that list—and Mr. Wicherly and I are busy men."

George felt himself flushing. "I thought—I thought I ought to," he stammered. "After all, I'm a trustee, too——"

"If Mr. Green had listened to me——" began Mr. Wicherly, but a look from Mr. Millar stopped him.

"Of course you are," said Mr. Millar kindly; "but the fact is, we know the late Mr. Green's affairs inside out. Why not leave it to us?"

"I haven't had much experience," said George.

"How could you?" inquired Mr. Millar. "There's time enough for you to gain experience."

After that George gave up the struggle. The documents were passed round rapidly, signed by each trustee in turn and sorted out into neat piles.

"That is all," said Mr. Wicherly at last.

"Good," declared Mr. Millar, glancing at his watch. "Good work—eh? You'll let me know if you want another meeting?"

176

"Oh, quite," agreed Mr. Wicherly. "But I can do a great deal now. It is all a matter of routine."

"D'you mean the meeting is over?" inquired George incredulously.

"Yes," said Mr. Millar, smiling. "Hustle and bustle—no time to waste."

"But what about—what about Highmoor House—and the servants and everything?"

"The governess manages all that," declared Mr. Millar promptly. "She always has managed it—even in Green's lifetime. Everything goes on as before. As a matter of fact, Green wasn't down there much. We've given up his flat in Pont Street. Haven't we, Wicherly?"

"That is so. I took it upon myself——"

"Quite right," Mr. Miller said, "quite right. We don't want to waste time on details."

They all stood up. Mr. Bennett drifted away, and Mr. Wicherly began to collect some of the papers and to put them into his case. George found himself at the door, shaking hands with Mr. Millar.

"Er—thank you, sir," he said, with the vague idea that he was taking leave of his host at a party.

"Thank *you*, Ferrier," replied Mr. Millar, smiling.

George lingered, fingering his hat. "I say, do we—have we any personal responsibilities?" he asked. "I mean, I suppose we should take an interest in Miss Green herself, shouldn't we?"

"Oh, undoubtedly."

"I thought perhaps she should get away for a bit."

"Get away?"

"For a holiday—a change of air," George explained.

"H'm," said Mr. Millar thoughtfully.

There was such a curious look on his face all of a sudden that George began to wish he had left the matter alone. He felt as if his words had put in motion some force which he had no means of stopping—a sort of avalanche. "Perhaps I'm wrong," he said hastily. "Perhaps it's just as well for her to stay quietly at home."

"She lives near you, doesn't she?"

"Yes—but——"

"How old is she?"

"Eighteen," said George, and he added hastily, "but she seems much younger, of course. She's had such a sheltered life, she's very—very——"

"You seem to know all about her," said Mr. Millar, and suddenly he was smiling again, and smiling very pleasantly.

"Why—yes. I thought as I was her trustee——"

"Quite so," said Mr. Millar. He paused a moment and then he added in some surprise: "Eighteen?"

"Yes," said George, "but young for her age—very, very young."

"Well, we'll see what can be done about a change of air for her," said Mr. Millar in a final sort of tone.

15

CLEARING THE AIR

GEORGE stepped out into the street, and the glare of sunlight reflected from the pavement hit him in the eye. The street was like an oven, and it was full of people—a surging mass of clerks and typists and secretaries and company promoters and stockbrokers and all the other busy denizens of the city hurrying forth from their offices to snatch a mouthful of lunch. He hesitated before plunging into the crowd and tried to make up his mind where to go for lunch, and how to find his way out of this unfamiliar part of London to the district that he knew; but he was so dazed and muddled by the ordeal through which he had passed that he did not know which way to turn and he could not concentrate his thoughts upon the immediate problem of where to feed, because his thoughts insisted upon dwelling on the meeting which had just taken place, and of the miserable part which he had played in the proceedings. They knew all about the business of the Green money, and he knew nothing. They had done exactly what they wanted with him, and he had been forced to acquiesce. It was probably quite all right, but George didn't like it. He didn't like the responsibility; he didn't like groping in the dark; and he didn't like the way they had rushed it through. Mr. Millar had been very decent, really, but somehow or other George did not quite trust him. George knew nothing about business men—they were outside his experience—but he knew a good deal about horses, and he could always tell when a horse was untrustworthy, no matter how beautifully it behaved; there was a look in its eyes, there was a sort of *feel* about it, and you just *knew*, by some sixth sense, that you had better be careful. George had this feeling about Mr. Millar.

This was bad enough, but it was not all, for there was another uncomfortable feeling worrying George. He had had the feeling all the time the meeting was in progress—the feeling that something was wrong, that there was something he ought to remember. It kept on knocking at the back of his mind, nagging at him . . . something that he ought to remember—something important . . . but for the life of him he couldn't think what it was.

It was this feeling of something being wrong that had led George to try to assert himself, and consequently to make such a complete fool of himself.

George was still thinking about all this in a confused way and hesitating in the doorway of Mr. Millar's office when the swing-door opened and Mr. Millar himself appeared.

"Hallo, Ferrier!" he exclaimed. "Here we are again! Are you going anywhere special, or will you come and have a snack with me?"

George hesitated. He had been thinking so hard about Mr. Millar that he felt as if his thoughts must show on his face. "No—at least—no," he babbled. "Nowhere special, I mean."

"Come along, then," Mr. Millar said.

He took George lightly by the elbow and piloted him through the crowd, and, whereas it had seemed to George an absolute impossibility to push through this surging mass of people without using physical violence, he found himself sailing through with scarcely a jostle or a bump.

"You must swim with the stream," declared Mr. Millar. "There's a knack in it, like there is in everything else. Here we are! It's a funny little place; but they know me, and the food's good."

In a few moments they were sitting at a small table in a crowded room and a black-haired waiter, with a white apron tied tightly round his middle, was offering them a menu card.

"Cold beef and salad as usual, Jacques," said Mr. Millar, waving the card away. "What about you, Ferrier?"

"I'll have the same as you."

"And two lagers," added Mr. Millar. "That suit you?"

George said that it suited him admirably.

Everything had happened so quickly. At one moment he had been standing outside Mr. Millar's office wondering where to go, and how he was going to get there, and the next moment he was sitting at the table order-ing his meal—at least it seemed like that.

"Quick work, eh?" said Mr. Millar, smiling. "Hustle and bustle, that's the motto—no time to waste here."

"Yes, so I see."

"I'm glad I caught you," continued his host, suddenly serious. "It came over me sud-denly that it would be a good thing to have a chat. You aren't too happy about this business, eh?"

George made a deprecating noise.

"You thought we rushed things a bit," said Mr. Millar. "But we didn't, really. It's all in the day's work to us, and we could do it in our sleep. We're doing this sort of thing every day of our lives—settling up estates, buying and selling securities. It's nothing to us to deal in thousands."

"Oh, I know, but——"

"This business is just one of a whole lot of estates to us; but, of course, you feel differently about it. You feel you ought to be doing more. You don't want to shirk your job—that's it, isn't it?"

"Yes," said George, "but——"

"I like you all the better for it," declared Mr. Millar, smiling.

"I thought——" began George diffidently.

"I know, I know. But, you see, the whole thing is a matter of routine. Wicherly is a pompous old ass, but he's a capable man of business, and he's doing this sort of thing every day. We can leave all that side of it to him. I'm dealing with stocks and shares every day, so I can deal with that. It's all plain sailing."

"It isn't plain sailing to me," said George ruefully.

Mr. Millar laughed. "I thought not," he said. "But you know about other things, about country things—horses and cows and trees—eh?"

"Horses," admitted George.

"Well then," said Mr. Millar, as if that settled the matter once and for all.

"Yes, but——" began George in a doubtful tone.

"There's no 'but' about it. Put me down in front of a horse and I'm all at sea," declared Mr. Millar, cocking one black eyebrow in comical apology for his metaphor. "Put me in front of a horse," he continued, "but don't put me on the top of it. I've only once been on the top of a horse, and I didn't stay there long," and he laughed heartily.

George laughed, too. He was beginning to like Mr. Millar much better. "Oh, well——" he said. "But, then, you wouldn't take on the job of vetting a horse and get paid for it."

"I'd take on the job like a shot," declared Mr. Millar, picking up his knife and fork and attacking a plate of pink beef and green lettuce which had appeared before him on the table. "Of course I'd take on the job, and I'd

185

get hold of the best vet in the country and go by his advice. 'There's the horse,' I'd say. 'You go ahead and do your stuff. Test it for spavin and glanders, and everything you can think of and give me your opinion.' "

George roared with laughing.

"That's what I'd do," declared Mr. Millar, smiling in sympathy with George's mirth.

George had not missed the point in Mr. Millar's little parable. He examined it carefully. "Then you mean that I——" he began.

"Yes," said his host. "You get an expert opinion. Get your own stockbroker to vet the securities and give us his advice. Why shouldn't you? I shall be only too glad to let him see the list. You'd be satisfied then, I take it?"

George was surprised; he was also embarrassed; he did not know what to say.

"I should welcome it," said Mr. Millar earnestly. "Don't hesitate on my account. Fix it up and let me know, or give me his address and I'll fix it. Have anybody you like."

"It isn't that I don't trust you," George declared. And this was true, for now he had reversed his opinion of Mr. Millar. The man was obviously sincere. Besides, if he was willing to allow an expert to look into the late Mr. Green's financial affairs, everything must be perfectly straight and above-board.

George felt more of a fool than ever. It just showed that it was no use trying to do anything unless you knew the ropes.

"Think it over," Mr. Millar said.

"Of *course* I trust you," said George. "It was only that I didn't understand, and I felt that I ought to be doing something about it—taking an interest in it. Five hundred pounds is a lot to get for doing nothing at all."

"Think it over and let me know," said Mr. Millar, smiling kindly. "And now, what about a spot of Stilton to fill the corners? The Stilton is marvellous here."

They ordered Stilton and biscuits and, like magic, these comestibles appeared before them.

"No time wasted," Mr. Millar pointed out as he dug and scooped for a generous portion of cheese. "The people who come here have no time to waste. Time's money to them. I've got to rush back to see a man at two o'clock. I'm glad we've had this chat—cleared the air, hasn't it?"

George was glad also, and said so. "It was awfully good of you to take the trouble," he declared. "I mean I *was* rather—er—worried. I felt I wasn't pulling my weight."

"There may be plenty of opportunity for you to pull your weight. When we're all dead and gone you'll still be here. If Miss Green marries with the consent of her trustees, the trust ends, of course; but if she marries without their approval the money is held in trust for her children, and if she doesn't marry——"

"I don't think that's likely," George said.

Mr. Millar looked a little taken aback.

"Most girls marry," George pointed out, " 'specially if they're as pretty as she is."

"Pretty, is she?"

"Yes," said George.

Mr. Millar looked at his watch. "Four more minutes," he said. "Just enough time to settle up the matter of this holiday. It's a good idea, and I'm glad you spoke to me about it."

"I just thought," began George in a deprecating manner.

"Of course, of course," agreed Mr. Millar. "Good idea of yours. The girl would be all the better for a little change after her father's death and all that. As a matter of fact, Miss Wilson might have thought of it if she'd been worth her salt."

"She's rather—er—old-fashioned," George said.

"Old-fashioned, is she? Well, I'll send her a note and tell her to fix it. I suppose she can do that, eh?"

"I suppose so."

"You're doubtful," Mr. Millar declared. He was extraordinarily quick. "Wait a minute. I've got an idea. I'm going down to Bournemouth tomorrow—must have a bit of a holiday. How would it do if they came to Bournemouth—eh? I could keep my eye on them and see that they were comfortable. I could fix up rooms for them at my hotel."

George saw at once that this was an excellent plan. It would do Elma no end of good to get away from Highmoor House, and if she were under the eye of her elderly trustee, she could come to no harm. George would get the responsibility of Elma off his shoulders and would be able to breathe freely for a bit.

"It's splendid, sir," he said enthusiastically. "I couldn't have thought of anything better."

"I'll do that, then," said Mr. Millar, nodding. "I'll fix it all up and write to Miss Wilson. To tell you the truth, it will be a bit of a bore. . . . I really feel I need a complete

189

rest. But still . . . I'd do a good deal for poor old Green."

"It *is* good of you," George said. "It's a great relief to my mind. The fact is, Miss Wilson doesn't—isn't—I mean she——"

"Hasn't much control over the girl, I suppose?" suggested Mr. Millar, smiling.

"Not as much as she thinks she has, anyhow," replied George, somewhat cryptically. "I mean, Elma doesn't always—well, it's rather difficult to explain."

But apparently there was no need to explain. Mr. Millar shook his head and laughed and called for the bill.

"I know," he declared. "Girls will be girls. I've got one of my own, so I'm pretty knowledgeable about girls. I bet *you* know a bit about them, too," he added with a sly glance at his companion.

"Perhaps—a little," agreed George, laughing.

"My girl will be at Bournemouth, too," said Mr. Millar, "so they'll be able to play about together. Yes, that's the thing: I shall hand her over to Pauline. Does she play tennis?"

"I don't know," said George; but somehow

or other he felt pretty sure that Elma Green did not play tennis, for he could not see her dashing about a tennis court in drill shorts.

16

VARIOUS KINDS OF MYSTERY

MR. MILLAR hurried away to keep his appointment and left George standing in the street. There was no need for George to hurry—he had plenty of time to catch his train home—so he found his way into the Strand and dawdled along, gazing into the shop windows and incidentally causing a good deal of obstruction to the other pedestrians. He did not come often to this part of London, and, when he did, it was usually on some business for his father, and he was in a hurry to get it over and return to the more interesting and (to George) more glamorous West End. But today he had no business and there was no hurry, so he strolled. Presently he passed a shop which displayed in its window a large assortment of curious objects for the deception and annoyance of the king's lieges: stink bombs and plate-lifters and hideous masks and false hair and other necessities for that curse of civilization—the practical joker. George paused and looked in. A tall, lanky man with a sad face was standing in the doorway of the shop and, when he saw George was interested, he took a strip of paper out of his pocket and tore it into small pieces.

"See that?" he inquired.

George nodded.

The man put the pieces in his hand, raised his hand to his lips and breathed on them. Then he opened his hand and showed George the strip of paper whole once more.

"I say!" George exclaimed.

The man smiled sadly. "Plenty more inside," he declared.

George followed him into the shop.

"Ever done any conjuring?" inquired the man, opening a large drawer and taking out various little boxes and mirrors and handkerchiefs and rolls of coloured paper.

"No," said George; "but the fact is, we're going to have some children to tea—girls, you know. Do you think girls like conjuring?"

"Everybody does," replied the man mournfully. "Girls and boys and men and women— they all like it. Conjuring always goes down well, especially if you can do a little practice beforehand. Though, as a matter of fact, these things don't need much practice. Fool-proof, that's what they are."

"They ought to suit me down to the ground," said George a trifle bitterly.

"Somebody been having you on?" inquired the lanky man sympathetically. "Been sold a pup, have you?"

"Not exactly," replied George. "I've been having myself on—if you know what I mean."

"Nothing like a few conjuring tricks to raise the spirits," said the man, still in the same mournful tone. "I do them myself when I feel a bit down in the mouth. Here's a nice one now," he continued, pointing to a little wooden box. "Take it up and look at it. Nicely made, isn't it? Nothing odd about it, is there?"

"No," said George. "It's just an ordinary little stud-box."

"Just an ordinary little stud-box," agreed the man. "Now, then, you put a coin in it—any coin will do—thank you, sir. I shut the box—so—and place it on the table, and cover it with my handkerchief—so. Now, sir, if you'll just remove the handkerchief and open the box. . . . Thank you, sir."

"It's gone!" said George in amazement.

"Why, so it has!" said the man sadly. "Your half-crown's vanished. Never mind, I think I can find it for you. It's here, I think," he added, slipping a somewhat grimy but flexible, long-fingered hand inside the opening of George's waistcoat. "Yes, here it is, large as life. . . . That's the right coin, isn't it?"

"If you can teach me to do that . . ." exclaimed George.

"There's no teaching necessary," declared the man, and he proceeded to disclose the secrets of the box, and several other equally intriguing mysteries which required different and equally intriguing apparatus for their demonstration, and presently George might have been seen issuing from the little shop with a brown paper parcel under his arm.

He had lost his train, of course; but there was another in half an hour—a slow one which stopped at every station and was therefore fairly empty. George was able to obtain a compartment to himself. He sat down and thought about his day. The brown paper parcel lay beside him on the seat, and he looked at it with affection. It would be tremendous fun to show those tricks to Dan's friends—it would be the making of the party.

He would practise them, and practise the
"patter," which was obviously an important
part of the effects. He would get Paddy to
help him.

It might be thought that now, when he was
actually on his way home in the train,
George's adventures were over for the day;
but such was not the case. There was another
adventure waiting for George, an adventure
of the mind, and a very curious one.

George sat in the empty compartment
listening to the rattle of the wheels and
thinking about the conjuring tricks and Dan's
party and staring unseeingly at an advertise-
ment of a Life Assurance Company on the
opposite wall of the compartment. "Insure
Your Life," it said. "The Beta Gamma
Assurance Company is Safe and Sure." And
beneath, in smaller letters, it pointed out the
peculiar advantages offered by the Beta
Gamma to those who insured with them.

George gazed at this notice for some time
without seeing it at all, and then, somehow,
the information penetrated to his brain, and
there was a sudden quite audible click—and
George remembered.

"Crikey!" he exclaimed, almost leaping to
his feet in his excitement. "Oh, crikey!

That's what I've been trying to remember all day. . . ."

The point which George had remembered so suddenly was that Mr. Green had insured his life for £20,000. He had told George so, and also told him that the purpose of this insurance was to cover Death Duties. George remembered the whole thing clearly now. He remembered it so clearly that is seemed incredible that he had not remembered it before. He remembered it so clearly that there was no possible doubt whatever in his mind.

"Crikey!" he said again, in awful consternation (and it was a mercy that there were no other travellers in the compartment, for they might have received the impression that there was a lunatic at large). "Then, why did Millar have to sell out all these shares? He didn't have to, of course! . . . Oh, my giddy aunt!" said George, running his fingers through his hair so that it stood straight on end. "I knew there was something I ought to remember. . . . I must write to him at once."

He must write at once—that was his thought—but, unfortunately, he could not write till he got home, and the wretched train seemed to be dawdling on purpose to annoy

George and torture him beyond endurance, and the sickening taxi (which he was forced to take to Winthorpe station, because obviously it was quite impossible to wait ten minutes for the bus) was so old and decrepit that it crawled up every hill like a steam roller on low gear, so that when George did at last arrive at Swan House he presented to his fond parents the appearance of a man distraught.

They left their dinner on the table and followed him to his study, where he was already setting out paper and searching feverishly for ink; and they hovered round him asking questions and gradually becoming acquainted with all the facts of the case.

"I'll tell you all about it," George kept saying; "but I must write first. He needn't sell out the things, don't you see. . . . If I get him in time—he needn't sell them out. I knew there was something I had to remember. . . . Where the devil is my pen?"

"Extremely interesting," Mr. Ferrier said. "Extremely interesting. The workings of the subconscious are wrapt in mystery."

"Dinner——" began Paddy doubtfully.

"Oh, *dinner!*" exclaimed George with scorn, and then he added, more kindly: "Afterwards, Paddy, afterwards. . . ."

George could neither rest nor eat until he had completed his letter to Mr. Millar and had addressed it to his London office (since he did not know the name of the Bournemouth hotel), and had gone out and posted it in the pillar-box in the Winthorpe road. He felt better then, and was quite oblivious of the fact that the pillar-box had been cleared for the day and that his letter would lie there for nearly twenty hours before proceeding a step farther on its journey. In George's mind— as in the minds of many who are not in the habit of regular correspondence on important business matters—a letter posted was a letter well on its way, and when George heard the gentle thud of his letter falling into the box he breathed a sigh of relief. Mr. Millar would get the letter, and he would put everything right; everything was as good as put right already.

The letter was a curious one, for George had written it in haste and excitement, half off his own bat and half to the dictation of his father, who had been anxious to be of service in the matter. The two styles did not blend very well, and indeed no attempt had been made to blend them; but, in spite of this, the letter was perfectly clear and Mr. Millar,

199

when eventually he received it, was too upset
by the news it contained to notice the peculiar
mixture of language in which it was couched.

17

BREATHING SPACE

ON Wednesday George went for a long walk with Nadia to refresh himself after the troubles and trials of his visit to London, but on Thursday he rode over early to Highmoor House. He had promised to ride with Elma on Thursday morning, and the promise must be kept. He was not particularly keen to ride with Elma, because he had not yet made up his mind about her: at one moment he decided that she really was very sweet indeed, and that the man who married her would be an extremely lucky fellow, but the next moment some inner voice would whisper to him, "Yes, but could she ever develop into a real companion? Remember, it's for your whole life!"

It was the thought of marriage as a "life sentence" that frightened George. Life seemed so long; it stretched before him into eternity. He could not believe that there was anybody in the world with whom he could live for ever and not become bored. He was not bored with Paddy, of course; but, then, Paddy was at least twenty different people. She was a different person every hour, and you never knew which person she would be next. You might be annoyed with Paddy, you might even dislike her—George was aware that some of her neighbours disliked Paddy a good deal—but you couldn't possibly be bored with her. . . .

Oh, well, thought George, I must just be very careful with Elma until I can make up my mind whether I love her or not. . . . and he rode on with a little frown between his eyes.

He rode across the moor and up the hill to the stable gate; but when he reached the big stone entrance it was Miss Wilson who was waiting there for him, and Elma was not to be seen. George hesitated for a moment. He did not like Miss Wilson. For one thing, she made him feel a fool and, for another, she was so terribly pedantic and old maidish that he was frightened to open his mouth in her presence in case of shocking her. He hesitated and then rode on, because, of course, there was no escape; and as he went forward he seemed to see her in a different light. There

202

was something rather pathetic in the droop of her shoulders as she leant against the gatepost. She was old, and miserably thin; she was a dried-up slip of a woman who had obviously never known what it was to enjoy herself and have a good time. Poor wretch, thought George commiseratingly, as he drew up his horse beside her and looked down into her pinched sallow face.

"Good-morning, Mr. Ferrier," she said. "I wish to speak to you for a few moments."

George dismounted and shook her by the hand. "Of course," he said. "It's a lovely day, isn't it? Is Elma ready?"

"Elma is not riding this morning," said Miss Wilson dryly.

"Not ill, I hope?"

"No, she is perfectly well, I am glad to say."

"Splendid," said George, a trifle too heartily. There was a little silence.

"The fact is," said Miss Wilson, "Elma has deceived me. I was not aware that you and she were riding alone together every morning before breakfast. The early morning is not my best time—to tell you the truth, I do not feel at my best until the day is well advanced—and Elma has taken advantage of this unfortunate weakness."

George was taken aback. "Oh!" he said feebly.

"You were not aware of this deception?"

"No," said George. "I never thought about it. But, as a matter of fact, Elma is perfectly safe with me. I mean, I know all about horses. It's my job."

"You do not understand," said Miss Wilson. "I consider it unsuitable for Elma to ride alone with a young man. I was under the impression that the groom was accompanying you; and, indeed, I was stretching a point in allowing her to go at all."

"Oh, I say!" exclaimed George. "That's *very* old-fashioned, isn't it? Carruthers is a decent fellow, but we don't want him tagging along."

"Carruthers knew that I expected him to go with you."

"I told him he needn't come."

"He should have informed me," she declared. "He deliberately deceived me. I cannot understand it at all."

George was annoyed. "I don't know why you're making such a fuss," he said. "After all, I'm Elma's trustee." And it seemed to him, as he made this point, that he was for ever trying to impress this point upon people,

204

and that people for ever refused to take this point into their minds and keep it there.

"I am aware of that," Miss Wilson replied doubtfully. "But you are so young, so very young. It seems strange that Mr. Green should have chosen such an extremely youthful trustee."

"But he did," said George.

"I wonder why," said Miss Wilson.

George knew the answer to that, but he did not think it fit to enlighten Miss Wilson. It would be better for Miss Wilson to believe that he had been chosen for reliability and moral worth rather than for actuarial reasons.

"I suppose he must have trusted you," Miss Wilson added after a short but thoughtful silence.

"It certainly looks like it," agreed George.

Miss Wilson sighed. "Perhaps I am foolish and old-fashioned," she said; "but Elma is my responsibility. Mr. Green wished her to be brought up in what might possibly be considered an old-fashioned manner. . . ."

"Oh, I know that," agreed George. "But there *are* limits, aren't there, and——"

"——and I have endeavoured to carry out her father's wishes to the best of my ability."

"I'm sure you have," said George gravely;

"and, honestly, I wouldn't have done it if I thought you wouldn't approve."

Miss Wilson was impressed by his sincerity. "We shall say no more about it," she declared. "In any case, you and Elma will not be able to ride together for some time because we are going away this afternoon." And she smiled at George quite humanly.

George smiled back. "Yes," he said, "that's all right, then. I suggested it to Mr. Millar. I thought it would be nice for you to have a change of air."

"How kind of you!" she exclaimed. "I received a letter this morning from Mr. Millar to say that he has taken rooms for us at Bournemouth at the Kenilworth Castle Hotel. He is staying there himself with his son and daughter. It will be a pleasant change!"

"Yes," said George; but he said it doubtfully, for the Kenilworth Castle was not the hotel which he would have chosen as a holiday resort for his ward; and, in fact, if he had known before that it was the Kenilworth Castle which Mr. Millar had in mind he would have registered a strong protest instead of encouragement to the plan. George had never actually stayed there himself, of course, for the place was run on the champagne standard and inhabited almost entirely by millionaires, but he had dined there once with a friend who had won on an outsider and wanted to celebrate, and on two other occasions he had partaken of Angel's Breath in the American Cocktail Bar, and somehow or other he could not envisage the Misses Wilson and Green in that galère.

"It is a relief to my mind," continued Miss Wilson, quite oblivious of her companion's forebodings. "I had been of the opinion that a change of air and scene would be beneficial to the child after the sorrow of her bereavement. I had been considering the matter and wondering how best to accomplish the project. Mr. Millar has arranged everything. It is exceedingly kind."

"Yes," said George thoughtfully. "H'm. . . . What does Elma think of it?"

"Elma is aware that I know best. She will do as I say."

"Yes," said George more thoughtfully still; and then he added, "Yes . . . well, that's all right, then. . . . But you'd better keep an eye on her when you get there."

Miss Wilson bridled. "I shall most certainly do so," she declared. "I do not think it necessary that I should be told by you——"

"Oh, I know!" cried George hastily. "Of course, you will. I only meant——"

"What did you mean?"

George had meant exactly what he said, so he found it difficult to qualify his statement. "Oh, well," he said. "I hope—I hope you'll have a good time. The food at that place is tophole, that's one thing."

"Not very rich, I hope," inquired Miss Wilson with a shudder.

"Pretty rich," replied George, licking his lips.

The conversation was obviously over, and George was about to make his adieux when Miss Wilson took a sudden decision.

"Would you care to stay to breakfast, Mr. Ferrier?" she inquired.

George accepted with alacrity.

It was rather a strange experience to meet Elma again under the eye of Miss Wilson. She was an entirely different person from the Elma of Monday morning. She was demure and monosyllabic, her eyes were cast down upon her plate of porridge and cream, and her lashes lay upon her cheeks like fringes of dark silk.

They talked about Bournemouth, which

208

Miss Wilson had visited with her ancient aunt in nineteen hundred and three, and George tried to explain that the resort had changed a good deal since then.

"It is larger, no doubt," agreed Miss Wilson complacently.

"Different," insisted George. "All sorts of people go there now, and not just people recovering from illnesses."

"The people will not affect us," she replied. "Elma and I will lead our usual quiet life together with our books and our needlework. I am told that the gardens of the Kenilworth Castle Hotel are renowned for their beauty. We shall find a secluded seat and enjoy the sunshine and the sea air."

It was at this moment that Miss Wilson rose to replenish her plate at the massive sideboard, and Elma chose the opportunity to raise her eyes and look at George. She looked at him and smiled—it really was a delicious smile, friendly and provocative, and full of meaning and mischief—and George smiled back; he could not help it.

Afterwards, as he rode home, having taken leave of his hostesses with conventional courtesy, that smile of Elma's worried him a little. There was a good deal in that smile.

She'll forget about me, he thought, as he cantered across the moor. She'll forget all about me when she gets to Bournemouth, and it will be just as well. But, strangely enough, the thought gave him no pleasure—none at all. He wanted—well, he wanted to be friends with Elma—plain, honest friends—that was what he wanted. He didn't want her to forget him, and he didn't want to be rushed into anything more than friendship. He wasn't ready for that—not yet.

Well, she's off, thought George, half in regret and half in relief at the breathing space which had been granted to him, and she won't be back for a fortnight, and then we'll see.

A fortnight seemed a long time and a great deal could happen in it. When Elma returned she might be different; she might have developed a little; she might be more like other girls and consequently easier to deal with. George made up his mind that when Elma returned they would ride together again—he must fix that with Miss Wilson. In the meantime, there was plenty to do. There was Peter, for instance. He had intended to see a good deal of Peter—and hadn't. He had neglected Peter completely (or was it that

Peter had neglected George?). He hadn't seen Peter since that first expedition to Highmoor House. So much water had passed under the bridge since the fateful expedition that George felt as if he had not seen old Peter for *months*. Perhaps he'd like a day's rabbiting, thought George. The place is alive with the brutes—they want shooting. I'll ask him.

George was passing Rival's Green as he came to this decision and, obeying a sudden impulse, he dismounted and went in at the side gate which opened on to the moor. He hitched his horse to the garden seat and, avoiding the drawing-room, where Mrs. Seeley was sitting in state, he strode into the hall and shouted for Peter at the top of his voice.

Peter came slowly down the stair. "Hallo, George," he said in a quiet voice. "Hallo, what's up?"

"Only that I haven't seen you for ages," George replied. "What have you been doing with yourself, eh?"

"You saw me on Friday, didn't you?"

"It seems ages," George declared. "So much has happened since Friday."

"Nothing much has happened here," said

Peter dryly; "but, then, nothing much ever does."

There was a distinct coolness in the air, and George was at a loss to account for it. He was taken aback. He did not know what to say.

Cathy had been doing the flowers in a small pantry which opened off the hall. She had heard every word of the conversation (indeed, it would have been impossible not to hear), and she was very much annoyed with Peter. Peter had been disagreeable all week—ever since that Highmoor House expedition he had been simply unbearable—cynical and aloof and intransigent, and Cathy had borne with him nobly because she felt certain that something was worrying him, and because she was aware that he was tired and nervy and therefore not altogether responsible for his evil humour. She had borne with his "horridness" when it was directed against herself and the other members of his family; but it was quite a different thing if he was going to be horrid to George. George was not used to the give and take of a large and somewhat difficult family. George was vulnerable.

Cathy seized up a bowl of variegated flowers and issued from the flower-room prepared for battle. She glanced at George and she saw he was hurt. He looked rather like a puppy—a very large and friendly St. Bernard puppy—who had come dashing up to his master with his tail awag and had received a sharp smack on the nose.

"Hallo, George!" she said. "How nice to see you! Peter's got a tummy-ache this morning. Come and talk to me while I finish the flowers." She put her bowl on the hall table and returned to the flower-room.

George lingered in the hall uncertainly—it was Peter he wanted to see—but Peter had lighted his pipe and had strolled towards the front door with his hands in his pockets, and was now surveying the sunlit garden with a nonchalant air.

"All right," said George under his breath. "I'm sure I don't care. . . ." and he followed Cathy into the flower-room.

It was not a very propitious sort of mood in which to start a conversation. Cathy knew that he had come to see Peter (and knew that he knew that she knew it), but she was so used to being a second-best companion that the knowledge did not worry her at all.

"Tell me about the new horse," she said. "Sit there, on the edge of the sink. How lovely for you to be able to buy it for Paddy with your own money!"

"It's simply marvellous," George agreed, and the clouds vanished from his brow at this miraculous understanding of the situation. "It's simply *marvellous* to be able to give Paddy something worth while. Nobody else seems to realise how marvellous it is for me."

"Of course it's marvellous for you," nodded Cathy. "It would be lovely to have lots of money and to be able to give people things—real things, I mean, not just silly little odds and ends of Christmas and birthday presents——"

"It's worth all the worry and bother," agreed George.

"Worry and bother?"

"Yes," said George. "I'm such a fool, you see." And he proceeded to tell her all the different kinds of fool he had been, and to lay before her a full account of everything that had taken place.

It was peaceful and sunny in the flower-room and the roses had a lovely smell. Somehow or other (George thought) Cathy seemed just right when she was surrounded by flowers. She was not like a flower herself, for she was much too human and much too

interested (flowers were soulless things), but
Cathy was a sort of flower-general, marshall-
ing her troops. Nobody that George had ever
seen could make flowers stand up and look in
the right direction and show off their beauty
as Cathy could.

George talked and talked, sitting on the
edge of the sink and watching the bowls and
vases filled one by one by Cathy's deft
fingers; and Cathy worked and listened and
nodded and smiled. She was aware that to
George she was merely an ear—but that could
not be helped—and she was glad that at least
she had been able to banish from his eyes that
surprised-and-hurt-St. Bernard look.

". . . And so you see what a fool I've been,"
said George, but he said it with a slightly
more cheerful air.

"You don't know about business," Cathy
pointed out in her sensible, matter-of-fact
way. "If you had learnt about business you
would have understood as well as they did."

"Oh, I know," said George. "At least, I
might have understood; but the silliest part
was forgetting about the insurance. You can't
say that wasn't damn silly, can you? No
amount of knowing about business or not
knowing about business makes any difference

to that. Dad says it was my subconscious mind that kept on trying to make me remember about it all through the meeting, and that it couldn't get through until I sort of relaxed. Odd, isn't it?"

"Very odd," agreed Cathy thoughtfully.

There was a little silence and a bee, which had been brought in from the garden fast asleep in a flower-bell, woke up and began to bumble round the little room.

"I'll put it out, shall I?" said George, and the spell was broken.

He caught the bee in his handkerchief and put it out of the window and then, after a little more desultory conversation, he went away.

18

THE WORM TURNS

WHEN George had gone the house felt strangely empty and strangely silent. Cathy finished her flowers and bestowed the bowls of roses in their usual places about the house; and all at once, as she placed the big brown pottery bowl on the hall table and stood back to admire the effect, the futility of the thing swept over her. "What is the good?" she demanded of herself. "What *is* the good of wasting all that time doing flowers? How often have I filled these same silly bowls with flowers—spring flowers, summer flowers, or great shaggy-headed chrysanthemums—and how often shall I go on doing it? Does anyone ever notice them? Would anyone care if I stopped doing it? Would father or mother or Peter or anyone look round and say, 'Hallo, no flowers!' "

She stood quite still, looking at her handiwork, and it seemed to her that life went on and on and nothing ever happened, and the thought depressed her beyond measure. She seemed to see, in the cycle of the flowers, the cycle of the years of her life—daffodils, sweet-peas, roses, delphiniums, chrysanthemums, and beech leaves—and then daffodils again—hundreds of bowls of flowers representing hundreds of hours' work—and all quite useless. Cathy had never felt before that her life was useless and static, but now she could not dismiss the idea. Her reason told her that she was a useful member of society, for her family depended upon her in all sorts of ways, and she gave each member of it something that he or she would have missed had it been withdrawn; but, in spite of this, her life seemed suddenly flat and stale and empty—and, worst of all, uneventful.

If Cathy could have stood apart and looked at her life from a distance, or stood still, poised between the past and the future, she would have been able to see that her life was not uneventful, and that it was certainly not static. Nobody's life is static. There is movement and development in every life all the time. Even those people who are stuck fast in a backwater looking at the stream of life flow past are subject to the law of eternal movement; for, if nothing else is happening to them, there is change taking place in their own souls.

Cathy was unused to self-analysis. She was too busy thinking of other people to bother much about herself, so her sudden mood of self-pity took her by surprise, and after a few moments she gave herself a little shake and lifted her chin. . . . After all, I'm me, thought Cathy, and that's always something. Nobody has ever been me before.

It was a strange thought, and strangely comforting. Nobody had ever been Cathy before. Nobody had ever, in all the long history of the world, possessed that inner being, that parcel of complexities, which was Cathy Seeley. And, this being so, it seemed to her that a miracle might happen for her especial benefit, and that some day George might look at her differently, and not as though she were a sister or a favourite horse—not with kind, friendly eyes. Cathy felt that she would almost rather George should look at her with anger and hatred . . . she felt there would be more hope then . . . and perhaps she was right.

It was no new idea to Cathy that she loved George—she had always loved him, and she was perfectly certain that she always would.

Her love for George was part of her life; it had grown into her; it had developed with her as she grew and developed; but hitherto Cathy had loved George in a placid, friendly way, and there had been no bitterness or pain in the knowledge that her love was not returned. Today, however, she found that her feelings had changed—her rage with Peter for the way he had treated George showed her how changed they were—Cathy had felt that George was hers and had done battle for him on that account. She had been furious with Peter; she had been shaking with anger, and her whole being was upset with the violence of her unaccustomed emotion.

Cathy was still angry with Peter, though not quite so angry as she had been, for her quiet talk with George had calmed her a good deal. There were several things which she ought to do, but, for the moment, she felt disinclined to do anything. Her emotional disturbance had tired her. She sat down on the front doorstep in the sun and rested herself in the peace of the garden. In spite of the dry weather, the garden was "quite good," she decided—it was wonderful, really. There was a dusty sort of look about the foliage, but the flowers were very gay.

Cobham was wonderful with flowers—they were lucky to have him; it was a pity he was getting old. . . .

Cathy was still sitting there when Peter strolled up with his pipe in his mouth. He looked at her in surprise.

"Hallo!" he said. "Haven't you got anything to do?"

"Anything to *do*!" echoed Cathy, waking from her dream . . . and then quite suddenly her rage flared up. "Can't I sit still for five minutes?" she inquired. "Have I got to go on slaving from morning to night while you stroll about with your hands in your pockets?"

Peter was astonished. It was so unlike Cathy to talk like this that he could hardly believe his ears. He gazed at her to see what had happened to her, but, beyond the fact that her eyes were very bright and her cheeks rather pinker than usual, she looked exactly like herself.

"But, Cathy . . ." he began, and hesitated.

"Well, what?"

"I didn't mean anything. I just meant——"

"You just meant that I oughtn't to be slacking," said Cathy, with an edge to her voice. "Other people can do what they like—they can stroll about and sulk as much as they please; but I've got to keep on doing all the silly little jobs that nobody else wants to do. I can't sit down for five minutes without you coming and moving me on—like a policeman——"

"Are you—are you feeling quite well?"

"Quite well, thank you. Perhaps you'd like to see my tongue," said Cathy furiously. "Perhaps you'd like to take my temperature and feel my pulse."

It was all very silly, of course, and an outsider would probably have thought it extremely funny; but neither Cathy nor Peter was in a condition to see the humour of it.

"What on earth's the matter?" Peter demanded.

"You're the matter!" cried Cathy, rising from the step in her wrath. "You're selfish and rude and horrible. You're simply unbearable. I suppose you think it's nice for us to have you here. . . . Well, it isn't. You snarl and snap at everybody. You think you're so wonderful—and all the time you're just a horrid, bad-tempered little boy—you ought to be smacked."

Peter was so taken aback by this outburst

that he quite forgot to be angry. "I say . . ." he began. "I say, Cathy. . . ."

"I can't stand you any more!" she exclaimed. "No, I can't. You've done nothing but sulk for days, and your manners are absolutely foul. It was bad enough when you snapped and snarled at all of *us*—and a frightfully bad example to the children—but how dare you be beastly to George? George hasn't done anything. You don't deserve to have a friend like George——"

"You don't know what George——"

"I *do* know," Cathy cried. "I know that George is kind and good and wouldn't hurt a fly. George hasn't done anything, and yet you treat him like dirt—and it hurts him. You're a stuck-up *beast*. . . . I've tried to bear you because I was sorry for you, but I shan't bear you any longer. . . ." and, so saying, she turned and fled, for she was aware that she was going to cry. She fled upstairs and locked herself into her room, and Peter was left standing on the steps with his mouth open and his heart full of angry words and nobody to listen to them.

A quarrel begun and abandoned is the worst sort of quarrel that can afflict a family, for the protagonists are obliged to consume their own smoke. Peter and Cathy did not re-open their quarrel, but it smouldered silently. They did not address each other unless it was absolutely necessary, and they were icily polite to each other at meals. There was a feeling of strain in the air; even Mrs. Seeley felt the strain, and was disturbed by it.

The Seeley family was used to quarrels, of course—most large families are—Peter often quarrelled with the twins, and the twins frequently fell out with Dan; but Cathy had never been known to take any part in these imbroglios except the part of a peacemaker. The Seeley family was shocked and astounded at the spectacle of its peacemaker at war.

It was very much easier to start a war than to call a truce, so Cathy and Peter found, and before long they had both decided that this quarrel was a perfect nuisance, and they would have been glad of an excuse to patch things up. Cathy was a little ashamed of her outburst, but she comforted herself by the reflection that Peter had richly deserved it, and that it had done him good—he was not nearly so disagreeable now, and his manners had improved a good deal. She was also ig-nobly amused by the attitude of the family; by the way they all chatted pleasantly at meals to cover any embarrassing silences. She was aware of their eyes gazing at her speculatively, and turning away when she happened to look round. I believe it's good for them, Cathy thought. I've always been the buffer. . . . I've always tried to make things pleasant and easy for them . . . and now it's their turn. Perhaps it would have been better for them if I hadn't always tried to smooth things over, perhaps I've been too bufferish. . . .

This was such a strange thought that she fell into a reverie over it and awoke to find Jim proffering her the mustard with an ingratiating smile.

Peter took a little longer than Cathy to arrive at the conclusion that the quarrel was a nuisance, for Cathy had said her say and Peter had had no opportunity of saying his. He was furious with Cathy, but all the same her words had made an impression on him. Of course, Cathy had not known what he was suffering (she had no idea of the misery and wretchedness which filled his heart), and she had exaggerated his rudeness and bad temper out of all proportion; but afterwards, when he considered the matter in cold blood, Peter was forced to admit to himself that her accusations were based on fact. He *had* been gloomy and difficult, and he *had* been a bit off-hand with poor old George. Poor old George was a perfect fool, of course, and a very annoying fool, but it was not George's doing that they had gone over to Highmoor House. . . . It was *my* doing, thought Peter wretchedly. I made him go—in fact, I took him—I filled him up with the idea that it was his duty to take an interest in Elma. . . . It isn't George's fault.

Having come to this conclusion, Peter searched for some means of propitiating Cathy without losing face, but he could find no means. A button came off his shirt and a hole suddenly appeared in the heel of his favourite pair of socks, and Peter was helpless. It never occurred to him to ask his mother to darn the sock or to sew on the button—Cathy was the person who did these things. Peter put the offending garments in the bottom of the drawer and searched harder than ever for material to heal the breach.

19

PRACTISING MAGIC

THUNDERCLOUDS were brooding over Rival's Green, but Swan House was bathed in sunshine. George had no idea, of course, that his visit to his friends had caused so much hostility, so much inconvenience, so many heart-burnings. He had ridden home quite cheerfully after his soothing talk with Cathy and had put in a good day's work in the stables. Then he had dined with his parents as usual and had discussed Elma Green's visit to Bournemouth. Mr. and Mrs. Ferrier did not know Elma, but they were interested in her, and they liked to hear any little items of news that were going.

"She'll be there now," said George, glancing at the clock, "and I only hope she has the sense to appreciate the food."

"Why shouldn't she, the creature?" Paddy inquired.

"Girls don't appreciate decent food,"

replied George. "You take them to a top-hole restaurant and spend pounds on a succulent repast, and half the time they don't know what they're eating."

Mrs. Ferrier was immediately in arms for her sex, but Mr. Ferrier sided with George, and the argument lasted until dessert was put on the table. The gentlemen were two to one, but Paddy was more than a match for them. She was so agile and fiery and so amazingly illogical that you never knew where you were—so to speak—and Mr. Ferrier and George presently retired from the unequal battle feeling thoroughly bamboozled.

There was silence for a few moments, and then Paddy smiled at them tenderly. "But you're right. I shouldn't wonder," she declared. "Men are such greedy creatures—it would be no wonder at all if they knew more about food."

"That's what I said," murmured George feebly.

"And you were right, darling," Paddy declared. "It's myself knows how right you are, for I've lived me whole life amongst the creatures, and I've always found it paid to feed them like fighting cocks."

After dinner George inveigled Paddy into his study with the mysterious announcement that he "wanted to show her something." He was aware that Paddy would rise to the bait, and he was not disappointed.

"But what is it, then?" she demanded, pricking up her ears like a terrier.

"Ah!" said George, smiling in a secret sort of way.

Paddy was vastly intrigued. She followed him up the stairs, pestering him with questions. "Would it be a hedgehog, George, darling?" she inquired. "Because if that's what it is——"

"No, it isn't a hedgehog."

"Well, what, then?"

"I'll show you," George said firmly, and he would say no more. And soon Paddy was sitting in one of the ancient basket-chairs waiting to be shown, and there was an expression of eager and child-like anticipation on her small bright face which was pleasant to see.

"Now, then, Paddy," said George. "Now, then, are we all ready? Here goes. . . . Take a look at this box, will you? Nothing odd about it, is there? Just an ordinary box, eh?"

"Yes," said Paddy, "a neat box, it is."

"Quite ordinary?" inquired George anxiously.

"It is, indeed," said Paddy—this was obviously what he wanted her to say.

"Quite ordinary," said George with relief. "Now we've got to have a coin—here's a half-crown—take a good look at it, please. Now put it in the box and shut the box—that's right. I put the box on the table—so—I cover it with a handkerchief and I wave my wand—abracadabra!" said George with profound gravity. "Abracadabra. . . . Now open the box."

Paddy leant forward and opened the box. "George, where it it?" she exclaimed. "George, it really *is* magic!"

"Pretty good, isn't it?" he agreed with becoming modesty, though secretly he was enchanted with his success.

"It's amazing!" she declared.

"Yes," said George. "Of course, I really ought to find the half-crown down your neck, or something, but I'll have to practise that. D'you think they'll like it?"

"Who?"

"Dan and Co., of course."

"George . . . yes . . . what a good idea! Of course they'll like it. Have you got anything else?"

"Heaps of things," he replied. "I've got a magic coin—a thing like a half-crown with a little hook on it—that does all sorts of queer things, and some paper strips, and an odd sort of double handkerchief, and a ball on a string, and a cigarette-case—where is it? Ah, here it is. Have a cigarette?" (He opened the cigarette-case, and it was empty.) "See that?" he asked.

"It's empty," she said, "and that's not surprising. It usually is empty—your cigarette-case—when you offer me a cigarette."

"Ah, but look here!" he adjured her. "Look here, Paddy. I put this empty cigarette-case down on the table—I wave my wand—I open it—and there you are!"

The cigarette-case was full.

"Have one," he said.

Paddy accepted one doubtfully. "Is it real?" she inquired. "I mean, it won't go off with a bang or anything?"

"It's perfectly real," George assured her, taking one himself to give her confidence. "As a matter of fact, it's the neatest thing of the lot—that cigarette-case—so astounding, and yet as simple as ABC." And he proceeded to lay bare the mystery to Paddy and to show her how the empty drawer—a sort of false bottom—could be pulled out, leaving the real drawer full of cigarettes inside.

He showed her some more tricks, and they were all successful, more or less, for George had the long, flexible fingers of a born conjuror, and after the display was over he put his treasures away in a drawer and sat down on the window seat.

It was dark now and the sky was full of stars, and the narrow lamp-lit room seemed as if it were floating above the tree-tops in space.

"I don't wonder Dad's keen on stars," said George after a little silence. "Wonderful things, they are."

"Yes," said Paddy. But she was not thinking about stars; she was thinking about something nearer at hand. She had been thinking about it for several days, and now seemed a good time to speak of it. "Have you ever thought of giving up this trustee business?" she asked.

George hadn't thought of it.

"That's one of the reasons I didn't want you to spend the money," she continued. "You could refuse the money and give up the whole thing. It's worrying you, isn't it?"

"It isn't only the money," said George. "I promised, you see."

"I know; but you didn't realise what you were letting yourself in for."

"That's true," he agreed. He was silent for a few moments, and then he continued earnestly: "You see, Paddy, it's all so queer. It started in such an odd way—such a chancy way—and now it's suddenly got so important. What I mean is, I only met the old boy once, by accident, and I only saw him for a few hours, and most of the time I was half-tight—at least," amended George with a praiseworthy attempt to avoid the slightest exaggeration, "at least I wasn't *really* half-tight, I was just happy—everything seemed rather far away and I didn't care if it snowed."

"You *were* half-tight," declared Paddy. "That explains it. I've often wondered why you took it on."

"I wasn't, honestly. How could I have been? We had a bottle of hock for lunch," said George reminiscently, "and very good, it was. Afterwards when I told him it was my birthday he was quite vexed and said we should have had fizz—rather nice of him, I thought. We had hock, and then port, and then we had brandy with the coffee. I couldn't possibly have been tight."

"I would have——" Paddy began.

"Why, of course you would," said George, smiling at her tenderly. "One cocktail, and all your inhibitions vanish—not that you have many inhibitions at the best of times——"

"Indeed!" said Paddy, bridling.

"But the point is, *I wasn't*," George rushed on, for he was anxious to keep strictly to the matter in hand and not to be led away by an argument over Paddy's reactions to strong drink. "*I wasn't*. I took on the job when I was in my sane and sober senses; and, now that I've put my hand to the plough, I can't turn back."

Paddy chuckled involuntarily, for the simile amused her.

"Why are you laughing?" he inquired.

"I'm sorry," she said hastily. "I know it's all very serious. Go on, George, darling."

"Well," said George. "Yes—where was I? Oh, yes. You see, I feel I've got to do what the old boy wanted—that's what I feel—and the thing is, what would he have wanted? If I hadn't been happy I might have got a better idea of what he really wanted me to do. He must have wanted me to do *something* or he wouldn't have chosen me, would he? He knew jolly well I wouldn't be any use at the

234

money part of the business. Of course, if I'd known this was going to happen so soon, and that I should never see the poor old blighter again, I wouldn't have taken the brandy. I'd have said 'no' (well, I did say 'no' at first, but I'd have stuck to 'no') and I'd have tried to find out exactly what was in his mind. I'd have asked him all sorts of questions." George paused for a moment and then added with a sigh: "If only I'd *known*—or if he could come back. . . ."

"We always feel that," said Paddy, quite serious now. "When anybody dies we always wish we could have them back—even if it was only for an hour—just to ask them something, or to tell them how much we liked them."

"I *did* like him, Paddy. I feel as if I'd known him quite well. He was a funny old boy and awfully fussy and fumy, but I liked him quite a lot."

"Then you probably know what he would like you to do," said Paddy promptly.

"Yes," said George. "That's just it. There was something he said . . . and I believe I do know what he wanted."

Paddy had the sense to remain silent. She waited patiently.

"It's about Elma, you see," continued

George. "She's such a lonely sort of creature, and it really is a frightfully dull life for a girl, shut up in that big gloomy house with a dry-as-dust old maid, miles from everywhere, seeing nobody from one month's end to another."

"She sees you," Paddy pointed out.

"I know," said George, and he blushed.

"George!" cried Paddy in alarm. "George, you're not going to marry her!"

"No," he burst out. "At least—well—that's the whole thing. Somebody's got to marry her, because she won't be *safe* until she's safely married—she's so lonely and defence-less—and I believe the old boy would like me to marry her. I believe that was in his mind, somehow."

"But you're not in love with her!" Paddy cried.

"I'm not sure," said George. "She's very sweet, you know, and very, very beautiful, and there's something so appealing about her—she's so unusual—not like other girls at all—old-fashioned and quaint and innocent as a child. . . ."

"You're *not* in love with her," cried Paddy. "You're *not*. Oh, George, don't do anything silly. If you were in love with her, it's not like that you'd be talking. You wouldn't be wondering whether the father wanted you to marry her. . . ."

"Why wouldn't I?"

"Because you wouldn't care whether he wanted it or not—or (if you cared at all about what he wanted) you'd be busy deluding yourself into the belief that he *did* want it. It's the wrong way round you're looking at it," cried Paddy, her eyes flashing with earnestness and with the effort to explain what it was she really meant. "Oh, George, don't you see that if you loved her you'd look at it from the other end—from her end? The girl would come first, and all the rest of it wouldn't matter a hang."

There was silence for a moment and then Paddy added with conviction, "You may be sure he wouldn't want you to marry her unless you love her."

George saw that this was true. "I must be sure first," he agreed thoughtfully. "But Elma isn't like other people, and I've got to make up my mind before I go any further. How can I be sure? There are so many girls, and I like them all. Am I ever going to like one best of all?"

"My dear, of course you are," said Paddy gently.

George smiled at her. "But I think you'd like Elma," he said. "I really think you would."

Paddy was sure she would not like Elma, but she was too wise to say so.

Part 2

1

ARRIVALS AT THE KENILWORTH CASTLE HOTEL

"*T*HE *Kenilworth Castle Hotel is situated some miles from Bournemouth on a cliff overlooking the sea. It is large and commodious and beautifully appointed. Every bedroom has its own bathroom and telephone and the cuisine is up to the standard of the best London hotels. The gardens are the best in the neighbourhood, tastefully laid out in terraces from which magnificent views may be obtained, and a winding path leads down to the shore, where a secluded bay offers unequalled bathing. The tennis courts are unrivalled, and there are ample facilities for golf, riding and sailing. The hotel is a splendid centre for motoring, being within easy reach of the New Forest and of interesting historical monuments. There is a specially built dancing floor and an excellent band plays dance music three times a week.*"

It is thus that the prospectus describes the

amenities of the Kenilworth Castle Hotel, and the prospectus does not lie. Everything is of the best, and the prices charged are such that the best can be offered and the shareholders of the company which owns the hotel can pocket a substantial dividend every year. They can pocket it cheerfully and with good conscience in the knowledge that they have left no stone unturned to procure the comfort of their guests.

Mr. Arbuthnot Millar was a director of the Kenilworth Castle. It was therefore his duty to stay at the place occasionally and keep his eye on the way things were run. He had an arrangement with the manager by which he procured the best rooms for himself and his family at a nominal charge, and the fact that part of this nominal charge came back to him in the form of a dividend was a source of satisfaction to him. He found other sources of satisfaction when he stayed at the hotel: the staff was aware of the fact that he was a director, and rushed to do his bidding and to anticipate his every wish, and it was extremely pleasant to stroll through the big airy rooms and to feel that—in a sort of way—the whole place belonged to him. The Kenilworth Castle was only one of many irons which Mr. Millar kept heating in the fire, but it gave him more real satisfaction than all the other irons put together. It was a safe and lucrative iron, and one which he could see heating with his own eyes. He could see that it was prosperous, and that it would continue to be prosperous for as long as there were people in the world with money to burn. Mr. Millar wished that he had more shares in the Kenilworth Castle and less shares in oil mines in foreign countries where cataclysms of nature and stupidities of man seemed banded together to deprive him of his hard won capital.

It was for these reasons that Mr. Millar liked staying at the Kenilworth Castle Hotel when he wanted a little holiday and a breath of sea air, and his son, Wilfred, and his daughter, Pauline, were quite willing to accompany him and to remain with him as long as he pleased. It was a good spot and suited them down to the ground, for the tennis courts really were excellent and the dancing floor as good as any in town.

The guests who took advantage of the amenities of the hotel had one thing in common—they were rich. It was the only thing they had in common, for they were of all classes and of all nationalities—a constantly shifting kaleidoscope of colour and form. South Americans, Spaniards and Jews, Indian princes and Italian counts rubbed shoulders (metaphorically, of course) with London financiers, Big Business men, Wall Street operators, oil kings and company promoters. There was a family of Japanese, small and dainty as porcelain figures, and a family of Russians, tall and gaunt, with the haunted eyes which seem to be the most striking characteristics of the Slav.

These people pursued pleasure all day long and far into the night. They pursued it in all the different ways which the Kenilworth Castle put at their command, but it seemed as if few of them had managed to catch up with it—far less to seize hold of it and make it their own.

The young of the different species made friends with each other on the tennis courts or in the sea, and by so doing caused their elders anxiety or amusement, but always gave them matter for conversation. For instance, when young Skein of Skein's Patent Dog Food danced assiduously with Miss Trim of Trim's Seedless Jam, Mrs. Trim was exceedingly put out, for she had heard that the dog food was on the downward grade; but Mrs. Wordless (whose husband had made his money by the sale of shares in doubtful companies and was therefore a cut above commercial kings) was considerably diverted by the circumstance, and remarked to her cronies as they took their seats at the bridge table that it looked as if the dogs would be having jam on their biscuits before long.

The Kenilworth Castle Hotel did not bother to turn its head when Miss Green arrived with her faithful companion. She was tired and pale and dowdy—she might have been a fly on the wall for all the notice she attracted. Mr. Millar had made proper arrangements for her reception, of course, and she was received by the reception clerk and conducted to the rooms which had been set aside for her, and (since she was a friend of Mr. Millar's) the manager was informed of her arrival, and hastened to present himself and to inquire if the rooms met with her approval. Miss Green said nothing at all in answer to his inquiries, but Miss Wilson said that the rooms would do very well. She was not enthusiastic about them, partly because she did not wish to give him the impression that they were any better rooms than those to which she was accustomed, and partly because the journey down by car had upset her and given her a violent headache. Miss Wilson's one idea was to get rid of the manager and lie down on her bed and allow the headache to have its way with her. So she merely said that the rooms would do very well and edged him towards the door, and the manager departed, feeling a little sad to think that the beauty of the rooms was not appreciated.

They were beautiful rooms—the best in the hotel—with balconies overlooking the gardens and the sea. Each room had a separate bathroom, and there was a double door between the rooms, so the ladies could communicate with each other. Although Elma had said nothing to the manager, she was enchanted with the place—it was excitement that had rendered her dumb. She liked the big airy rooms with their pretty colouring; she liked the bathrooms with their mirrors and coloured fittings and all the fascinating little taps for hot and cold showers and sea-water baths; but most of all she liked the view from the windows of the wide, heaving, blue expanse of sea. She was still admiring everything and trying all the different gadgets when Mr. Millar knocked on the door. His appearance had a sobering effect upon her, and he found her a little difficult to get on with. He persevered, however, and explained who he was, and inquired after Miss Wilson.

Elma pointed to the door and told him in as few words as possible that Miss Wilson was tired after the journey and was lying down.

"Well, perhaps you'd better have tea sent up," he said. "Will she be better by dinner-time?"

"Yes," said Elma.

"Good," said Mr. Millar heartily. "Well, you must both come and dine at our table. Will you tell her?"

"Yes," said Elma.

He went away after that with the impression that his ward was a pretty girl, but possessed no manners and less sense. It was very unfortunate—so he felt—but it couldn't be helped. He had often noticed that people with a great deal of money had little else to recommend them.

Miss Wilson had recovered by dinner-time and was quite pleased to receive Mr. Millar's message. They dressed themselves in their black silk dresses, which had been made by the little dressmaker in Winthorpe, and went downstairs, quite happy, and quite unaware of the curious spectacle they presented amongst the gorgeous and multi-coloured dresses worn by their fellow-guests.

Pauline Millar gasped when she saw them. "Heavens above!" she exclaimed, seizing her father's arm. "And she's quite pretty, too! Where on earth did they get those clothes? You don't expect me to go about with those clothes, do you?"

"You can take her in to Bournemouth tomorrow," declared her father soothingly. "Take her to Bobby's and fit her out. Money no object."

Pauline was so delighted with the prospect that she was able to greet Miss Green and her companion in a cordial manner, and they all went in to dinner and took their seats at the table which had been decorated with pink carnations and smilax in honour of Mr. Millar's friends.

"My son is playing in a tennis tournament," said Mr. Millar to his ward. "You will meet him tomorrow."

Elma signified her agreement in her usual monosyllabic manner.

"Do you like tennis?" inquired Pauline.

"No," said Elma.

"Not like tennis!" cried Pauline in amazement.

"Elma has never tried tennis," said Miss Wilson pleasantly. "I have no doubt she would enjoy the exercise if she were afforded the opportunity. Perhaps it might be possible to purchase a tennis racquet at Bournemouth——"

"No," said Pauline firmly.

"No?" inquired Miss Wilson. "I was under the impression that Bournemouth was quite a large town now. A friend of Elma's informed us that it had increased considerably in size, so I naturally assumed that it would be possible to purchase—er—sports accessories. But perhaps," she added, struck by a sudden brilliant idea, "perhaps it would be possible to *borrow* a tennis racquet for Elma to use. I have no doubt that there are more than four tennis racquets in the hotel, and if they were not all in use their owners might be willing to lend——"

"Oh, *no*," said Pauline, more firmly than before. "I didn't mean—what I meant was, she had much better stick to golf or swimming, or whatever it is she does best. It's no use trying to do everything—there isn't time."

Miss Wilson was somewhat taken aback. "Elma has not had much opportunity——" she began; but she did not get any further with her explanation, for the wine waiter had appeared with a large bottle wrapped in a table-napkin and was filling Elma's glass with sparkling amber wine.

"Is it—is it champagne?" inquired Miss Wilson in alarm. "Oh, no—please—I beg of you—Elma is not accustomed to wine."

"It won't do her any harm," declared Mr. Millar, smiling. "I assure you it won't. We must celebrate our meeting, you know."

"She will not like it," said Miss Wilson desperately; and the wish was both father and mother to the thought.

"Try it," Mr. Millar commanded.

Elma obeyed. She sipped it daintily and screwed up her face, and then she sipped it again—and smiled.

"She likes it," Mr. Millar declared.

"Yes," said Elma, taking another longer sip.

"Of course she likes it," Pauline said. "Who wouldn't like it? Is this the first time you've tasted fizz?"

"Yes," said Elma; and then, to the amazement of all her companions, she added gravely, "but it will not be the last."

"Elma!" cried Miss Wilson in horrified accents.

Elma was immediately subdued, and for about ten minutes she was once more monosyllabic; but, after that, the champagne and the gorgeous food, the discreet homage of her trustee and all the unwonted sights and sounds of the big dining-room began to go to her head, and she paid no more attention to Miss Wilson's restraining exclamations. Her cheeks grew pink and her eyes brightened and she chatted and laughed with the best, and Mr. Millar reversed his opinion of his ward and decided that she had plenty in her, and that all she wanted was bringing out.

Miss Wilson gave up the struggle. She felt exactly like a person who has been driving a familiar and well-tried motor car, and, coming to a steep decline, suddenly discovers that the brakes will not act. She could do nothing but sit back and let things rip, but she made up her mind that afterwards in the privacy of her pink and silver bedroom she would make up for lost time. "I must *speak* to Elma," she decided. "I really must speak to her seriously.

251

We should not have come here at all. It is not the right milieu. . . . But how was I to know?"

Poor Miss Wilson was so distraught by all these reflections that she scarcely knew what she was doing, and presently she found herself finishing a large plateful of chocolate ice pudding without being aware that she had helped herself to the dish. It happened to be her favourite pudding, but unfortunately it always disagreed with her so disastrously that she never allowed herself to indulge in it, so it was doubly unfortunate that she had eaten it, and eaten it unknowingly and therefore without enjoyment. Perhaps it will not disagree with me tonight, thought the wretched woman; but, even as she thought it, she was aware of a cold, dull, leaden feeling in her vital parts, and before she was able to tear Elma away from her new friends and drag her upstairs to bed there was no doubt at all in Miss Wilson's mind that the pudding was going to disagree with her as usual.

There was a little mist in the morning, and Miss Wilson, lifting her fevered and aching head from her fiery pillow, beheld it seeping in through her open window. She groaned and

252

lay back again. Hateful place! she thought. Why, oh, why, did we not remain quietly at home? She rang for tea and sipped a few mouthfuls, but it did her no good, and she became aware that it would be impossible for her to rise from her bed and accompany her charge down to breakfast. She had just reached this appalling conclusion when Elma bounded into her room, ready dressed and as bright as a bee. Miss Wilson looked at her with positive loathing. Nobody had any right to look like that, or to feel like it, at eight o'clock in the morning. Life was extremely unfair. Health and strength and money were showered upon the favoured few. . . .

Miss Wilson pulled herself together and wrote a little note to Mr. Millar—a very straggling, feeble sort of note—informing him of her indisposition and asking if it would be possible for him to have Miss Green to breakfast at his table. She rang the bell and despatched the note and returned to bed full of the most frightful forebodings. "It is dreadful," she said to herself, "and Mr. Millar is not at all the right sort of person . . . he had such a curious effect upon Elma. But what can I do?"

She was a little reassured by Mr. Millar's

prompt answer to her SOS. It was a kind note, sensible and to the point: he was exceedingly sorry that she was unwell, but she was not to worry, for Miss Green would be a welcome addition to his party. He was her trustee, and would be responsible for her welfare. He was sending his daughter along to see that Miss Wilson had all she required, and to escort Miss Green down to breakfast.

Pauline appeared soon after and was unexpectedly sympathetic and capable. She rang for the chambermaid and gave orders that Miss Wilson was to be well looked after; she refilled a cold hot-water bottle with her own hands; and, best of all, she removed Elma, and Miss Wilson was left in peace.

Elma was very sorry for Miss Wilson, but she could not help being a little glad on her own account. She had realised last night that Miss Wilson was going to cramp her style—Miss Wilson was old-fashioned, of course, and Elma was anxious to subscribe to new-fashioned ways. This was obviously a modern place, and Elma thought it was absolutely perfect, and her new friends were the most delightful people she had ever met. The whole atmosphere was so different from anything that she had ever experienced, or even imagined, that she felt she was moving in a dream and, as one is never surprised in a dream, no matter what happens, so Elma was unsurprised by anything that happened to her at the Kenilworth Castle. She was not even surprised when Mr. Millar handed her fifty pounds in notes and made her sign a receipt and told her to go to Bournemouth with Pauline and buy herself some clothes.

"It's your own money, so you needn't thank me," he said, smiling at her kindly.

Elma obediently forbore to thank him. She stuffed the notes into her bag. "Must they be black?" she inquired, looking at him with her large and innocent eyes.

"Black?" inquired Mr. Millar doubtfully.

"The clothes," said Elma.

"No," said Mr. Millar firmly. "No, they needn't be black. People don't wear mourning now—not to the same extent."

"I like new-fashioned ways best—in everything," declared Elma with unaccustomed fervour.

Pauline drove her into Bournemouth, and they parked the small sports car before starting their morning's work. "We're going to be *hours*," she explained, "hours and hours and hours, so we don't want to be bothered with the car—and we're going to have a perfectly marvellous time."

Pauline's predictions were fulfilled; they were about six hours over their shopping, and a marvellous time was had by both girls. They shopped assiduously all morning, lunched together at Stewart's, and continued their quest for ravishing garments in the afternoon. They were both young and strong, and the orgy of buying in which they indulged did not begin to tell upon them until tea-time. By then they had spent a great deal more than fifty pounds, but apparently that did not matter. Pauline had instructed her new friend in the mysteries of credit. "If you buy *enough* at a shop, you needn't pay for it," she declared; "and, of course, you never pay out *money* for frocks and coats and hats and things like that. It simply isn't *done* . . . the shop people would have a fit if you offered to. You just tell them to put it down to your account."

"I suppose I shall have to pay some day," said Elma, a trifle anxiously.

"Oh, yes, *some day*," Pauline replied. "But you needn't worry about that *now*. When they send you the bill you can send it on to Dad. You've got heaps of money, so you'd better learn how to spend it." (She found Elma was a quick learner.)

"Yes," said Elma. "But what was the fifty pounds for?"

"For undies and things," replied Pauline vaguely, "and for anything we don't want to buy at Bobby's."

As most of the things they wanted were procurable at Bobby's, the fifty pounds remained intact until lunch time; and, indeed, when Elma and Pauline returned to the Kenilworth Castle Hotel, Elma still possessed forty-odd pounds of the sum entrusted to her that morning. Her room was already full of cardboard boxes containing entrancing clothes, and yet she had spent hardly any money at all. It was more like a dream than ever.

Miss Wilson was no better; in fact, she was a good deal worse, for nobody except the chambermaid had been near her all day, and she had not the slightest idea where Elma was nor what she was doing. Elma put on her old dressing-gown (she had bought a new one, of course, but she was aware that the sight of it would disturb Miss Wilson and lead her to ask all sorts of unnecessary questions) and went in to see the invalid. She had bought some grapes and a copy of *The Literary*

Review—a somewhat dry periodical to which Miss Wilson was addicted. These gifts were a peace offering—a sort of burnt sacrifice—to propitiate Miss Wilson and ease Elma's conscience and they fulfilled both purposes.

Miss Wilson had made up her mind to "speak" to Elma, and had thought of all the harsh and reproachful things she would say; but it is almost impossible to be harsh and reproachful to somebody who comes to your sick bed bearing gifts of hothouse grapes and *Literary Reviews*—especially if you labour under the delusion that these expensive luxuries have been bought out of the frugal pocket-money of the donor.

"Oh, Elma!" cried Miss Wilson. "*Where* have you been all day? I have been so *worried*. Oh, my dear child, what lovely grapes. How good of you. And the *Review*! I shall look forward to perusing it when my head is slightly better. Oh, Elma, what *have* you been doing? Yes, I believe I could take a few grapes—just three, perhaps. Three grapes could not harm me, could they? Where have you *been*, Elma?"

"To Bournemouth," Elma said.

"With whom did you go?"

"With Pauline Millar."

"Oh, well," said Miss Wilson feebly. "I

suppose it is fortunate that Miss Millar is here. We must be thankful, I suppose. I hope you behaved nicely, Elma?"

It was a question, so Elma replied in her usual manner. "Yes," she said.

"I was afraid last night . . . I was not sure. . . . Miss Millar is not a *fast* girl, I hope?"

"No," said Elma. She was a trifle hazy as to what Miss Wilson meant, but "no" was obviously the correct answer.

Miss Wilson was not completely reassured. "She looks as if she were. She paints her mouth," said Miss Wilson, doubtfully.

"Everybody does nowadays," replied Elma promptly.

"Oh, well," said Miss Wilson, lying back wearily. She must just hope for the best. There was nothing else for it. "I do hope," she murmured, "I do hope that you will not forget yourself at dinner tonight, Elma, but that you will behave with decorum."

"Yes," said Elma, and she added, "I must go and dress now."

"Look in and see me before you go down," said Miss Wilson.

Elma did not reply. She had no intention of looking in and seeing Miss Wilson.

2

THE SUGAR-STICK FROCK

ELMA shut the doors between the two rooms before she began to dress, for she did not want to disturb Miss Wilson by the rustling of tissue paper. She had already decided to wear the "sugar-stick" frock—it was so bright and pretty after the dull black clothes which she had worn for so long. It was made of thick silk and was striped in bright shades of cherry and green and white, and it was so stiff that it almost stood by itself. The skirt was long and very wide, and the bodice fitted tightly. When Elma had bathed and donned her new crêpe de chine undies she slipped the dress over her head and looked at herself in the mirror.

"Oh!" she said aloud. "Oh, how pretty!"

She was enchanted with the vision in the glass—and, as a matter of fact, anybody would have been enchanted. She pointed the toe of her new green satin slipper and lifted her full long skirt and curtsied to her reflection in the glass. "Good-evening, Elma Green," she said. "You are a new-fashioned girl. How are you liking things?" And then she laughed. Her eyes were very bright and her cheeks were pink with excitement.

It was at this moment that Pauline arrived upon the scene. She stood in the doorway for a moment, quite dazzled by the metamorphosis of her new friend.

"Well, I'm blessed!" she said.

Elma ran to her and took her hand. "Do you like me?" she asked. "Am I all right, Pauline?"

"Turn round slowly," Pauline said. "Yes . . . yes, you're all right. In fact, you're very much all right."

"Should I not have had my hair waved like you?"

"No, I told you before. It would spoil you. You're a special sort of type—not like other people at all—so it's much better to stick to what you are. . . . You'd better powder your face. I'll do your mouth for you."

"You are kind," said Elma.

"I'm not kind," replied her new friend quickly, so quickly that you might have thought she had been accused of some major crime. Pauline prided herself on being hard boiled. There was no soft, silly nonsense about *her*, and, truth to tell, although she had given up a whole day to the refashioning of her father's ward, she did not feel that she had been "kind." She had enjoyed it thoroughly, and she now felt the same sort of pride in, and responsibility for, Elma as a man might feel for a work of art which he had made with his own hands. She therefore did Elma's mouth with great care and gave a few finishing touches to the sugar-stick frock, and they went downstairs together.

"I shall see your brother tonight," said Elma as they went down.

"Yes," replied Pauline. And then she added somewhat cryptically, "And he'll see you."

"Yes," said Elma. It was obvious, of course, but she was far too much excited to wonder why Pauline should have made such a silly remark. They were going down the stairs now, and on every landing there was a large mirror and Elma saw the new-fashioned girl in the sugar-stick frock coming towards her, and turning sideways, and disappearing out of the edge of the glass—it was a thrilling sight.

The Kenilworth Castle Hotel had not noticed

Miss Green before, but it made up for its lack of interest now. Nobody recognised her as the dowdy girl in the queer black clothes who had been dining with the Millars the previous night. "Who is she?" everybody wondered (and a good many people put their wonderment into words) when they saw Miss Green tripping into the dining-room with the Millar party.

The four members of the little party took their seats at the table. Mr. Millar was pleased and surprised at his ward's appearance. He looked at Pauline and nodded, and she knew what he meant. She knew a good deal about her father—they understood each other—sometimes Pauline wished that she did not understand him quite so well. Wilfred Millar had not met Miss Green before, so he was not surprised at her appearance. He decided that she was very pretty and attractive, and he was attentive and friendly to her. At the present moment he was in the toils of a beautiful South American woman—a créole—who was suing her husband for divorce. Her sad face and beautiful liquid brown eyes filled Wilfred's mind to the exclusion of every other woman on earth. He was aware that his passion for this woman was hopeless; and, in fact, he hardly wanted anything else. It was enough for Wilfred to walk on the terrace with her and to hold her hand and listen to the soft, husky voice reciting the list of brutalities which she had endured. In comparison with Mariana, Elma Green was nothing but a child, rather crude and uninteresting. When dinner was over the Millar family scattered. Wilfred pursued his créole, Pauline made a bee-line for the dance room, and Mr. Millar, after seeing his ward comfortably ensconced in the lounge with a copy of the *Tatler* to keep her happy, announced his intention of playing Bridge in the next room.

"I hope you won't feel dull," he said kindly.

"Oh, no," said Elma. It was pleasure enough to be here in this beautiful place; to be sitting here by herself without the somewhat boring presence of Miss Wilson to disturb her rosy thoughts and dreams; to watch all the strange people and wonder about them. "Oh, no," said Elma. "I *couldn't* be dull *here*."

"Well, I shan't be far away if you want me," said Mr. Millar, smiling, and he left her there.

He had no sooner gone when things began

to happen, and, as before, Elma was unsurprised. She was still moving in a dream, and the dream was more dreamlike than ever. Before, even in the dream, Elma had been herself, but now she was not herself any more. She did not look like herself and she did not feel like herself, either.

Dick Skein was the first on the field. He had seen the sugar-stick girl in the dining-room and had watched her leave the room with the Millars. He had seen the Millars scatter, and now he was approaching Miss Green with a lace handkerchief in his hand and an ingratiating smile upon his fair and somewhat florid face.

"Excuse me, I think this is yours," he said. "You dropped it in the dining-room."

The handkercheif changed hands and was examined. The initials in the corner were "D.S." (Strangely enough, they happened to be the initials of Mr. Skein's sister.) "No, it is not mine," said Elma.

"Not yours?" inquired Mr. Skein in surprise. "I could have sworn . . . Well, whose can it be?"

Miss Green had no idea at all.

Mr. Skein drew up in a chair and they discussed the matter thoroughly and, having

265

come to no satisfactory conclusion, passed on to other and more personal topics. There were a good many people in the lounge and Mr. Skein felt the eyes of his friends boring into him from all directions, but he took no notice at all.

Later, when he drifted into the American Bar to refresh himself after his protracted conversation, he was greeted with shouts of welcome and a hail of questions:

"Who is she?"

"What's she like?"

"How did you pick her up?"

"She's mad," he said tersely.

"Stark, staring or balmy?" inquired Bertie Trim with interest.

"All three. . . . Gimme a drink, someone," was the enlightening reply.

In the strange jargon of present-day youth, the word "mad," even when qualified by such adverbs as stark, staring or balmy, need not be taken to mean a jibbering lunatic with straws in its hair, and in this particular case it was obvious that nobody was put off by Mr. Skein's alarming report of the new arrival. On the contrary, the interest which had already been manifest was considerably quickened. Several people, anxious to know more, stood Mr. Skein drinks, while others, who preferred to gather their own information, were seen to slope off in the direction of the lounge.

It was discovered that no introduction to Miss Green was necessary—not even the hackneyed gambit of opening or shutting the window—Miss Green smiled at everybody alike and made delicious use of her violet eyes.

She was so beautiful, and her frock was so sophisticated, that her admirers could hardly be blamed for thinking that she was other than she was. Her artless manner, and her old-fashioned—absolutely archaic—diction was recognised to be the most priceless wit, and Elma was soon surrounded by a circle of young men who hung upon her every word and roared with delighted laughter every time she opened her mouth.

"I shall stay here for ever," declared Elma, when asked how long she might be expected to grace the Kenilworth Castle Hotel with her presence. "It is the most delightful spot I have seen or, indeed, imagined in my wildest dreams. I have a luxurious home, of course, but I must admit that I find it gloomy." She paused to allow the laughter to subside and then added, "So I intend to remain at the Kenilworth Castle Hotel indefinitely and to drink champagne every night."

"You're marvellous!" cried Bertie Trim, wiping his streaming eyes.

"Are you staying here alone?" inquired another young man with interest.

Elma opened her eyes very wide. "Oh, no!" she said reproachfully. "That would not be correct. My companion is indisposed."

"That's lucky, isn't it?" he chuckled.

"You poisoned her, I suppose?" suggested another acquaintance.

"Oh, *no*," cried Elma indignantly. "How could you imagine such wickedness!" She paused a moment for more laughter and then added, with a sideways glance, "Indeed, there was no necessity to poison Miss Wilson. I was aware that she would be confined to her room for some days when I observed her eating ice pudding last night."

The little circle rocked with joy.

Elma had never suspected that she was witty and clever, and her success went to her head. It would have taken a pretty strong head to remain sober under the circumstances. Two cocktails, pressed upon her by her admirers, did not help to steady her. She was scarcely aware that she was playing up to her audience, that she was intensifying her personality for their benefit. She only knew that she was happy, and that they were happy, too, and the world seemed more dream-like than ever.

"I have never had such a delightful time," Elma declared, and she added confidentially, "I like gentlemen better than ladies."

The howls of laughter, which greeted this announcement, brought Mr. Millar from the Bridge room. He happened to be dummy at the moment, and he strolled into the lounge to find out who was making the confounded row, and it was a most unpleasant surprise to discover that his ward was the cause of all the trouble. Drastic measures were necessary, and Mr. Millar took them: he removed Elma from her circle of admirers and sent her up to bed.

Elma went quite meekly, for she was used to being ordered about, and the habit of bowing to superior authority is hard to break. There were large cracks in this habit of Elma's, but they were only cracks—as yet.

Elma removed her finery and went in to see Miss Wilson, and found no improvement in her condition. She was not glad of this, of course (for that would have been unkind), but it was quite impossible to feel very sorry. The fact that Miss Wilson would probably be confined to bed for several days meant that Elma would be at liberty to enjoy herself. She had already received several pressing invitations for the next day, and her only difficulty was to decide whether she would go sailing with Mr. Skein, or motoring with Mr. Trim in his super-charged Bentley, or whether it would be more pleasant to walk along the shore with that extremely romantic and incredibly handsome Spanish count. There is no hurry to decide, thought Elma as she put out the light. I can make up my mind tomorrow.

It was no part of Mr. Millar's plan that his ward should make friends with every Tom, Dick and Harry in the place. He had a plan, of course, for he never did anything without reasonable forethought. He had intended to wait a little and allow his plan to develop slowly and naturally; but it was now obvious that he must hurry it forward. So when Elma departed meekly to bed, Mr. Millar made his apologies to the Bridge table and went in search of his son.

Wilfred had been walking on the terrace with

his créole, and quite suddenly he had begun to get a little tired of her sorrows, and he received the impression that she was beginning to get a little tired of reciting them to him. He had left her sitting on the stone balustrade, wrapped in mystery and in coloured net scarves, and had betaken himself to the American Bar to refresh himself and to ponder on the mutability of love.

Mr. Millar found him there, long before he was properly refreshed, "I want to speak to you," he said.

Wilfred was not anxious to take part in a private conversation with his father, for he was aware that nothing pleasant could come of it, but he saw that his father was determined, so he had no choice in the matter. They went out on to the terrace and found a secluded seat.

"This must cease," Mr. Millar said. "You'll get yourself into trouble with that woman. If you don't get cited as co-respondent, you'll probably get a knife in your back. South Americans are pretty handy with knives."

"Yes," said Wilfred; "but there's nothing in it."

"Nobody would believe that."

"It's true."

"Oh, I believe it all right," declared Mr.

271

Millar rather scornfully. "I know you, Wilfred, and so I know you've got milk and water in your veins instead of good red blood; but other people who didn't know your little peculiarity would not believe it for a moment. Look out for that knife, Wilfred."

"It's practically over, anyhow," said Wilfred sullenly.

"That's a good thing, because I've got other work for you."

"Work!" exclaimed Wilfred in dismay.

"Do you intend to remain idle for the rest of your life? Do you expect me to support you indefinitely?"

"Oh, I say!" exclaimed Wilfred. "I mean, I've told you I'm sorry. Somehow or other, I don't seem to have found the right kind of job yet."

"Very strange!"

"You can't say I haven't tried," Wilfred pointed out.

"You've tried at least half a dozen jobs," agreed his father dryly.

"I know, but none of them——"

"None of them were soft enough. If you could find a job with plenty of money coming in regularly and nothing at all to do——"

"Oh, I say!" said Wilfred reproachfully.

272

"That would suit you, wouldn't it?" insisted his father.

"I thought of being a tennis pro."

"Too much work. You like tennis *now*; but you wouldn't like it if you *had* to play—it would lose all its fascination at once."

"Well, what do you suggest?" inquired Wilfred anxiously. "What sort of job, I mean?"

"I've told you," declared Mr. Millar. "You want a job with plenty of money in it and nothing to do. I've found a job for you—a job that will suit you down to the ground. Now, just you listen to me. . . ."

3

AT SWAN HOUSE

IT was breakfast-time at Swan House and, contrary to their usual custom, the three Ferriers were all partaking of their morning repast at the same moment: Paddy, as usual, standing by the mantelpiece, eating mouthfuls of grape-fruit and skimming through the pictures in the *Daily Trumpeter,* and George and his father working through an Englishman's breakfast with solemn satisfaction. When the post arrived, and was brought into the dining-room, it was discovered that the only letter of interest or importance was a bulky-looking package addressed to George, and addressed in an unknown spidery hand. His father and mother, though much intrigued, buried themselves in their papers more deeply than ever, for they were of the opinion that their son's correspondence was his own business and none of theirs. If he invited their interest, of course, they were at liberty to show it. But would he?—that was the question.

George opened his letter and looked at the signature. "Victoria Clara Wilson!" he claimed. "Who on earth is she?"

The spell was broken and Paddy gurgled with delight. "Oh, George!" she cried. "It's one of your lovelies, of course, and you've forgotten her name; or perhaps you call her Vicky or Tootsie—or something more intimate still."

"What's that?" inquired Mr. Ferrier, looking at them over the top of his *Times*.

"It's a letter for George," Paddy pointed out. "Pages and pages of it, and he doesn't know who it's from."

But George had now discovered the identity of his correspondent and was busily wading through the sheets.

"Oh, hell!" he exclaimed, frowning prodigiously. "This *is* a nuisance."

There was such dismay in his tones that his mother was seriously alarmed.

"What is it?" she inquired anxiously.

George did not reply; he was so deeply engrossed in his letter that he had not heard the question. He came to the end of a sheet and turned it over and read on.

Paddy watched him, and she too was frowning, for her active and unbridled imagination had presented her with at least half a dozen explanations of the letter and of George's dismay. The least unlikely explanation (and therefore the one which Paddy was forced to choose) was that the letter heralded the advent of an illegitimate grandchild. She glanced at her husband and he met the glance with a bland smile. Quentin is a dear, she thought, a dear old donkey. He's trying to tell me that George is all right. He *is* all right, of course, but still . . . things do happen. . . .

"What is it, George?" she demanded—louder this time—for her scanty stock of patience was exhausted and she felt that she could not stand the uncertainty a moment longer.

"I suppose I shall have to go," murmured George, still reading. "The wretched woman is ill, and the whole thing is my fault, really. I got her into this trouble, and I shall have to get her out of it——"

"Oh, George!" cried his mother in dismay. "Then it is what I thought . . . but perhaps it isn't *true*. Perhaps it's just—just biliousness or something."

"It *is* biliousness," declared George, "but that doesn't make it any better."

"Of course it's better—if it's biliousness it can't be a baby, can it?"

George looked up in astonishment. "Miss Wilson——" he began. "Miss Wilson—good heavens, what *are* you talking about?"

"This girl—the girl you've got into trouble."

George laughed uproariously—he could not help it—for, although he was considerably worried over the letter, the idea of Miss Wilson in that particular kind of trouble was amusing in the extreme. "My dear lamb," he said, when at last he was able to speak, "my very dearest lamb of a Paddy, you have got completely adrift. You're determined that your son is a Don Juan and all the time he is only a grave and serious trustee whose ward seems likely to turn his hair grey before he's much older. Read that," he added, cramming the letter into her hands and applying himself to his neglected bacon and eggs with an appetite which even the vagaries of an errant ward could not impair.

Paddy was quite disappointed at the humdrum solution of the mystery, but she was also extremely relieved. It is quite possible to harbour these two apparently irreconcilable emotions at the same time in the same breast—at least Paddy could.

"Read it aloud, Paddy," said Mr. Ferrier, who had been more perturbed than he would have admitted—"at least, if George does not mind."

"Read it aloud, by all means," said George, with his mouth full. "As a matter of fact, I couldn't read half of it. Her writing is like the wanderings of an inebriated spider, isn't it?"

Paddy spread out the letter and began to read:

Kenilworth Castle Hotel,
Bournemouth.

"DEAR MR. FERRIER,—You will be surprised to receive a letter from me, and indeed I have delayed to write to you on this account, hoping that there might be an Improvement in the Situation and that I should not need to trouble you. If I could have Dealt with the Situation by any other means in my Power, or could have looked for Help from any other Source, you may be sure I should have done so. Nor would this letter have been written if Mr. Arbuthnot Millar were still at hand, for although his Influence upon Elma is not all that I could Wish, he certainly exercised a

278

Modicum of Restraint upon her behaviour. Unfortunately, Mr. Arbuthnot Millar has been forced to return to the Metropolis on Urgent Business. He received a letter yesterday morning which seemed to cause him deep Anxiety and Dismay, and, although no word of explanation was vouchsafed, I feel sure that this letter must have contained News of the Gravest Importance. He left here in great haste, and his daughter, Miss Millar, accompanied him, but his son, Mr. Wilfred Millar, remained. Mr. Arbuthnot Millar's departure has increased my Responsibility, for Mr. Wilfred Millar, though exceedingly Kind and Attentive, does not possess the forceful personality of his father, and is therefore less able to Deal with Elma's Extravagances."

Paddy stopped reading and looked up in perplexity. "Is the woman a lunatic?" she inquired.

"No," said George, "not exactly. She's just a bit old-fashioned, that's all."

"But what does she mean, the creature?"

"She means that Elma is on the war-path," said George. "I'm not altogether surprised, to tell you the truth."

"Go on, Paddy," said Mr. Ferrier impatiently.

Paddy continued:

"In the midst of my Anxiety and Trouble, I remembered Your Cryptic Words to which I was so misguided as to take exception. You remarked that I should be well advised to keep my eye upon Elma! I ask myself now, in the light of all that has happened, whether this remark was made with a Fuller Knowledge of the Pitfalls before me than I myself possessed. At the time, of course, I was Confident of my Ability to watch my charge and to Guard and Guide her, no matter what Dangers or Difficulties should lie before us at the Kenilworth Castle Hotel, but I did not Anticipate the unfortunate Circumstances that I should be laid low by a severe attack of gastritis—a distressing complaint by which I am occasionally victimised should the even tenor of my days be unduly disturbed. . . ."

"What on earth is it all *about*?" demanded Paddy, looking up from the letter and meeting the broad smiles of her listeners with one eyebrow cocked inquiringly.

"She got ill, so she couldn't keep an eye

on Elma like I told her," replied George, chuckling.

"Well, why doesn't she say so?" Paddy asked. "And why, in heaven's name, are you both laughing? I can't see anything funny in it at all."

"The fact is, Dad and I are enjoying Miss Wilson's language in your voice," said George; and he looked at his father for confirmation.

"The voice is the voice of Paddy," agreed Mr. Ferrier, smiling more broadly than before, "but the words are the words of Miss Wilson. Go on, my dear, perhaps we shall come to the kernel of the nut before very long."

"Where was I?" said Paddy. "Oh, yes:

". . . the even tenor of my days be unduly disturbed, nor did I Anticipate the Unfortunate Circumstance that we should meet with a Snake in the Grass in the person of Miss Millar—Mr. Arbuthnot Millar's daughter. You may think it unduly harsh to apply this term to a young lady of pleasant appearance, but it is by no means Unwarranted, I can assure you; she filled hot-water bottles for me with one hand and, with the other, encouraged my charge in Extravagance and Debauchery. Elma's Purchase of Expensive and Unsuitable Raiment at the Bournemouth shops is only one of many perversions which can be laid at Miss Millar's door. It is the most Flagrant and Far Reaching in its consequences, of course, for you would be astounded if you beheld Elma clad in this raiment. . . ."

"I bet I *would* be astounded," interrupted George. "I bet she's a stunner in that raiment. I always said Elma wanted someone to take her in hand."

". . . for it has not only altered her Appearance, but her Character. I discovered these deplorable facts when at last I recovered sufficiently from my indisposition to leave my room; discovered that Elma had succumbed to the subversive influence of her new friend and was indeed an Entirely Different Person. No longer is she Modest and Maidenly, but is become Positively Brazen, welcoming and encouraging the Attentions of the Opposite Sex. I spoke to Mr. Millar, beseeching him to Uphold my Authority and to give orders that we were to leave the precincts of this Modern

282

Babylon and return to the peaceful seclusion of Highmoor House, but Mr. Millar—although extremely courteous and pleasant—did not seem to Appreciate the Gravity of the Situation. I spoke to Miss Millar, to young Mr. Millar, and to Elma herself, but my words were Unheeded. Now Mr. Millar has departed and the Situation has become worse than before. At this present moment, as I write, Elma is in the American Bar, surrounded by Gentlemen who are encouraging her to Excess. They follow her wherever she goes and laugh at everything she says. Oh, Mr. Ferrier, you are my only Hope. Will you come to my assistance Without Delay?

"With many apologies for troubling you,
    "I remain,
        "Yours sincerely,
            "VICTORIA CLARA WILSON."

"Poor soul!" said Paddy as she came to the end of the letter and began to fold it up, for the end of the letter was quite easy to understand. Miss Wilson had obviously become so distraught that she was unable to pick her words with her usual care and judgment. "Poor soul, what a time she's having with

283

that girl! I thought you said the girl was shy," she added.

"Only the first day," replied George. "She's a quick worker when once she starts; but, as a matter of fact, the whole thing is my fault. You see, Paddy, I told her——" But what George had told Elma was destined to remain in oblivion, for Mr. Ferrier dropped a bombshell which changed the appearance of the whole affair.

"I do not care for the appearance of Dusty in the picture," declared Mr. Ferrier thoughtfully.

"Dusty!" cried George.

"The letter refers to Mr. Arbuthnot Millar," Mr. Ferrier pointed out. "I knew him some years ago in Mesopotamia—Iraq, as it is now called—I believe you have heard me speak of him once or twice."

"Dusty!" cried George again.

"We called him that. All Millars are Dusty, you know—at least, they were in my day."

"My hat!" cried George. "You mean they're the same person—your corkscrew and my co-trustee?"

"I was not aware of the fact until now," said Mr. Ferrier apologetically. "Millar is not an uncommon name, and it was not until I

284

heard him referred to as Arbuthnot Millar that I realised he must be the Millar I knew."

"This is frightful!" declared George, as the various implications of the discovery unfolded themselves before him. "This is positively frightful. What did he do? You'll have to tell me, Dad."

Mr. Ferrier saw that he must. "It was a little trouble over the mess accounts," he said reluctantly. "Dusty was Mess President, you see. The affair was hushed up because the C.O. considered that a scandal in the battalion would be undesirable. I happened to be aware of the facts, because—er—my mess account—er—but Colonel Protheroe refunded the money out of his own pocket. It was a little matter of twenty pounds."

"Dusty *has* come on, hasn't he?" said George bitterly. "It's a little matter of twenty thousand pounds this time."

"What do you mean?"

"Why, it's as plain as a pikestaff. He's put that insurance money in his pocket, of course. Gosh, what a fool I've been!"

There was a horrified silence.

"But, George, are you sure?" demanded Paddy. "How could he do that?"

"He could do it easily. I was in such a

maze, that day at the meeting, that he could easily have slipped in an extra paper for me to sign, and old Bennett is half dotty. It means that Wicherly must be standing in with him, of course; but that wouldn't surprise me—I didn't like Wicherly from the very beginning. He's bald and slimy like a slug—yes, it's as plain as a pikestaff." He was silent for a few moments, and then he continued: "Why, of course he could have done it. He's as clever as paint and frightfully plausible. I didn't trust him at first—I had a sort of feeling about him—but he talked so frankly and pleasantly that I changed my mind. I see it all now," declared George, frowning with the effort involved. "That was why he said I could have my own stockbroker to vet the list of securities—he didn't mind, you see. There was no hanky-panky about the securities. He merely concealed the fact that old Green's life was insured, and, if I hadn't happened to remember, he could have got off with it."

"It is almost incredible!" exclaimed Mr. Ferrier.

"And don't you see," continued George, holding his head so that it should not burst with the thoughts that were crowding into it. "Don't you see it was *my* letter—our letter—

that caused him all that Anxiety and Dismay and sent him tearing off to London at a moment's notice. It all hangs together, you see."

"It may have been as you say," said Mr. Ferrier, still doubtful; "but surely it would have been a difficult matter to conceal the fact that Green's life was insured."

"It was easy," cried George. "It was as easy as falling off a log backwards. Old Bennett and I probably signed the receipt—or whatever was necessary—we signed everything. Old Bennett was a thousand miles away and I'd already made such a fool of myself that I was willing to do anything they told me."

"It is most regrettable," Mr. Ferrier said. "I do not know if you could be held responsible. . . . I feel that a legal opinion should be obtained. Would you allow me to arrange for you to see Mr. Crane, my lawyer?"

"If you think it would be any good," replied George doubtfully. "It's so complicated, isn't it? It would be difficult to explain."

"Mr. Crane is exceedingly intelligent."

"Well, we'll see," said George; "but I'd better deal with the girl first."

"George, what girl?" cried Paddy.

"Elma," he replied. "You read the letter, didn't you? She's run amok at the Kenilworth Castle, and it's a dangerous place to run amok——" He rose and pushed back his chair.

"George, you don't mean——?"

"Yes, I do," declared George. "I simply must go—you'll lend me Grandpa, won't you? It's all my fault, you see. I should never have trusted him . . . and it's my fault she's run amok—I practically told her to. . . ." He paused at the door and added with a rueful grin: "I shall have earned that five hundred quid before I'm through."

4

THE PURSUIT BEGINS

GEORGE had the foresight to wire to Miss Wilson that he was on his way to her assistance, so she was waiting for him when he arrived. She was standing on the steps of the Kenilworth Castle Hotel, and, if the truth were told, she had been standing there for nearly an hour. George saw her as he drove up, a small, thin figure bowed by the cares and anxieties which she had endured.

"Oh, Mr. Ferrier!" she cried, hurling herself down the steps and seizing his arm. "Oh, Mr. Ferrier, you're too late."

"Too late!" echoed George. "How can I be too late? What's happened? Where is she? Let me get at her and we'll soon see——"

"She has gone," declared Miss Wilson in a choked voice. "Yes . . . gone. . . ."

"Gone where?"

"I do not know . . . I have not known what to do . . . I am completely finished. . . ."

She looked it, too, thought George, but he did not say so. He wanted to hear the whole story before he started to sympathise with Miss Wilson. "Look here," he said, "we'll go and have lunch and you can tell me all about it."

"Lunch!" cried Miss Wilson in horror-stricken tones.

"Yes."

"But I could not eat."

"Well, I could," said George firmly.

They found a table and sat down.

"If it had not been for the unfortunate circumstance that I found myself eating an ice pudding without being aware of it," began Miss Wilson. ". . . and, although it sounds a sheer impossibility, I can assure you that it is no more than the sober truth; but when I saw Elma about to partake of champagne—and most unfortunately she enjoyed it—if this had not occurred, I might have been more able—but I am afraid that I am not making myself perfectly clear."

"No, you aren't," said George frankly; "and, besides, I know all about you being ill. I think you'd better start from where your letter left off. Start from there, and tell me all about it in words of one syllable, please."

"In words of one syllable!" exclaimed Miss Wilson in surprise.

"Or two syllables," said George kindly. "If you can't manage less. Start from where you got up and came down and found Elma on the warpath."

Miss Wilson had never been spoken to like this before; but her morale was completely shattered and, far from being annoyed with George, she felt positively grateful for his masterfulness. She looked at him as he sat before her at the table—he was so large and masculine that she was reassured—and the calm manner in which he was working through the menu from the hors d'oeuvres to the dessert helped to give her confidence. She sat there and watched him eat, and crumbled a piece of dry toast on the tablecloth, and wondered why she had ever thought him too young and irresponsible for the position of trustee.

"Go on," said George. "Tell me about the letter—the one that caused Anxiety and Dismay. What did old Millar say when he got it?"

"Oh, I could not——" began Miss Wilson in distress. "I am aware, of course, that gentlemen occasionally use words of which in

291

calmer moments they are incapable, but it has never been my misfortune to be associated with one who was liable to forget the presence of ladies. My father was in Holy Orders, and his conversation——"

"He swore like a trooper, did he?" said George, who had begun to get the knack of translating Miss Wilson's circumlocutions into plain words.

"No, indeed!" cried Miss Wilson. "How could I possibly have conveyed such an erroneous impression! My father's conversation was entirely free from——"

"I mean Mr. Millar, of course," said George hastily. "Old Millar swore like a trooper. Did he say anything about me?"

"No?" said Miss Wilson, in some surprise. "No, he did not mention you, Mr. Ferrier. Why should he?"

"Oh, well . . . I just thought he might have," George replied. "I thought . . . well, what did he say?"

Miss Wilson frowned with the effort to remember. Her head was positively bursting with pain, but she was anxious to help George as much as possible. "Mr. Millar was extremely angry with his unknown correspondent—so I gathered——"

"Yes," said George eagerly. "Yes, he was angry, was he?"

"Exceedingly angry," Miss Wilson declared. "Indeed, he proceeded to the extreme length of referring to this unknown person as an interfering young swine."

"Ah, I thought so," said George, nodding gravely. "An interfering young swine—yes."

"You know this person?"

"Well, I have a sort of idea . . ." said George, waving his hand vaguely. "What happened next?"

"He had a serious conversation with his son. They walked up and down the terrace for some little time, and I could see that the matter under discussion was of grave importance. I hope you will not think that I was spying upon them," she added; "but the fact is, I was writing letters in the lounge and I could not help seeing them."

George reassured her. "Go on," he said. "What happened after old Millar buzzed off to town? That was the day before yesterday, wasn't it?"

"Yes," said Miss Wilson meekly.

"Well, what happened yesterday? We mustn't waste time, you know."

Thus adjured, Miss Wilson proceeded with

her tale. Yesterday had been a "good day." The Situation had taken a turn for the better; and Elma, instead of wandering about the grounds followed by a train of admirers, had gone off for a drive in Wilfred Millar's car. Miss Wilson had been glad to see her go; she was under the impression that Wilfred was trying to help matters, to reason with Elma and to persuade her to go home. It was more pleasant for everybody when the other young men, instead of pursuing Elma, returned to their former flames—Dick Skein to Miss Trim, and Harold Glendinning to Sylvia Wordless.

"I was quite grateful to young Mr. Millar," declared Miss Wilson pitifully. "I was able to sit in the lounge without feeling that everybody was staring at me and hating me. I was even able to come down to dinner and take a little soup."

So much for yesterday. This morning at breakfast Elma had been "more like her old self," quiet and reasonable and docile as a lamb, and Miss Wilson had hoped that the strange madness which had attacked her charge was passing off. They had talked of returning home at the end of the week, and Elma had seemed to agree.

"Why on earth didn't you suggest that before?" George inquired.

"Suggest it!" cried Miss Wilson. "I pled with her to return, but she would not listen. I pled with her over and over again. I had lost all control of the child, Mr. Ferrier, and I could not regain it. At home I had only to 'speak' to Elma and she obeyed me without question, or if any slight punishment were necessary I could send her to bed, or regulate her diet. Here I had no possible way of disciplining Elma. She defied me openly. It was unprecedented."

"Go on," said George. "What happened this morning?"

"She came with me to the shore," said Miss Wilson miserably, "and we sat and watched the people bathing—it is not a pleasant sight, in my opinion, but Elma seemed to enjoy it. We had taken our needlework with us. The sun shone, and we talked together—almost in the old way. I was almost happy," declared Miss Wilson pitifully. "I was *almost* happy, Mr. Ferrier. I did not scold the child for her behaviour, for I was afraid she would resent it. I deliberately avoided any controversy. We sat there for some time and then Elma discovered that she had not brought the right shade of silk for her work. It was a particular shade of green which she required for a leaf. I suggested she should substitute another shade, but she declared it would not be suitable. She decided to go back to the hotel and fetch the green silk. I remonstrated with her, for the path up from the shore is steep and the sun was very warm, but she would not listen to me. 'There is no need for you to come,' she said; and, so saying, she rose and left me.

"I waited for a long time," continued Miss Wilson, taking a little sip from the glass of hot water which stood beside her on the table; "but at last it became obvious that Elma was not coming back. I was afraid she had fallen in with some of her new friends and had found their society more amusing than mine, so I returned to the hotel and sought for her. Mrs. Wordless was sitting in the lounge, and presently she called out to me that if I was looking for Elma I could save myself the trouble, I asked her if she had seen the child, and she replied, 'Elma has gone for a spin in Wilfred's car.' (Nowadays even strangers persist in calling each other by their Christian names, a curious and most undignified custom, in my opinion.) I did not give Mrs.

Wordless the satisfaction of knowing that Elma had gone without my permission, for she is a most unpleasant person," declared Miss Wilson fervently. "There is something positively malevolent about her personality. I merely said that I had forgotten the arrangement and thanked her courteously. I was hurt, of course, to think that Elma had gone without informing me of her intention, but not unduly anxious, for—as I told you—I trusted young Mr. Millar and was grateful to him for his help. It was not until I went upstairs and found that Elma had taken a small suitcase with her that I——"

"What!" cried George.

"Yes, a small suitcase. I do not know what garments she has taken, for I had no list of the new and eminently unsuitable clothing with which she——"

"But what did you *do*?" cried George. "Where have they gone? Good heavens!"

"I did nothing," Miss Wilson admitted helplessly. "What could I do? I did not know what to do, so I did nothing." She twisted her hands together in the extremity of her distress and added, "I did not want anybody to know— the scandal—her reputation—I am afraid you must think I am quite useless and incapable—but I do not feel well."

"Great Scott!" said George. "Great Scott, this *is* the limit! Wilfred Millar . . . and old Millar is Dusty. . . . Great Scott! Something will have to be done."

"Oh, I *know*," agreed Miss Wilson. "But what can we do? I would have gone after them in the car—but I did not know where——"

George did not know where, either, but he saw that something must be done without delay, and that he was the only person to do it. Miss Wilson was quite useless. The woman was ill—if appearances counted for anything, she was very ill, indeed—for her face was sallow and drawn, her eyes were glazed, and her hands trembled so that she could scarcely lift the glass of water to her lips. Poor wretch, thought George, she ought to be in bed; in fact, bed is the only place for her. She wouldn't be the slightest use.

"Now, look here," said George firmly. "You go straight to bed and stay there. I'm taking charge of the whole thing, see?"

"But, Mr. Ferrier——"

"I'm taking charge," repeated George. "You wouldn't be the least use in the world.

In fact, you'd only be a nuisance. You're ill, you see."

"I do feel *very* unwell," admitted Miss Wilson in trembling accents.

"Of course you do," he said. "I expect you got up too soon. It's no good trying to do things when you feel like that—you'd only hinder me."

"What are you going to do?"

"I'm going after them in my car," said George. "Don't you worry. I'll bring her back."

He spoke with a good deal more confidence than he felt, for he had no idea how he was going to accomplish the feat. He only knew that it must be done. Somehow or other, Elma must be found and brought back—and that without delay.

George paid his bill and left the dining-room, and Miss Wilson followed him, uttering fervent protestations of gratitude and fervent apologies for her incapacity.

"It is dreadful," she declared, wringing her hands. "Nothing so terrible has ever happened to me before. I have betrayed my sacred trust. I have failed——"

"Go to bed," said George firmly. "Go to

299

bed at once. You're only worrying me. I've got to think."

"Well, if you really mean it—" said Miss Wilson, thankful beyond measure for this masterful handling, "—if you really mean that you can manage better without me——"

"Go to bed," said George.

Miss Wilson went.

5

THE PURSUIT CONTINUES

HAVING got rid of Miss Wilson, George was free to make his own plans for the pursuit of his errant ward. He had told Miss Wilson that he had got to think; but unfortunately thinking was not his strong point, and he was fully aware of this. "Give me something to do," he would say, "and I'll do it as well as most people, but don't ask me to think." George had got to think now, because he was entirely on his own, the responsibility of the whole thing was on his shoulders. He had got to prepare some sort of plan, he had got to find out where they had gone before he could leap into the car and go after them. Where had they gone?—that was the question—and how on earth was he to find the answer to it?

Oh, curse, thought George to himself, hesitating at the door of the lounge. Oh, curse, what *am* I to do? If only Peter was here. . . . Peter would be able to think of some way. . . . Shall I ring up old Millar's office and see if I can find out from him?

His hand was on the door of the telephone-box, but he hesitated before going in. Old Millar was Dusty. Old Millar was a cork-screw. It was quite possible that old Millar knew all about it—in fact, it was possible that old Millar was at the bottom of the whole thing. George had not thought of this before, but, now that he did think of it, he saw that it would suit old Millar very well if he could get hold of Elma Green for his son. It would suit him admirably. If he could marry his son to Elma, he was safe. The trustees could not very well sue Elma's father-in-law for a return of that wretched twenty thousand pounds. I believe that's his game, thought George. And Elma is such a silly little ass—my goodness, what a mess!

It was at this moment, when George was still hesitating, that the hall porter approached. He was a tall, broad-shouldered man with the presence of a church dignitary and an imposing strip of war ribbons on his chest.

"Can I get a number for you, sir?" he inquired politely.

"Yes . . . no," said George. "The fact is——"

"If I can be of any assistance——"

"Well, why not?" said George, with sudden inspiration. "I say, is there anywhere we can talk?"

The hall porter showed no surprise at this unusual request, for he had met with many unusual requests during his tenure of office at the Kenilworth Castle Hotel. He led the way to his desk and, opening a door at the back of it, he ushered George into a comfortable little sanctum. There was a table and two chairs here, and the walls were hung with road maps, and there was a small bookcase in which reference books such as *Who's Who* and *Baedekker* rubbed shoulders with tourist guides and railway time-tables. By this time a pound note had changed hands with great dexterity and the least possible fuss.

"Now," said George, sitting down in the more comfortable of the chairs. "Now, can I rely upon you? Yes, of course I can. I can see you're just the sort of fellow to help me."

"I shall certainly do my best," declared the hall porter in a friendly manner. It was obvious that this was a young gentleman who knew what was what. The hall porter was

303

used to large tips, of course, but most people were more inclined to part with their money after certain services had been rendered rather than before. The hall porter preferred George's method—you knew where you were.

"Well," said George, "it's like this: I've come down here today to see my ward—she's Miss Green. I dare say you've seen her about the place, haven't you?"

"Yes, sir, I have."

"Yes, she isn't easily overlooked, is she? Well, I've come all this way to see her, and what do I find?—I find she's gone off in a car with a fellow called Millar."

"Ah!" said the hall porter, nodding.

"I should think it *is* 'Ah!' " agreed George. "You see, the whole thing, don't you? I thought you would. Well, the point is, I'm her trustee—she's an orphan," he added, struck by a sudden inspiration. "She's an orphan, and I'm her trustee. I've got to look after her, haven't I?"

He saw by the hall porter's face that he had played a good card, so he played it again in a slightly different form. "Her father and mother are both dead," he said, shaking his head sadly.

"I'm not supposed to notice things like that," said the hall porter doubtfully, "nor yet to speak of them, sir. I wouldn't be here long if I went about noticing things like that—if you know what I mean."

"This is absolutely confidential," declared George. "I don't want anything said either. You can see that, can't you? I'm putting myself in your hands, aren't I? You don't suppose I want everybody to know that she's gone off with that fellow in his car. It's a dead secret between you and me, and if you can help me——"

"You want to know where they've gone?"

"Yes, that's what I want."

The hall porter thought for a few moments. It was a ticklish business, and if it had been any other young gentleman he would not have moved a finger; but Wilfred Millar was the hall porter's *bête noir*—it would be rather pleasant to spoke his wheel and, at the same time, to earn the gratitude of this extremely frank and likeable young gentleman, who was as different from that young pup of a Millar as chalk from cheese.

The hall porter sat down on the other chair, "Well, it's like this," he said: "Young Mr. Millar came here this morning asking about the road to Exeter—what it was like, and all that. So I told him.''

"Oh, thank you!" exclaimed George, springing to his feet. "Exeter it is! I'll be after them like——"

"Hold on a moment!" cried his new friend. "Hold on, not so fast. I don't believe he's gone near Exeter."

"What!"

"Now, listen to me, sir. If young Mr. Millar's gone to Exeter, I'll eat my hat. . . . Now, listen—he's a bit too clever, you see. He came in here to this very room asking me about Exeter and wasting my time. Well, I told him about Exeter—it's part of my job— but I could see he wasn't listening—not properly. That's funny, I thinks to myself.''

"Damn' funny," agreed George in a doubtful tone.

"You see, sir, lots of people come and ask me about roads, so I know the sort of way they ask and the sort of things they want to know. It's the surface they ask about, and whether there's much traffic, whether it's a straight road or winding, and if it's pretty wide. Sometimes they write down the names of villages and towns on a bit of paper. Well, young Mr. Millar didn't ask none of the usual things, and he didn't listen or bother himself. It struck me at the time there was something funny about it, but, of course, he never meant to go there at all. It was a blind, if you ask me."

George was tremendously impressed. "I call that *clever*," he declared. "Damned clever of you, that's what it is. Fancy you noticing!"

"I was a bit fed-up, to tell the truth," replied the hall porter. "Coming in here and asking all those questions, and then not listening to what I said. Wasting my time, he was."

"Sickening," agreed George; "but clever of you, all the same. Where d'you think they've gone?"

"I think they've gone to London, if you ask me," replied the hall porter, who was now completely won over by George's whole-hearted admiration of his cleverness. "In fact, I'm pretty sure they've gone to London. It's like this: Miss Green and young Mr. Millar were looking at the play-bills yesterday afternoon (I don't know if you noticed that I've got play-bills of some of the London theatres hung up at the back of my desk in the hall); well, they were looking at them together—not just casual, but really serious. 'I don't think you'd like *Wine and Women*,' young Mr. Millar says. 'I don't think you'd enjoy it. Let's go to *Show a Leg*. There's more go about it.' 'I shall enjoy everything,' says Miss Green in an excited sort of voice. 'Why, of course you will,' he says to her, smiling at her. 'And it's about time you had a bit of fun.' Well, sir, that was all I heard. Mrs. Wordless came up to complain about her *Manchester Guardian* getting torn in the post—full of complaints, she is. If it's not one thing, it's another, and how I can be held responsible for a *Manchester Guardian* torn in the post is more than I can see."

"Most unreasonable," agreed George.

"Most of them are unreasonable," said the hall porter with a sigh. "Well, that's all I heard. They moved away when they saw Mrs. Wordless."

"It was quite enough," said George. "They've obviously gone to London—the silly little ass!"

"That's right, sir, you've said it. She hadn't ought to have trusted Mr. Wilfred Millar—a young bounder, if ever there was one—though I shouldn't be saying it. I've got a young daughter of my own," he added, as if that explained his attitude—which perhaps it did.

"Have you?" said George with interest—he was always interested in people's private lives—"but, then, she's got a father to look after her, hasn't she? That makes a lot of difference."

The hall porter agreed that it did. He certainly would not have allowed his daughter to behave like Miss Green. "Now what's to do?" he said thoughtfully. "That's the question. Have you made any plans, sir?"

George looked at him helplessly. "I'd never catch them, would I?" he said.

"They've had two hours' start of us," agreed the hall porter, who had now identified himself completely with George's quest. "Two hours' start. No, you'd never catch them. I wonder if they've stopped for lunch at the Woodstock."

"Why should they?"

"Why shouldn't they? It's a good place, run by the same company as runs this. Young Mr. Millar's father is a director of the company, and he always goes there on his way to London. Directors get special terms, you see, and I shouldn't wonder if young Mr. Millar couldn't wangle special terms on account of being his father's son. Pretty good

309

wangler, he is! Wait a minute, now, I've got an idea——"

"What?"

"The hall porter at the Woodstock—he's a friend of mine. I'll get him on the phone. . . ."

George waited impatiently while the hall porter went off to telephone to his opposite number at the Woodstock Hotel. He felt that it was a waste of time sitting here while every moment Elma was being whirled farther and farther away, and yet it was not really a waste of time, because he could not pursue them until he knew where they had gone. He spent a little time tracing the road to London on one of the maps on the wall and was interested to find that the Woodstock Hotel, being an offshoot from the Kenilworth Castle, was marked upon the map with a large red spot. It was between Alresford and Alton, and you went by Winchester, of course. It was a main road the whole way.

Nearly ten minutes elapsed before the hall porter returned, and George had become quite desperate; but when he set eyes on his new friend's smiling face he knew that all was well.

"You're lucky, sir," said the man.

"They're there *now*. They've had their lunch and they're sitting in the lounge."

"Good man!" cried George, seizing him by the hand. "Oh, good man! Why, you ought to be—you ought to be a general, or something."

"I'll be on the dole if you breathe a word of this," replied the hall porter, smiling rather ruefully. "His father a director and all——"

"But I won't," cried George. "Goodbye, and thank you a million times. I'll be off and——"

"Wait a moment."

"But I must——"

"No, wait. It's an hour's run to the Woodstock—more, really. Even in a Bentley, you couldn't do it under an hour. They would be gone long before you got near the place. . . ."

"Oh, my hat!" cried George. "Of course they will!"

". . . if it wasn't for a little trouble with the car," added the hall porter in a significant tone.

"What?"

"I said *a little trouble with the car*. Not much, of course, but just enough to delay them for an hour or so. I couldn't do more than that, so you'll have to hurry. I'll get into the most almighty—— Oh, thank you, sir, I'm sure. I never expected——"

George was gone. He leapt down the steps, flung himself into the car, and in less time than it takes to tell he was tearing down the drive at full speed. He knew now where he had to go; he had something definite to do. "Give me something to *do*," said George between his teeth. "Give me something to do and, by gosh, I'll do it!" He turned into the main road, and was off like a rocket. The old car seemed to respond to his urgency—it had never gone better—and for the first time in his life George felt that there was something human and friendly about a car. It was not merely a mass of machinery and metal and wooden parts: it had a distinct personality and was actually responsive to his need. "Good old Granpa," whispered George. "You shall have the feed of your life if you get me there in time. I'll never laugh at you again. . . . I'll polish your old brass nose till it shines like a beacon. . . . I'll change your gear-box oil. . . ."

Encouraged by these promises, Granpa gave of his best, and it was not much after three o'clock when they reached Winchester—coming in by way of Romsey—and turned into the High Street. They were held up there for a few moments in a traffic jam, but that was not

Granpa's fault, and George did not blame him for it. "Good old Granpa," he said again as they turned the corner at Bridge Street, and then to the right up Magdalen Hill. "Good old Granpa, it's not far now—we'll make it—or I'm a Dutchman."

So far, George had given all his attention to his driving, for he was not a practised driver and the speed at which he was travelling made it necessary to concentrate, but now that he was getting near his objective he began to wonder how he was going to tackle the situation. It was possible that they had gone on, of course, and if so he must pursue them to London in the hope of catching them before they arrived and were swallowed up; but if they were still here—and George had a feeling that they were—he must try to get Elma alone and persuade her to come with him. "I shall take her home with me," he decided. "She'll be much safer at Swan House. Paddy can keep an eye on her. If only I can get hold of her. . . . I'll just have to wait and see . . . I'll get hold of her somehow . . ." muttered George, swerving suddenly to avoid a farm cart which had come lumbering out of a field gate just in front of him.

313

6

THE PURSUIT CONCLUDES

THE Woodstock Hotel was quite a different sort of place from the Kenilworth Castle. It was new and ugly and somewhat ostentatious, and was built at the side of the road, and it was obviously intended to catch the eye of rich motorists looking for a place to lunch. George came upon the hotel quite suddenly at a twist in the road and disliked it at once—it really was hideous—but that did not matter, of course, and George wasted no time in vain regrets for the architect's lack of taste. He drove up to the door and parked his car with a view to a quick getaway, for you never knew what might happen, and he remembered Napoleon's maxim that a wise soldier always makes sure of his line of retreat.

Having seen to this, George strolled into the hall (trying to assume as casual an air as possible) and looked about him with interest. The hall was just the sort of hall that one

314

would expect (with marble pillars and palms in pots and horrible tubular furniture) and even the hall porter—who was standing beside his desk—was of an inferior breed compared with the Kenilworth Castle man. This was a little disappointing, of course, for George had assumed that any friend of the Kenilworth Castle hall porter would be of the same type as himself, and he had hoped to find another staunch ally of magnificent presence and courage. He could see at a glance that this man was no use at all—he was half the size and possessed only one medal, and his moustache was drooping and sandy and somewhat sparse.

There was a lady talking to the hall porter, an oldish lady in youngish tweeds, and George was obliged to wait until she had finished asking him what she should see in Winchester and where she should go for tea in that ancient and historical town. He felt inclined to advise her to go to a warmer and more ancient place than Winchester, but managed to resist the impulse.

"Look here," he said, when at last the lady had gone and the hall porter was at liberty. "Look here, I've just come from the Kenilworth Castle. Is Mr. Millar still here?"

The hall porter looked at him, and there was not a shade of recognition or expression upon his face. "Mr. Millar?" he said doubtfully.

"Mr. Wilfred Millar," amended George. There was a crackle of paper, and another good note went west.

"Ah, yes," said the man, doing the disappearing trick far better than George with all his practice was able to accomplish it. "Thank you, sir. They're still 'ere. Some little thing went wrong with the car—the coil ignition, it was—troublesome thing, the coil ignition, sometimes."

George looked at the man and saw that he was perfectly grave—solemn as a bishop, in fact.

"That was—unfortunate," said George.

"Ah," agreed the man. "Still, there's a good mechanic 'ere. 'E happens to be my son-in-law."

"A good mechanic is a useful sort of fellow," said George thoughtfully. "I like good mechanics. Give him ten bob with my compliments, will you?"

"Thank you, sir."

"Not at all. What's—er—happening now?"

"There was a little unpleasantness," said

316

the hall porter, still in that grave and perfectly detached manner. "The young gentleman said it 'adn't ought to have taken so long—not knowing about the difficulties of coil ignition, d'you see—'e's just gone out to the garage to 'urry things up. Very impatient and unreasonable young gentleman, 'e is."

"Yes," said George solemnly.

"The young lady's in the lounge," added the man, pointing across the hall.

"Quite so," said George, straightening himself. "I'll go and speak to her. I'm taking her back to Bournemouth. . . . You've heard me say so if any one should be interested enough to inquire," he added, taking a leaf out of Wilfred Millar's book.

"Very good 'earing, I've got," said the hall porter gravely.

George made for the lounge. (There was no time to waste, for Millar might return at any moment.) He found Elma sitting there by herself at a table in the corner; she was looking through a copy of the *Illustrated London News*, and he saw at once that her week in Bournemouth had changed her a good deal. It was not only that her clothes were different—and George was obliged to give full marks to whoever had chosen them—she was powdered and lipsticked and generally smartened up. "I always thought she was a quick worker," murmured George to himself, and he strode across the room and laid a hand on her shoulder.

Elma looked up and her mouth opened in dismay.

"Yes, it's me," said George. "You didn't expect to see me, did you? A nice chase you've given me!"

"I am going to London," she said.

"Oh, no, you're not," George told her. "You're coming with me—and you're coming now. You can't go tearing up to London by yourself with any young fellow that comes along. It isn't done—honestly."

"I am going to London," said Elma firmly.

"You don't understand," said George desperately. "You can't go to London with Millar. You can go later on. We'll arrange it."

"But it is all arranged——"

"Look here," said George. "If you don't get up and come with me at once, I'll pick you up and carry you. D'you want me to do that?"

It was an empty threat, of course, for George would sooner have died than laid violent hands upon her. Already several people in the lounge had looked up from their papers and were watching the little scene with interest.

"You cannot mean it!" Elma exclaimed. "Oh, George, please. . . . I want to go with Wilfred. . . ."

"I do mean it," said George.

Elma rose hurriedly.

"Come on," continued George, laying a hand on her arm. "There's nothing to be frightened about. We'll talk it over and I'll explain everything—I've got to talk to you. Come on."

So far, George had been lucky—in fact, he had been very lucky indeed (he had deserved his good fortune, of course, but people do not always obtain the fortune that they deserve). He had found his ward, and was on the point of removing her from the hotel—two minutes more and they would have been on the road to Winthorpe—but, alas, at the crucial moment George's luck deserted him. They had emerged from the lounge and were actually crossing the hall when they came face to face with a tall young man in a brown suit.

"Wilfred!" cried Elma, throwing herself into his arms.

"Hold up," said the young man. "Hold up, old thing. It's O.K. now. That mechanic was a damned fool. I've fixed the thing myself. I must just wash and then we'll be off."

"No," said George in a firm tone. "At least, you can wash, of course—and, as a matter of fact, you'd be all the better of a wash, for there's a streak of oil right across your nose—but you can't go off with Elma—that's flat."

"And who the devil are you?" inquired the young man.

"I'm her trustee," said George, "and I don't approve of her dashing about all over the country with strangers."

"You mind your own business," said Wilfred Millar quickly. "What are you doing here? My father's her trustee; and, if you *must* know, I'm taking her to London by his instructions."

"Oh, no, you're not," said George. "Elma's coming with me."

"I don't know who you are, but——"

"Ferrier is my name."

"Well, you can go and ferry, then—go and ferry your confounded boat," cried Wilfred Millar furiously.

"Why don't you go and grind your confounded mill?" retorted George with equal vigour.

It was at this moment that the hall porter saw fit to interfere. "Now, then," he said, coming across the hall towards them. "Now, then, young gentlemen, this won't do, you know. You can't make a row 'ere, you know. 'Tain't allowed, you know. I'll have to send for the manager, you know."

"Send for him, by all means," said Wilfred with a grand air. "It's about time something was done, if people can't have lunch in this beastly place without being annoyed by lunatics. Send for the manager at once—I've got something to say to him about that mechanic, anyhow."

The hall porter was somewhat taken aback. He had no real wish to send for the manager—especially if it meant a complaint about his son-in-law's work—as a rule, the mere threat to send for the manager had a soothing and calming effect upon young blood. . . .

"Well, I don't know," he said doubtfully. "The manager's engaged at present. Why can't you talk it over quiet and settle it amongst yourselves—eh?"

"There's no earthly need to send for him,"

said George firmly. "Miss Green is my ward. I'm taking her home."

"You are not," said Wilfred firmly.

"I am going to London with Wilfred," said Elma firmly.

The hall porter looked from one to the other in despair. "It's beyond me," he declared. "You'll have to fix it yourselves, that's all, only go out in the garden and fix it quiet. We don't want no rows 'ere . . . people don't like it, you know."

He opened a door at the end of the hall and hustled them out into a small courtyard where there was a plot of bright green grass and a few teak-wood seats and some painted tubs with orange trees growing in them. "Now, then," he said, "there's nobody 'ere, so you can 'ave a nice quiet talk. You talk it over and fix it up. There's no need for any fuss, see?" And, so saying, he left them and shut the door.

"This is nonsense," Wilfred declared. "We don't want to talk anything over—it's a waste of time. Elma wants to go to London, and I'm taking her."

"Elma is not going with you."

"This is absolute bilge," cried Wilfred

322

angrily. "What d'you mean by coming after us like this?"

"To fetch Elma, that's all," said George. "You've no right to go off with her——"

"I'm not 'going off' with her, you idiot. I'm taking her to London——"

"I have never been to London," Elma explained.

"I know all that," said George wearily. "The point is, you can't go to London with *him*."

"Well, I'll be damned!" cried Wilfred. "Of all the cheek! I suppose you think you'll take her to London!"

"I certainly shan't let her go alone with you."

"Let's all go together!" cried Elma, clapping her hands. "What fun that would be!"

"No!" cried both young men with one voice, and then they glared at each other furiously as if the mere fact that they were agreed upon one point had increased their antipathy.

"No," said George again. "You're to come with me, Elma. You don't understand what you're doing."

"I am going to London, that is all," Elma pointed out.

"It isn't all—that's the difficulty," declared George.

"Oh, come on, Elma," Wilfred said. "The fellow's mad or drunk—probably both. Don't let's waste any more time arguing with the fool. We can get through to the garage this way," and he took her arm and walked across the grass.

George was hot and tired, he was also extremely thirsty. He had pursued Elma for miles, and now, when at last he had run her to earth, she was once more escaping from his grasp. It was maddening, and George lost his temper completely. He bounded after them across the lawn like an infuriated tiger and, seizing Wilfred with one hand and Elma with the other, he forced them apart. He took care, of course, to exert a good deal more force upon Wilfred, and indeed used such a degree of violence that Wilfred, taken by surprise at the sudden onslaught, lost his balance completely; his foot caught against an orange tub and he spun round and sat down on the grass with a thud.

"There," cried George. "Get up and take what's coming to you. Get up, I say."

Wilfred did not get up. He sat there looking

at George with a very curious expression in his eyes. "That's an assault," he said slowly. "Do you understand, Mr. Ferrier? I shall have you up for assault."

"Get up," cried George, dancing with impatience. "Get up and I'll knock you down again—then you can have me up for assault twice over. You can have me up for assault as many times as you like—twenty times, if you like. . . ."

"You heard that, Elma," said Wilfred. "He threatened me."

"Oh, yes!" she cried. "Get up and fight him, Wilfred," and there was a new and thrilling note in her voice.

George looked at her in surprise and saw that her eyes were shining like twin stars.

"I have always wanted to see a real fight," she continued eagerly. "You are my knight, Wilfred. Why don't you get up and fight him?"

"You're crazy," said Wilfred firmly. "I'm not a savage. This is the twentieth century. Tell him to go away."

"Get up and fight him."

"I shall do no such thing," declared Wilfred. "It would be putting myself in the wrong. He will hear of this disgraceful business from my lawyer."

George looked at the beautifully dressed young gentleman sitting on the grass, and contrasted his solemn dignified expression with his somewhat ignominious attitude. It really was very funny, indeed, and George began to laugh.

Elma stamped her foot. "Can't you see he is laughing at you?" she cried.

Wilfred did not move. "Fetch the hall porter," he said. "Tell him to get the manager."

"Yes," agreed George. "Go on, Elma. Get the hall porter and the manager and the boots and half a dozen waiters and the lift-boy. I'll take 'em all on."

"He's mad," said Wilfred. "Raving mad!"

"Oh, why don't you get up!" cried Elma, seizing his arm and trying to raise him from the ground.

George realised now that the game was in his hands, it had been handed to him on a plate. "Don't worry him, Elma," he said. "He doesn't want to get up. He likes sitting on the grass. He's too proud to fight—or too civilised, or something. I'm afraid you haven't chosen the right kind of knight this time." And, so saying, he took her hand and led her away, gently but firmly, helped her into the car and drove off slowly down the road.

For a little while neither of them spoke a word, for George did not know what to say and Elma was struggling, not very successfully, with tears. They ran into Alton and turned north here, for George, as has already been stated, was making for home. He was aware that he must make for Marlowe, but beyond that he had only a vague idea of the direction he should take. Granpa was not going so well now, and this worried George a good deal, for he was a horseman and knew his limitations. If Granpa conked out, George would not be able to diagnose the trouble, far less to remedy it. He realised, of course, that it was extremely decent of Granpa to wait until now before showing signs of distress; it did not matter now—not to the same extent—because, even if Wilfred took it into his head to pursue them (and this did not seem likely) he would never think of pursuing them northwards. If he asked the hall porter, that worthy would say Bournemouth, and if he didn't ask the hall porter, he would probably make for town. In either case, they were safe from pursuit, and Granpa could take his time.

The hum of the car and the gentle breeze in her face soothed Elma considerably, and soon she dried the remains of her tears and began to look about.

"This is not the way to Bournemouth," she said in a very small voice.

"I'm taking you to my home," said George, and he added, "My mother will deal with you."

It sounded a frightful threat, and Elma relapsed into silence. What was his mother like, she wondered, and she visualised a tall, severe-looking woman—a female grenadier.

"I would rather go back to Miss Wilson," she said at last.

"Well, you can't. Miss Wilson's ill."

There was a long pause, and then George sighed. "I don't know what to say to you," he told her. "I think you must be crazy to go off with an absolute bounder like that. Any one with the least grain of sense could see what a bounder he is."

Elma made no reply—unless a small smothered sob could be interpreted as such.

"Yes, you may well be ashamed," said George sternly. "I've been chasing you all over England since nine o'clock this morning. You've nearly killed Miss Wilson—by the way, that reminds me. I must stop at the next village and send her a wire."

The car ran on for fully a mile before any more was said and George, who could never be angry for long, began to feel better. He remembered, too, that it was really his fault, for it was he who had started Elma on the downward path. He began to feel a little sorry for her, but he was not going to show it—not yet, anyhow.

"You see what a nuisance you are," he said at last.

The words were stern and more than a little unkind, but Elma realised from their tone that he was beginning to thaw.

"Why did you come after me if I am such a nuisance?" she inquired in an innocent voice.

"Because it's my duty to keep an eye on you," said George promptly. "Oh, you needn't think I *wanted* to chase after you like this—it doesn't amuse me at all."

"I am sorry, George," she said. "It was because I was so anxious to go to London, and Wilfred offered——"

"My goodness, don't keep on saying that. You've said it over and over again like a parrot. I'm sick of hearing it. Don't you realise that you can't go dashing off to London with any Tom, Dick or Harry that asks you?"

"Other girls——"

"Oh, I know other girls do it—and get off with it, too—but other girls are different. You're such a silly little ass. You don't belong to modern times at all. The fact is, you're an anachronism," added George, rather pleased with himself for thinking of this apt description.

"I do not think that is the right word," said Elma meekly (she had been educated by a purist, of course).

"Oh, yes, it is," declared George. "You're a female anachronism, that's what you are."

Elma sighed. She saw what he meant, of course. "I want to do things in the new-fashioned way," she pointed out.

"You can't," said George firmly. "You're different." He paused a moment and then added, "You're too pretty, for one thing."

"Wilfred said——"

"I don't want to hear what Wilfred said."

"No," said Elma meekly.

"The fact is, you're not fit to be loose. Something will have to be done with you—I wish I knew what."

"I do not think I like Wilfred very much, after all," said Elma after a pause.

"You surprise me," George told her with elaborate sarcasm.

7

THE MILLAR FAMILY AT HOME

WILFRED MILLAR gathered himself up and examined himself carefully to see what damage he had sustained. It was important to make sure of this, not only for medical reasons, but also for legal ones. The barbarous assault upon his person should not go unpunished, he was determined upon that. Assault and battery, with threats, thought Wilfred, and I believe the Habeas Corpus comes into it, somehow. I'll make him pay through the nose for this. People can't go knocking people down and get off scot-free—not in twentieth-century England, thought Wilfred, and he snorted with sheer rage. By this time he had discovered that his ankle was bleeding—he had scraped it against the tub as he fell—and another part of his body was considerably bruised (he could not see it, of course, but he was sure it would be black and blue tomorrow). His *amour propre* had sustained a pretty severe injury and his temper was in rags.

In one way, it was a little unfortunate that there were no bones broken, because a broken bone elicits sympathy, and requires the attention of a doctor, but in another way it was fortunate that Wilfred was not completely incapacitated, for it would have delayed matters a good deal. As it was, he could drive straight up to London and see his lawyer—or, rather, his father's lawyer—and put in motion the wheels of the law. He bound up his ankle with his handkerchief and limped into the hotel. Somebody should suffer for this, and suffer immediately.

It was obvious to Wilfred that the hall porter was the person upon whom to vent his rage. If the hall porter had been worth his salt, he would have taken Wilfred's part and sent that damned young swine Ferrier about his business. He did not actually suspect the hall porter of being in league with young Ferrier; but he was no fool, and he was beginning to smell something a bit fishy about the whole thing. I'll cook his goose for him, Wilfred thought, and proceeded to put his plan into execution.

Meantime, the hall porter had heard all about the *fracas* in the garden. He had heard about it from the boots, who had been watching from the staircase window and had seen Wilfred's downfall with unholy joy. The boots had hastened downstairs to tell the hall porter all about it—and the story lost nothing in the telling. The hall porter drank it down with avidity and unbent so far as to remark that it "served the pip-squeak right, so it did."

(Wilfred was unpopular with the staffs of his father's hotels, for he put on airs and was close with his money, and it was this unpopularity which had been his undoing. Hall porters and garage mechanics are human beings, with feelings like other people, with preferences and prejudices, and like the rest of us. If young Millar had been a favourite, they would have stood by him through thick and thin, and George's quest might have had a very different ending).

The boots and the hall porter discussed the whole matter in suitably lowered voices and, comparing the two combatants, they decided unanimously that the better man had won and that the young lady must be "a bit off the top" to prefer that pip-squeak to a fine, generous, upstanding young fellow like the other one.

"But wimmin are queer," declared the boots thoughtfully. "You never know with wimmin."

The hall porter agreed. "Pretty little piece she was, too," he pointed out.

"It's the pretty ones is the worst."

They were still discussing the peculiarities of the fair sex when the door into the garden opened somewhat violently and Wilfred Millar limped into the hall, and it was obvious from his expression that there was going to be a good deal of unpleasantness for somebody. The boots fled for his life, but the hall porter could not fly—he was chained to his desk, so to speak—and the whole force of Wilfred's rage and fury fell upon his head.

He knew, of course, that the whole thing *was* his fault, but Wilfred did not know this, so Wilfred was merely letting off steam, and the hall porter bore it as patiently as he could. There were a good many things that he could have said, and they were all perfectly clear in his mind; but instead of saying them, he remained dumb. The fact was, his wife was ill, and for this reason he was more than usually anxious to retain his post. . . .

But I'd like to push his face in, thought the hall porter, trying not to look at the tempting visage and clasping his hands firmly behind his back. It was not surprising that his dislike of Wilfred had grown into hatred before Wilfred had finished with him.

Having told the hall porter exactly what he thought of him and warned him that his tenure of office would probably come to an end in the near future, Wilfred limped off to the garage. He intended to see the head mechanic there, and vent some of his surplus rage upon him. Unfortunately for Wilfred, the garage hands had seen him coming and had made themselves scarce, so he found nobody in the place at all. He rang the bell and waited and looked about, but it was no use, and at last he got into his car and drove off in a worse temper than ever.

The hall porter had told Wilfred that Mr. Ferrier had announced his intention of taking the young lady back to Bournemouth, but Wilfred had shown no interest in this news, for he had no intention of pursuing them. He was through with Elma—they could go to hell, for all he cared. He was aware that his father would be angry with him for letting Elma slip through his fingers; but his father had been angry with him before, several times, and had got over it. He would just have to get over it again. Wilfred had done his best to carry out the plan and had actually been injured in the attempt—no man could do more. He intended to explain all this to his father, and then they would see a lawyer and justice would be done. London was therefore Wilfred's objective, and to London he went, driving furiously and even more inconsiderately than usual. His car was a powerful one, and he took a delight in ramming past his fellow-roadusers at inconvenient bends, and in accelerating suddenly to frighten pedestrians and make them leap out of his way. Several people shouted at him angrily, and Wilfred shouted back and sped on. It was really rather astonishing that Wilfred arrived in London without much more serious injury than he had already sustained.

Mr. Millar's flat was near Hyde Park Corner. It was a "Luxury Flat," and lived up to its reputation. Wilfred and Pauline lived there with him, because neither of them had any money to live elsewhere. They got on well enough, for they each had interests and friends and they did not interfere with each other's lives in the slightest. Wilfred put his car away and limped up Grosvenor Place, carrying his suitcase. He had noticed that

Elma's suitcase was still in the car and had decided it could stay there. It was bad enough to have to carry one suitcase . . . and she had treated him abominably. It was now about nine o'clock (for he had stopped and had dinner on the way) and he was pretty certain that the flat would be empty. The Millar family rarely indulged in quiet domestic evenings; their pleasures lay in other directions—in dining and wining and having a good time. Pauline would almost certainly be out with her latest young man, and Mr. Millar would either be playing bridge or dining his latest young woman at the Savoy. Wilfred was glad to think that his family would not be there when he arrived, for he wanted a good night's rest before seeing his father, or rather before his father saw him. He would be able to attend to his wounds and creep off to bed and nobody would know he was there until the morning.

This plan seemed flawless to Wilfred. The more so because his family were not expecting him and Elma at the flat. He had told young Ferrier that he was taking Elma to London to his father, but that had been a brilliant inspiration on his part—it had sounded well, he thought, and it was disappointing that it had not made more impression upon Ferrier. In reality, he and Elma had intended to spend a few days at the Ritz, and a room had been booked for them. . . . Mr. Millar had arranged the whole thing, of course, and had instructed Wilfred in his part with a good deal of care.

Wilfred thought of all this as he went up in the lift, and he reflected with an inward qualm that his father would be very angry indeed when he heard that his elaborate plan had failed; he had been extremely keen on the plan, and had overborne any objections upon Wilfred's part with the force of a steam-roller.

Wilfred sighed. He put down his suitcase and opened the front door of the flat—he had his latch-key, of course—and as he opened it he became aware that the flat was not empty: he heard voices in the lounge, and the tinkle of a decanter against a glass. . . .

It was a horrible moment, for he was not ready to face his father. He saw at once that he had been a fool to come here. Why hadn't he gone to the hotel by himself and stayed there comfortably? The reason was that he was tired and wretched and craved his own bed—perhaps even now he could creep in without being seen. . . .

Wilfred hesitated for a moment and was lost, for at that very moment his father came into the hall.

"Wilfred!" exclaimed Mr. Millar in amazement, and then, as he looked at his son and saw by his face that his well-laid plans had gone awry, he uttered a string of well chosen but wholly unprintable epithets.

Wilfred had not expected a warm and sympathetic welcome, but he was surprised at the vigour and force of his father's language. "It isn't my fault," he said sullenly. "What's the good of going at me like that before you've heard what's happened?"

"I can see you've made a mess of it," replied Mr. Millar furiously. "I can see you've ruined everything—fool that you are!"

"Everything was perfectly O.K.," declared Wilfred. "I got her to come with me and we were actually on our way when that fellow Ferrier barged in——"

"Come in here," said Mr. Millar, and he took his son by the arm and dragged him into the lounge.

Pauline was there, stretched out on the sofa with her silken legs crossed and a cigarette dangling between her lips. "Hallo!" she said, raising her head and looking at Wilfred in

340

surprise. "Hallo, what's up? What have you done with Elma?"

Wilfred was amazed to find his whole family at home like this, but he was given no time to inquire into the reason. He was too busy answering his father's questions and trying to make excuses for the failure of their plans. The whole story was dragged out of him bit by bit, his injuries were scoffed at and his stupidity condemned in no uncertain language. Wilfred had come in for condemnation before, but he had never seen his father so furious, so unreasonable, so completely lost to all sense of decency.

"How could I help it?" Wilfred kept on saying. "It wasn't my fault."

If he said it once, he said it half a dozen times, and every time he said it Mr. Millar cursed with renewed fury. "You've muddled the whole thing," he declared. "It was in your hands, and you've muddled it. Why didn't you go after them and get her back?"

"I didn't want her back," Wilfred replied. "I don't want to marry her now. She's crazy. I don't know why you're so keen on me marrying her. There are other rich girls in the world."

"I told you before I left Bournemouth that

it had become absolutely necessary for you to marry her," raved Mr. Millar.

"Yes, I know," Wilfred said, "and I did my best."

"Your best!"

"What more could I have done? I thought it was better to come straight home and tell you what had happened. We can sue him for assault."

Mr. Millar laughed, but it was not a pleasant sound. "That *will* be fun," he said. "You'll sue him for assault and he'll sue me for embezzlement and misappropriation—tremendous fun we shall have!"

"What!" cried Wilfred incredulously.

Mr. Millar repeated his statement slowly. ". . . and you needn't look at Pauline like that," he added. "Pauline knows. She's got twice as much brain as you have. If you hadn't been such a fool you might have guessed long ago how things were going."

"Embezzlement!" cried Wilfred in horror.

"Pretty word, isn't it?" agreed his father, pouring out a generous measure of whisky from the decanter which stood on a side table, and drinking it off at one gulp. "I thought I could get off with it, of course; and I would have, too, if it hadn't been for that young swine. I had everything arranged. Wicherly was standing in, and old Bennett is in his dotage. Ferrier is a fool—I had him taped. It was as easy as an old shoe and as safe as the Bank of England. There was nothing to stop me——"

"But why——?" cried Wilfred.

"Why? I had to have money. D'you think I can keep you and Pauline going on air? I lost heavily in oil, and I had to get money some-how—*had to*, I tell you—and the money was there. It was child's play compared with other deals I've put through. Green had insured his life for twenty thousand, and not a soul knew of it except Wicherly and myself—and then, when the whole thing was settled, that young fool re-membered. How was I to know Green had told him? How was I to know he'd forget all about it and only remember afterwards when the money was lodged in my bank? Even then I could have saved the situation if you hadn't messed and muddled the whole thing. I knew you were a fool, of course," said Mr. Millar scornfully, "but I didn't expect you to do any-thing except carry out a simple plan. Any fool could have done what you had to do. If you had played your part we shouldn't be in this mess. We should be perfectly safe. We should be sitting pretty. You'd have married the girl and the trust would have been wound up. Ferrier couldn't have proceeded against me if you were married to the girl."

Wilfred had listened to all this with his eyes like saucers. "But embezzlement!" he said again in horror-stricken tones.

"Yes," agreed Mr. Millar. "Say it again— keep on saying it if it gives you any satisfaction. You see what you've landed us into with your muddling."

"I can see what you've landed us into," replied Wilfred with more spirit than he had shown before. "How was I to know so much depended upon it? How was I to know you were a crook?"

"A crook! That's good. Since when have you got so squeamish? Did you ever stop to inquire where the money came from? No, and you didn't care as long as you got it out of me—money, money, money was what you wanted all the time. You couldn't hold down a job for five minutes because you were so damned lazy. You threw it up and crawled back to me holding out your hands for more money—and more—and more. Did you think money fell from heaven, or what?"

"I didn't think . . . I thought we were rich," said Wilfred miserably.

Mr. Millar laughed. "He thought *we* were rich!"

"I wouldn't have taken the money if I'd known it was stolen——"

"Shut up, Wilfred," said Pauline in a quiet voice. "You've been to blame as much as any one. You and I have both been in it up to the hilt. It's a bit thick to turn on him now."

"You—can say that," began Wilfred in a choked voice.

"I've been spending the money, too. We've all been spending it and having a dashed good time. *We* can't complain."

Mr. Millar was walking up and down the room. "It's so idiotic," he declared. "The whole thing is utterly and completely idiotic. I've put through deals that were a hundred per cent more complicated and dangerous. The thing is, I know where I am with business men and I know how to deal with them. That young Ferrier upset all my calculations. I put him down as a fool—and he is a fool, of course. I knew perfectly well that he thought there was something fishy going on, and I took the trouble to lead him up the garden path; he came like a lamb.

The whole thing was fixed, and then he—he bumped into it—yes, *bumped* is the word—and upset everything. There was only one way out of the mess—to get hold of the girl—and again that fool bumped in."

"Can't you diddle him again?" inquired Pauline anxiously.

"D'you think I haven't considered it?" cried her father. "I haven't slept a wink since I got his confounded letter. I've thought about it until my brain reels, but I've come to the conclusion that it's too risky. For one thing, I can't depend on Wicherly—he's got cold feet—he won't back me up this time, and the worst of it is, he's not in it as deeply as I am. Damned twister, he is! I had a hold on him, but this business has given him a hold on me, and I don't like it. No, it's too risky. The game's up."

Pauline looked at him questioningly, and he nodded. "You understand," he said.

"Yes," she replied. "But what about Wilfred?"

Mr. Millar smiled unpleasantly. "Wilfred can look out for himself. It's about time he did; and, to tell you the truth, I'm a little tired of friend Wilfred." He went over to the side table and poured out another drink. "Well, here's luck!" he said.

"Luck!" cried Wilfred.

"Why not?" inquired Mr. Millar. "Even crooks like to think there's luck in store for them, you know. Goodnight, my dear son, sleep well; and if you take my advice, you'll go while the going's good."

He went out, shutting the door behind him.

"Pauline!" cried Wilfred in agonised tones.

"Well, Wilfred?"

"This is—frightful."

"I suppose it is," she replied. "It's the end of a good many things—nice things, they were."

"But what are you going to *do*?"

"We're going away, of course," said Pauline calmly. "You heard what Dad said."

"You're going away?"

She nodded. "I've known for some time that he was prepared for something like this to happen. He has got money banked abroad in another name. I found out by accident and taxed him with it, and he admitted that it was true. It was a sort of insurance, he said. He's been sailing close to the wind for years, of course."

"Pauline!"

"I shut my eyes," she admitted.

"You knew—and yet——"

"Yes," said Pauline, and she smiled. "We all seem to be coming clean tonight, so I may as well join in the orgy. I knew the money was—well—not honestly come by; but I like a good time, you see. Sometimes it worried me a good deal and sometimes it didn't. It's wonderful how you get used to things like that. I'm like Dad, I suppose—unmoral, or something. He's so jolly clever that I didn't think he'd get caught."

"Pauline!"

"Well?"

"You're going away—with *him*?"

"Yes."

"You can't!" cried Wilfred. "You can't go away with *him*. Let's stick together, you and I."

"How could we?"

"I'll find something to do."

She swung her foot in its beautifully fitting shoe and watched it and did not meet his eyes. "What would you do?" she inquired.

"Anything," he told her earnestly. "Anything honest."

"You really are extraordinary," she said. "You've lived on him for years. You've bat-

348

tened on him and cadged from him and cheated him in all sorts of silly little ways, and now you begin to talk like a prig. Go and do something honest. You won't make much money by it. I'll stick to him, thank you."

"Pauline, you don't mean it!"

"I do mean it, and I'll tell you why. I'll be quite honest about it," declared Pauline, lifting one eyebrow in the whimsical manner of her father. "There are two reasons why I intend to stick to him. One is that he would be completely lost without me, and, as I have lived on him all my life, I believe he has a claim on me now that he's in trouble. The other reason is that I shall be more comfortable with him. I like my comforts, Wilfred."

"Can't you see he's crooked?" Wilfred burst out.

"Yes," she said slowly. "Yes, I can see it. He's deformed really, deformed in his soul. Perhaps something happened to him when he was a child—some injury that deformed his nature and twisted it out of line—just as a child's body can be deformed for life by a blow or a fall. The queer thing about Dad is that he doesn't *know*, he isn't a bit *ashamed*. He tells me a good many things. Sometimes I wish he wouldn't tell me so much. It almost frightens me sometimes, and I can't help wondering what it feels like to be him—to be so much off the straight as not to be able to see straight any more—but I shall never know that, because he doesn't know himself, so he couldn't tell me even if he wanted to. I suppose, really, that I'm worse than he is because I see the difference between right and wrong, and he doesn't; but I'm not cut out for poverty, that's all."

"Oh, good heavens!" cried Wilfred. "Is everybody *mad*?"

"Perhaps we are," said Pauline wearily, "perhaps we're all mad. Anyhow, I'm going with him."

"When are you going, and where?"

"I don't know," she replied, "at least I do know where we are going, but I shan't tell you. It will be better for you not to know—and safer for us. You might come all over honest and let the cat out of the bag. If you take my advice, you'll disappear yourself for a bit; it will be healthier for you."

"I haven't a bob," said Wilfred simply.

Pauline took off a diamond ring and held it out to him. "Here you are," she said. "It's the only decent thing I've got, and you ought to get at least thirty pounds for it. That should keep you for some time if you're careful. It's mother's," she added, "so you can take it without any qualms—it hasn't been bought with stolen money."

He took it and looked at it. "Mother's!" he said. "Thank God she's dead."

"Yes, it *is* nice, isn't it?" replied Pauline in a queer, strained voice.

"Oh, Pauline!"

"Go away," said Pauline carefully. "Go away and stay away."

He turned towards the door and then stopped and looked back. "Goodbye," he said. "I say, I suppose—I suppose I shan't—see you again."

"No," said Pauline. "I don't suppose you will."

"You're taking it very calmly!" he exclaimed.

There was no reply, and after a few moments he opened the door and disappeared.

Pauline waited until she heard the front door of the flat close with a thud, and then she burrowed her head into a cushion and cried as if her heart would break.

8

MR. AND MRS. FERRIER

MR. and Mrs. Ferrier spent a long and somewhat trying day. They saw George start off to Bournemouth in the car, and then started upon their usual day's employments, but Mr. Ferrier was so worried and unhappy that he found it impossible to work. Pure science is admittedly an enthralling pursuit, but it requires a placid mind, and on this particular day it had lost its power to enthrall Mr. Ferrier—the troubles of his family eclipsed the stars.

Having considered the matter carefully for about half an hour, Mr. Ferrier came to the reluctant conclusion that it was possible George was right in his surmise that Arbuthnot Millar had appropriated the twenty thousand pounds. Everything pointed to that conclusion, and his previous knowledge of the man was the deciding factor in the case. (Dusty had been a twister, and Mr. Ferrier did not believe he could have changed. It was a great pity that

Green had trusted the man—but, of course, Green had never heard of Dusty's little mishap in Mesopotamia, and Dusty had always been a plausible sort of chap.) Mr. Ferrier was very much alarmed when he reached this conclusion, and the stars receded farther than ever; for twenty thousand pounds is a large sum, and he was not sure whether George—as one of the Green Trustees—might be held responsible for a part of it. Mr. Ferrier was fairly well off, but he was aware that if he had to raise even a third of that sum his income would be uncomfortably reduced. Swan House was run on simple lines, but it took a good deal of money to run it at all, to keep the old house wind- and water-tight and to pay all the men. Mr. Ferrier's books brought little grist to the mill, and George's horses provided him with pocket-money and no more.

It was exceedingly worrying, and Mr. Ferrier hoped against hope that George was wrong, and that the twenty thousand pounds was perfectly safe. He hoped this not only for financial reasons, but also for moral ones. Mr. Ferrier liked to think the best of his fellow-men, and it was terrible to have to think that any one could be so lost to honour and decency as to steal twenty thousand pounds from the dead body of his friend—of a man who had trusted him.

Mr. Ferrier could not sit still any longer, he could not bear to be alone with his thoughts, so he got up and left his study and went in search of his wife. He did not say much to her, of course, for it was no use worrying Paddy with business matters, but he wandered about after her all the morning like a lost dog. He followed her up and down the stairs and round the house as she went about her business of housekeeping, and he stood and watched her while she cleaned the lamps and arranged the flowers.

"Quentin, darling," said Paddy at last. "It's almost demented, I am, with being followed."

"I am sorry, my dear," he declared.

"It's not much head, I have, at the best of times."

"I wonder you are not worn out," said Mr. Ferrier gravely. "I had no idea that house-keeping was such an arduous task."

"It wouldn't be if I did it properly."

Mr. Ferrier could not agree with this. He had noticed, of course, that Paddy had rushed upstairs to the top of the house three times when once would have done, but he had also noticed—somewhat to his surprise—that, in spite of her haphazard methods, Paddy got through a good deal. She knew what she was doing, and she did it. He adored Paddy, of course, but he had always believed her to be incapable and her housekeeping a farce.

"It is a pity you are obliged to work so hard," he said with a sigh, and the sigh was due to the reflection that if his fears materialised she would probably have to work a good deal harder.

"But what would I do if I didn't?" demanded Paddy. "And, to tell the truth, I don't."

Mr. Ferrier looked a little puzzled.

"I don't do much," Paddy explained kindly. "That's what I meant. We're quite lucky with servants compared to other people; I can't think why."

Mr. Ferrier could not think why, either. He was aware that the servant problem bulked large in the lives of his friends; but Paddy seemed to be able to get servants and to keep them without much difficulty. Swan House was far from the town, it was large and old-fashioned, there was no electricity, nor gas, and therefore no labour-saving devices. Mr. Ferrier thought of all this and then he said, "It is indeed a mystery."

"It's a miracle," Paddy said seriously, "just like when manna fell from heaven for the starving Israelites. They didn't know how it was done, and neither do I. We must just be thankful," she added.

The explanation of Paddy's own particular miracle was a psychological one: servants liked Paddy. She talked to them as she had talked to the servants in her old Irish home— as if they were human beings like herself. She was good to them, and exceedingly generous in a haphazard way. She was interested in them and trusted them implicitly. Sometimes she got furiously angry for no reason at all, and sometimes she laughed at things that would have made other mistresses furiously angry: you never knew where you were, so to speak. But this, instead of annoying the servants, amused them and kept them interested, for if you have to do the same things at the same hour every day of your life, anything out of the ordinary is welcome. Paddy was a champion monotony breaker. This was all to the good, of course, but perhaps the chief attraction which outweighed the obvious disadvantages of Swan House was the fact that Paddy's eccentricities gave her servants food for conversation: they discussed her endlessly in her own kitchen and

356

in the kitchens of her friends. They did not discuss her unkindly, because they were fond of her in a queer sort of way and very proud of her, too. Other servants had ordinary mistresses—they had Paddy.

"D'you know what she said to me this morning . . . ?" was a gambit warranted to produce instant silence and attention from any audience for miles around, and the bursts of laughter or the incredulous exclamations which punctuated the tale were most gratifying to the teller:

"Go on, do—she never!"

"Well, she *is* a cure, and no mistake!"

Domestic crises sometimes took place at Swan House, but these were usually occasioned by accident, illness or marriage, or some such intrinsic cause. Paddy was rarely left in the lurch or badly let down by her staff, and she remained silent (and thought about the Israelites) when her friends discussed their troubles and trials in this connection.

The day wore on and no message came from George. Mrs. Ferrier had a good many small duties to attend to in the house and the garden and the stables, and Mr. Ferrier wandered after her and watched her doing them and tried to help. Unfortunately, like many exceedingly clever men, he was also exceedingly handless, and it was impossible for him to draw a pail of water and carry it to a horse without spilling more than half of it over his own feet.

"Quentin, darling, couldn't you go and write your book?" cried his wife more than once; but, somehow or other, Quentin could not.

After tea Paddy could stand it no longer, and she decided to take him for a walk, so they set forth together across the moor, taking the two spaniels with them. (Nadia's babies were now quite old enough to be left alone for a little, and it was good for Nadia to have some relaxation from maternal cares and responsibilities.) It was not so hot today, and there was a pleasant breeze, and a few great, billowy clouds, high up in the blue sky, sailed past with the slow dignity of galleons. Their shadows moved with them over the hills and the moor and changed the colour of the burnt-up grass from bright yellow to pallid grey.

Mrs. Ferrier hung on Mr. Ferrier's arm and chattered inconsequently of everything that passed through her head. She had started chattering to "take Quentin's mind off," and, strangely enough, her chatter had taken her own mind off, too.

Belt and Nadia gambolled about together—they were obviously delighted to see each other again—and the thought crossed Mr. Ferrier's astronomical mind that the dogs were like the satellites of Jupiter, for they circled round and round himself and his wife, and the whole party moved onwards to some fixed and appointed spot. They crossed the stream by some stepping-stones and began to climb Ingram Hill and soon came to the Roman Road where George had ridden with Elma. It was Mr. Ferrier's turn to talk now (you could scarcely call it chatter) and he began to tell Paddy about the Legions of Rome. He explained that the moor was a swamp in those far-off days, and that this was why the road had been made on the lower slopes of the hills, and he added that it must have annoyed the Roman engineers a good deal for they preferred to rule their roads straight from point to point. "They were a great nation," Mr. Ferrier said. "They were brave and hardy."

"So far from their homes!" said Paddy sadly.

Mr. Ferrier took the point. (He had often found that Paddy's remarks, even when they seemed irrelevant, were not really irrelevant at all, but usually followed a definite train of thought missing out several stations on the way.) "It is curious to think that the Romans, here in Britain, were farther from their homes than is possible in modern times," he said thoughtfully. "I have not studied the matter seriously, but I believe it may be taken as a fact. There is no place in the world today so far from another place *in time* as the distance from here to Rome in 55 B.C. Many of the Romans who came to this land were exiles for life, exiles from their own sunny land and from their loved ones."

Paddy stood on the narrow causeway and looked from right to left. "I never realised they were human beings," she declared.

It was a curious remark, but Mr. Ferrier did not misunderstand it—perhaps he understood what she meant better than Paddy herself—for he smiled and said, "Human beings like you and me."

"Shouldn't it be 'you and I'?" inquired Paddy.

"No, it shouldn't," said Mr. Ferrier firmly.

"Oh, well," she said, "it's an ignoramus

you have for a wife, but you knew it from the first, so you can't complain. . . . And to think they laid down these stones with their own hands, the creatures!"

Mr. Ferrier agreed that it was a curiously moving thought, and they walked on together at peace with the world. They talked of many things as they went along, and they enjoyed themselves so much that each of them wondered why they did not go for walks together more frequently. The dogs were enjoying themselves, too, nosing into a hundred entrancing smells, investigating rat-holes, and hounding rabbits into their burrows with energy and spirit. Sometimes they were in front of their human companions and sometimes behind, and sometimes they forgot all about smells and rabbits and chased each other madly all over the moor. If George had been there he would have been horrified at the freedom accorded to his shooting dogs; but George was otherwise engaged.

"Perhaps there will be a wire from George," said Mr. Ferrier as they came back through the garden together, but he said it quite cheerfully, for he felt a good deal better after his walk. The situation was unchanged, but he had decided that, even if his income were reduced and they were obliged to economise, he would always be a rich man as long as he had Paddy.

There was no wire from George, and this was taken to mean that he was staying at Bournemouth for the night. . . .

". . . And that's all to the good," Paddy declared, "for it's a long drive there and back in one day, and George not used to it and all . . . it feels like a week since he left here this morning," she added thoughtfully, and Mr. Ferrier replied that it felt the same to him.

They dined together quite peacefully, and then Mrs. Ferrier left her husband to enjoy his port, and went into the drawing-room, and no sooner had she gone than a wire arrived. It was brought to Mr. Ferrier on a silver salver, and he took it and opened it. He read it carefully several times, and then he put on his glasses and read it again; but the glasses made no difference.

"Is there an answer, sir?"

"Oh! . . . no answer, thank you," he replied.

When the maid had left the room he read the telegram again and then laid it on the table beside the decanter of port and thought about it seriously.

Handed in at Bournemouth
8.15 p.m.

Ferrier Swan House Winthorpe many thanks all your kindness agree you keep child great relief to my mind Wilson.

Mr. Ferrier realised that the telegram was not for him at all: it was for George. He would not have opened it if he had known this before, but, now that he had opened it, there was not the slightest use in shutting his eyes to its obvious meaning. . . . "Agree you keep child," murmured Mr. Ferrier to himself in horror-stricken tones. . . . "Agree you keep child." And he suddenly envisaged George's study changed back into a nursery—a nursery for an illegitimate grandchild.

His first thought was to rush to Paddy with the news, and he half-rose from his chair with this, very natural, intention; but before he had risen completely he had changed his mind and sat down again. No, he thought, no, it would worry her, it would upset her. I shall not tell Paddy tonight. . . .

There must be some explanation, of course, there *must be*. Miss Wilson was an elderly woman—it could not be her child—George had laughed wholeheartedly at the mere idea (Mr. Ferrier remembered this distinctly). But, if it were not Miss Wilson's child, whose could it be? Could it possibly be Green's daughter's child? No, for it was only about a fortnight since George had met Green's daughter for the first time—not yet six weeks since George had met Green. Whose child, then?

I must wait . . . thought Mr. Ferrier, gazing round the familiar room with unseeing eyes. . . . It is no good trying to . . . perhaps George . . . I must wait for George's explanation. . . .

Having reached this decision, Mr. Ferrier put the telegram into an envelope, sealed it carefully and addressed it to his son and, going into the hall, he hid it beneath two bills and a circular which had arrived for George by the afternoon post. It was now high time for him to join Paddy in the drawing-room, but he realised that it would be impossible for him to sit opposite to her for the whole evening with this appalling secret on his mind. She would discover that something was wrong, and before he knew where he was

364

he would have told her the whole thing.

Mr. Ferrier opened the drawing-room door and looked in and saw Paddy sitting on the window-seat reading a book. "My dear," he said, "I have done no work all day. I think if you will excuse me . . ."

"Why, of course, Quentin, darling," she replied, smiling at him across the room. "I shall go to bed early."

Mr. Ferrier shut the door and went away. He felt like a criminal of the deepest dye.

Paddy carried out her intention of going to bed early. She had been asleep for hours when she was suddenly awakened by a strange pattering sound upon the window-pane. She lay still and listened. She had been dreaming of the time when she was young, of the time before she met Quentin Ferrier and married him and left her own land to come and dwell in his. It had been quite a usual occurrence—in those far-off days—for Paddy to be awakened in the middle of the night by handfuls of gravel thrown against her window. Paddy's brothers were stirring young men and, on returning from nocturnal adventures of which their father might disapprove, they used this means to awaken Paddy and

365

gain entry to the house. Paddy was a light sleeper, so she always heard, and it was her practice to light a candle and go down to the little side door near the pantry and let her brothers in. Nobody knew how she dreaded these nightmare journeys through the big silent house—the banshees and witches hid behind the big old-fashioned furniture and tried to catch her bare legs as she scurried by. . . .

Paddy had been dreaming about this, but now she had awakened and, instead of awakening in the cold bare room in the old Irish house, she had awakened in her own comfortable English bedroom . . . and there was Quentin sleeping peacefully in the other bed. What a horrid dream, Paddy thought. It must have been the cheese soufflé. She snuggled down comfortably and pulled up the sheet, but even as she did so the pattering came again—and it was louder this time, much too loud to be rain, or even hail.

Paddy jumped out of bed and ran to the window and saw George standing below her in the garden. She saw him quite clearly in the light of the moon, and she saw his shadow, large and inky black, spread out upon the ground.

"Come down and let me in," he said. "I've rung the bell till I'm tired . . . thought you were all dead, or something."

Paddy put on her red flannel dressing-gown and crept downstairs. She shot back the bolts of the big front door and was immediately enveloped in a bear's hug. (Strangely enough, this was the way her brothers had always greeted her appearance, for they adored Paddy, and were a demonstrative family.) Paddy was still half-dazed with sleep, and for a moment she almost thought that this was Pat . . . and then she remembered that Pat had been killed on the Somme more than twenty years ago.

"Dear, darling Paddy!" George said. "It feels at least a month since I've seen you. I've had a ghastly day."

"We thought you were staying there," she told him breathlessly.

"Where? Oh, at Bournemouth. . . . I've been all over England since then. The car died on me near Marlowe—yes, Marlowe—I'll tell you about it later. They had to get a spare part and fix it up. It took hours. I don't know what they did, so you needn't ask me, but it seems to go all right now. Give me a horse every time," said George a little ungratefully. "You know where you are with a horse—only, of course, I couldn't have done a fraction of the mileage with a horse; but, then, *they* couldn't either, so it would work out much the same. I lost my way after that and wandered round the home counties like a lost soul——"

"Yes," said Paddy hopelessly. "But what does it all mean? And why in the Name of Fortune are we standing here in the cold? Come in and shut the door, darling," she added, pulling his arm. "Meredith can stay where he is till the morning."

"But I've got her there, you see," objected George, jerking his head towards the car. "She's fast asleep, poor little wretch, so I thought I'd tell you before I woke her and brought her in."

"For the love of Mike!" exclaimed Paddy. "Who have you got there, and how, and why?"

"I'd better fetch her in," George said in a decided sort of voice. "You'll get cold standing here in your dressing-gown. What a ticket you look!" he added tenderly, and he ruffled her hair, which was already standing straight on end.

"But, George—who?" she demanded, clinging to his arm.

"Elma, of course. You've got to be decent to her—decent but firm—and you've got to explain to her why she can't go tearing off for a weekend in town with any young fellow who happens to ask her."

"For the love of Mike!" cried Paddy again in despairing tones.

"Well, I can't," George declared, "and somebody must, so you'll have to do your best. I'll go and wake her up."

Elma was awakened and brought in. She was dazed with sleep and very subdued. George's mother was no grenadier, but there was something a little frightening about her and, although she spoke quite kindly and hospitably, Elma was aware that she was not particularly pleased at the advent of her unexpected guest. So Elma behaved with meekness and respect. (Miss Wilson would have been delighted if she could have seen her.) She drank a cup of hot milk and followed her hostess upstairs and helped to make up the spare room bed. Unfortunately, Miss Wilson had not considered that a sound knowledge of domestic arts was desirable for a young lady, and Elma had never made a bed in her life.

She did her best, of course, but she was more hindrance than help, and Paddy became somewhat annoyed with her handlessness.

"My goodness patience alive!" she exclaimed. "Can you not see it's crooked, the sheet? Pull it across and tuck it in. . . . No, not that way, the other side of it. . . ."

Elma pulled and tucked manfully, but to no good purpose.

"We'll *never* get it done at this rate," declared Mrs. Ferrier impatiently. She was boiling with curiosity. She was longing to get the girl settled for the night so that she could go downstairs and hear all about it from George. George *must* tell her the whole thing. She had tried to question the girl, but it was no use—nothing sensible could be got out of her. This was not really surprising, of course, for the girl was obviously a fool. And what (thought Paddy) could you expect from a pig but a grunt? She had been pretty sure that she would not like Elma Green, and she did not like her.

"Have you left your suitcase in the car?" she inquired when at last the bed was made.

"No," said Elma.

"Where is it?"

Elma did not know where it was and said so.

370

"In the Name of Fortune!" exclaimed Mrs. Ferrier irritably. "Did you not have a suitcase with your night things in it?"

"Yes," said Elma.

"Did you lose it, then?"

"Yes," said Elma thankfully. She had no wish to give an account of all her strange adventures to Mrs. Ferrier.

"You lost it!" cried Mrs. Ferrier in horror-stricken tones. "You mean you lost it out of the car!"

"No," said Elma.

"Where did you lose it?" demanded Mrs. Ferrier, and she stood and waited for an answer.

Elma struggled for a few moments and then decided that it was hopeless to begin to explain. "Perhaps if you asked George . . ." she suggested.

"H'm," said Mrs. Ferrier. She was confirmed in her suspicion that there was a mystery—and a somewhat peculiar mystery—attached to this sudden and totally unexpected arrival of Elma Green. She would ask George—most certainly she would ask George. George was crazy to think of marrying this girl—a helpless, hopeless idiot, if ever there was one.

371

Mrs. Ferrier fetched one of her own nightdresses for her guest and provided her with a brush and comb. "There," she said. "Now you can get into bed and go to sleep. You'll be quite comfortable, I hope." And with that hospitable valediction Mrs. Ferrier left her and went downstairs to find out what had happened.

"Oh, there you are, Paddy!" exclaimed George, looking up from the large plateful of veal and ham pie which he had commandeered from the larder.

"Yes, here I am," said Paddy. "You can tell me about it while you're eating."

"But are you quite sure she's all right?"

"All right?"

"You're sure she's really going to bed?" inquired George somewhat anxiously, for he had been at such pains to capture his ward that he almost felt as if he ought to mount guard at her door, or spend the night doing sentry duty beneath her window. He would have liked to chain her to the bedpost, of course, but that was clearly impossible.

Paddy put down his anxiety to solicitude for their guest's comfort, and her heart sank into her bedroom slippers.

"Am I sure she's going to bed!" exclaimed

Paddy in despair. "I've made the bed, George. Are you wanting me to undress the creature and put her into it?"

"It mightn't be a bad plan."

"I will not, then. I've given her a bed and a nightdress and all. She can get into them both and go to sleep. I'm nearly dead with curiosity. Will you *tell* me what it's all about?"

"In the morning——"

"It is the morning, and you'll tell me now," said Paddy firmly. "There's no sleep in me at all. . . . And what's this?" she added, picking up Miss Wilson's telegram, which was once more lying open on the dining-room table.

"Oh, that!" said George, with his mouth full of veal and ham. "Oh, well, you can see for yourself. It doesn't need explaining. I wired to Miss Wilson from Marlowe, and that's her reply. She's quite pleased for us to keep Elma."

Paddy saw for herself that Miss Wilson was delighted for them to keep Elma—and that was all she saw. Unlike her husband, she had received the simple explanation of the telegram before reading it.

"Is she going to stay here *long*?" Paddy inquired, and it was obvious to the meanest intelligence that she hoped for an answer in the negative.

"Well, that depends. . . ."

"Depends on what?"

"On lots of things," said George vaguely, and then he added, "I'd better tell you the whole story."

This was what Paddy wanted, of course, so she sat down beside him at the table and prepared to listen with all her ears, and George set to work and gave her a pretty full account of his adventures. He was aware that Elma had not made a good impression upon his mother, and he was anxious to present his ward in the most favourable light. For this reason he glossed over Elma's foolishness and tried to point out that she was more sinned against than sinning. She was so innocent and unworldly, declared George, trying to soften Paddy's heart, and she was really a dear little thing when you got to know her. Unfortunately, his championship of Elma, far from softening Paddy's heart, hardened it into granite, for Paddy misunderstood the situation completely. George is besotted with the creature, thought Paddy in dismay. George is besotted with her; and she's not only a fool, but a minx as well.

"You *will* help me with her, won't you?" George was saying, for this was his fondest hope. He had brought Elma to Swan House so that Paddy could take her in hand, kindly but firmly, and make her see sense.

"Help you with her!" echoed Paddy with a mulish expression upon her small face. "How would I help you with her, pray?"

"By talking to her and explaining things like I told you," replied George in desperation; but, even as he spoke, he was aware that his plan had miscarried. He knew Paddy so well that he could read her like a book: she had taken one of her unreasonable dislikes to Elma, and no power on earth would alter it.

They talked for a long time without getting any further, and parted in the small hours of the morning feeling more annoyed with each other than they had ever felt before.

"Paddy might try to help me," thought George as he crawled wearily into bed and blew out his candle. "Paddy must see that I couldn't do anything else except bring her here. . . . Paddy is so unreasonable. . . ."

At the very same moment Paddy—already snug in *her* bed—was thinking much the same thing about George. Who would ever have thought that George could be such a fool

(Paddy was thinking). It's a pretty face she has and nothing else at all . . . the mimsy, wimsy creature . . . she's no wife for George . . . he would be tired of her in a month. . . .

9

ELMA AT SWAN HOUSE

ELMA made no attempt to escape from
Swan House—the idea never entered her
mind. She seemed to take it for granted
that she was to remain at George's home
indefinitely. In some ways, she was a very
pleasant guest—amiable and accommodating
and decorative. Mr. Ferrier liked her; he was
so delighted to find that she was not an illegitimate grandchild that he started with a
distinct prejudice in her favour. He liked the
deferential manner in which she sat and
listened to his conversation, and he liked the
way she spoke, and, perhaps most of all, he
liked to look at her—Elma was extremely
pleasant to look at.

He was delighted with his new guest and
with the discovery that the telegram, which
had worried him so much, had such a simple
and satisfactory explanation, but there was
still one matter troubling his peace of mind—
it was the matter of the twenty thousand

pounds. Mr. Ferrier felt that he could neither work nor rest peacefully in his bed until he knew for certain whether "Dusty" had appropriated the money and, if so, whether George could be held responsible for it. The first thing to do was to take legal advice, thought Mr. Ferrier, so he persuaded George to write a full account of all that had happened, to Mr. Crane. George suggested that they should ring up Mr. Crane and tell him about it (for George disliked the labour of writing letters, and preferred the spoken to the written word), but Mr. Ferrier would not hear of this. He pointed out that they could set out their case more clearly on paper, and that when Mr. Crane had all the facts before him he could consider the matter at his leisure.

It was a joint letter, on the same lines as the letter they had written to Mr. Millar, but much longer, of course, because there was so much to explain. Its composition took Mr. Ferrier and George a whole morning, and it was exceedingly hard work. They started from George's meeting with Mr. Green and worked conscientiously through the whole story. The letter was like a young novel when at last it was done.

"My goodness!" said George with a sigh as he collected the sheets and pinned them together. "My goodness, what a time he'll have reading it! What will he charge, I wonder?"

"He will charge the correct fee," replied Mr. Ferrier, "and we shall know exactly where we stand. You had better go out and post it at once, George."

"Where's the hurry?"

"This is Thursday. He will get it tomorrow, and we shall have his answer on Saturday," replied Mr. Ferrier, with sublime confidence in the rapidity and efficiency of His Majesty's Mail.

"But there's no need to worry," George pointed out. "Old Millar won't run away."

Mr. Ferrier smiled. He reflected that the slang of the present-day youth was extremely crude. "I was not anticipating anything of that nature," he replied; "but the fact is, I shall be more comfortable in my mind when we have obtained a legal opinion."

During the writing of the letter Elma had been sent out into the garden to amuse herself as best she could. She had plenty of time to explore it thoroughly. She walked down the path and looked at the flowers and she walked down to the paddock and looked at the horses. It crossed her mind that Swan House was very dull and quiet compared with Bournemouth; but, to tell the truth, that short episode had been so short and so highly coloured and so completely different from the rest of Elma's life that she could scarcely believe it was real. It had seemed like a dream at the time, and, now that it was past, it seemed more than ever like a dream, and it was fading from her mind as dreams will.

Elma sighed and returned to the garden and walked up and down, and presently, when Mrs. Ferrier came out to cut some roses, Elma hid in the greenhouse so that her hostess should not see her.

Unfortunately, Mrs. Ferrier kept her garden scissors in the greenhouse, so she came straight down the garden and opened the door and found her unwelcome guest crouching on the floor. "What *are* you doing?" she inquired a trifle irritably, for it seemed absurd that, with the whole garden and the paddock at her disposal, Elma should choose to lurk in the greenhouse and frighten her out of her wits. "What *are* you doing?" she repeated with increased irritation.

380

"Nothing," Elma said.

"Why don't you go down to the paddock and look at the horses?"

"I did."

"Well, do it again," said Mrs. Ferrier firmly.

This little encounter did not help them to understand each other any better, and Elma was confirmed in her conviction that she liked gentlemen better than ladies. They were more reasonable, she thought.

Two days passed. They were uncomfortable days and, to everybody at Swan House, they seemed to contain more than the average number of hours. It was Paddy's fault, of course, for Paddy was miserable, and when Paddy was miserable she made no attempt to hide the fact. She went about her daily business with the mournful air of a woman who has buried her best friend, and her manner to her guest was as chilly as an iceberg.

George bore it as long as he could, but at last he decided that something must be done. He pursued Paddy to the lamp-room and tried to reason with her, rushing in where angels would have feared to tread.

"I say," he began, with an assumption of carelessness which would not have deceived an imbecile. "I say, Paddy, it's about Elma. I think she's feeling a bit dull, you know."

"I wouldn't be surprised," declared Paddy.

"She can't *help* being here," George pointed out. "I mean, there's nowhere else for her to go."

Paddy did not reply to this. She took up her shammy and began to polish a lamp with tremendous vigour.

"Don't you think you could—er—talk to her a bit . . . make jokes, and that?" inquired the poor fool ingratiatingly.

"Make jokes, is it?" exclaimed Paddy in well-affected amazement. "The creature wouldn't understand my kind of jokes——"

"You might try her."

"—and, what's more, I couldn't make jokes to order if you paid me."

"If you could just be a bit more matey . . ." said George, blundering further. "I mean—well—I can't think why you've taken such a dislike to her. Dad likes her quite a lot——"

"Dislike to her!" exclaimed Paddy. "For the love of Mike! Who said I had taken a dislike to her? Herself, I suppose."

"No, no," declared George, hastily and untruthfully and without much conviction.

"No, no, of course not. Elma wouldn't—I only meant—I mean you——"

"Am I not polite to the girl?" inquired Paddy, turning upon George and assuming the offensive.

"Oh, yes, of course," babbled George. "Of course you are. I didn't mean—I mean that's just it. You're far too polite."

"Too polite, indeed! How could I be 'too polite' to a guest?"

It was useless to pursue the matter further, and George retired from the field of battle with the conviction that he had done more harm than good. The worst of it was, he could see no prospect of relief from the strain, for Miss Wilson's indisposition had developed into a severe attack of jaundice and she was laid up at the Kenilworth Castle Hotel with a doctor in attendance. Frantic letters of apology arrived from her by nearly every post, and George had already spent a small fortune in soothing telegrams. Miss Wilson was likely to be *hors de combat* for some time, and Elma could not return to Highmoor House alone. Where else could she go?

George approached his father on the subject, but Mr. Ferrier had started work again (he had ample confidence in Mr. Crane's ability to solve his problem), and there was no help to be got from him.

"Paddy will come round," said Mr. Ferrier vaguely, and he added, "Shut the door when you go out, George."

On the second day Elma's trunks arrived from Bournemouth full of the enchanting "raiment" which she had bought under Pauline Millar's supervision, and to Mr. Ferrier's delight and Mrs. Ferrier's dismay, she became more decorative than ever. Elma obtained a good deal of pleasure from wearing her lovely clothes, but she was not really happy at Swan House, for she had too much time on her hands, and she was not accustomed to filling in her own leisure. Miss Wilson had ordered her days according to a time-table compared with which the Laws of the Medes and Persians were loose and variable: so many hours of each day were devoted to study, so many hours to exercise, and so many to needlework. Of course, it had been different at Bournemouth—the trouble there had been to choose between all the different delightful employments and the delightful young men who clamoured for her company.

There had been too much to do at Bournemouth, and there was too little to do here. Fate was exceedingly capricious, in Elma's opinion, but the idea of rebellion never entered her mind. George had brought her here, and here she must stay until she was taken somewhere else. The cold politeness with which her hostess treated her did not trouble her greatly, for (when she thought about it at all) she thought that cold politeness was Mrs. Ferrier's natural manner. "My mother will deal with you," George had said, and Elma had shaken in her shoes at the threat. She not unnaturally supposed that Mrs. Ferrier was dealing with her faithfully. Elma avoided Mrs. Ferrier as much as possible and frequented the society of George; in fact, she attached herself to him and accompanied him wherever he went, and George bore it as patiently as he could, because he was sorry for her and because he realised that there was nothing else for her to do. It was a vicious circle: Mrs. Ferrier was cold, so Elma attached herself to George, so George was kind to her, so Mrs. Ferrier became colder and more polite, so Elma attached herself to George more firmly . . . and the atmosphere at Swan House was about as cheerful and

385

peaceful as the atmosphere of a Russian play. The only person who was unaware of tension and strain was Elma herself; she followed George everywhere he went, prattling like a three-year-old babe.

10

THE MYSTERIOUS SECRET

WHEN Friday came, George—despite his good intentions—had almost reached the end of his patience. Elma accompanied him to the stables in the morning and watched him groom the horses and feed them. She showed no desire to help him; and, indeed, her clothes were so obviously unsuitable for stablework that George did not suggest it. He spent his time telling her to "Look out!" or to "Stand back!" or, warningly, "Don't lean against that dirty bin," and Elma obeyed these commands with admirable meekness.

She was so meek that George's heart ought to have warmed to her, but strangely enough he found her meekness annoying. He wanted to shake her till her teeth chattered in her head. How on earth could he ever have imagined himself in love with the silly little ass? She was very pretty, of course—prettier than ever in her dainty new frocks—and she was really very sweet and innocent and good. . . . But, oh, how she bored him!

. . . And what *is* to be done with her? George wondered, as he curry-combed the sleek withers of his favourite mare. What on earth is to become of her—*eventually*! It was a problem which troubled George a good deal, and troubled him increasingly as the days went by. Miss Wilson would recover, of course, and presumably she and Elma would return to Highmoor House and their daily round, but somehow or other he had a feeling that Elma would never settle down again into the narrow groove. She had tasted Life (with a capital L) and had obviously found it good.

George had tried to sound his ward on the subject of her future, but without much success, and he had a secret and most disquieting conviction that Elma envisaged a future of married bliss, and that she had chosen him for her partner in the enterprise. He had tried to impress upon her as tactfully as possible (in the course of casual conversation) that trustees were as a race apart, their almost sacred duties debarring them from matrimonial entanglements, but he was doubtful whether Elma had taken the point.

After lunch, George escaped from his guest

(it required a good deal of guile, but he managed to give her the slip) and fled upstairs to his study and shut the door. He stood there for a few moments panting with relief, and then he flung himself into a basket chair and gazed round the room. Its familiarity was soothing; it's solitude was balm. He remembered that Peter had commented on the fact that it was "peaceful here." Peter's right, he thought. You simply have to get away from people sometimes. You have to relax.

George relaxed. He found it extraordinarily pleasant. His head fell back against the well-known cushions and his fingers trailed on the floor. He raised his legs and propped his feet upon the table. . . . Bliss. . . .

Five minutes passed and George—if the truth be told—was very nearly asleep, when the door opened and Elma peeped in.

"Oh, there you are!" she said, and she smiled at him a trifle timidly.

"Er—yes," said George, removing his feet from the table. "Er—yes. Here I am."

"I wondered where you had gone," she continued, coming in and shutting the door. "I looked everywhere for you."

"Did you?"

"Yes, I looked all round the garden and the

stables. I might have known you would be here. It is such a nice room, isn't it?"

"Yes," said George.

"I like it immensely," said Elma, looking round with a cheerful air. "It seems so far away from the rest of the house . . . and it is so high up. I like the way one can see for miles over the tops of the trees. I wish I had a room like this at home. Do you think I could build one?"

"Build one!" echoed George in surprise.

Elma nodded. "On the top of the house," she explained. "A room just like this that would be my very own."

"No," said George. "It would cost hundreds——"

"But that would not matter," Elma pointed out. "I am very rich, you see."

"You've discovered that, have you?"

"Yes," replied Elma complacently. "I think it is very pleasant to be rich, because one can do as one likes. I intend to buy a new car and to build a room like this. I also intend to buy a new car for Mrs. Ferrier."

George sat up in his chair. "You can't do that!" he cried in alarm. "Here, I say, Elma, you don't understand——"

"Her car is exceedingly shabby and uncomfortable," Elma pointed out, "and I feel that she requires a new one. I shall buy one for her at the first opportunity and she will be grateful to me."

"But, Elma——"

"I wish to be friends with Mrs. Ferrier," added Elma thoughtfully.

George was thunderstruck. "You can't!" he declared. "My goodness, you don't understand *anything*. Paddy wouldn't accept a car from you . . . she'd be furious if you suggested giving her one. Of course, it's very kind of you to think of it," he added, as he saw Elma's downcast expression, "very kind, indeed, but Paddy *likes* Granpa. She wouldn't part with the old thing for worlds."

Elma considered the matter. "Then I shall give her something else," she declared.

"You won't give her anything," said George firmly.

"But I want——"

"I know, but you don't understand. You can't go about giving people things—they don't like it."

Elma sighed and abandoned the project. It seemed queer to think that people did not like receiving useful presents; but she accepted George's word.

"Are we going to sit here all the afternoon?" she inquired, taking up her position on the window-seat, and then, as George did not reply, she added, "I think it would be very pleasant. It is extremely warm in the garden."

"Look here," exclaimed George in desperation. "Look here, Elma. I'm awfully sorry and all that, but couldn't you find something to do?"

"Something to *do*!" she echoed in surprise.

"Yes, something to *do*," repeated George firmly. "I've got a lot of things to do—I mean—er—I'm going to—er—to be very busy, you know."

"I will sit here with you," Elma said.

"No," said George. "No, Elma. I simply couldn't work with you here—and I've got to work, you see."

"But I will be very quiet indeed."

"No," said George again. "The fact is—er—well, you see, it's a bit worrying having somebody following me round all the time. You find something to do, there's a good girl."

Her eyes filled with tears. "You do not want me," she said rather pitifully. "Nobody wants me here. Mrs. Ferrier does not like me at all."

"What nonsense!" cried George. "What absolute rubbish! Of course Paddy likes you—we all like you. It's just that I'm going to be very busy this afternoon."

"I am so glad *you* like me," said Elma with an April smile. "I like you, too—very much. I like you better than Wilfred Millar and——"

"I know," George interrupted hastily. Elma had already made this preference too plain. "I know all that. We like each other tremendously and we're friends. We decided that ages ago."

"Yes," said Elma doubtfully.

"And, of course, I'm your trustee."

"I think it would be much nicer if you were not my trustee."

"Well, I am," said George in a firm and final manner.

There was a short silence and then Elma sighed. "You're so brave," she said softly.

George pretended not to hear. He had heard quite enough from Elma on the subject of his encounter with Wilfred Millar, and he was fully aware of her views on the subject. He had tried his best to persuade her that he had just "pushed the fellow gently" and that the orange tub had accomplished Wilfred's downfall; but Elma did not believe that. Elma

393

preferred to think that George had fought for her with the strength and ferocity of a lion. She would have liked to see them fight, of course, and George could imagine her standing by, holding their coats and urging them on with screams of excitement. It was very strange and it just showed how little her father had understood her when he had spoken of her as being "like a flower" and "easily shocked and frightened." Elma *looked* like a flower, of course, but in reality she was hard-boiled and bloodthirsty; she belonged to the period when men were *men* and swaggered about the world with feathers in their caps, when they enjoyed cock-fighting and bull-baiting and repaid an insult with a hastily drawn sword. Elma was an anachronism, and George had told her so. All this George knew, and Elma knew that he knew it, and the simple statement, "You are so brave," had meant all this—and more.

"Look here," said George. "I'll give you a book to read—a modern book that will teach you about the modern world. It's no good filling up your mind with Sir Walter Scott and—and all that. Things are different now. You've got to live in Today, so you had better learn about it."

"Yes," said Elma meekly.

George looked at his shelves and selected a couple of "Peter Wimsey" books. They were his own favourites and, as far as he could remember, they contained nothing which could bring a blush to the cheek of the most innocent maiden on earth. "You take these," he said. "They're all about a fellow called Peter Wimsey. You read them carefully and you'll see what's what. He's a modern sort of chap, you know—not like Pendennis."

"I like Pendennis," Elma declared. "I think you resemble Pendennis. I thought so from the very——"

"Oh, no, I don't. And I don't resemble Peter Wimsey, either," said George hastily. "It's just your imagination. You mustn't imagine things like that."

"But I like imagining things."

"You imagine far too much," said George quite sternly.

"But I can't help it."

"Well, you must try. Now, you take these books and find some nice sheltered place in the garden and settle down. You can read till tea-time."

Elma took the books reluctantly. She was not very fond of reading, and she would much rather have spent the afternoon with George. She hesitated and smiled at him wheedlingly. "Couldn't I stay here?" she asked. "I would be very quiet."

"No," said George. "No, I'm afraid not. I'm going to be *very* busy, indeed."

Having got rid of Elma for a couple of hours, George lay back in his chair and sighed. He had intended to devote the afternoon to the practise of magic, for tomorrow was Saturday (the day of Dan's party), but somehow or other the desire to practise magic had left him—he was not in the mood for it at all. What he really wanted was a little chat with Paddy, one of their nice friendly chats.

George sighed. I wonder if it would be any good, he thought. I wonder if I could wheedle her into a proper friendly chat. . . . Perhaps if I didn't mention Elma at all, but just began talking about something else . . .

George sighed again, more deeply than before; it was simply unbearable to be at odds with Paddy, it took every bit of pleasure out of life. He was aware, of course, that the rift was not his fault—what else could he have done but bring Elma here?—but that did not make things easier. Paddy was miserable, and he was miserable—it was simply unbearable.

He rose and put away his conjuring effects which were scattered about on the table and went downstairs to look for Paddy. He looked for her all over the house, but she was not there, and then he looked in the rose-garden, but she was not there either. Finally he went out on to the terrace and looked down on to the tennis court, and there she was, sitting on the seat near the shrubbery, and Cathy was there too. George smiled when he saw them, for they were such a funny pair, and they were talking so earnestly—Paddy waving her hands, as she did when she was excited, and Cathy nodding her head. He might have known that Cathy would be here, for she always walked over from Rival's Green on a Friday afternoon with a basket of eggs for the Ferrier household.

George watched them for a few moments and then he was seized with a mischievous idea: he would steal up behind them through the shrubbery and bounce out on them and make them laugh, and then, when they had finished laughing, he would sit down beside them and they would have one of their good old talks, the three of them together—all friends—and Paddy would be happy and comforted, and the clouds would disappear.

George made a circuit and came up through the shrubbery. It was years since he had used that path, but he had not forgotten it. He had played here when he was a child, hunting Red Indians and bears, or exploring the jungles of the Amazon. The path had been disused for so long that it was now hardly a path at all. The rhododendrons had spread their branches until they met, and the gravel was embedded in moss. George pushed on manfully, however, and he had almost reached his objective when Cathy's voice halted him in his tracks:

"But George must never know!" she cried. "Never—never—you promised me—you promised me!"

There was such agony in the tones that the listener was appalled. He turned and blundered back through the bushes with feverish haste—his one idea to be out of earshot before any more was said—and it was not until he reached the other side of the shrubbery and emerged into the light of day that he stopped to consider the meaning of what he had heard. The incident, though trivial in some ways, was not trivial to George. He was both shocked and hurt to discover that these two friends of his—so old and tried—had some tremendous secret from which he was excluded. He knew them both so well and he had believed them to be transparent as mirrors, yet here they were with some deep secret, sharing it and guarding it—a secret that he was never to know. "Never, never!" Cathy had cried. He had approached them with confidence, and with his heart full of friendliness and affection, and this had made the shock a good deal worse. George felt shut out from them and wounded to the core. "It's some silly woman-secret," he told himself; but even as he said it he knew that it was not, for he could still hear Cathy's anguished tones ringing in his ears: "But George must never know—never, never—you promised me."

At first George was hurt, and then he was angry, but after a little his natural curiosity awoke and he racked his brains to think what on earth it could be—this secret which was to be guarded from him at all costs. He thought of all sorts of explanations, but nothing that he thought of would fit, and he remained unsatisfied. He realised, of course, that it was his own fault—he should not have tried to play such a silly childish trick—and, indeed, now that he thought about it, he wondered at himself; for the mischievous, light-hearted spirit in which he had conceived his plan had vanished and the whole thing seemed incredibly foolish.

Meanwhile, Paddy and Cathy were continuing their conversation, quite unaware that any part of it had been overheard:

"You see why, don't you?" Cathy was saying in slightly calmer tones. "You see why it's so important that George must never know? George is so *kind*, you see. He's so kind that it's almost a fault. Look at how kind he is to Dan."

"You mean the party tomorrow?"

"Yes, and he's promised to go to the school concert on the twenty-fourth. It will be a frightful affair, and George knows that as well as I do."

Paddy was too much worried to think about school concerts. "I believe you're right," she said thoughtfully. "I believe George *is* too kind. That's the trouble."

"He can't bear to see anyone unhappy," Cathy pointed out. "He just *has* to do something for them."

"Yes," said Paddy. She was silent for a moment or two, and then she went on, "That's what's so dangerous. The fact is, George ought to be shut up; he's not fit to be loose . . . all those young women languishing at him . . . and George too kind . . . dangerous."

"Yes, dangerous," Cathy agreed. (She was fully aware that Mrs. Ferrier's reference to "all those young women" who were languishing at George was merely a fashion of speech, and that one young woman only was dangerous, in Mrs. Ferrier's eyes.) "But you mustn't say a word," Cathy declared, bending forward a little and scraping a hole in the gravel with Paddy's stick. "You won't, will you? You've promised, haven't you?"

"Yes," said Paddy reluctantly. "Yes, I've promised."

Cathy patted her knee. "You know what I feel," she said. "I can't say it properly, but it's *dear* of you to—to want—to want—well, you know what I mean——"

"It's not dear of me, it's selfish," Mrs. Ferrier declared. "George is as blind as a bat, I could shake the creature . . . and you know as well as I do that I want what I want because I really do want it," she added with firmness and conviction.

"I know," said Cathy gently, "but you won't say anything, will you?" And then she raised her pointed chin in the air and added defiantly, "If he asks me—and I don't suppose he ever will—it must be because he can't do without me, and not because he's sorry for me or because he thinks I can't do without him."

There was another little silence, and then Paddy sighed. "Of course I see that," she admitted. "I see the sense of it, darling, but it's hard to sit back and watch your only child rushing to destruction. . . . I could strangle that Elma creature with pleasure."

"Fierce woman," said Cathy, smiling.

"There she is," continued Mrs. Ferrier, pointing to her guest, who was wandering across the tennis court with the "Peter Wimsey" books under her arm. "There she goes, looking as if butter wouldn't melt in her mouth, and all the time she's after George like a—like a vampire. She hangs on his arm and gazes up into his face. I declare the man isn't born who could resist her!"

Cathy shivered a little. "But I think you're wrong about her," she said. "I think she really—likes George. She's childish and innocent, I think."

Mrs. Ferrier snorted. "Do you?" she inquired. "Well, you may be right, but it comes to the same thing in the end: I don't want a moron for a daughter-in-law."

11

DAN'S PARTY

LIKE many another host or hostess, George discovered that a party has the same strange capacity to grow and develop as a jungle plant. He had intended to have Dan and perhaps three of her friends to tea in the garden, to play tennis with them, to show them his conjuring tricks and then to take them home in the car. Dan understood this perfectly, of course. She invited three friends and then fell out with two of them and invited two others. Then she made it up with the first two and found that her party had grown to five. By this time the news of the party had spread all over the school, and girls who had never before shown the slightest interest in Dan proceeded to woo her with acid drops and chocolate bars. The situation was difficult, and Dan could not deal with it, so she telephoned to George and pointed out that "several other people wanted to come," and George told her to "go ahead."

Dan went ahead joyously, and soon she had no idea how many girls she had invited to spend the afternoon at Swan House.

"I think there will be twenty," she declared, when Paddy rang her up to inquire how many guests there would be. "I *think* there will be twenty, but I'm not sure. There may be more, of course. You see, Elaine asked me if she could bring her cousin, and I didn't like to say no."

The explanation seemed inadequate to account for the growth of the party, but Paddy accepted it nobly. "Of course, you couldn't," she agreed, trying to make her voice sound pleased and hospitable. "You couldn't say no to the creature. And why should you? It was just that I wanted the numbers for the ice-cream."

"Ice-cream!" said Dan. "Oo, how lovely!"

"Have you counted in your family?" asked Paddy, still struggling manfully with numbers.

"Cathy's coming," said Dan. "I haven't asked the others. George said I could ask who I liked."

"Hadn't you better——?"

"No," said Dan firmly. "They're beastly to me, so now I'm being beastly to them—it isn't often I have the chance. The twins are

405

fed-up to the back teeth, but they're pretending not to be. They'll be more fed-up than ever when I tell them about the ice-cream."

Paddy was rather taken aback by these un-Christian sentiments, but she felt unable to cope with them over the telephone. She hung up the receiver and added Cathy's name to her list with a feeling of relief. Cathy could be relied on to be pleasant and kind and helpful.

So much for Dan & Co., but the party had grown in other directions also. There was Elma, and, although Elma was but a single person, she bulked largely in George's mind, for he could not conceive how Elma would fit in with Dan's schoolgirl friends; she might be an asset or she might be a liability—you could never tell with Elma. . . . and then there was Harry Coles. George had asked Harry because he thought Harry would enhance the value of the party and give it tone. Two men for tennis was almost essential, and Harry—having had the advantage of spending five years at Harrow—would presumably appear in an O.H. blazer. Harry was fair and blue eyed and extremely good-looking, and George could not help feeling that Harry was a much superior answer to a maiden's prayer than he was himself. Harry had been asked at the very beginning, when the party was first mooted, and he had accepted in spite of the warnings with which the invitation was accompanied. "Of course I'll come and help," he had declared. Then, the day before the party, he had rung up and asked if he could bring Clarice Morton, who was staying with the Coles for the weekend.

"Clarice!" George had cried in dismay. "But look here, Harry, I say. . . ." and he had said a good deal, for Clarice was the last person George wanted; but his repeated warnings that it was a "children's party," and that it would be a "frightful show," fell on deaf ears, and Clarice was coming. George hung up the receiver in the dazed manner of a person who has been dealt a mortal blow: the party had got completely beyond him, he had no control over it any more. Having thus resigned himself, he was able to bear the further blows of fate with equanimity, and this was fortunate, for on the Saturday morning Paddy let fall the information that she had asked Mrs. Snipe to come over from Wandlebury, and that she was bringing three children whose parents were in India.

"Poor little pets!" said Paddy. "They'll enjoy the fun of the party."

"If there *is* any fun," said George doubtfully.

"Party!" inquired Mr. Ferrier, suddenly waking from a trance. "What party is this?" And then, before his question could be answered, he added, "By the way, Liston ffoulkes is coming over this afternoon. He has been asked to read a paper before the Royal Geographical Society, and I have promised to give him my latest observations on the spots of Jupiter, by which—as you are no doubt aware—the revolutions of that planet upon its axis are calculated. He is bringing his wife and daughter with him, so perhaps you would be good enough to entertain them for me. Liston ffoulkes and I will be occupied. I trust this will cause you no inconvenience?"

Paddy screamed with horror. "That woman!" she said. "How d'you think I'm going to entertain that lackadaisical woman— and the whole place crawling with children?"

"Dear me!" said Mr. Ferrier in dismay. "Dear me, I had no idea . . . I am extremely sorry, Paddy, but I fear it is impossible to alter the arrangement. . . ."

"Let 'em all come!" George said. "What does it matter? We'll make her play kiss in the ring with the children."

Fortunately for the Ferriers, the drought was still unbroken, and it was a beautifully bright sunny afternoon when the guests began to arrive. The party, which had grown and spread like a jungle plant, now began to resemble a tidal sea full of cross-currents and whirlpools. George felt like a swimmer struggling to reach the shore and never succeeding in his attempt. He was swept hither and thither and battered by the waves; he was caught in eddies and could not escape. There was Clarice, for instance—Clarice arrived clad in suitable apparel for a sunny day at Ascot, in pink chiffon accordion pleats and a pink picture hat. She expected a good deal of attention from George, and he could not really blame her, for he had encouraged her a good deal during that ten days in town. Clarice was completely out of her element at the party; she clung to George pertinaciously, for she was the kind of person who must have someone to cling to, and George was her only hope. Elma clung to him, too, because she was literally terrified of the schoolgirls. Dan's friends were certainly very overpowering; they were large and bulky and amazingly clumsy. They rushed about all over the house and grounds, playing some strange modern version of hide-and-seek, and they became so excited that their eyes blazed with the light of battle and their faces shone like tomatoes. (There were "only thirty" of them—or so it appeared—but to George it seemed that there must be double that number.) He did not blame Clarice and Elma for their alarm, nor for their dependence upon him, but he did blame them for their manifest hatred of each other—it made things so much more difficult.

Miss Liston ffoulkes was another trial to George. She was dressed in mannish tweeds, for she had not expected to find herself plunged into a party. She strolled about on the terrace and, whenever George passed, she waylaid him and described the games which she played with her Girl Guides—described them at great length and with a wealth of detail. She was anxious for George to marshal his young guests and to induce them to play these games which were "so much more sensible than rushing about aimlessly in this heat." George agreed with her in principle, of course, but it was quite impossible to marshal his guests, for they were scattered far and wide over the house and grounds, and it seemed to him that if they were enjoying themselves, it was better to let well alone and to allow them to enjoy themselves in their own way.

Mrs. Snipe and the three children whose parents were in India had retired beneath the shade of a tree and were playing independently of the rest of the party. George was aware that something should be done about this, but he could think of nothing to do. The children were too small to join in the general saturnalia, and they seemed quite happy in their own way. Paddy was trying to entertain Mrs. Liston ffoulkes, and not succeeding very well (he could see that by Paddy's pleading expression as he passed). Mr. Ferrier and Mr. Liston ffoulkes had retired to the former's study and locked the door. They had found this somewhat drastic measure necessary to preserve their privacy from the hordes of young women who were hiding or seeking all over the house. Harry Coles had given the party one horrified glance and fled for his life. It was discovered later that he had sought sanctuary in George's study and had spent most of the afternoon reading *Gaudy Night*.

Of all the people to whom George had looked for help, Cathy was the only one who really tried to fulfil her obligations, and even Cathy seemed different today, and not so

411

comfortable as usual. This was not entirely Cathy's fault, of course, for George found himself unable to speak to her, or even to meet her eyes with his usual frank cameraderie. He could not help remembering—every time he looked at her—that she and Paddy shared a mysterious and alarming secret which he must never know.

Everybody was supposed to be taking part in the game of hide-and-seek, but it was not ordinary hide-and-seek, and George never really mastered the rules; and, in any case, it was impossible for him to hide efficiently with Clarice, attired in pink chiffon, and Elma, attired in blue muslin, sticking to him like leeches the whole time. For one thing, their brilliant colour scheme was visible a mile away, and, for another, Clarice could not be expected to hide behind a water butt in the stableyard, nor even behind a holly bush in the garden.

George wandered about, visiting the various little groups and trying to diffuse an atmosphere of hospitality and cheer—and Clarice and Elma trailed after him. Large overheated schoolgirls lurked in the bushes and bounded out upon them, shrieking, "You're my prisoner, now! You're *it*, Mr.

Ferrier!" But, although he was caught every time, George never actually became "it," because it was obvious to the meanest intelligence that his two companions would not be parted from him.

The fat girl (whom George had seen before when he was waiting for Dan at the school gates) was a brilliant exponent of the game. She seemed to be everywhere at once, and George began to wonder whether the fat girl could possibly be twins—or even triplets. Dan was also very much in evidence; she was enjoying herself thoroughly, for she had all the honour and glory of a hostess without any of the responsibility. At first she ran about with tremendous energy and shrieked herself hoarse, but after about an hour of continuous exercise she began to feel tired. Dan was not built on the Atalanta pattern, and the afternoon was warm. She decided that she had had enough running about and that she was hot and hungry. Fortunately, when this idea occurred to her, she was in the kitchen garden. There was no fruit yet, of course, but there was a whole line of peas. Dan filled her hat with the pale green pods and retired into the raspberry canes to eat them at her leisure. She was rather surprised to find that she was not the only person who had evolved this brilliant plan. Mary Byrd was there before her, sitting with her back against a stake, and, all round her, the ground was strewn with empty pea-pods.

"Hallo," said Dan a trifle shyly.

"Hallo," said Mary Byrd, and then she added anxiously, "They won't mind, will they?"

"I shouldn't think so," replied Dan. "Why should they mind? Besides, they'll never know."

"It's too hot," Mary explained.

Dan agreed that it was. She thought for a few moments and then she said, "Look here, I'll tell you what: we'll go up to the loft in the old part of the stables. Nobody'll find us there."

Mary agreed at once. They picked a few more peas to take with them, and then Dan led the way to the stables.

Fortunately, there was nobody about, so they were able to reach their objective without being seen, and they managed the ascent of a very rickety ladder which had lost most of its rungs. They crawled through an open trap-door and found themselves in the old loft which had not been used for years. The loft

414

was empty, except for a rope, which had once been used on a pulley for taking in hay, and a pile of empty sacks in the corner. There were cobwebs everywhere, and shafts of bright sunlight fell like spears through the holes in the roof.

"What a gorgeous place!" exclaimed Mary Byrd.

Perhaps it may be thought that gorgeous was a strange adjective to apply to a very dirty and dilapidated old loft, but it was the word of the moment, and Dan and her friends applied it to everything that gave them pleasure.

"Yes, isn't it *gorgeous*," said Dan, and she sank down on to the dirty floor with a sigh of pure bliss. The party was gorgeous, of course, but this was the most gorgeous moment of all—it was quite too incredibly gorgeous for words.

Mary Byrd was the idol of Dan's young heart. Mary Byrd had "everything." She was pretty and popular and good at games, and she had a lovely home and gave "gorgeous" parties, and now here she was alone with Dan in the old loft and obviously delighted to be here. . . .

Mary sat down, too, and they began to talk in low voices about all sorts of things—about all the funny little happenings at the school, and about the mistresses and the other girls. Their heads were very close together and they giggled a good deal, and as they talked they kept on splitting the pea-pods and eating their contents. (They must have eaten several pounds of peas between them, but it did them no harm at all—nor did it prevent them from enjoying a thoroughly sound meal when tea-time came.)

Presently they heard voices and they peeped out of the window and saw George and Clarice and Elma standing in the yard below.

"I'm afraid I'm just letting them rip," George was saying. "They're just falling down. You see, we've plenty of room for the horses in the other part of the stables."

"Why don't you pull them down and build a swimming pool?" inquired Clarice in her languid and somewhat high-pitched voice.

"Because I'm not a millionaire," replied George shortly.

Mary nudged Dan. "Aren't they silly?" she whispered. "Those two girls, I mean. Can't they see he's fed-up with them?"

"Is he?" Dan asked eagerly. She was

delighted to think that George was bored with his companions.

"Why, of course he is. Let's play a trick on them, shall we? Let's make him come up the ladder." Mary did not wait for Dan's consent to her plan. She stretched out her hand and loosened a piece of glass from the broken window-frame and threw it down into the stone-paved yard, where it splintered into a hundred fragments at George's feet.

"Good Lord!" cried George, jumping back.

Clarice and Elma screamed in unison and ran to the other end of the yard.

"What on earth——?" began George. "Who on earth—I say, is anybody up there?"

There was silence. The two conspirators crouched down on the floor, smothering their giggles in their pocket handkerchiefs.

George called out again several times, but there was no reply.

"That's funny!" he said, and then he reacted to the incident in the exact manner foreseen by Mary Byrd: he began to walk across the yard to the stable door.

"Where are you going?" inquired Clarice, following him.

"There must be somebody up there," he

replied. "I'll just go up and have a look——"

"No," cried Clarice and Elma with one voice.

"But I must find out who it is."

"It's a cat, that's all," Clarice declared.

"It's burglars!" cried Elma, clinging to his arm.

"It's probably a tramp," said George. "Tramps often find their way into that old loft—they camp there, you know, and we can't have that, because they might set the place on fire."

His companions were extremely unwilling to let him out of their sight, but he shook them off and dived into the stable and began to climb the rickety ladder without more ado.

Clarice and Elma had followed him into the stable, but they could follow him no farther. They waited down below and watched him disappear through the square trap-door in the roof. . . .

There were queer scuffling sounds and then peals of laughter.

"George, what is it?" cried Clarice.

Elma was speechless with anxiety.

The sounds died away and all was quiet. They waited for some moments and then

418

Clarice called out again, "George, what's happened? Come down, George!"

There was no reply.

"They have killed him!" cried Elma, wringing her hands.

At this moment two round rosy faces appeared in the square opening and looked down at them. The faces were wreathed in smiles.

"It's those idiotic children!" Clarice exclaimed.

"Yes, it's us," said Mary Byrd sweetly, "and it's no good calling him, because he's our prisoner. Are you coming up to rescue him?"

"How can I?" inquired Clarice, looking at the crazy ladder in horror.

"It's quite easy, really."

"Don't be silly. Mr. Ferrier was showing us the stables. Tell him to come down."

"We aren't silly," cried Dan indignantly. "It's the game. You have to take people prisoners, and then their friends come and rescue them."

"We aren't playing the game," Clarice declared.

Mary Byrd giggled. "You don't know how to play the game, do you?" she said with a *double entendre* which was completely lost upon her victim."

"No, and I don't want to know."

There was a short silence and then Clarice raised her voice. "George!" she cried. "Do stop this nonsense and come down."

"I can't come down," replied George in stentorian tones.

"No, he can't," declared Dan, chuckling delightedly. "That's just the joke. We've tied him up, you see."

"You've tied him up!"

"With a rope," explained Dan.

Clarice was exceedingly angry. She was angry not only with these idiotic children, but also with George. George could easily have escaped from them if he had wanted to. She explained this to Elma in a loud voice, and Elma agreed somewhat timidly. It was the first time they had spoken to each other directly all the afternoon.

They waited for a few minutes to see whether George would take the hint, but nothing happened.

"It's ridiculous," Clarice said.

Elma agreed that it was. "Perhaps we could go up the ladder . . ." she suggested doubtfully.

"Nonsense," replied Clarice. "Just look at it! . . . Well, I suppose we had better go. We can't stand here all the afternoon. . . ."

They drifted away.

12

DAN'S PARTY CONTINUES

IT was true that George could have escaped, of course, though perhaps not very easily, for his captors were fairly strong young women and exceedingly determined. They had been waiting for him when he had emerged from the trap-door and had dropped the rope round his body, pinioning his arms to his sides. The attack was skilful and had taken him unawares; before he knew where he was, he found himself lying on the floor wound up in coils of exceedingly dirty rope. Some men might have been angry, but George saw the funny side of it. He lay on the floor and chuckled while his captors exchanged pleasantries with their enemies down below. It was not until Clarice and Elma had gone, and his captors were standing before him looking at him with triumphant airs that he realised the gravity of the affair.

"Look here!" he said, suddenly serious. "Look here, you've done it! I mean, they'll be simply furious—at least, Clarice will be——"

"You don't mind, do you?" inquired Mary anxiously.

George examined himself and found with surprise that he did not mind at all. "N-no," he said doubtfully.

"We only did it to get you away from those hags," said Dan. "You hate them, don't you?"

He denied this, of course, but his denial was not taken seriously.

"You had to say that," Mary Byrd pointed out.

"We did it neatly, didn't we?" put in Dan.

"Very neatly indeed," agreed the prisoner.

"And you're quite comfortable, aren't you?" Dan inquired. "I mean, the rope isn't hurting you anywhere?"

"Yes—no," said George, smiling. "But I suppose prisoners aren't allowed to smoke?"

He was immediately put on parole and his bonds loosened. Mary lighted his cigarette for him and Dan brought an old sack and put it behind his back.

"That's better," said George, "but you'll let me go in time for tea, won't you? Paddy couldn't manage it all by herself."

"Of course, darling George," said Dan affectionately.

There was silence for a few moments. George lay back and smoked contentedly. He was feeling remarkably cheerful. As a matter of fact, it was very pleasant indeed in the old loft, cool and quiet, and the atmosphere was friendly and companionable.

George looked at the round, honest faces of his jailers and thought, "Decent kids!" And he fell to wondering what they would be like when they were older. Would they grow up into artificial nonentities like Clarice? Neither of them could ever be like Elma—he was sure of that—for already Dan and Mary knew more about the world than she did; they were infinitely more independent and self-assured.

"Don't grow up," said George suddenly and somewhat foolishly.

"What! Why?" inquired Dan in amazement; but Mary Byrd understood.

"We never would be like *them*," she declared. "We're different, you know. Lots of girls—even grown-up girls—are quite sensible."

They discussed the matter quite seriously while George finished his cigarette, and then they chatted desultorily about other things. By this time George had learnt the name of

Dan's friend and had realised that this was the girl who had "everything," this was Dan's ideal of what a girl should be. He thought Dan had chosen well, for Mary Byrd was a whole person and a very attractive one.

"I suppose you two are tremendous pals," he said with some guile.

Dan hesitated, but Mary replied at once and without the slightest embarrassment, "We're going to be from now on—at least, if Dan will."

"Oh, *rather*," said Dan, and she smiled at Mary with her heart in her eyes.

When the tea-bell rang the prisoner was liberated and helped his ex-jailers down the ladder—which was much more difficult in descent—and they all three walked up to the house together, joining the stream of hot and dishevelled maidens trooping in to tea.

Paddy had provided sufficient food for twenty boys—she had taken that as her standard of capacity—so there was ample for thirty girls. They had to eat it standing, for there was no room for chairs, but nobody minded that. The dining-room was filled with the sound of chatter and the tinkling of teacups and spoons.

"They're enjoying it, the pets," whispered Paddy to George as she pushed past him, carrying a tray of food.

George was willing to believe that they were. He had begun to think that it was quite a good party. It had started somewhat stickily, but it was going strong now. Clarice would not speak to him; but that did not trouble him at all—in fact, he was tremendously relieved to find that he had offended her so seriously—for Clarice had been much too possessive in the earlier part of the afternoon; her assumption that George was her own particular property had alarmed him a good deal.

George handed plates of cakes, and laughed and joked with his guests, and he would have been exceedingly happy but for the thought of his conjuring performance, which hung like a cloud in the otherwise cloudless sky and approached nearer every moment. He had thought it would be rather fun to show a few tricks to Dan and half a dozen of her friends, but he had never bargained for an audience like this. He was afflicted with stage fright. He was certain that he would make a complete fool of himself. His fingers would be all thumbs.

Unfortunately, he could not back out of it now, for Dan had told everybody that there was going to be magic, and it was impossible to let Dan down.

"This is awful," he said to Cathy as they all streamed into the drawing-room with expectant faces. "This is positively frightful. Sit near me, for heaven's sake."

"Yes, of course, I'll sit near you," said Cathy soothingly. "But don't worry, George. Everything will be all right."

"It won't," he declared. "My hands feel twice their usual size—look at the crowds of people—— Oh, goodness, why did I say I'd do it?"

"Don't think about the people," Cathy whispered. "Pretend they're not there. Pretend you're just doing the tricks yourself, or showing them to Paddy."

It was excellent advice, and George tried to follow it, but without much success. The older people were sitting on chairs all round the room and the girls in rows on the floor, and George was conscious of something like a hundred eyes fixed upon him as he stood behind his table. His brow was wet and his collar was sticking to his neck, and his hands trembled as he arranged his paraphernalia; it

427

was indeed an ordeal for a novice in magic. He noticed suddenly as he looked round at the sea of faces that Elma was absent. (Clarice was sitting on a high-backed chair near the window with her hands folded and an exceedingly sulky expression marring her pretty face, but Elma was nowhere to be seen.) Where the dickens was Elma? Now that he thought of it, he had not seen her at tea either. . . . Oh, well, thought George, I suppose she's somewhere about. I've got enough to worry about without worrying about Elma. . . .

He cleared his throat and began his entertainment in a voice that sounded, in his own ears, strangely creaky and high pitched.

"Now, then, ladies and gentlemen, you see this box. . . ."

The girls made a very appreciative audience; they clapped and cheered vociferously at suitable moments, and indeed everybody seemed delighted with George's efforts—everybody except Mr. Liston ffoulkes. He and Mr. Ferrier had finished with Jupiter's spots and came into the drawing-room just as the amateur magician was starting to perform. There were no chairs left, so they had to stand, and they took up their positions uncomfortably near the table.

Mr. Liston ffoulkes was a scientist, of course, and therefore exceedingly scornful of magic. He was also a very tiresome old gentleman—one of those people who always "butt" into everything and upset their fellow-men whenever they can. He started to "butt" into George almost at once.

"*But* you did not put the coin beneath the handkerchief," said Mr. Liston ffoulkes. "*But* that small box has a false bottom, so, of course——"

"But I did . . . but it hasn't," replied George—somewhat impudently, it must be admitted—and he displayed the coin beneath the handkerchief and handed the box to his tormentor so that he might examine it at will.

It was fortunate that Mr. Liston ffoulkes had not hit on the right solution and therefore could be crushed so easily. Indeed, his interference enhanced the mysteries which he had intended to expose and raised George's stock a good deal.

"Oh—er——" said Mr. Liston ffoulkes. "No, I see—er—very strange."

George went ahead more cheerfully after that, his spirits rising and his patter improving with every trick he did, and his audience laughed and clapped and appeared to enjoy themselves immensely. They were especially vociferous in their applause when the magician made his magic coin disappear into thin air and then discovered it down the fat girl's neck.

"Lena!" they shouted. "Hurrah for Lena! She keeps half-crowns in her ears!"

The fat girl was as pleased as punch at the sudden notoriety (George had felt sure that she would be pleased). She giggled delightedly and begged him to do it again. *Lena*, thought George, as he complied with her request. What an extraordinary name for her! What an unsuitable name! . . . But, of course, her parents could not see into the future when they chose it for her.

There was only one slight contretemps during the display. George had made his magic coin vanish and had promised his audience that he would shake it out of his father's top hat (which he had borrowed for the occasion). Something went wrong with this trick and George, as he lifted the hat, was suddenly aware that the coin was still reposing peacefully in the box. He hesitated for a moment and looked instinctively at Mr. Liston ffoulkes.

"Ah," said that gentleman nastily. "Ah, yes, let us see the coin. I fancy you have not removed it from the box. However, shake the hat, by all means."

George shook the hat half-heartedly and a half-crown rolled out.

For perhaps half a second George gazed at the half-crown with incredulous surprise, and then he picked it up and held it in the air for his audience to see.

"Here it is!" he said. "I told you——"

The remainder of his speech was drowned in the deafening applause.

It was by far the best effect of the performance, and, like a wise general, George decided to retire upon his laurels. He intimated that the magic was at an end, and immediately everybody rose and began to say goodbye. In the resulting confusion it was easy to get hold of Cathy and slip the half-crown into her hand.

"This is yours, I think," he said, smiling at her in the old comradely manner, "and when I say, 'Thank you for the loan,' I jolly well mean it. How on earth did you manage to drop it in?"

Cathy's eyes were twinkling. "I had to do it," she whispered. "It would have been such a score for that horrid old man. You aren't angry with me for interfering, George?"

431

"Angry!" said George in amazement.

There was no time to say any more, but he made up his mind to get to the bottom of the mystery some other time. . . .

First, he wanted to know how Cathy had become aware of the fact that the trick had gone wrong; and second, he wanted to know how she had managed to get the half-crown into the hat without his seeing the manoeuvre. It was dashed clever of her, he thought.

The party was now melting rapidly, each guest assuring her hostess in exactly the same words that she had enjoyed herself "frightfully," and that it had been "simply gorgeous." Dan, however, struck out a line for herself. "Oh, darling, darling!" she cried, squeezing her small hostess till she gasped. "Oh, darling, *darling*, I'll love you for ever!"

Everybody had gone now except Clarice, and it was impossible for her to go until Harry Coles was found to take her home. His car was still standing in front of the door, which was accepted as proof that he "must be somewhere about."

"Well, I wish to goodness you'd find him, then," said Clarice, who was so disgusted with her afternoon's entertainment that she was almost in tears.

"He cannot be far away," declared Mr. Ferrier in a soothing voice.

"Elma has vanished, too," said George, remembering this disquieting fact quite suddenly.

The two culprits were run to earth in George's study, and they were both surprised when they heard that the party was over. George, who had found them, received the impression that they had been enjoying themselves thoroughly in a quiet way.

"Nice girl, that," whispered Harry as he followed George down the winding stair. "No nonsense about her, what?" But George was so annoyed with Harry that he did not reply.

Later in the evening George was even more annoyed to receive the same sort of confidence from Elma. "I like Harry," she declared with a thoughtful smile.

13

POST-PRANDIAL CONVERSATIONS

ON Sunday night there was still no word from Mr. Crane in answer to George's letter, and there was no word from Mr. Millar, and no summons for assault from Wilfred.

"It is very strange, indeed," said Mr. Ferrier as he and his son discussed a post-prandial glass of port. "I have given the matter a good deal of consideration, and it seems to me that the situation is unresolved. Arbuthnot Millar received your letter. Why does he not reply? He must make some move."

"It's his turn to play," said George thoughtfully.

Mr. Ferrier agreed. He was secretly very proud of the masterly way in which George had carried out *his* move: a knight's move, thought Mr. Ferrier, sideways and forwards, threatening Dusty's queen. In fact, thought Mr. Ferrier with an inward smile, you might say that Dusty's queen was taken, and, as every chess-player is aware, the loss of his queen is a serious matter and usually signifies the loss of the game.

"I wonder what they're up to—the Millars, I mean," said George, twirling his glass thoughtfully and watching the waves of port circle round and round like a miniature whirlpool.

"I wonder," Mr. Ferrier agreed. "One would hardly think that Millar could sit back and do nothing. You explained the situation, and your letter requires a reply. Personally, I feel no anxiety as regards the summons for assault with which young Millar threatened you."

"He would look a bit of a fool, wouldn't he?"

"And Elma is his only witness."

"I know," nodded George, "and she's fed-up with him."

"On the other hand," continued Mr. Ferrier, "there might be a case against you for abduction. Millar's contention being that he had instructed his son to bring his ward to London and that you had interfered and carried her off in a forcible manner. That would not be pleasant, George."

"Elma would have something to say to that, too," said George promptly. "She was absolutely fed-up with him, you see. She changed her mind about going with him to London when she saw what he was like. As a matter of fact," he added somewhat diffidently, "Elma's told me half a dozen times that she—er—well—prefers me to Wilfred Millar, now."

Mr. Ferrier was not surprised, for he had quite good eyes when he liked to use them. George obviously held the queen, and held her pretty firmly. Mr. Ferrier was certain that if the worst came, and they were obliged to take the case to court, Elma would not only withhold any evidence which might harm George, but would lie like Ananias to save him from a moment's pain. George's feelings were less easy to read. He was kind to her, of course; but George was always kind.

"I don't know what to do," said George with a sigh. He was still thinking of the Millar imbroglio, of course.

"I am quite unable to advise you," his father replied. "And I cannot think why we have had no word from Mr. Crane."

The words had scarcely fallen from Mr. Ferrier's lips when the telephone rang, and,

436

as the telephone was in the dining-room, George rose and answered it.

"Hallo!" said George.

There were the usual cracklings and clickings, and then suddenly a voice, a somewhat querulous voice, sounded in his ear. "I have waited for thirty-five minutes," it said.

"Hallo," said George. "Who is it?"

"Is that Mr. George Ferrier?" inquired the voice.

"Who is it?" inquired Mr. Ferrier.

"I don't know yet," said George.

"You don't *know* who you are?" inquired the voice in tones of amazement.

"What?" said George.

"I asked if that was Mr. Ferrier."

"Yes, it's me," said George.

"Mr. George Ferrier?"

"Yes."

"This is Mr. Crane."

"Oh, good."

"Who is it?" inquired Mr. Ferrier again.

"The lawyer fellow," replied George.

"What did you say?" inquired Mr. Crane.

"Nothing," said George hastily.

There were more cracklings and clickings and then the voice sounded again, much louder and clearer. "Is that Mr. George Ferrier?" it inquired again.

"Yes," said George, waving his hand to keep off his father, who was buzzing round him like an old and extremely anxious bee. "Yes, this is me, all right. Did you get the letter?"

"I have just this moment received it. I have been away for several days and my clerk sent it round to my house. It is important that I should see you immediately. Can you hear?"

"Yes, but can't you tell me?" asked George, who had no desire at all to go up to London in this boiling-hot weather.

"Tell you?" (the voice sounded as if its owner could scarcely believe his ears). "Tell you what?"

"Tell me what you think about it, of course."

"No, that is—that is *impossible*."

"Oh, well!" said George. "Well, can't you write, then? Go ahead and do what you think . . . write to Mr. Millar and ask him——"

"Mr. Ferrier, I must beg you not to discuss this matter on the telephone. It is a most serious matter. Please mention no names."

"What is he saying?" inquired Mr. Ferrier,

trying to approach his ear to the receiver.

George waved him away. "I'll tell you all about it afterwards," he declared.

"But you have already told me," Mr. Crane pointed out; "and too much time has been wasted—valuable time. I consider it absolutely necessary for you to come up and see me."

"Well, perhaps on Wednesday——" began George in a reluctant tone.

"Tomorrow, please. I cannot explain on the telephone, but I can assure you that the matter is urgent."

"But look here, tomorrow is——"

"You cannot have anything to do which is of more immediate importance," said the lawyer firmly. "I shall expect you tomorrow at eleven o'clock."

There was a crackle and a buzz and a feminine voice inquired, "You do really love me, don't you?" and George became aware that his conversation with Mr. Crane was at an end. He hung up the receiver.

"Well?" asked his father anxiously.

"He's in a flat spin," said George with a little frown.

"A flat spin!" echoed Mr. Ferrier incredulously.

"Yes, absolutely. I've got to go up and see him tomorrow or the skies will fall."

"Did he say that?" inquired Mr. Ferrier, who was unable to recognise his lawyer in George's report of the conversation. "Are you quite sure it was Mr. Crane?"

"Oh, rather," said George. "It was him all right—fairly gibbering, he was."

Mr. Ferrier's heart sank into his boots. If Mr. Crane was gibbering, the matter must be serious indeed. He had consulted Mr. Crane several times about a right of way which had been formed across his property, and had always found him a model of clarity and dry legal acumen. "Gibbering!" repeated Mr. Ferrier in dismay.

"Absolutely. He wouldn't discuss anything . . . kept on saying there'd be hell to pay if I didn't come."

"Dear me!" said Mr. Ferrier. "Dear me—tut-tut—this is dreadful, George. It does not sound like Mr. Crane at all."

"Oh, I could see he'd fairly gone off the deep end," said George. "I could see he was all of a doodah—at least, of course, I couldn't *see*, but you know what I mean."

"You couldn't see?"

"Not down the telephone."

"Oh, I see," said Mr. Ferrier. He ran his hand over his head and was surprised to find that what hair he possessed was standing on end. "Oh, dear! Oh, dear!" he exclaimed. "It is all most unfortunate. I wish you had never met Green or accepted any responsibility in the matter."

George became aware that his father was really upset, and he immediately changed his tune. "Good Lord, there's no need to *worry*," he said. "The lawyer fellow will fix it up in half no time—that's what he's for."

"But, George——"

"And, anyhow, they can't do anything to *me*. I haven't done anything wrong, have I? come and finish your port."

It took several minutes to soothe Mr. Ferrier, but George put his mind to it, and soon they had resumed their seats at the table and were talking quietly again.

The curtains were still undrawn and the french windows stood open; it was dark and starry, and not a breath of air stirred the heavy foliage of the trees. They had discussed George's visit to Mr. Crane and all that he must remember to say, and now they were silent. George was peeling an apple.

441

Suddenly there was a step on the gravel path and a figure appeared, outlined against the dark-blue sky.

"Hallo, here is Peter!" Mr. Ferrier exclaimed. "Hi, Peter, come and have a glass of port."

Peter stepped over the threshold, blinking a little in the lamplight. "Hallo!" he said. "Yes, please, Mr. Ferrier. I know your port. It's much too good to refuse."

George had already pushed the dessert plates aside and made room for his friend at the table. He was glad that Peter had come, for the last time he had seen Peter there had been that slight unpleasantness, that feeling of coldness and estrangement between them. George had no idea how or why that unpleasantness had arisen, but he was glad that it was past. He was very fond of Peter. Yes, he thought, glancing at the thin, clever face with its high student's forehead and the straying curl of hair which, no matter what Peter did to it, would never lie down obediently with its fellows. Yes, I'm dashed fond of old Peter; he's a good fellow.

"I felt I had to see you—to tell you," Peter was saying, addressing the words equally to his two hosts. "I knew you'd be pleased and

442

interested. The fact is, I've heard of an opening—it's in Devonshire, a country practice—as assistant to a G.P. Sounds the very thing. I'm buzzing off on Saturday to let him have a look at me."

"Great!" exclaimed George. "It's what you wanted, isn't it? I'm jolly glad for your sake . . . of course, it's a bit of a blow for *me*. I mean, I hoped to see a good deal of you this summer."

Mr. Ferrier congratulated his young friend gravely and then he rose. "I'll leave you to have a talk," he said. "You had better finish the decanter between you . . . but don't delay too long," he added, and he looked at George to see if he had understood.

George nodded. He was fully aware that Paddy and Elma should not be left to entertain each other for long periods.

This little by-play was lost on Peter, for he was too intent upon his own feelings to notice it. He had come to tender an olive branch, for he felt that he could not leave Winthorpe until he had made it up with old George. As a matter of fact, the unpleasantness seemed much more definite and important to Peter than it seemed to George, for George had been so busy that he had not had time to think of it, and Peter had thought about it a good deal. He had thought about it himself, and he had heard about it from Cathy in no uncertain terms.

"What are you thinking about?" George inquired. "I suppose you're gloating over all the wretched people you'll be able to cut up when you get to Devonshire!"

Peter laughed. "You're quite wrong," he said. "As a matter of fact, I was thinking about Cathy. We had a most unholy row."

"A row?"

"Yes. It's odd, because I don't think we've ever had a row before in all our lives—I can't remember one, anyhow—not a real blazing row like this."

"Oh, that's it, then!" exclaimed George.

"That's what?"

"Nothing," said George. "I knew there was something up, that's all. Cathy's been worrying about it."

"Oh, has she?" inquired Peter in surprise. "Did she tell you? I thought—I thought she didn't want you to know about it."

"Of course, she didn't tell me," said George. "Of course, she didn't want me to know about it," and he smiled happily, for all at once he was feeling extraordinarily light-hearted and gay. George had not known until now, when the puzzle was solved, how much it had worried him and clouded his skies. The puzzle was solved and there was no mystery, no deep, dark secret between Paddy and Cathy from which he was shut out. Life was good.

"Then how on earth did you know?" inquired Peter, and he took out his pipe and began to fill it carefully.

"I just knew," said George, chuckling. "A little bird told me . . . and you needn't start filling your pipe; there's no peaceful smoky evening in store for you, my lad. You've got to come and make yourself agreeable to the ladies."

"Ladies!" exclaimed Peter in dismay.

George laughed. "We've got a guest," he said. "You'll never guess who it is. Somebody you know—at least you've met her. My goodness, Peter, I'll have to tell you the whole thing!"

Peter looked towards the open window as if he meditated escape. "A guest!" he said doubtfully.

"Well, a sort of guest," declared George, helping himself to the remainder of the port, "but not a very welcome one, I'm afraid.

Paddy would give a good deal to get rid of her—and so would I, for that matter. Didn't Cathy tell you about it?"

"No," said Peter. "As a matter of fact, Cathy and I—well, I told you we'd had a row. But why do you want to get rid of the woman?" he inquired, changing the subject hastily.

"Because she's a confounded nuisance, because she's a regular old Man of the Sea. Here she is and here she's got to remain——" said George with a little frown between his eyes. "It wouldn't be quite so bad if Paddy didn't hate the sight of her—that's what makes it so awkward—and I can't move a step without treading on her. She's under my feet the whole time—from early morn to dewy eve—and I'm getting a bit sick of it, to tell you the truth."

"Who on earth is it?"

"Elma," said George. "Have some more port, won't you? Oh, sorry, I've finished it. Elma Green—*you* know—old Green's daughter with the violet eyes. She's learnt to use them, too, and—here, I say, what's the matter!" he cried, for Peter had leapt to his feet with such force that his chair fell over backwards on to the floor.

"What's the matter?" Peter cried furiously. "You can sit there with that smug smile p-plastered all over your face and—and——"

"I say!" cried George. "I say, hold on——"

"You c-cad!" cried Peter, stammering a little as he always did when he was unduly excited. "You c-c-cad! How dare you talk about her like that? You're not fuff-fit to tie her shoes, you great, hulking, insensible brute! You don't understand her. How could you? She's like a fuff-flower . . . she's innocent and good and—and beautiful. . . . What d'you mean by it, I say?"

George had been listening to this outburst with amazement. His eyes were goggling out of his head and his mouth had opened as if to speak; but no sound came.

"Well, aren't you angry?" demanded Peter, when he had recovered his breath, and he leaned across the table and glared at George. "Aren't you angry?" he shouted.

"N-no," said George doubtfully. "I don't seem to be."

"You're *impossible*!" Peter cried. "I tell you you're a c-c-cad, a great, hulking b-brute with no more understanding than a louse— and you aren't even angry. I've stood aside all this time because we're friends, and I wasn't

447

going to butt in. I saw how the land lay that first day; but now—well—I'm d-damned if I'm going to stand aside a m-moment longer—I'm going to make fuff-friends with her now—this very minute. I'm going to—to——"

"Woo and win her," suggested George. For George, during this second outburst, had suddenly seen light. Light had flooded the dark places of his mind and everything was perfectly clear.

"Are you making fuff-fun of me?" inquired Peter suspiciously.

"No," said George. "Oh, *rather* not. I can't understand it, that's all."

"You idiot, can't you understand I want to m-marry her?"

"Yes, but why? I mean, you don't know her, do you? How d'you know you want to marry her when you've only seen her once?"

"I suppose you think I'm after her money?" roared Peter with renewed fury. "Well, I'm not. I don't want her b-blasted money. It's *her* I want, and I know what she's like a damned sight better than you do—I knew what she was like the m-moment I laid eyes on her—so *there*——"

"Here, I say, keep your hair on!"

"I suppose you'll try to queer my p-pitch—because you're her trustee . . . fine trustee *you* are. . . . You'd never have gone near her if it hadn't been for me!"

"My dear old boy——"

"If you t-try to queer my pitch——"

"But I won't!" cried George, hammering on the table in his excitement. "I wouldn't for worlds queer your pitch. If I'd thought for a *year*, I couldn't have thought of anything better."

"D'you mean you approve?" inquired Peter, unable to believe his ears.

"Wholeheartedly," said George with fervour.

They looked at each other in silence.

Peter found his voice first. "But I thought you——" he began.

"No," said George, shaking his head violently.

"Do you mean . . . ?"

"Yes," said George, violently nodding. "Oh, well, to tell you the truth, I did at one time . . . well, I mean, I did just consider it vaguely, you know. She's rather a dear little thing, and so pretty——"

"Beautiful," amended his friend.

"Yes—well—beautiful," George admitted;

"but after I got to know her better I saw that she wasn't just quite my—I mean, I'm such a fool, you see, so I ought to have a wife with brains. You see the point, don't you?"

"Flowers haven't got——"

"Oh, I know," agreed George hastily; "and you've got all the brains you *need*. She's just the very wife for you."

Peter smiled. It was an exceedingly fatuous smile. "Gosh, I can't believe it!" he said.

"That's fixed, then," said George firmly.

There was a little silence and then a sudden thought assailed Peter. "But look here," he said anxiously. "What about *her*? Supposing she doesn't like me, or something?"

Strangely enough, George had not considered this possibility before. He was unwilling to consider it now. "Nonsense," he said. "You can make her like you if you take a little trouble. It isn't difficult."

"I must be careful not to frighten her, not to go too fast or anything," said Peter, frowning anxiously.

George laughed. "Good Lord, you won't frighten her in a hurry," he declared. "She likes men who *are* men. What you want to do is to seize her by the hair and drag her off to your cave. As a matter of fact, there's a fellow called Pendennis that she admires tremendously—a fellow in a book—I don't know what it's called."

"Pendennis," said Peter.

"No, that's the fellow's name," said George. "Well, never mind; the point is you'd better get hold of the book and read it—you might get some ideas. He was a swashbuckling sort of chap—got tight, and knocked people down by the score and made off with the girl—you know the sort of thing."

"I don't remember that bit," said Peter, in some perplexity. "Besides, I can't go about knocking people down. Don't be such an ass."

"You could knock me down," suggested George.

"You know perfectly well that I couldn't!"

"I mean I'd let you," said George. He was willing to suffer a good deal to rid himself of the responsibility of his ward.

"Oh, don't be an *ass*," said Peter wearily.

"I was only trying to help," George complained. "Trying to give you some idea of how to go about it. You'll never make the slightest headway if you treat her like Dresden china—she isn't that sort. I know she looks that sort, but, believe me, she isn't. Now listen to me: you take her out in your car tomorrow and kiss her. Tell her you're madly in love with her——"

"But I am!"

"Then it won't be difficult at all," George pointed out, "you can just let yourself go, can't you? You can talk about love at first sight, and all that. She'll be *thrilled*," declared George earnestly.

"Do you really think——"

"Yes," said George, "yes, I believe you'll do it if you put your back into it. I believe she's *ready* to fall in love."

"Ready? What d'you mean?"

"I just mean ready," George said. "She thought she was in love with that cad Millar until I knocked him out, and then she liked Harry Coles quite a lot . . ."

"Harry Coles!" exclaimed Peter in a voice of extreme disgust.

". . . and she'd fall in love with *me* if I'd let her—but I won't," George added hastily, as he saw Peter's face. "Good Lord, no. Don't you worry about *that*. The fact is her head's full of love stories—Sir Walter Scott, and all that—and she's just waiting for someone to come along. She's a princess in a tower," said

George seriously, "waiting for a Knight to ride past and give her the come-hither, that's what she is."

"A princess in a tower," nodded Peter, delighted with the idea.

The conversation ended soon after this, and the two young gentlemen joined the ladies in the drawing-room. It had been rather a curious conversation in several ways. For one thing, Peter and George had changed places, and their friendship had taken a new turn. Before this conversation Peter had always been the leader, and had laid down the law to his friend; but now George, quite unconsciously, had taken command. The fact was that Peter's clever head was full of the theory and practice of medicine, he was interested in people's bodies, and not in their minds—Peter had never had time for girls. George, on the other hand, was intensely interested in all sorts of people, and liked them, and understood them. He had had ample opportunity of studying the psychology of girls in general and of his ward in particular, to him she was an open book.

If only Peter will go it, he thought to himself, as he looked at the two of them seated together upon the sofa at the other end of the room, if only Peter will go it hard, everything will be grand. He'll pull it off all right . . . I'll keep on gingering him up. . . .

"What on earth are you smiling to yourself like that for?" inquired Paddy suddenly, "It's like a Cheshire Cat, you are, so mysterious and all."

14

GOING TO LONDON

LEAPING into the train at the very last minute, when in fact it was already moving with considerable speed, George found himself in a compartment labelled "Ladies Only," and in the company of one member of that sex.

"I say, I'm frightfully sorry——" he began, and then he saw that it was Cathy, and ended with a laugh.

Cathy had seen him coming, of course, she had seen him at the gate, and had opened the door of the compartment to enable him to get in; had gone the length of grasping his sleeve and giving him a firm and decisive pull just at the right moment, and her actions had been crowned with success: George had caught the train. Cathy had acted instinctively (she had realised that he would lose the train if somebody didn't do something about it, and do it quickly) she had not really wanted George to come into her compartment and sit there opposite to her all the way to London, in fact there was nothing she wanted less; for Cathy had decided to cure herself of George, she had suffered from the painful complaint for years—and it was hopeless.

It was after her talk with Paddy that Cathy had made up her mind to take herself in hand, and she had laid down certain rules by which she hoped to overcome her disease: she must avoid George whenever possible, she must interest herself more deeply in household affairs, above all she must not think about George, and whenever she found herself thinking about him she must think deliberately of something else. These were good and wise rules, and, in time, they would almost certainly have effected a cure, it was therefore unfortunate that out of sheer common humanity Cathy had been obliged to open the door and help George into the train.

"Granpa and Paddy between them," gasped George. "First he wouldn't start, and then she ran out of petrol—lord, what a sprint!" and he lay back against the cushions and mopped his face.

Cathy said nothing. She was too full of thoughts and feelings all jumbled up together, and her heart was thumping as if she, too, had raced to catch the train.

"I didn't know you were going up today," he continued, when he had got back his breath. "I'm going up to see Dad's lawyer about the Green money. What are you going to do?"

"Dentist and shopping," said Cathy briefly.

"I tell you what," George said. "You get all your stuff done this morning, and then we'll lunch together and do a flick—what say?"

Cathy hesitated. Her appointment with the dentist was at one fifteen; she had in her bag a list of shopping which would more than fill her day; she had decided to cure herself of this absurd and absolutely hopeless infatuation for George.

"Do let's," said George, smiling at her.

"All right," said Cathy. "Where shall I meet you?"

"What about Fortnum's?" he suggested.

I'm mad, thought Cathy, I'm absolutely crazy. I can't possibly go to Gooch's about Dan's gym tunic, and get a hat, and have my fitting, and go out to Harrod's about mother's curtains, and back to the Army and Navy for Peter's suitcase . . . I'll have to ring up Mr. Manning and tell him I can't come and have my tooth stopped . . . I'm a perfect fool to dangle after George like this.

"All right, what time?" she said.

"One," said George, "or as soon after as I can manage, I don't know how long this lawyer fellow will keep me. I've got a lot to talk to him about."

"Mrs. Ferrier told me."

"Yes," said George. "It's all very complicated, of course. I'm perfectly certain that old Millar's a crook, and that he's pocketed the money, and I believe they hatched a plot—he and that precious son of his—to get Elma into their hands and marry her to the son."

"It was a good thing you were able to prevent it," said Cathy without much conviction.

"It was almost kidnapping," George pointed out. "Elma had no idea what she was doing—she's such a child."

"She's very beautiful," said Cathy, pressing deliberately on her wounds.

"And very rich," added George. "Very beautiful and very rich—it was the money Millar was after."

"Money is useful," said Cathy.

"I should just think it *was*," said George.

458

They talked about other things then, and George remembered his desire to get to the bottom of the half-crown mystery, and made searching inquiries as to how Cathy had managed to get the half-crown into the hat just at the right moment.

Cathy's answers were vague:

"I just slipped it in when nobody was looking," she said.

"Well, it was *very* clever of you," declared George. "You saved my bacon. It was a frightful moment when I realised the trick had gone wrong . . . and *there* was that old blister gazing at me with the light of battle in his eyes. You were a real pal."

"Oh, well," said Cathy, looking out of the window so that she should not see the friendly admiration shining in his face. "Oh, well, I just thought it would be so bad for him to be right. That's why I did it, you see."

George was a little disappointed. He would have liked to think that the noble deed had been done for him, for friendship's sake, and not for the good of the professor's soul. He pressed Cathy on this point but she stuck to her guns.

"He's the sort of person who is always right," she declared—"or, at least, he always thinks he's right—and he must be so horrid to live with. I just felt I had to give him a lesson. Perhaps he won't be so ready to butt into things for a day or two—he looked pretty silly." She chuckled reminiscently, and added "You should have seen his face when the half-crown rolled out of the hat . . . it was funny."

"I expect it was," said George, rather flatly.

"Oh, it *was*," Cathy assured him. "The old man's eyes positively goggled—he was so sure, you see."

"Yes," said George. He really felt absurdly hurt and disappointed.

They buried themselves in their papers for the remainder of the journey.

They buried themselves in their papers, but in reality neither of them took in much of the day's news. Cathy was too agitated to concentrate, and George had suddenly thought of Peter and Elma. He had glanced out of the window and had seen a small car chugging along the road which ran for some miles parallel with the railway. It was not Peter's car, of course, but it was sufficiently like Peter's car to make George think about Peter;

and, thinking about Peter brought Elma to his mind. He wondered what they were doing now—at this moment—and whether Peter was working on the Pendennis lines, as George had advised. Ten minutes to eleven, thought George, glancing at his watch, they've been out for nearly an hour . . . I wonder . . .

It was rather a pity that George was not gifted with second sight, and was therefore unable to see his two friends, in whose affairs he took such a benevolent interest. They were sitting on a bank under a shady tree, and Peter had taken Elma's hand and was holding it fast. "I was simply knocked out," he was saying, "I had never seen anyone so beautiful in all my life. Well, of course I hadn't, because there isn't any one in the world as beautiful as you are . . . your eyes. . . . Oh, Elma, your eyes are wonderful! . . . English wood violets, that's what they're like."

"Oh, Peter!" sighed Elma.

"I expect you thought I was stupid . . . that first day . . . but it was because of you . . . because you were so marvellously beautiful. I couldn't breathe——"

"Oh, Peter—I never knew——"

"You're so innocent," he told her earnestly,

"you're so good and sweet. Oh, Elma, I shall die if you aren't kind to me."

"Oh, Peter——"

"You're like a flower," he told her, "you're like a star. You're like a fairy princess . . ." and he continued to tell her all the delightful and beautiful things she was like, and Elma listened, enthralled. Peter was the perfect lover, the lover she had sought for in every man she had met. Peter was a romantic like herself.

15

A DEAD SECRET

IT was one o'clock, and Cathy was waiting for George to arrive. She was waiting at the top of the steps which led from Fortnum and Mason's shop to the restaurant on the first floor. A buzz of talk filled the air, people came up the steps, and met other people who had been waiting for them, and laughed and chattered and pushed on into the restaurant for lunch. There were men and women and dozens of young girls with fair curls and dark curls and gaily-painted mouths, their eyes quested round eagerly, passing over Cathy as if she were invisible; tired eyes, they were, almost without exception, tired and hungry, but hungry for something other than food. Cathy wondered if her eyes were hungry, too, when she looked at George . . . she hoped not. There was something rather horrible about those hungry eyes. . . . Already she was regretting her foolishness in accepting George's plan for it was so dangerous to be alone with George. Supposing he saw that hunger in her eyes, and guessed what it was she craved. . . . George was clever about people, she had told him that, and it was true. . . . and then she remembered that he had never been clever about *her*. He knows me too well, she thought, and the reflection brought a queer mixture of relief and pain. He knows me so well that he never sees me, she thought, and at that moment George came in.

Cathy saw him first, pushing his way through the crowded shop, and she saw that his face was unusually grave and thoughtful, but when he came to the bottom of the steps he looked up and saw her, and smiled in his old friendly way.

"Sorry," he said, as they went in together and found a table in the corner and sat down side by side on the cushioned seat. "Frightfully sorry to keep you hanging about. I was hours with the man. I came straight here. What will you have?"

"I don't know," Cathy said. "Tell me first—I can see something's happened."

"It jolly well has. The fact is Millar has disappeared."

"What?'

"Vanished . . . done a bunk . . . vamoosed," explained George. "At least, it looks like that. Come on, Cathy. What are you going to eat?"

She chose something at random, and returned to the subject. "But, George, how awful!" she said. "Has he taken the money?"

"He's taken it," nodded George. "Old Crane found out this morning—I must say he doesn't let the grass grow under his feet—he found out which Insurance Company it was, and he found out that they've actually paid the money—twenty thousand pounds!"

"George!"

"I know. It's pretty steep. Fortunately for me I hadn't signed the receipt. I didn't have to, you see, because I'm not an executor. Old Crane explained all that. I'm one of Elma's trustees, but I'm not an executor, so I'm not responsible in any way. I've sent Dad a wire—he was worrying."

"What happens next?" Cathy inquired anxiously.

"Mr. Crane's going to Take Steps."

"What kind of steps?"

"To verify—er—everything. Once it's all Verified he can Take Further Steps—steps to find old Millar and make him disgorge, I suppose. I don't know what he's going to *do*—not

465

actually—he was very careful what he said, and he told me to be 'guarded.' I mustn't go about shooting my head off or I'll get taken up for libel or slander or something."

"Is that what he said?"

"It's what he meant, anyhow," George declared. "And he said I wasn't to worry, but just leave it in his hands," continued George more cheerfully; "so let's do that. What have you been up to? Did the dentist hurt?"

"No," said Cathy truthfully.

"I thought of you several times," George told her, as he took up his knife and fork, and started on the grilled steak which he had chosen from the menu. "I hate going to the dentist. He always hurts me like hell," and with that they began to talk about other things.

Although George had been told not to worry about the Green affair, and had decided to take this excellent advice, his interview with Mr. Crane remained at the back of his mind, and the subject kept cropping up during the course of the conversation like King Charles's head. Every now and then George remembered something he had said to Mr. Crane, or something that he ought to have said, or something that Mr. Crane had said to him; and, because he was so completely at ease with Cathy, these troublesome recollections came tumbling out just when and how he thought about them.

"Old Crane says we'll have to appoint new trustees," said George suddenly, in the middle of a discussion about Nadia's puppies. "But I told him to hold on a bit. We shan't want any new trustees if Elma gets married!"

"Oh . . . no . . ." said Cathy faintly.

"No," said George smiling. "The trust gets wound up if she marries with the approval of her trustees, and the only trustees left will be Mr. Bennett and me. I can square old Bennett quite easily, of course, so there's nothing to stop Peter going ahead——"

"Peter!" exclaimed Cathy.

George's face was a study in consternation. "Oh, My Hat!" he exclaimed. "I *am* a fool! I shouldn't have . . ." he stopped and looked at her.

"You don't mean that Peter——"

"Look here, it's a dead secret," said George earnestly. "I shouldn't have said a word. It was just because I was chatting away to you without thinking—we're such friends, you see. Of course, nothing's settled yet, but Peter is absolutely mad about Elma. Didn't you know?"

467

"Peter!" said Cathy again.

"Mad about her," nodded George. "I didn't know myself till last night."

Cathy looked at him with eyes like saucers. "I don't understand," she said.

"I know," he agreed, "it *is* difficult to understand, but really and truly she's quite a nice little thing. Paddy doesn't like her, but honestly she's quite nice. She's been brought up in a silly way, and her head's full of silly ideas, but I believe she would improve tremendously if she got half a chance. . . . You won't try to put him off, will you?" added George in an anxious tone. "You see, it would be such a relief to my mind to get her safely married to Peter."

Cathy could not answer—she was speechless with amazement—and George, misinterpreting her silence, continued earnestly, "I know it must be a bit of a shock to you, Cathy, because of course you and Peter—well, I mean you've always been such pals, and marriage changes people—but he'd have to marry somebody, some time, and he might do worse, you know. There isn't any *harm* in Elma. I honestly believe she'd be all right if somebody took her in hand."

"Yes," said Cathy helplessly.

"And Peter's the very man for the job."

"Is he?"

"Yes, of course he is. You won't try to put him off, will you?"

"No."

"That's splendid!" declared George, smiling all over his face. "That's tremendously good of you," and he sighed with relief.

There was a few moments' silence, and then he leaned towards her and continued confidently; "I really believe she'll suit Peter down to the ground. As I told him last night, he's got all the brains he needs. Now I'm quite different, of course. I should need a wife with brains. Not anybody frightfully clever, you know," said George, shaking his head, "not a sort of blue-stocking or anything, but somebody clear-headed and helpful. Look at the smart way you helped me with that half-crown, and the way you seized hold of me and hauled me into the train this morning!" said George, smiling at her in a friendly manner. "You see what I mean, Cathy. I should need somebody like that for a wife. Somebody with all their wits about them."

Cathy smiled back at him. She could not

469

speak to save her life, but she hoped the smile looked fairly natural.

"I've often thought what sort of a wife I'd like," George declared, as he helped himself to cheese, "but I've never seen any one to fit the bill. I've been—well—a bit keen on one or two girls but there's always been something . . . you want to be absolutely *sure* before you start thinking about marriage. You can't go and marry a girl because she dances divinely, or because she's marvellous to look at, or because she's sweet, or kind, or because she's amusing, and a good sport, or because you've got lots of things in common, and get on like a house on fire. You want *all those things* in the same person—at least I do—and it looks as if I shall have to remain a bachelor for the rest of my life."

He laughed, and Cathy laughed too.

"Aren't you going to finish your ice?" he inquired.

"I'm full up," said Cathy. It was perfectly true. She felt as if she would never be able to eat anything again.

16

THE PRIVATE VIEW

GEORGE paid the bill, and they came out of the restaurant and hesitated for a few moments at the top of the stairs; and suddenly it seemed to Cathy that she could not bear any more—she had come to the end of her tether. She could not go to a picture house with George and sit beside him in the dark for the whole afternoon; she could not listen to any more confidences from him—it was impossible.

"Look here," she said incoherently. "Look here, George—I ought to have told you—I forgot to tell you—I haven't done half my shopping—I can't come—there's Harrods and—and lots of things—mother's curtains— I'm sorry—I can't come, George."

"Oh, I say!" exclaimed George in dismay.

"I ought to have told you——"

"But look here——"

"I can't," she said. "I'm sorry . . . thank you . . . awfully . . . it's been lovely . . . thank you, George." And with that she ran down the steps and plunged into the shop.

George was disappointed. He was quite ridiculously disappointed if the truth were told. He felt like a child who has been deprived of a long-anticipated treat, and deprived of it for no fault of his own. He stood quite still at the top of the steps and watched Cathy go. He watched her thread her way between the counters which were piled high with biscuits and caviare and bottled fruit; he watched her absurd little hat, perched jauntily on her fair curls, bobbing in and out of the people—he watched and waited for her to turn back and smile at him, but he watched in vain—and at last she reached the door where the flowers are, and the marvellous baskets of fruit; and there, after pausing for a moment to allow an old lady to come in, Cathy passed out and disappeared from view.

Cathy disappeared from view, and all at once the whole place seemed to grow darker—it was as if a cloud had come over the sun. The place was full of people, but it was empty; George was in the midst of a jostling chattering crowd, but he was alone. He was alone and miserable . . . Cathy had deserted him . . . he was alone. . . .

And suddenly George *saw*. He saw with amazement, but also with absolute certainty, that Cathy was the girl he had been looking for all his life . . . *Cathy* . . . and without waiting to reflect further, or to decide what he would say to her if he managed to catch her (or indeed to think of anything at all, except of the absolute necessity of catching her now, this very moment, and of never letting her out of his sight again), George rushed down the stairs and fought his way through the shop like a madman.

She was getting into a taxi when he burst through the swing doors, and without a word he leapt in after her. The commissionaire slammed the door and they moved off.

"George?" she exclaimed in surprise.

"Cathy," said George breathlessly. "Cathy, look here, I must talk to you—I must—where can we go and talk?"

"We can't."

"We must—you don't understand——"

"I'm going to Harrods."

"You aren't," said George firmly. "I mean you can't. I mean I've *got* to speak to you. It's frightfully important. Let's get out."

They were still in Piccadilly, not five yards from Fortnum's, in one of the most complete

473

and hopeless blocks that George had ever seen. He laid his hands on the door to open it.

"George, don't be silly!" she besought him. "We can talk tomorrow—or any time——"

"I'm not silly," he replied earnestly. "I *was* silly—I was absolutely crazy—but I'm sensible now. I've got to talk to you, Cathy. Where can we go?"

"We can't go anywhere," said Cathy desperately.

"Yes, we can," he declared. "We can go to the Academy, to Burlington House," and he pointed to the big grey archway on the opposite side of the street.

"But, George——"

"It'll be empty at this hour," he told her, "and we can talk—come on, Cathy."

"No."

"Yes, honestly you must. I won't ever ask you to do anything for me again—at least only one more thing——"

He opened the door and got out; he paid the taxi in a royal manner; he took Cathy's hand in a firm grasp and led her across the street, threading his way with difficulty between the buses and cars and commercial vehicles jammed nose to tail as far as the eye could see. He led her through the archway and across the court and up the steps to the turnstiles without a word, and it was not until they had found their way to the Statuary Room, and were quite alone, except for the strange white gleaming figures, that he let go her hand and prepared to speak.

"Now," he said. "Now.... Well, of course you think I'm mad, but I can't help it . . . you see, it came over me suddenly . . . it was when you disappeared. Somehow I couldn't bear it when you disappeared . . . I don't know why . . . yes, I do know why . . . it was because I love you."

"George," she began, stepping back from him a little.

"Stop," said George hastily. "Please stop, Cathy. I know what you're going to say. You're going to remind me of all that rot I talked at lunch . . . only it wasn't rot, it was true . . . the only thing that *was* rot was my saying that I couldn't find the girl who was everything I wanted . . . it was you all the time! Of course," said George, gasping a little, because of a queer tight feeling in his chest, which seemed to interfere with his breathing. "Of course, I know it's a surprise to you—I mean, it's difficult for you to—to think of me like that all of a sudden—but if you'd just try to—to think of me like that——"

Cathy gazed at him. She could not believe her ears. She was struck dumb.

"Say something," said George rather pitifully. "Say you'll—you'll think about it or something. I know you're astounded—well, so am I for that matter, simply astounded—but please do say *something*, Cathy. Say you'll think about it. Say you don't—altogether—hate the sight of me."

She couldn't say anything at all—it was impossible—but she turned towards him and raised her face, and George saw her blue eyes looking up at him, full of love and tenderness, and swimming with bright tears.

"Cathy!" he cried. "*Cathy*! D'you mean it's all right?"

"If you—really—mean it," said Cathy tremulously.

He put his arm round her shoulders. "Cathy, darling!" he cried. "Darling, darling, Cathy!" And the words came out of him—flowed out of him with the elemental force of a river in full flood. He felt as if they'd burst out of his chest instead of issuing from his mouth in the usual manner of words. He was blinded and dazzled by the sudden revelation of what the words meant and of how deeply and sincerely he himself meant them. "Cathy, darling," he heard himself saying. "Darling, darling, Cathy."

Cathy leant against him as trustfully as a child, and presently he bent down and kissed her cheek, and the sweet fragrance of her golden curls was in his nostrils.

(It was at this moment that an attendant paused to look in at the door—they did not notice him, of course—and he, having been married for twenty years to a nagging wife—smiled in a somewhat scornful manner and went away.)

"I've been blind," said George.

"We were too near to see each other properly. You were too used to me, George."

"And you really love me? . . . It's marvellous! I can't think why you do. I mean, I'm no use. I just footle about with horses and things. Why do you love me, Cathy?"

"You're George," she whispered. "That's all that matters."

"Darling," said George fervently. "I simply can't tell you how much I love you! I see now I've loved you the whole time."

"No," said Cathy firmly. She could not pass this remarkable statement.

"Yes, honestly," he replied. "It was because I loved you all the time that nobody else was just right. Let's sit down while I explain."

They sat down, and George kept his arm round her shoulders while he explained very carefully and gravely, exactly how it was, and Cathy listened. She was dazed, she was almost drunk with happiness. The naked statues stood all around them and looked on with complete indifference.

"Look at that woman!" said Cathy suddenly, "that marble woman with the mirror—she doesn't care!"

George glanced at her scornfully. "And we don't care about *her*," he pointed out. "For one thing, her legs are too short from the knee to the ankle! Let's see . . ." he added, running an experienced hand down Cathy's silken leg. "Yes, yours are just right. I knew they would be, of course. I couldn't possibly marry a woman with deformed legs."

After that the conversation degenerated into lunacy too crazy to record, and it was not until the Academy began to fill up, and people began to wander into the Statuary Room that they came to their senses once more.

"I suppose we'll have to go," said George, looking about him, as if he did not know where he was.

"I suppose so," said Cathy vaguely.

"What about—er—your shopping?"

"I couldn't," said Cathy, still in that strangely vague way. "I couldn't—do shopping. I don't know which way up I am."

"I know," agreed George. "I feel rather—odd, too. But there's just one thing I *must* do before we go home. . . . Cartier's in Bond Street."

They drifted out of the door and down the steps, and as they were crossing the courtyard they came face to face with Clarice Morton and a somewhat vacuous-looking young man.

"My dear!" cried Clarice, seizing Cathy's arm. "My dear, how marvellous meeting you like this—and George—you can tell us what to look at. What did you see?"

"Oh, they're marvellous!" said Cathy brightly, "you'll love them, Clarice. We liked the landscape in the south gallery—and there are some adorable children, of course."

"I liked the statues best," put in George, playing up nobly for his side.

"Naughty, naughty man!" cried Clarice, with a sideways glance. "I'm not going to take Douglas to see the statues—he's too young."

They shook themselves free from Clarice and her swain and pushed on, chuckling together over the encounter.

"How awful of us!" Cathy said.

"But how did you know what to tell them—how did you know there were adorable children and landscapes?"

"There always are," she pointed out, "and I had to say something. I suppose you're going to Cartier's for Paddy," she added, as they turned into Piccadilly and walked on.

"No," said George.

She slipped her hand into the curve of his arm—it was a nice strong safe arm—and what a marvellous feeling to know that it was hers! George squeezed the hand—they were country cousins, but who cared.

"What then?" asked Cathy. It intrigued her somewhat that George should have business at Cartier's.

"Can't you guess?" he asked.

"Studs," said Cathy—it was the only thing she could think of that a man might buy for himself at a jeweller's shop.

George laughed. "My dear lamb," he said, "I always get my studs at Woolworth's——"

Something in the way he looked down at her, something in the crinkling of his eyes, in the whimsical loving curve of his mouth told her what it was he wanted to buy——

"Oh, George!" she cried, pulling his arm. "Oh, George, no, not *there*!"

"Yes, there," he said firmly. "It's the best place, isn't it? Only the very best place in London is good enough to provide a ring for you."

"Oh, George!" she sighed. "It'll be so expensive."

"I should just hope it would be," said George.

As they turned up Bond Street the old feeling of stimulation filled George's heart. (He wondered if Cathy felt it, too—he would ask her about it some time.) He remembered the last time he had been here—a great deal had happened since then, but the street had not changed—it wore the same air of history, of luxury, of glamour. The sun shone on the plate-glass windows, and was reflected from the silver fittings of the brave cavalcade of cars. He remembered how he had toyed with the pleasant conceit that the sun was shining for him, and that everything was glittering for him because it was his birthday. Today, the

481

sun was shining for him and Cathy, and the Spirit of Bond Street was wishing them long life and happiness.

Cathy gave his arm a little pinch. "George," she breathed, "George, darling, isn't Bond Street *wonderful*? It's—it's smiling at us, George!"

THE END

ROMANCE TITLES
in the
Ulverscroft Large Print Series